# BONES

## GABRIELLE LORD

McPHEE GRIBBLE PUBLISHERS

McPhee Gribble Publishers
Penguin Books Australia Ltd
487 Maroondah Highway, PO Box 257
Ringwood, Victoria 3134, Australia
Penguin Books Ltd
Harmondsworth, Middlesex, England
Viking Penguin, A Division of Penguin Books USA Inc
375 Hudson Street, New York, New York 10014, USA
Penguin Books Canada Limited
10 Alcorn Avenue, Toronto, Ontario, Canada M4V 3B2
Penguin Books (NZ) Ltd
182-190 Wairau Road, Auckland 10, New Zealand

First published by McPhee Gribble Publishers 1995

3 5 7 9 10 8 6 4 2

Copyright © Gabrielle Lord 1995

All rights reserved. Without limiting the rights under copyright reserved above, no part of this publication may be reproduced, stored in or introduced into a retrieval system, or transmitted, in any form or by any means (electronic, mechanical, photocopying, recording or otherwise) without the prior written permission of both the copyright owner and the above publisher of this book.

Produced by McPhee Gribble
487 Maroondah Highway, Ringwood, Victoria 3134, Australia
A division of Penguin Books Australia Ltd

Typeset in 11/13½ Palatino
Printed in Australia by Australian Print Group

National Library of Australia
Cataloguing-in-Publication data:

Lord Gabrielle, 1946-
Bones.

ISBN 0 86914 359 X.

I. Title.

A823.3

**BONES**

Gabrielle Lord was born in Sydney in 1946. After studying at Armidale University she worked variously as a saleswoman, teacher and fruitpicker, and spent nine years with the Commonwealth Employment Service as an employment officer. Her first book, *Fortress*, was published in 1980 and the film rights to this were sold in 1983, allowing her to begin writing full-time. *Bones* is her sixth novel. Gabrielle has also written for ABC television. She has one daughter, Madeleine, and lives in a beach suburb of Sydney.

By the same author

*Fortress* (1980)
*Tooth and Claw* (1983)
*Jumbo* (1986)
*Salt* (1990)
*Whipping Boy* (1992)

ACKNOWLEDGEMENTS

I am grateful for the assistance of the Literature Board of the Australia Council in the writing of this book.

I also acknowledge the debt I owe the profound and honest work of Alice Miller, and the loving support of all my friends, especially Virginia, Margie, Jeanette and Philippa, who sustain me in my own soul work.

And with heartfelt thanks to Roger Johnson.

# Prologue

WOOLLAHRA, 11.20 PM, 10 NOVEMBER 1991

The length of the lane, the back of the surgeon's garage and house flashed mauve like a set in a horror movie as lightning zigzagged the sky. The crash followed a few seconds later. Only an occasional car at this hour, headlights shining on the wet black road, picking up the heavy rain in slanting crystal lines, swished past. He'd stood for hours in rain in the Mekong Delta when he was a young man, and this violent electrical storm was just what the doctor ordered.

At the corner of the lane he looked left. From this position, he could see the the high wall that enclosed the front garden of the house where it faced the main road. Another brilliant flash, the crash closer now, showed him the unmarked car parked outside. He couldn't see the driver through the heavy rain but he knew the other cop was in the house, and that every so often the inside man checked the back area of the building, the courtyard outside the kitchen and the garden that gave onto the garage. He knew the surgeon was hot because of the trial; he'd demanded another fifteen on top of his usual fee because of that.

The house itself was well secured; previously he'd noted the recessed video cameras in the back and front gardens. Formwork on top of the garage that opened onto the lane showed the skeleton of a second-storey addition that was going up, delayed by the rain. And it was just as well, and the reason he'd decided to do the job this way, because the builders had disconnected the electricity. Their powerboards and materials were all stacked away in the garage.

He went back down the lane to the garage door, looked quickly each way and squatted to fix the lock. The tiny, intense beam of his flashlight was hidden by his crouching figure and it was only a few moments before he eased the door up. He stood, breathing fast. It excited him, this work; made him feel alive.

The floor of the garage was wet from rain flooding in under the roller door. There was enough light from the lane to show him the doctor's big car, safe and dry, beside his wife's red Saab. Earlier in the day, he'd walked around the pewter Mercedes in the hospital car park and noted the winking alarm system. He didn't have to wait long. At the next thunder crash, he raised his gloved fist. He always gave them a chance. 'I'm here, you bastards,' he said, chopping the Mercedes hard. The alarm started screaming. He turned and ducked under the door, pulled it down and fastened it, and moved quickly down the lane as the *blar-blar-blar* punctuated the night. He went into a phone box in the street behind the house and made a call.

As he hung up, he heard the alarm stop. Now he was aware of several other distant bleepers, set off by the storm. He came back to the house and made himself invisible in a garden opposite as the unmarked car cruised slowly down the lane. It pulled up outside the garage just as the roller door was raised by the inside man wielding a powerful flashlight. The driver stayed put while he conversed with the other, then he pulled the car away and turned at the end of the lane. The inside man walked a little way in each direction, inspecting the ground where the garage gave onto the wet tar of the lane. It showed him nothing, just the rain running along the narrow gutter, bits of broken leaf and twig from the earlier wind.

He waited unseen in the dripping garden opposite. Rain was a good ally; it washed things away. The unmarked car reappeared at the other end of the lane, without lights this time. The storm was almost directly overhead now, so that there was hardly any delay between the thunderclap and the lightning that showed the driver's white face: young, bored. Then the headlights came up on high beam to light the empty lane. The car cruised past him and turned back into the roadway. Even if the driver had done his job properly, got out of the car, got his tootsies wet, he would have been doing well to find me, thought the man hiding in the wet garden.

Fifteen minutes went by.

He crept back to the garage, undid the lock and rolled up the door. There were drops of water on the driver's door of the Mercedes where the inside man had opened it, turned off the alarm and reset it. He whacked the Mercedes in time with the next overhead crash, pulled down the door, and melted back into the garden.

A few minutes and the alarm was silenced. The unmarked car returned to check the lane; the inside man checked the garage and the back street. The storm was moving away.

But he was in no hurry. There were other nights, other storms over Sydney. Other ways of dying. He'd seen most of them. He waited.

A third time he went back to the garage, stooped down, lifted the door, noted the winking red alarm light, waited for the next crash of thunder and hit the Mercedes hard. *Blar-blar-blar!* it screamed. This time he moved smartly back to his car parked two streets away.

The rain was heavier now, even though the electrical violence was easing. He unlocked his boot and drew a small device out of a bag, smaller even than the one he'd used to frag the sergeant twenty-five years ago. The alarm had stopped and all he could hear now was the steady drip of rain from trees hanging over back walls, and the rushing of the nearby stormwater drain.

This time the unmarked car didn't bother to check the lane, nor did the inside man appear with his flashlight. He gave them plenty of time to come back for a last check-up. Neither returned.

But he did.

He lifted the door carefully. The dashboard of the Mercedes was in darkness. No red light.

### WOOLLAHRA, 6.15 AM, 11 NOVEMBER 1991

'Get out of that shower, Polly. Hurry up. I'll be late.' Alan banged on the bathroom door. A muffled shout from inside did not satisfy him. 'I've got to be there at eight. Dad, tell her, will you?'

His father, preoccupied, didn't answer him; he hurried downstairs doing up his tie to take a call on the hall phone. Alan went to his parents' bedroom and knocked. Sybil was still in bed, lying awake, staring at the ceiling.

'Mum? Tell Polly to get out of the bathroom.'

His mother came back from wherever she'd been and smiled at him. *'Ella,'* she said opening her arms. *'Linos, ella 'tho.'*

'Mum,' he said, irritated. 'Talk Australian, will you.' He didn't want to kiss her good morning. 'Tell Polly to get out of the bathroom. She's been in there for ages.'

'Use mine,' Sybil said, pointing to the closed door that led off the bedroom. She was frowning and he could see the packet of pain killers by the side of the bed. He remembered the argument he'd heard late last night, pulling the pillow over his head in his bedroom and screaming *shut up shut up shut up* into it through clenched teeth.

'Your shower's too low,' he told her. 'I bang my head all the time.' He was well over six feet already, at fourteen. He left the bedroom and jumped down the stairs. His father was on the hall phone, angry, his voice hard.

'And you saw fit, Doctor, to decide not to inform me?' There was a pause. Alan crept into the kitchen and opened the refrigerator, pulling out milk and yoghurt.

'Are you telling me now that you didn't notice?' His father's voice had become menacingly soft. 'I want you in my room this morning when I come out of theatre to tell me why you didn't notice not only that she was going off – don't interrupt while I'm speaking – not only that she was going off, but that she was an acute abdomen.' Alan heard the sharp intake of his father's breath before he continued. 'It was a fluke that I happened to drop by the hospital last night. And you can thank your lucky stars that I did. The night sister told me you'd checked her only fifteen minutes earlier. We nearly lost her. My patient almost died because of your negligence.'

Alan gritted his teeth and shut his eyes. He hated that know-it-all hardness in his father's voice; the terrible importance of his father's work. And he hated that his father was always *right*. He filled a bowl with muesli, chopped a banana onto it, poured yoghurt on top and watched it slowly slide down the muesli hill.

'I call it gross negligence, Doctor. That's what I call it.' His father's voice, hard, strong and *right*.

Alan found the walnuts and started making a wall of them around the top of the yoghurt hill.

'Am I expected to believe that you checked her thoroughly and missed an acute abdomen? Control yourself, Doctor.'

Alan couldn't stand listening any more. He carried the yoghurt and muesli hill out of the kitchen and slid past his father, who didn't notice him; carried his breakfast upstairs away from that dark angry voice. But still it pursued him.

'I find that impossible to believe, Doctor Mitchell. Nor do I wish to discuss it now.'

Alan was trying to run along the upstairs hall to his room without upsetting his overloaded bowl when Polly swung out of the bathroom in front of him. As they collided the bowl went flying and muesli, yoghurt, banana and nuts hit Polly, the wall and the carpet.

'Oh shit, Alan. You dork!' The front of Polly's towel dripped white with yoghurt. Discs of banana stuck to her damp arms and chest.

'Sorry,' he said.

Their father suddenly loomed up behind them. Alan noticed his father's neck; the way he favoured one side. 'Is your mother up yet?' he asked. Then he saw the food splattered everywhere. 'What on earth is this? What's going on here?'

'Sorry, Dad. Polly bumped into me.'

'She wouldn't have bumped into you if you'd been watching where you were going. And what are you doing bringing food upstairs like that? Where's your mother?'

Polly backed into the bathroom and slammed the door.

Sybil appeared at her bedroom door, tying an ancient dressing-gown, staring first at her husband then at her squatting son as he tried to shovel cereal and yoghurt back into the bowl with his bare hands. Her husband glared at her.

'If you'd been up at a decent hour – ' He stopped and noticed what his son was doing. 'Get a cloth, for goodness sake, Alan. You're bloody useless.'

'Don't speak to him like that.' Sybil's voice was as angry as her husband's, her accent always more marked when she was distressed.

Please, thought Alan, gathering banana discs, just all be quiet. Just don't anybody say anything more and it will all be all right.

'If he gave as much thought to his studies as he does to his damn stomach, he'd be a lot better off.'

'Leave him alone. You're always on at him.'

'If I didn't keep on at him, he'd do nothing. I've just had a lethal female junior doctor almost kill one of my patients. Please spare me the lecture on raising my own son.'

Alan scraped the last of the banana into the bowl and stood up, watching his father follow his mother back into the bedroom. 'If you hadn't drunk so much last night,' he heard him say, 'you might have been able to keep your hands off Rod Angstrom during dinner and been able to get up to prepare breakfast for your children – '

The bedroom door slammed shut on the rest of it.

Alan hated thinking of his mother's hands on Doctor

Angstrom's body. He hated to think of the phone calls Doctor Angstrom made on the nights his father was in theatre, hated the way his mother's voice seemed different when she was speaking to this man. Laughy and young, he thought.

Polly rushed out of the bathroom, squealed as she slid in some yoghurt, regained her balance, swore at her brother, and vanished into her room leaving a vapour trail of perfume and talc. Alan went to her door and knocked. She turned round as he came in and he looked away because she was in her underwear.

'I failed physics,' he said, head down. 'I saw my report.' He was aware of her pulling on a blouse.

'How come you saw it? You're not supposed to open them, Al. You didn't throw it away, did you?' He was silent. 'Oh Al. That was crazy.'

Alan looked up at his sister. 'Please, Poll. Don't bring yours home. That way he might forget.'

'Al. He's not going to forget. Honest.'

'But please. He might. Just don't bring yours home.'

His sister's face showed him it was useless. 'I'm sorry, Al. I can't do that.'

He stood dejected, staring at the tiny flecks in the carpet.

'I heard Annabel Oswald really likes you,' Polly added to cheer him up, twisting to do up her skirt.

He shook his head. 'I don't think so. Lucy told me she just wants to go with me because of Dad and the trial. You know, the publicity and the thrill of it and everything.'

Alan glanced at her dressing-table, at the framed photograph of the four of them taken last Christmas – Mum, Dad, Polly and him. He thought he looked like a dill. He stared at his parents' photogenic smiles; the elegant mother, the hero father.

'Did you hear them last night?' he asked. She nodded.

'I hate it,' he said. 'How much longer's it going to go on for? I reckon that Angstrom is a real jerk. A *gynaecologist*.' He repeated his father's contempt. 'They only have to worry about four inches.'

Polly sat down on the bed. She started rubbing something on a pimple, looking at herself in the mirror as if she were some strange girl she didn't like very much. Then she shrugged. 'They have to sort it out,' she said. 'It's their business. Bloody so-called grown-ups.'

Polly looked beautiful, Alan thought, even though she was his sister. Her long eyes and hair like their mother's. 'But Poll,' he said, 'why don't they talk to us about it? Aren't we part of this family too?'

She was so intent on plucking her eyebrows now that he knew he would get no answer from her. He left her room and went downstairs for something to clean up the mess with, and was startled to see the cop that he didn't like standing in the lounge room, looking out the front window, nursing a cup of something. He couldn't get used to this. He hated the idea that everything his family said and did was seen and heard by an outsider. He hated the security cameras.

Outside, the weather had cleared. Alan decided he'd skip a shower, found some scouring powder and a cloth and was on his way upstairs when he met Polly coming down. She looked at what he had in his hand, shook her head slowly as if to suggest that he was utterly hopeless, and passed him without comment.

'What?' he said, turning to talk to her descending back. '*Tell me.*' He looked down at the scouring powder and the cloth in his hands. Somehow, girls always *knew*. 'What am I supposed to use?'

His father appeared at the top of the stairs, frowning. 'Are you going to clean up this mess?'

'I'm coming, I'm coming.' Alan raised the scouring powder to show his father, and continued upstairs, along the hall, to the scene of the crime. He stood in front of the muesli and cereal spread across the pale green carpet, unsure where to start, then he shook the scouring powder over it. He heard his mother yelling.

'*Oxi*! No, no. *Linos. Oxi*, not that. Just the sponge cloth. You need to clear this away, not add more to it.' She grabbed a towel and squeezed it dry over the bathroom sink, then she came to stoop beside the spill. Swift strokes of the damp towel and she seemed to make the mess disappear into its folds.

'I didn't know,' he said. 'I didn't know what to use.'

'Go and get me a plastic bag and we'll get rid of this.' She rolled the stuff in the towel and was getting another damp one to clean the yoghurt out of the carpet. Her pink dressing-gown had slipped off one shoulder and she looked soft and young with her coppery hair in a loop on her neck. He smelt her special bed smell.

'I'm sorry, Mum. It was an accident.'

'I know. It's okay. You get the plastic bag for me? Or some paper?' she called out after him, because he was already halfway down the stairs.

Polly leaned over the banister of the landing. 'Al,' she said in low voice,' ask your teacher for another report. Tell him you lost it. Tell him you're suffering from post-trial stress trauma or something. This'll only make it worse, Al. Truly.' She looked at him with anxious love and Alan continued downstairs thinking his whole life *was* post-trial stress trauma, even in the years before the trial.

In the kitchen his father was putting on his suit coat, looking at the big diary with the surgical lists which lay open on the counter next to his medical bag. Alan wanted to ask him what exactly was an acute abdomen. But his father was still too angry; he hoped he would stay angry enough not to think about the missing school report. The surgeon jerked his coat collar to pull his jacket down and winced as he moved his neck. He looked at his watch. 'Have you cleaned up that mess?'

'I'm doing it now.'

They looked at each other. Alan looked away. He always felt in the wrong. He felt he always irritated his father.

'Tell your mother I'm going now,' the surgeon said, looking past Alan, and his son turned to see that the cop he liked was waiting at the door. His father stepped outside, Alan dawdled after him and the three of them walked down through the sunny, sodden garden.

Everything looked rinsed and clear after last night's storm; it would be hot later on. Alan realised he was still carrying the scouring powder. He tried to put it in the back pocket of his shorts, but it was too big. Sometimes, he thought, Dad noticed him, and not just to go on about applying himself to his studies. Sometimes Dad took him flying. Just the two of them in the Cherokee and he let Alan sit in the pilot's seat and fly it, straight and level. Sometimes his Dad smiled at him and told him he was a real character. When that happened, Alan wanted to laugh stupidly or jump around.

As they walked towards the garage, he wished he knew something wonderful, some astounding fact, something no one else in the world knew, just for the delight of his father, the great surgeon.

'Lightning makes more nitrogen,' he said hopefully, looking at the tall suited figure walking ahead of him. 'That's why everything looks greener after a storm.' It wasn't very good, but it might catch his father's interest. His father didn't even look up at the five sulphur-crested cockatoos that squawked overhead on their breakfast run.

The nice cop opened the door from the garden to the garage and checked inside before letting Alan and his father through. 'Is that a fact?' said the cop to Alan. 'I never knew that.' The cockatoos had landed in the blue spruce next door and most of them were swinging upside down.

Following his father into the garage, Alan noticed the alarm was not winking. 'Doesn't it work?' he asked, putting the scouring powder on the bench.

'It's fine,' said his father. 'It kept going off in the storm last night.'

'I'll get the roller door, Dad,' Alan called out. His father was unlocking the Mercedes, sliding his medical bag across the seat, climbing into the car. The nice cop was already at the roller door, lifting it up, looking fast in each direction like a cat, up and down the lane. He spoke into his radio and Alan knew that the other man would be starting the unmarked car at the front, ready to follow his father to the hospital.

Brilliant early sunshine fell into the garage interior and Alan blinked. His father slammed the car door shut, switched on the ignition and the Mercedes warmed up, singing its fine-tuned German hum. Pilots had respect for engines, Alan thought. Dad had once told him that motors were like people. They needed to warm up before they could work efficiently. Alan came up to stand beside the driver's door. He saw his father wince as he stretched his left arm along the top of the passenger seat, turning his head stiffly to check the rear.

'Dad?' Alan said, hating to see his father hurting.

'What is it?' Alan heard a little irritation, but hoped it was just the pain in his neck. His father turned back and looked at him. It seemed like the first time in months that his father had actually looked at him, noticed him, *seen* him. Alan's heart filled. 'Dad? Let me back the car out for you. I'll be really careful?'

Something in his son's voice touched the surgeon's heart. Sybil was right, he neglected his children. He looked at Alan's face and saw with a pang that he was scared of him. Scared and desperate to please.

'Can I? Please?'

The surgeon made a decision. 'Okay.' He got out of the car and let his son get in.

Alan adjusted the seat and moved the rear vision mirror, absurdly pleased with himself. 'I'll guide you out,' his father called, going out to the lane. Alan nodded and concentrated hard. No seatbelt while reversing. He watched his father in the rear vision mirror, then he craned his neck to see where the edge of the garage door was on one side and his mother's red Saab on the other.

His father made the beckoning movement that indicated it was safe to reverse out of the garage. Alan raised a hand to show he'd understood, touched the horn, selected reverse gear, and as it engaged the fireball erupted from under the gearbox of the Mercedes, blowing the front seat apart in a wide V-shape so that the top half of Alan hit the roof just as the entire vehicle split open along its width, exploding in a mighty burst of flame and metal shards and thunderous noise as Alan, the Mercedes, the garage and the timber frame on top were blown sky high.

White cockatoos screeched into the shocked silence and the air filled with dust and feathers and scouring powder and screaming as Sybil and Polly and the other cop ran down the garden.

SYDNEY, 10 DECEMBER 1991

The surgeon moved his head and peered through the slit in his bandages. He could see his grostesque swathed head reflected in the curved steel of the basin on the bedside cupboard. His left eye, damaged by a piece of shrapnel as he'd been blown backwards into the fence of the house opposite the garage, was aching. Each time he blinked he could feel the area of damage like a plank in his eye. His groin ached from another, larger, piece of metal. After consultation, they'd decided to leave that one alone. It was difficult for him to remember to be just another post-operative patient, a nobody; passive recipient of another surgeon's expertise. Difficult to remember to stay silent as procedures were discussed in his hearing without his contribution. It was a security measure.

The drugs made day and night hard to distinguish. His wounded eye didn't like the light, and the heavy curtains of his room were mostly shut during daylight hours.

A knock and Polly walked in. She pulled a chair over and sat by his bed. His right hand, flash burnt and stiff, lay inert beside him. She touched it gently with a fingertip. 'What's it like today?' she asked.

'It's all right,' he said. 'How's your mother?' He watched his daughter's face, bony with grief.

'She's okay.' Then she stopped. 'No she's not. She's terrible. She's mad. She won't get out of bed. I don't know what to do. They've put us in this house in Ramsgate.' His daughter leaned over, closer. The pain and fear in her face were terrible for him to see, useless and wounded as he was. 'Dad. *Please* do it. A new life. New identities. I can't stand how it is.' She fumbled for something in her bag. 'You haven't seen this yet. Malcolm will be here in a while to talk with you. Look.' She pushed a postcard into his hand.

He turned it over. It showed four stick figures, crudely drawn. One was already crossed out. He stared at it. This was his family. Someone had drawn his family in this crude way after killing his son. And then sent this new obscenity to his house. He crushed the card in his not-so-injured left hand and his skin burned anew at the movement.

Polly took the card back, then laid her fingers lightly on the healthy skin of his hand, near the flash burn. 'We can make a new life. I'll make Mum come with me tonight and visit you. We can put it all behind us and start again.'

Put it all behind us and start again. After she'd gone, the words kept circling in his mind like a mantra. He was too dazed to do anything except let them.

He had managed to swallow part of his evening meal when Polly, Malcolm and Sybil came in. He pushed the tray away and looked at his wife, who was wearing black like a Greek widow. This was her first visit and she stood awkwardly by the door. He spoke her name and reached out his hand, but she did not move.

'*Sivilla mou. Ella,*' he pleaded. '*Ella 'tho, Sivilla mou.*' She stared at him and he couldn't say what was in her haggard eyes. Her lips were bitten, the once beautiful face a mask of suffering. He let his neglected, burnt hand drop. Then he could smell the acetone of last night's alcohol around her as she sat silently next to Polly in the furthest of the two chairs near his bed.

Their case officer Malcolm stood a little behind what was left of the surgeon's family, separate and untouched by their loss. 'Your triple-bypass friend in the Prime Minister's department,' Malcolm was saying as the surgeon brought his attention back from the pain in Sybil's face and her rejection of him, 'has leaned on all the right people for you.' For a second he didn't understand what Malcolm was saying. 'We don't often work with people from your – ' Malcolm searched for the words, 'walk of life. But he's come up with a position for you, something academic. Set you up interstate. A new name, a new life. He's had a couple of preliminary talks with some people and we can create a vacancy at a university. A nice university town in another state.' Malcolm straightened up. 'You're in a very good position,' he said, and the surgeon thought he was mad. 'They think you're dead, remember.'

He thought of Sybil's wild grief as he had moved in and out of consciousness after the explosion. The way she screamed, 'The bomb was for you and you weren't *there! You're never there and my Linos died instead!*' Then there'd been the funeral that he had not attended, and Sybil's grief in the newspaper photos had been for her son, not her husband, despite what the press had been told.

'I need time to think about it,' he said.

'We haven't got time, Dad,' said Polly. '*Please.*'

'You get brand new names, birth certificates, all your papers fixed up. Your solicitor can organise the sale of your property. We'll pay your expenses. You won't be out of pocket. You agree not to contact relatives and friends except through us. We'll fix up secure meetings for you from time to time.'

'There are no relatives,' said the surgeon, thinking of his dead parents and Sybil's fragmented family in Alexandria and Crete. Friends, he was thinking. I don't have friends, only colleagues and subordinates.

'Think about it,' Malcolm was saying. 'How does the University of Western Australia sound?'

After he'd gone they sat in silence, Polly anxious and tense, Sybil avoiding his eyes. The soft rush of the airconditioner filled the hospital room.

'Please, Dad.' He looked at his daughter. He looked away. He looked at his wife and looked away from her too, bringing his focus back to the pain and tension in his own body. Sybil, Sib. Talk to me. But all he encountered were those eyes and the bitter, exhausted mouth.

'Mum. We've got to do it. They'll kill us all.' Polly the elder child, the *only* child now, the umpire, trying to get her father and mother to negotiate. Trying to pull what was left of the family together. She seemed more adult than either of her parents just at the moment.

He closed his eyes and let his wounded head sink into the pillows. He thought of Alan and felt something move in his heart. He thought of the tickets to St Moritz that were somewhere on his desk at home, of Alan yelling on the double black runs; the sailing, the beautiful house. The dinner parties, the entertainment. The life of the successful surgeon and his lovely family. The good life. The phrase made him want to weep.

'*Please*, Mum. Tell him. Tell him we've got to do it. It's our only chance. Tell him.'

There seemed to be a long silence before Sybil started to speak.

Then she told him. But what she told him was not about a change of identity or a new life. It was not about putting it all behind them and starting again. What she told him was something he could scarcely believe. As the meaning of her words unfolded in his mind and Polly started to cry then raced out of the room, the surgeon looked at his wife and saw not the woman he'd lived with for nearly twenty years, but someone he didn't know at all. He saw the stranger.

# 1

Inside, the house was already dark but Joss didn't want to put the lights on yet. It was a second or two of peace. Some fifty years slipped away and he was waiting for his grandmother to come downstairs to the window seat and read him the story of Peter Rabbit. Outside, the afterglow of sunset washed the foothills mauve. A late Beechcraft flew towards the nearby airfield, a plover shrieked at the disturbance in the air. Joss stood quite still, looking through the steel bars. Beside him the mauve light, drained of its warmth by the darkness of the house, fell on the worn cushions of the window seat. The poignant mood faded.

Sometimes, it was his particular horror to imagine them already in the house. Sometimes he imagined Lombard upstairs, sitting in his bedroom, grinning, as he walked in. Or the killer waiting in Polly's wardrobe until she went to pull out her dressing-gown. Lying under her bed to grab her ankle as she stepped up. And sometimes, he actually heard the creak on the old staircase behind him as someone crept down with a knife. These days, he steeled himself against swinging round as he had done in the first year.

The mantel clock ticked and clicked, then donged out six o'clock. Above it hung his father's faded WAC chart of the southern Philippines and the South China Sea, showing all the airfields he'd helped lay down late in the war on the islands. The magic island of Samsura.

She should be home by now. Last lecture at four on Wednesdays. A coffee in the union with some friends, maybe some time in the library, then into the white Celica he'd bought for her and the fifteen-minute drive out here. Joss turned quickly, crossed the dim room and went upstairs to his bedroom. Of course it was quite empty with just the double bed, the stern dressing-table with only hair-brush and aftershave visible, the silver-framed photographs of the parents he'd never had, the leather chair near the window. And the medico-legal book of gunshot wounds he'd been reading until yesterday, when the bound and beaten body of little eight-year-old Jeremy Smiles had been found by school kids at Spring Caves.

Joss switched on the bedside lamp and caught sight of his figure in the mirror as he straightened up. He examined himself, this tall man of fifty-three, as if he were someone else. He noted the slight stoop developing behind shoulders that seemed narrower these days, thick hair just greying near the temples, the face relatively unlined except for the furrows from nose to mouth. He hadn't realised they were so deep. Together with his deep-set eyes, they made his face seem corroded somehow, the skull showing through like a face painted by Munch. Just beyond his field of vision, Joss imagined he could see in the glass the shadowy outline of someone close behind him. He stared at himself. Not too bad, he thought. I am coping, as I know I must.

He picked up the book on gunshot wounds and went downstairs to his study, where a malachite desk set declared it was the sixth of July 1994. Joss flinched against the pain of the date: Alan's birthday. He would have been seventeen. Joss could barely stand the thought of it. He stacked the book on a tower of others and straightened up the mess of papers on his desk, sorting and making neat piles, clearing and smoothing until the surface was orderly again. His hand movements were still those of a surgeon's: quick, precise, deft.

On the left wall of the study hung a painting of Spitfires, and opposite that was a Mustang with its guns blazing. He sometimes worried about them, because they were from his old life, but he told himself it was all right to have them there. A lot of men had pictures of Spitfires on their walls, a lot of men flew aircraft, and the world was full of men who made model aircraft. And anyway, he thought, by the time they find us, by the time they get to this house, it will be the end, and far too late for me to be anxious about betrayal by *mise en scène*.

Above his desk hung Leonardo's magnificent anatomical drawings of the musculature of the human neck and torso. Joss leant with his hands on the desk, head lowered. The stiffness was still there in his neck. He stood for a minute like that until he felt the tear running down his face. He pulled out his handkerchief and wiped it away with irritation. The man who cries but does not feel, he remembered Ashley saying. Feelings were not for him, he thought. He remembered Prof Gainsborough saying that destructive emotional involvement had ruined many professional people, that if they valued their careers they must steel themselves against suffering – sentimentality he called it. Joss straightened up against the pain. I am dealing with this, he thought. I am coping with the loss of my son, my old life.

But his mind was filling with forbidden thoughts and banned memories. He knew he had to get out of the house until the keenness of the impulse faded. He locked up and walked down the driveway to the Niva. The frosty air of the tablelands made him draw his coat closer. Under brilliant stars the old-fashioned windbreak of cypress pines along the driveway made a dark wall, above which a chill half-moon was rising. He thought of that other car from that other life: the huge, dark grey Mercedes. He slammed the Niva's door, strapping himself in and starting it roughly, shoving it into first gear as if it were a brute that needed punishment. He drove past the dark mass of the old Boys' Home on the rise and another tear rolled from his right eye. He fumbled for his handkerchief and wiped his face, still watching the road and the lights of Maroonga ahead. The teariness came in waves, quite unconnected to any emotion he might be feeling, as involuntary as breathing. Some days he hardly noticed it. On others his eyes streamed constantly. Joss called it hayfever. Ashley called it something else. He suspected she was right, but there could be no expressing the enormous store of grief in him. It was better left alone. He was doing well, he believed. He was putting it all behind him.

He took the road into town, relaxing a bit with the movement and at the sight of the university lights winking through the darkness. He turned into the main gate and drove to the top of the hill where the humanities buildings clustered. Further on were the student union, the bookshop, the bistro and bar. His department, the law school, was out of sight on the other side of the hill and had its own canteen and common room.

Groups of students still walked up and down the hill carrying notes and briefcases. Joss could see their breath steaming under the haloed lights of the drive. Stars pierced the clear air and as his right eye overflowed again he noticed a wide blurred ring around the moon. Part of his mind recalled that in three days it would rain, while another, deeper, part resettled into its habitual resigned despair.

Joss's teaching load in the law school was not as heavy as other staff members'; at his request, time for consultancy work had been written into his contract so that he could be available to the local and other police forces. He wanted as much distraction from his own mind as possible and his teaching work didn't engage him sufficiently for that. He was used to action, not teaching.

Usually, when he wasn't lecturing on criminology, Joss worked on the ambitious national cross-referencing system that he and Detective Sergeant Dennis Johnson were collating: an index of murder, of weapons and styles and *modi operandi*, so that unsolved killings could be checked against other killings of like manner. If a hammer were used, Joss and Dennis could retrieve and compare all killings in which a hammer had been used; cases of strangulation were cross-referenced to itemise the use of belts, stockings, ropes, wires, neckties, underwear, electrical flex and, more recently, octopus straps. It was a huge project and Joss had a lot of help from senior students. He couldn't bear time alone with himself. It was essential, he believed, that he stay busy. He knew from old that if he kept the surface of his mind agitated with continual mental noise, observation, chatter, work and worry, the deeper layers where the pain was embedded were unable to break through.

But with the discovery of the body of Jeremy Smiles the day before, Joss knew that a lot of his time would be spent on the case. It sometimes struck him with surprise that his life still revolved around death.

He passed the low-lying admin buildings, all in darkness at this hour, parked the car and hurried up the steps to the dining hall. A queue of students moved along the food bar, taking ready-made meals from the shelves or ordering specials from the whiteboard. He saw his daughter immediately, her sleek hair and curving jaw line, Sybil's beautiful bones.

Joss walked up, nervous and uncertain of what to say to her, and she came over to greet him. 'Dad. What brings you here?' He could smell the rose soap she liked to use.

'You know. The usual.' They looked into each other's eyes, where the fear hid. Sybil's vivid eyes.

'Dad, I told you yesterday I was going to the Gold of Egypt exhibition and I'd be late.'

She had told him and he'd forgotten. He clicked his tongue and nodded. 'Sorry.'

'I'll walk you to your car,' she said, wanting to make sure he left. Then her gentle side. 'Have you eaten? Do you want something? You can have some of mine. The meals here are always too big for me.' Sometimes she sounded more like a mother than his daughter. The events of the last years had matured her too quickly, he thought.

They were calling her, saying her meal was ready, and Joss could see the servery attendant with her nurse's cap waiting near the till with a steaming plate.

'Get it for me, will you Ignatius?' Polly called back to her boyfriend. 'I'll be there in a tick.'

They walked back towards their reflections in the glass

doors of the union – Joss's bulky six feet and Polly half a head shorter than him – out into the cold tableland night. Joss was pleased to see her Celica standing in the middle of a pool of light in the parking area.

'What time will you be home, do you think?' he couldn't help asking.

'Dad,' she said and her voice was damning. 'Don't *do* this. It drives me mad. You know that.'

'I can't seem to help it,' Joss said sadly. 'Today's the sixth.' He felt her give a little shiver beside him.

'I don't care what date it is,' she said and her voice was harsh with trying not to. 'It's finished. It's over. Stop it.'

He fumbled in his pocket for the keys. 'How was it,' he asked, trying to ease her distress with a change of tack. 'The Gold of Egypt?'

'Too much black velvet. Too many boring jars. Too many hieroglyphics. Too many scarabs.' She paused and shivered as the wind lifted her dark hair. 'There were cases and cases of gold jewellery made for the dead. There was a golden collar of the vulture goddess. When I came out, I was in sort of a gold daze. There was a mummy there too, in his winding sheet.'

Her last four words made him hesitate as he got into his car. They sounded like the refrain from a ballad by Dunbar. For almost a year after the explosion he hadn't been able to read anything, his mind seemed incapable of comprehending words. Then he found that poetry, with its smaller segments, was manageable, especially the border ballads of death and betrayal. The phrase, *in his winding sheet*, arrested him. Polly had leaned down to kiss him through the Niva's window.

'Just don't be late home,' he said automatically and she exploded.

'Don't do this! I can't stand it!'

'I'm only concerned about your safety.'

'That's not true. You're concerned about me doing exactly as you want.' It was absurd, this fight of theirs, Polly standing screaming through the window at him, while he sat tensely in the Niva. She drew back from the vehicle. 'You forget I've got my life to lead. I'm nearly twenty! I'll drive home when it suits *me*, not you.'

'I bought you that car to keep you safe!' he said, hurt by what he felt to be ingratitude, her unfairness.

'Safe!' There was scorn as well as pity in her voice. 'Since when have you been able to keep anyone *safe*?'

This was a direct hit, the shocking truth, and Joss felt it physically. Too angry to respond, he started the car and jerked off down the drive. Then he stopped the vehicle, jumped out and ran back to her; she had almost reached the dining hall. He called her name and she turned, her face defiant. 'What?'

'It's not working. How we're doing it isn't working.'

'How *you're* doing it isn't working,' she said. She took a step nearer so as not to shout at him. 'Do I hassle you all the time?' she asked. 'You're always at me.'

'I worry about you.'

She shrugged. 'So? Worry. But just don't bully me because you choose to worry.'

Feeling his anger mount again he said goodnight and turned away. Then he heard her footsteps as she came up to him. This to-ing and fro-ing of theirs. 'Dad. I'm sorry. I know I hurt you. But you've got to learn to let me live my life. You've got to let me do it my way. You've got to respect my right to my own life.'

'What do you know about life?' he responded, stung by her words. 'You're only an ignorant little girl.'

He saw the tears of anger spring to her eyes and knew he'd done it again.

'Don't abuse me like that!' she cried. 'I know what's important to me. And I don't have to stand here and be insulted by you just because you're not getting your own way. You always start abusing people when they don't do what you tell them. You always think you know better.' She looked as if she were about to say something else, thought better of it and instead said in a softer voice, 'Back off, Dad. You're out of order.'

She turned and ran back into the light, leaving him standing, furious and hurt, in the darkness.

Too distressed to go straight home, he took the Spring Caves road and drove the fifteen kilometres to where the school kids had found the little boy. The cave was now taped off and he could hear the motor of a generator. A circular patch between the cave and the mobile police station was brilliantly lit so that the crime scene looked theatrical, illusory, like a UFO's landing field. Joss stopped the Niva and got out. A few straggly eucalypts picked up the light behind the mobile van, but apart from them the area around the cave mouth was bare.

'It's the criminologist,' he overheard one police officer say in the silence that followed the slamming of his car door. He walked over to the van. Once, Dennis had told him, the police rarely used to call criminologists in on an investigation, and when they did it was only because the press was demanding solutions and the minister was leaning on the commissioner. But things were changing, and Joss had an intelligent colleague in Detective Sergeant Dennis Johnson. This was the second job Joss had worked on with Dennis since the younger man had come up from Major Crimes two years ago on the Buchanan case, fallen in love with the relaxed lifestyle and the university computer system that Joss had invited him to use, and decided to stay on with a transfer from Sydney. Dennis was keen, observant, a dangerous man.

From inside the van, Joss could hear Dennis's voice on the telephone as he rang off. Joss climbed the steps and Dennis's tired face turned to him, his eyes hidden under the shadow of his brow.

'Where have you been?' he asked Joss. 'I've been trying to get hold of you. Eddie Chandler's finished the report on Jeremy Smiles. He wants you to pick it up first thing in the morning.' Dennis stood up and went to the cupboard where he'd hidden his cigarettes. This was a new ploy devised by his hypnotherapist to break the automatic reach, grab and light sequence of thirty years. He took a cigarette and sniffed along its length, running it under his nose. Then he lit it with a lighter bearing a naked woman in black garters, inhaled deeply and closed his eyes.

'I'm about to pack it up out here,' he said. 'We've been over and over it. Five knives, forty-something .22 shells, rabbit traps, and most of a three-0. Broken down and wrapped in oily rags and plastic. Lots of animal bones. Maybe even a fossil. Look at this.' He passed over a section of a long bone, honeycombed at one end, bitten at the other.

Joss picked it up and turned it over. Perhaps dingoes or wild dogs had crunched it open for the marrow. It was a femur, possibly a steer's or horse's. He ran his finger over the holes where nerves had once maintained their vital network, where muscles had attached. Old bone, cold in the tableland air. 'It's a big animal of some sort,' he said, putting it down.

Dennis was jiggling a tin can. 'Any vehicle marks have been obliterated by all the official and unofficial cars that came through here before we closed it off.' He paused to open the tin. 'And we found three-and-fourpence in old currency.' He pushed the tin across to Joss, who put his hand down to block it, glancing at the old currency, the dirty pennies and the blackened silver. He picked up a small coin and rubbed it. Threepence. The silver ears of wheat. He remembered the thrill of finding one in his Christmas pudding, the extravagance of the bigger sixpence hitting his teeth, his grandmother's smile. He dropped it back in the tin.

'What about the sheet he was wrapped in?' Joss asked and recalled Polly's words: *in his winding sheet*. 'Anything there?'

'Chinese flannelette. Sold in most of the big chains. Cheap as chips. Looked like grass stains at one end.'

'What about the towel under his head?'

'Maybe from a hotel or institution. Eddie might get something off it.' He leaned back in his chair. 'I remember you saying that the FBI profilers reckon it's the killer's way of showing the world he isn't such a bad sort of bastard after all. But it doesn't convince me.'

'It's only a theory,' said Joss. 'I was wondering ...' he said a moment later and Dennis looked alert.

'Yes?'

'Whether this killing might be related somehow to the Gold of Egypt exhibition. It's a long shot, I know, but it may have kicked off someone who was affected by the treasures from the land of the dead. The mummy. The fact that Jeremy Smiles was wound up so tightly in that sheet – strangled through it. And the cave is like a tomb.'

Dennis nodded but he still looked dejected. 'It's worth a try. Someone into Egyptian stuff. Possible occult connections.' He sighed. 'Remember the Sons of Satan?' Joss didn't, nor did he want to know about them at this stage.

'I thought I might go there tomorrow,' said Joss. 'To the exhibition. After I pick up the report from Eddie. I'll ask the attendants if they've noticed anything.'

'Worth a try,' Dennis said again. 'We've got sweet F.A. at the moment. Let's see what Eddie comes up with.'

Joss found himself looking at the tiny mark just left of centre above Dennis's top lip. He looked away; he was finding it easier these days to remain silent on medical conditions. Excusing himself he stepped down into the night and walked over the bare ground near the cave's entrance. It yawned much blacker outside the magnesium brilliance of the police lights, and his long shadow made a track that was swallowed up by the darkness of the cave. It *is* like a tomb, Joss thought. Beyond the pointer of his shadow, in the utter darkness, he could hear intermittent drips from the ancient mineral springs that had been a feature of the caves last century. He didn't want to climb down there just now. Shielding his eyes against the lights he went back to his car.

He drove back thinking of Jeremy Smiles, the eight-year-old St Callistus Junior School pupil who had disappeared two days ago on his way home from school – in under two minutes, in the street where he lived, and no one had seen a thing. Jeremy had walked with his schoolmate to the corner shop, waited outside while the other bought bubblegum, and vanished. Joss thought of what Jeremy's parents must be going through.

How does a person steel himself against suffering? he wondered. One way was to call it something else: sentimentality, or destructive emotional involvement. Another way was to laugh at it, like Prof Gainsborough. Joss found himself thinking of how Gainsborough and the lecture theatre of students – Joss among them – had laughed about Liston's notorious amputation operation that had resulted in a 300 percent mortality rate. Medical jargon: 300 percent mortality.' It sounded like a successful weed killer, Joss thought. Why didn't Gainsborough just say plainly, 'Liston killed three people with one operation'? The patient had died of shock and gangrene. The assistant, who lost his fingers during a bloody flourish with the bone saw, also died of gangrene a few days later. An observing surgeon who had his coat tails cut in the general slashing died of fright, a heart attack on the spot. In the lecture theatre, a lifetime ago, forty men and twenty-eight women had laughed as Gainsborough told the story in his amusing way. The fun of amputation without anaesthetics.

Joss was only now becoming aware of the way doctors spoke with a half-smile about things that were almost too horrible to imagine: 'And there we were with half his gut spilled out on the road trying to keep this dog away and all I had was my tie and and my fists.' He thought again of the visiting professor who had been delivering a lecture on diseases of the heart and who had suddenly flushed, paled, clutched his chest, staggered against the rostrum saying, 'Gentlemen, I am unable to continue, I'm having a heart attack,' and died. The reins of control held tight to the last. Completely unmoved even by his own death; not allowing himself to be touched in the slightest by the enormous, earth shattering, body shattering, mind shattering experience that he was undergoing. Controlled to the very last spasm.

He remembered the surgeon he'd assisted as a young resident who would say, 'Pass me that swab, sister,' and while the nurse was distracted, this man would stab at the fallopian tubes of women he judged to have had enough children. The arrogance, the violence, the *criminality*, had not been so apparent to Joss all those years ago. He recalled too the humorous brutality of the oncologist who used to tell his patients that their chemotherapy was going to be like 'having a Mack truck run over your body and then backing up and reversing over you again, just to make sure.' Even the patients would laugh. Joss couldn't remember the last time he'd laughed.

How did I do it? he asked himself. He realised that back there in the hospitals, when he had been doing his rounds, he had blocked out suffering by an emphasis on procedures: method, diagnosis, prognosis. He realised now that he had replaced the people he operated on with their organs and operations – another order of transplant, he thought. The gall-bladder in bed seventeen, the hyster in room thirty-four. Of course he was gracious, courteous even, but he was distant. Pulled right back from their human fear and suffering. He had meetings with other doctors to discuss and evaluate surgical lists, and as he strode through the hospital checking his patients, there was not the time, nor was it really appropriate, to dwell on the human suffering of his work, the mangled human pieces that he and the team carefully put back together. Even his questions to patients, although they might refer to their suffering, were asked purely in order that action be taken.

But now, there was no action to take. Joss was aware that he was still agitated by his fight with Polly. Was he a bully? Was it true that his concern for her was selfish, that he only tried to control her so that he would feel less anxious? Why did he continue to hurt his daughter? As he turned into his driveway, Joss felt his heart melt with relief at the sight of her car. She was home safely. He pulled himself together.

He stepped up to the front door and disarmed the security system, unlocked the door and went inside. The house was dim and warm, the familiar sofas and tables lit softly by the low flames of the stove. For a second, the house even felt safe.

He went upstairs and passed her door, through which he could hear the Gregorian chant she liked to play. He paused for a moment, wanting to knock, then he heard the music click off and Polly pad to the door. He was moving back when she threw it open. The terror in her face was shocking. Then the relief.

'Poll. I wish we could communicate better.'

She stood there in her pale blue dressing-gown, her face shadowed with a similar bluish tinge. He saw her features harden.

'Do you? Do you really? Because I've come to the conclusion there's no point in trying to talk to you. If I have a different point of view you just start insulting me. I'm not prepared to let you do that to me any more. You seem to be unable to treat me with respect.' She started to shut the door and impulsively he put up his hand to prevent her closing him out. She looked from his face to his hand on the door and shrugged. 'See? You just can't help it. You're a bully, Dad. You just don't know how to behave. You're so used to giving orders and being the great man. The world doesn't work like that. I don't work like that.'

He could feel the seriousness of her stand against him, its depth and breadth. He took his hand away from her door, ashamed of playing the heavy father.

Her voice was softer when she spoke again. 'I just want you to get on with your life and let me live mine. Is that asking too much? If it is, I'll move out any time.'

That thought was unbearable. He knew he could not be alone. 'You're my daughter and I love you. I'm trying to protect you.'

'Haven't you learned anything yet? You *can't* protect me! And bullying me to get things your way isn't loving me.' He could see she'd been crying and his shame bit deeper.

Her mother's eyes looked hard at him. 'What's it going to take for you to let some humility in?'

He stood there outside her door and she stood just inside her sanctuary, guarding it against him. Then she pushed the door. 'I'm tired, Dad. I've got a big day tomorrow. Semester piano theory. And anyway, it's not possible to discuss things with you.' The door shut with a gentle click and he felt like a clumsy, stupid oaf hitting out against the grace of her protest.

He went to his own room and locked the door behind him. After he'd turned on the bedside lamp he switched off the main light. He had never really known how to be with his daughter, and now it seemed impossible. She had gone a long way from him. He went to the windows and drew the curtains across. Then he looked around the room, as if someone might be crouching in the shadows of the corners. He sat in his leather chair and leaned back. On the top of his chest of drawers, several model aircraft threw long-bladed shadows against the wall: the Lancaster, the Halifax and the Stuka. For a second he might have been back in his study in Woollahra ten years ago with the children playing quietly downstairs. Sybil was supposed to keep them quiet so that he could read in peace after a day at the hospital. But she often failed and he would have to walk out onto the landing and yell down at them. He recalled their faces looking up at him. Their silence as he went back into his study to whatever it was that he found much more important than mere children of his. He remembered how they had loved to play with Mr Diggly-Bones, his skeleton from medical school who was packed in a box in the spare bedroom downstairs. Joss didn't like them touching the bones – it made him uneasy and he'd ordered them not to. But the narrow ivory lengths seemed to exert some sort of charm over the children, and he knew they disobeyed him. Once, returning suddenly from the hospital, he had caught Alan pushing the femur under a chair. He remembered the fear in his son's eyes. In fact, now that he looked back on it, the most common reaction

Alan had had to him seemed to be fear.

Then the thought came to him unchecked that perhaps Alan had wanted to become acquainted with the bones because he'd known, in some way, that in just a few short years he too would start reducing to that dry yellowness.

# 2

At 8 am forensic pathologist Eddie Chandler was as chirpy as any other man who enjoyed his work and liked to get started early. Eddie had a way of staying detached from what he did that prevented him from engaging with the dead. He split his life into work and other. His wife complained that he was detached from her too, but, he would say, you know what women are like. His subjects, the sites of their endings, and the forensic details that connected them to their lost lives were items of immense curiosity, and even delight, to him. He investigated and weighed and probed and analysed, and like Professor Gainsborough he used a macabre humour to cover inexpressible horror.

'Come in, come in,' he said to Joss in his quick manner, taking him by the arm like an aunt might. He was a very short man, worn and leathery like a jockey, Joss thought, and wondered about early hormonal upset.

Eddie proffered the folder of notes in his hand. 'This little fellow took a terrible beating,' he said, as if he were describing the fate of the favourite in the last at Randwick. 'I've had these photocopies made up for you to give to Dennis. I think they'll be helpful. And here are the police photos.'

The pale body of dead Jeremy Smiles filled the first picture: the head tilted in death; the terrified, lifted chest; the belly falling away to the narrow pelvis; arms falling loosely at the sides; the tiny penis hidden in its cowling. His frail body was covered with criss-crossed marks, like the tread of a tyre. There were close-up shots of these as well as other odd, grainy welts and bruises.

'I waited until yesterday morning to take those,' Eddie was saying. 'Came in early. You get much better bruise pictures from children if you wait a while.'

'What are they? Bootmarks?' Joss pointed to the cross-hatched marks in the close-up pictures of the buttocks and thighs. He felt a headache hit his forehead like a thunderclap, so that he had to physically step back to clear the explosion of pain. He sat down, blinked, and recovered somewhat. The headache melted and ran down his neck and he was aware of a twinge near his kidneys. Not for the first time he wondered if he were coming down with a virus.

Eddie shook his head. 'No. They're not kick marks. These were made by something flat and narrow, and the force was pretty evenly distributed over the length of it. Must have been some sort of strap. It's split his skin in places. Might be a piece of fine metal or something on one side of the strap. Some sort of reinforcement. That's why I'm inclined to think it's not a trouser belt. It's something boned with metal. It could even be part of a corset. Do you remember them? They had metal struts through them.'

'What do you think happened?' Joss asked, staring at the wounds to the child's body.

Eddie shrugged. 'He was probably holding the child with one hand. Some of the blows were inflicted with the child standing, then with the child supine – unconscious, maybe dead or dying – the worst of them were done when he was still.' Joss swallowed, trying to prevent his mind creating the scene that Eddie's matter-of-fact voice was describing. 'Maybe he used a belt from machinery. We could try machine shops. Maybe a fancy fan belt. It's too short for a clothes belt. Unless he rolled most of it around his hand, which would have been awkward. Look, you can see the pattern clearly there, as well as a bit of stitching. It shouldn't be hard to track down. It's very distinctive.' He pointed again. 'And there. And there. See? There's the split skin again.'

Joss stared at the regular marks. On some of them the crosshatching was split in the centre by a dark line that indicated where the child's skin had been sliced by the force of the blow. Something hurt his stomach and he realised his own belt was pressing into him. Some sort of saddle stitch? he wondered. 'Maybe it's a stirrup leather, or a girth strap?' he suggested.

Eddie Chandler shrugged his narrow shoulders. 'Maybe,' he said. 'I don't know much about saddlery. It's a long time since I was astride a steed. Looks a bit wide to me. Might not even be leather. Lot of synthetics are stitched – plastics, polys, all sorts of things. Could be a fabric veneer on something else. Anyway, I've done what I can. It's all there in my report. The exact measurements, a tracking of that herringbone pattern, the fine metal strip, the size and width. Good as a fingerprint if you can find the article that made it.'

Joss leafed through Eddie's folder. The measurements of death, he thought, all neatly noted in a manila folder: the estimated time, the cause or causes, the damage to the body before and after. The details and weight of the contents of stomach and organs.

'He was beaten and then strangled through the sheet,' Eddie was saying. 'I've got some fibres – hemp, or something coarse like sacking. Looks like he put the child in or near sacking at some stage. Red dye marking, could be a potato sack. I've got some canine fibres, too, but I've sent them away to the expert analysts. And I've got two sorts of human hair from the sheet and the towel. The boy's and one other. Could be the killer's. Or it might have come from the local laundromat. I won't know until I have something to match it against. I've got some soil. Some of it matches the soil round the cave area, but there's also a fine clay that might have been brought in by either the killer or the boy.

'That towel that was rolled up under his head? It's a common brand used in cheap hotels around the state. And I've got a very small sample of a filamentous green weed from the sheet.' Joss remembered Dennis mentioning the grass stain. 'Green means chlorophyll and the presence of sunlight. I've sent it off to the botanist. There was certainly nothing green growing down in that underground cave. I've checked out the upper cave and there's nothing growing there that's anything like it. Only woody weeds and the usual pasture grasses outside. It might be something from the killer's garden, unless it's from the boy's missing clothes.'

He paused before adding in a quieter voice, 'And you can tell Dennis I could find no evidence of sexual assault on the child.' For a second, Joss thought Eddie Chandler's professional overdrive had faltered, that there was human relief in his voice. 'We've got quite a lot, considering we've got none of the boy's clothes.' He accompanied Joss to the door. 'I've put the time of death at somewhere between four and six on Monday evening.' Joss thought of the low winter sunshine as the kids walked home from school, and of how it was almost dark by a bit after five these days.

He felt Eddie's hand on his arm, heard the urgency in the voice. 'Tell Dennis he's got to find me whatever made those marks.'


At the police station Joss, having discovered Dennis was out, sat in his colleague's office and went over Eddie's notes. He tried to remember what he had been doing late on Monday afternoon, the time of Jeremy's death. Something mundane, he imagined. Like in a sixteenth-century painting where the saint is being martyred, and on the other side of the field sit a lover and his lass picnicking under a tree, while on a hillside behind the martyr's killers a shepherd tends his flock. He looked at his watch again and went out to the front desk, where he learnt that Dennis was at court and would be there all morning.

Joss left the folder of notes on Dennis's desk and left the building. Back in his car he drove to the civic centre gallery, where the Gold of Egypt exhibition was being held. Egypt, the land of gold, the land of the dead. The land of Sybil's birth. He bought a ticket and went inside.

It took a while for his eyes to adjust to the lighting. Here and there, enveloped by pools of dim light, cocoons of gold and polished jewels hung suspended in the darkness. Then he saw that they were housed in barely visible glass cases. They lay on black fabric under light that was dull and focussed so as to minimise damage – some of the pieces were several thousand years old. Joss peered at the first one. It was the exquisite gold collar Polly had mentioned, in the stylised form of a vulture. He walked from case to case staring at the gold and faience, the gems, the jewel-like enamels, the lapis and glass. Delicate fluted cups, necklets, rings, bracelets, even finger stalls of pure gold to protect the drying flesh.

At the end of the room was the huge carved sarcophagus of an ancient king, and beside this lay the mummy itself, in gold and lapis with the sloe-eyes of ancient Egypt, the crossed and swaddled arms holding the crook and flail of power. Joss squinted to read the notes beside the exhibit. This ancient boy-king had lived in upper Egypt three thousand years ago. There was nothing to connect him with another little boy murdered and dumped in a sheet at Spring Caves in northern New South Wales, Australia. Crazy idea, he told himself. It says a great deal more about my processes than any murderer's. Because I can't let go. I'm the one locked in the land of the dead and I can't move forward.

Two dainty feet of bones protruding from the mummy's disintegrating bandages reminded Joss of the denuded bones in the foot of a man almost fatally electrocuted when the kite he had been flying with his son hit power lines. The tendons and bones were shockingly exposed; the flesh and muscles vaporised; his skin scored like pork crackling, stripped and wrapped backwards from the electrical violence. Joss had cut pieces of full-thickness skin, down to the flesh, from the man's abdomen and sutured them in to fill the wounds.

He was staring at these bones, three thousand years old, complex and delicate as porcelain, when the sheer endlessness of death suddenly hit him in waves, until he felt swamped and sickened and had to leave the darkened room. He stood a moment to gather himself into the present before he went out through the exit. In the lobby he introduced himself to the attendant who was selling programmes and gave her his card. Feeling foolish he asked if she'd noticed anyone odd in the past few days. 'No, not really,' she said. 'We don't have odd people in this town,' she laughed, then suddenly stopped, remembering the murder.

Joss heard his name and, still feeling dazed, wasn't sure for a second if it really was Ashley calling him. 'Joss,' she said again and walked over to him, shifting her briefcase to take his hand and pull him away from the attendant. 'What a nice surprise.'

They stood without speaking and Joss kissed her on the forehead, beneath the red-gold hair. His mood lifted and he wanted to hurry her out of there and find somewhere they could make love, so that just for a while the pain in his heart would stop. He kissed her again, feeling the softness of her lips, the warmth of her neck and cheek. 'Let's meet for coffee,' he whispered into the hair near her ear. He felt her nod in his arms.

'What time?'

'Three-thirty,' he said. 'The Seven Sisters.' He kissed the top of her head again and looked into her face, searching for something there.

'I haven't heard from you in a couple of days. I miss you,' she said frankly.

'Me too,' said Joss. 'The murder.'

'Of course,' she said and her vivid eyes softened. 'The little boy.' Then she tilted her head to one side and crossed his mouth with a soft kiss. She hurried away, calling, 'Have to go, see you later,' over her shoulder.

Joss stepped outside into daylight and blinked. After the intense focus of the gallery, the world did not seem real to him. It was as if he had wandered onto the set of some elaborate drama – a feeling he'd experienced many times. Leaving the hospital after countless exhausting hours in the theatre he would step out into a world where an empty chip packet might be blowing up the road, or a gardener was pushing a barrowfull of lawn clippings. Joss was often appalled by this real world – everything felt so rough and coarse after the tense, highly magnified world of clamped veins, forceps and microsutures. Everything looked gross, shocking, ordinary. Uncontrollable.

He was hit by freezing water. The fountain outside the civic centre was being blown sideways by a stiff north wind. He ducked and got into his car and sat for a moment shivering with cold. Then he started the Niva and drove out of town. He wanted to see Spring Caves by daylight. He had a peculiar feeling that he might faint. He shook his head and blinked until the feeling passed. I should have a better breakfast, he said to himself.

At Spring Caves a lone police car with a bored constable just moving out was all that was left of the crowds of police, photographers, experts and onlookers of the past two days. Joss walked up to the murder cave. It had a long opening under a wide arch, about four metres high, where someone had left a bunch of drooping garden flowers. There was nothing else green, Joss noted, thinking of the filamentous weed Eddie had told him about, only dry winter colours: fawn, ash, grey and silvery brown.

Joss stepped past the little bouquet into the centre of the cave. Daylight showed dirty limestone walls covered with graffiti – dates, lovers' initials – and fire-blackened areas where people had camped or cooked. On the back wall, to the right, was the narrow passage blocked up by masonry and barbed wire carrying the prohibition sign of the Tablelands shire council. The entrance to this lower cave had long been closed because of dangerous subsidence in the ground. Just beside the council sign was the hole in the masonry through which the killer had entered with his victim.

Joss made his way carefully through the hole, wary of strands of barbed wire, and down the crumbling pathway. The powerful police lights had been dismantled and all he had now was his torch. He reached the end of the sloping path and stood on the floor of the lower cave, flashing his light around a high-ceilinged area about the size of his two-storey house. Joss shivered and his breath steamed in clouds past the torch's beam. There was a strange odour of dust. Dry stalactites, reminding him of withered pedicles, hung from the cave's limestone roof. On the walls, tracings of ornate Victorian brackets where kerosene and carbide lamps had hung long ago could still be seen. From other dark chambers around him came the desolate plop of an occasional drip hitting the black surface of a pool.

Around the perimeter of the cave and cutting through to bisect it, Joss could see the remnants of mineral baths built in the previous century so that visitors could take the waters. A few broken ramparts of walls remained; the rest had long since collapsed. Litter, ancient leaf drift and old tins had filled the cavities until yesterday, when the contents had been bagged and removed by investigators. But the place still held the smell of rubbish and old bones.

Jeremy's body had been found on the right-hand side of the cave, on a low stone shelf, tightly wrapped in a sheet. Two schoolgirls who had sneaked away from the main party of the excursion and pushed past the masonry had almost fallen over him in the darkness, and then had scrambled screaming to their classmates and teachers.

Joss retraced his steps and breathed deeply in the fresh air. He blinked a little as he stepped out from the overhang of the upper cave. Crows jeered overhead and the morning was building up to a warm winter day. The commercial flight to Sydney was just vanishing over the mountains when he became aware of the sound of a car. Dennis's Commodore came into view and pulled up nearby. Dennis ambled over.

'I thought I might find you here,' he said to Joss. 'I felt like a drive in the fresh air. Thanks for the report. That herring-bone pattern from the belt or whatever it is goes in tomorrow's paper. Someone might recognise it.'

'I thought you were in court,' said Joss.

'Another adjournment,' said the younger man. Dennis was forty-six but looked older and there was a lot of grey that didn't show up in his fair hair. He just misses out on being handsome, Joss thought. There was something solid and dependable in the square features and well-set, tired eyes. Joss tried not to stare at the potentially deadly little blemish on Dennis's top lip, but he saw that the other man had noticed his scrutiny from the widening of his eyes and the tiny frown.

'I just had another look down there,' said Joss too quickly. 'What happens beyond the two caves that I've seen?'

'More caves. More bloody great holes,' said Dennis. 'The local Aboriginal people won't come within cooee of the place. Not anywhere round here. It's a bad place. They reckon it's stompie ground. You can't put cattle here, they won't settle down. Something to do with hearing the echo of their hooves underground. They sense they're not standing on reliable ground.' The two men looked at the earth beneath their feet.

'It's a terrible thing,' Dennis continued. 'The murder of a little kid. I never get used to it. I've got sons.'

He was touching the spot above his lip, feeling it as he spoke. Child murder, thought Joss. The most common form. And eight times out of ten, it's mummy or daddy.

Suddenly Joss was assailed by terrible memories of the explosion and his ear drums nearly bursting as the garage went sky high. He coughed and shifted his feet.

'You don't have any sons, do you,' Dennis was saying in the clear blue day and Joss remembered to shake his head.

'No, no, I don't,' he managed to say, and cleared his throat. He waited until he felt it was safe to look at Dennis again and then he encountered his vigilant eyes. This is a very observant man, Joss reminded himself. The silence was fractured by the screaming of crows.

'I want to go back and reinterview the parents,' Dennis said. 'And I want to talk to Jeremy's young mate again, the Hammersmith boy.' He pulled a tin out of his overcoat pocket and Joss recognised it as the one that had had the old currency in it. He watched as Dennis removed layers of sticky tape, unwinding it like the wrappings on a mummy. Finally, he got the the lid off and drew out the lone cigarette that lay in the tin. The burnt cork smell of tailor-made tobacco hung in the fresh air. 'Because if what that young fellow says is right,' Dennis paused to inhale deeply, 'we've got a killer who's like the invisible man. Hey, remember him? He was wrapped in bandages, too.' Joss recalled the early movie and television series, when tastes were simpler and more naïve.

The two men turned towards their cars. 'Fancy something to eat?' Dennis asked, looking at his watch.

'It'd have to be back at the university,' said Joss. 'I've got a lecture to give at 1.50 in the law building.'

'Sure,' said Dennis. 'I'll meet you there in twenty minutes.'

Dennis was waiting for him outside the reception area of the law school, an L-shaped building of three floors given over to lecturers' and tutors' offices, a large lecture theatre and three tutorial rooms. They bought themselves hot soup and sandwiches from the canteen, then Joss led Dennis down a flight of steps and along narrow corridors until they came to room 203 on the second level. The name 'Dr Jocelyn Haskell' was affixed in black and white plastic to the door. Joss unlocked it and they went into a small, serviceable office with a tidy desk and a terminal linked to the big mainframe of the law school. Joss stooped to pick up several messages slipped under the door by students – requests for meetings or extensions of final dates for the term essay. Several of these essays waited in a tray on the desk for Joss to mark. He drew up the blind to reveal wintry European trees in the courtyard that served as a lightwell for the second level, pulled up a chair for Dennis and sat down himself.

Dennis put his lunch aside and opened his briefcase.

Passing Eddie Chandler's notes to Joss he said, 'There's a lot in here but until we've got a suspect to match it against, it's just paper in a folder. We're getting nothing out of our known offenders.'

He foraged in his briefcase again and pulled out a single cigarette. 'Taped the little bugger on the inside. I almost forgot him. Well, that's not quite true.' He stood up and went to open the window. 'Do you mind if I smoke in here?'

Joss shrugged that he didn't. 'Are you finding it helpful?' he asked Dennis, taking the lid off his soup. 'The work you're doing with ... with the hypnotherapist?' He felt strange, talking about Ashley like this, with this man.

Dennis nodded. 'Very,' he said. 'I'm finding out all sorts of things about myself too. She doesn't like the term hypnotherapist though.' Joss remembered this. 'She says hypnosis isn't a therapy. Just a way of allowing deep absorption to develop.' Joss could hear Ashley's voice in these careful words repeated by Dennis. 'She tells me that most of the time we're not even conscious,' he went on. 'In trance states all the time. I'm learning about body signals. Ashley says she can feel when someone's telling a lie. And I certainly don't disbelieve her.' Joss thought of the steady, sherry-coloured eyes. 'It's great fine-tuning for a humble cop,' said Dennis. 'It's the best thing I ever did. I might not ever give up smoking though.' He laughed and inhaled deeply.

'I had a funny phone call this morning,' he added, sitting down and retrieving his soup.

'Oh?' said Joss, tensing, warned by some subtle change in his companion as much as by the change of topic.

'He'd only give me his first name – Malcolm.'

Joss felt his heart lurch. He was aware that Dennis was leaning forward, scrutinising him, and he kept very, very still.

'Wanted to know if we had a criminology department in the law school of this hallowed hall,' Dennis continued.

There was a knock at the door. Joss could see his fingers

on each side of a sandwich, his thumb and fingertips huge, as if he were looking down an operating microscope. His field of vision had collapsed with shock. He turned to the door so that Dennis couldn't see his face. The sandwich fell from his fingers. 'Come in,' he managed to say through the darkness of his paralysed perception. *Jesus. God. Malcolm. How does he know I'm here?*

The associate professor of law started to come in, saw Dennis and stopped. 'Oh, I'm sorry. I'm interrupting something?'

Joss shook his head, immensely grateful for the respite this interruption gave him. 'Not at all, Brian. Come in. We're talking shop.'

Brian Edgeworth stood in the doorway, stooped and thin in his English tweed, an unlit pipe drooping from his mouth. Joss pulled his mind back from where it had been with Malcolm, standing like a dark guardian angel behind Polly.

'Your 1.50 lecture,' Brian Edgeworth said, and Joss remembered that Edgeworth wanted to sit in. 'Can I make my apologies? I find I have a final-year seminar with the external honours people and I can't change it. Some of them have travelled a long way. I'm really sorry to miss it, I wanted to take some notes. I think I've got a 50 percent snooze rate.'

'That's perfectly fine,' said Joss, functioning again in faculty terms. 'I'll make sure you get full notes. 'Have you met Dennis Johnson?' Dennis crushed his cigarette out on the side of the metal bin near the window and the two men shook hands.

'Only by reputation, of course,' said Edgeworth. 'Dreadful business,' he added. 'We've never had anything like it in this town before.' There was a silence. 'I hear you two are doing grand things on the computer.'

Joss sensed that Edgeworth wasn't too comfortable with either cops or computers. 'A broad reference system,' he explained to Edgeworth.

Brian Edgeworth excused himself and left the room. Joss

forced himself to stay calm. *Malcolm. What's wrong?*

'Wonder why he'd ring me,' Dennis was musing. 'You'd think he'd ring the university if he wanted that sort of information.'

Joss was trying to chew and swallow food. His whole body was shivering at a cellular level. He hoped it wasn't noticeable; he prayed his face wasn't ashen and consciously tried to deepen his shallow breathing. 'And did he say anything else?' he asked in a voice that he hoped was light, a tone he hoped was normal. He risked a glance at his companion, tried to swallow some soup and burnt his top lip.

'He said something about a message in today's *Advocate*,' said Dennis, his voice flat and noncommital. 'I wondered if it might be the killer. Sometimes they like to help, as you know. But then he hung up on me.'

Joss grunted. Malcolm doesn't know where I am, he was thinking. No one knows where I am now, since Polly and I ran away from the job they organised for me in Western Australia. But Malcolm is smart, Joss remembered. Had he left the same message at police stations of other university towns?

'I had a look,' Dennis went on. 'There wasn't anything I could see that might be relevant. He started on his sandwich. 'Beetroot,' he groaned, pulling some out and placing it on the paper wrapping, 'is about the worst damn thing in the world. Reminds me of too many crime scenes I've attended. I forgot to ask them to hold it.' He opened the sandwich to remove all the offending material, reclosed it and bit into it. 'Did you hear what I said?' he asked.

'Yes.' Joss nodded. 'I did.'

'You've lived here – what? Two years? Three years?' Dennis asked lightly.

'Year and a half. Almost the same time as you,' Joss said. 'I came up here last year when they set up this new criminology department.'

'And where were you before that?' Dennis asked. 'I'm sure you've told me but I forget things.'

'I haven't told you,' said Joss steadily. 'And I haven't noticed you forget things.' He blew on his soup for something to do. He was feeling a little calmer now that he'd had time to absorb the news about Malcolm and process it through his shock absorbers. Dennis laughed, but he waited for Joss to speak.

'I was at Strathclyde in Scotland. Post-grad work in criminology the year before I came here.' Joss drank some soup straight after the lie and burnt his mouth again.

'Before that? What did you do?' asked Dennis, too casually.

'I worked as a counsellor – psychologist.'

'What area?'

'Lots of different areas. I did a lot of work with bereavement,' Joss heard himself say. 'That's my PhD area.' He had to stop this. 'Why all this interest in my CV?'

'Just curious,' said Dennis. 'You know what I'm like.' Joss forced some sandwich down his contracted throat. No, he warned himself, I don't know what you're like.

'I notice,' Dennis continued, finishing his sandwich and wrapping up the beetroot and paper debris, 'that you have a very elaborate house alarm linked up to the station. Unusual that. Round here, I mean.'

Joss felt the special fear of the liar, of having to put a story on top of the truth without slipping up. As always, he used part of the truth. 'My daughter is often alone out there. And country towns aren't what they used to be.'

There was a silence as the small ghost of Jeremy Smiles rose in their minds.

'I heard you got your twin endorsement in the minimum time,' Dennis was saying. 'I was having a Guinness with Wal before he went on the wagon. He was very impressed with your ability. Natural flyer, he said. Natural operator. You must take me up sometime.'

Wal Griffiths, the local flying instructor who ran the aero club, had taken Joss through his twin-engine endorsement earlier this year. After years of claiming – in what people imagined was a joke – that he could land an aircraft in an alcoholic blackout, he had caused a scandal by getting sober in AA. These days, now that his wife had thrown him out, he practically lived on the airfield, in a little room with a camp bed, littered with NOTAMS and WAC charts and dramatic posters about always putting the mains down first and never turning back during take-off.

Joss nodded. 'I did a fair bit of flying when I was young,' he said. 'This was more like a refresher course. I'm older and slower now.' He wondered why Dennis seemed so interested in his ability to fly. 'And you?' he asked Dennis to take the spotlight off himself. 'What's your history?'

'I joined the coppers too early. Got stuck, did my matric at night.' He tossed his lunch wrapper directly into the bin. 'I started law too but it gave me brain glaze.'

'Brain glaze is a prerequisite for studying law,' Joss attempted to joke.

'And here I am,' shrugged the other, glancing around Joss's office. His eyes were watchful, in spite of his casual manner. 'You were married?' he asked Joss after a pause. Joss nodded and the spear of ice in his heart turned to fire. Dennis noticed and didn't ask any more questions.

'I lost a wife along the way, too,' he said. 'Next time I'm determined to make my marriage work.'

'Oh yes?' Joss raised an eyebrow. 'And how are you determined to do that?' I couldn't make it work, he was thinking bitterly, and I tried for nearly twenty years. His shocked mind was starting to level out; grew busy classifying, wondering, questioning. *What does Malcolm want? It must mean something's happened to Sybil.* His body was quietening, the cells slowing down.

'By doing all the things I didn't do in my first marriage,' Dennis said breezily, as if all it took to change an entire way of living, of being, were a few finger-snapping decisions. 'I'd spend more time at home. More support for my partner. Time with the children. If there were any. I miss my boys. I only see them once a fortnight. You know, in my twenties and thirties I thought I had to get somewhere? Now it's different. I'm starting to see there's nowhere to get except where I am right now.'

The two men looked at each other in silence. Even in his shocked state, Joss wished he'd known this at forty-six.

Dennis was getting up, moving towards the door. Joss opened it for him, walked down the corridor with him and saw him to his car. He waited till Dennis was out of sight, raced back to his room, grabbed his folder of lecture notes and ran to Neville Grainger's room. He stood and collected himself for a moment before he knocked on the tutor's door. Grey-headed Neville looked up from his desk, saw the look on Joss's face and started to get up.

'What is it?'

'An emergency,' said Joss. 'I have to go into town. My daughter – ' he stopped. He had almost said 'my wife'. 'Can you take my 1.50 lecture for me? It's in A19. Third-year students and it's all here.' He presented the folder. 'Read it out if you like. It'll take nearly an hour to do that.'

'Well, I suppose – ' Neville took the folder and opened it. 'Cruelty in childhood,' he read, 'the hidden roots of violence.' He started leafing through the paper. 'This looks interesting. There's a heap here.' He riffled through the carefully typed notes.

'Apologise to the students for me, please,' said Joss. Then added, 'It would be a great favour.'

'Sure,' said the young man. 'I'll enjoy this. I'll have a look through – '

'I think you'd better start walking to A19,' said Joss. 'It's nearly time.'

He drove the few kilometres to town and found a parking space right outside the newsagent in the main street. He bought a copy of the *Advocate* and started racing through it right there in the middle of the shop, until he noticed that he was attracting attention. Steadying himself, he refolded the paper, tucked it under his arm and walked outside. The newsagent was opposite MacLachlan Park in the middle of town. He crossed the road and stood on the footpath just outside the park's main gates. He could see through to the other side of the square where the cathedral stood, its granite spires and buttresses forming a graceful backdrop to the bare English trees of the park.

Joss walked through the wrought-iron gates and crunched over the limestone gravel of the middle path that transected the lawns. In the centre of the park stood a dry fountain, a circular pool with a central column of snout-nosed fish twisting around one another to support a dry, open chalice. Vandals had clogged it up once too often and it hadn't played for years.

The newspaper burned under his armpit and he hurried out through the far gates and across the road. He raced up the steps and pushed open the heavy Norman door into the gloom of the cathedral. Sickly yellow light filled the centre aisle. He walked down its length until he came to the Lady chapel, hidden on the left of the main altar. A few candles burned in front of an image of the Virgin inclining herself stiffly towards sinners from a rosy cloud.

He sat in a pew and opened out the newspaper. Carefully he scanned each page. He skim-read every piece about the failing cattle and sheep sales. Sheep were bringing ten cents a head; it cost nearly a dollar a head to shoot them. The local production of *Midsummer Night's Dream* was worth seeing, according to Dryden, the pseudonym of the local drama critic, and the Gold of Egypt was one of the most successful exhibitions to visit the town in years. A brawl between student louts and town louts had wrecked one of the popular watering holes. Finally he came to the sporting pages, then the personal columns. He read them all. He was aware of a man coming out of the sacristy and stepping up to the altar, genuflecting then moving to set up candles and a missal. Joss looked over the ads devoted to escort services, massage parlours, lonely housewives, single European gents, until he was sure there was nothing there for him.

It was under Meetings that he saw it and nothing had prepared him for the thrill of love and pain and anger that the words caused in him. He threw his head back as the nine so-familiar words shot up his spine. Then he read them over and over, until he had to shove the paper on the pew beside him and try to calm himself.

He tore out the message, although he knew the words by heart. The man had vanished from the altar and four candles burned in front of the Virgin. Ten metres above him in a stained-glass rose window, enthroned between Alpha and Omega, holding the book of the law and thronged by fiery seraphs, a fierce and frowning Jahweh blazed down. Joss looked up, his eyes blurred, his breath coming hard. Everything I love you have taken from me, he thought in rage. What more do you want of me, you monster? Even my real self you have taken. All I have left now is Polly and I live in hourly dread of her loss. He thought of his daughter's hard tone and taut face as she denied the past. It's done. Over and done with. But then he turned again and saw the familiar words in the paper and knew that it wasn't over.

It could never be over and he had always known that.

# 3

He heard a footfall behind him and swung around. But there was no one there. He glanced at the Lady chapel and the four burning candles, shaking with fear. *Does Malcolm know I'm in this town? Does Sybil know?* No one in the world should know where we are. No one. Not even Malcolm. I'll have to find out if this advertisement was run in other newspapers. He thought of the huge job of checking police running sheets all over the country to see if Malcolm had left a message. Or at least those towns near a university with a law school.

Joss left the cathedral still half blind with shock, the torn page from the *Advocate* in his pocket. He turned a corner and almost knocked someone over. He grabbed her and steadied her.

'Sorry,' he said to the surprised woman and stooped to pick up the parcel she'd dropped. Then he remembered he was to meet Ashley for coffee. He looked at his watch. It wasn't 3.30 yet. He decided to go to the café and have a drink, collect himself before she arrived. He tried doing some deep breathing on the way.

When he stepped inside he saw she was already there, working on some papers at a table down the back, a half drunk coffee beside her. As he approached, she looked up into his face. Even with the light behind her she saw. 'What is it?' she asked.

His mind raced to find the right lie. Always use as much of the truth as possible, he reminded himself. 'Um ...' He came to stand next to her. 'Some news. I've had some shocking news.'

Her sherry-coloured eyes were soft and concerned. She put her hand on his arm. 'Sit down. What's happened?'

He shook his head. 'I just can't talk about it at the moment.' He straightened his shoulders. 'It's probably not so bad. It's just given me a jolt. I need to get home.' He kept standing there. He was aware of the waitress staring, of other people turning curiously to look at them.

'A jolt?' she said. 'Joss, you're in shock and I'm concerned for your physical safety.'

'What?' he said, because her words didn't make sense to him.

'I'm concerned that if you try to go home now, you might walk straight under a car,' she said slowly so that he could understand. 'Or if you make it to your car, I'm concerned that you might have a collision on the road home and be killed.'

He could feel the treacherous softening in his body at the idea that someone cared. Careful, he warned himself. This could be danger. 'I'm all right,' he said, trying to clear his mind, trying to work out what he should tell her.

'You are manifesting all the visible signs of shock,' she said, 'and I want you to sit down and spend some time here until I know you're in a fit state to walk safely, let alone drive.'

The visible signs of anaphylatic shock, he thought, running through them on automatic. Pallor, sweating – could she see that? Then the symptoms she couldn't see – the dramatic fall in blood pressure, cold peripheries, stomach contractions, nausea. The shut-down of all systems except those essential to survival; the fall in vascular volume, keeping blood only at the core, the heart, the brain, the gut, so that the threatened creature could take life-saving action. Run, his glands were telling him, run for your life. Sybil brings the past back with her, howling behind her, the hell creatures. Get Polly and run. Find the magic island of Samsura and fly there with Polly, where we'll be safe.

'I'll run you home,' she said, taking his arm. 'Your daughter can pick up your car.'

'No, no,' he said. 'I'm all right now.' He wanted to be

alone, his natural state, so as to think and decide and work out the best thing to do. He even tried to smile at her to show her how all right he really was. But she was relentless and he remembered how inexorable a counsellor she could be.

'Let's get you some water,' she was saying, turning to signal the waitress. Joss could see the concern in Ashley's eyes. Damn you, Sybil, he was thinking. Why couldn't you keep away? Her image rose before him and he felt the furious anger across his back, behind his heart, like a wave of lava. You dumped all of us. How dare you do this to me now. How dare you want to come back. *How did you find out where Polly and I are?* Too shocked to think this through just at the moment, he pulled out a handkerchief and pretended to blow his nose. He needed to cover his face, which he thought must betray him by its expression of fear. Images of his wife mixed with images of their child. My son, he was thinking in his confusion.

'What about some caffeine?' Ashley asked. He nodded meekly and she ordered two cappuccinos. They sat in silence.

'The colour is coming back into your face,' she said after a while. 'Your pupils are almost normal again.'

Just before the coffees arrived, Joss jumped up. 'Let's get out of here,' he said, suddenly able to act again. He took her arm and steered her out, leaving a bewildered waitress holding two steaming cups behind them. He ushered her to his car, overriding her protests. 'I'm fine to drive,' he said. It was almost true.

Fifteen minutes later, they were in Ashley's bed. He had kissed her in her living room near the little carved image of the Madonna with snowdrops in a vase. Her initial puzzlement turned to enthusiasm when he grazed over her cheek and neck, kissing gently. 'Are you sure you're up to this?' she whispered, with a slight frown. For an answer he took her by the hand into her bedroom. He didn't want to talk. 'Joss? Are you all right?' she asked again.

The room was dim and smelled of her body and her

cologne. On one wall was the large painting she'd done of the Madonna in a bright red robe dancing with the moon, the twelve stars spinning around her head and the redeemed serpent under her feet. He took Ashley's jumper off and kissed her breasts; he undid her bra and kissed them again, holding their fluid weight, blessing them. She helped him with her trousers and when she was naked, he covered her up in the doona while he got undressed. She threw back the covers to enfold him and they pressed together in her safe, soft bedroom. Soon she told him that she didn't know what she'd do if he didn't go inside her right now, this moment, and he carried out her urgent order. He needed sex for the strange space and time it gave him, time when he didn't have to think or be careful, time when he could let the anger and the fear and the shock take another form, just let his body do the running for a while. Damn you, Sybil, he felt in his body as he made love to Ashley.

And when he was sure from her signs and wonders that Ashley was on her way, he let himself go too, and for those radiant splintering moments, absolutely nothing else mattered.

They dozed in each other's arms for a while, until Joss stirred then groped for his watch on the table. It was dim and suddenly cold in the room. Ashley got out of bed, pulling her dressing-gown around her, to switch on the lamp and heater.

Half a face stared down at Joss from the wall and he was startled. For a second he thought of the scalp, right ear and cheek ripped off a patient of his in an industrial accident. The woman had made a complete recovery, despite the stretching, rupture and recoil, the terrible damage to tissues. They had literally stitched her scalp and half her face back onto her skull. Then Ashley switched the hall light on and he realised what it was he had been looking at.

'That's new,' he said, indicating the mask.

'Do you like it?' Ashley was hugging herself for warmth.

Joss looked more closely. The pale, drawn face above him on the wall had a blood-red teardrop running from one eye socket. 'He's a bit – I don't know – menacing for a bedroom. I liked the painting you had there better.' His mind returned to the hospital theatre and he recalled that while they were preparing the unconscious woman for surgery, he had glanced over to see her severed scalp and half-face sitting on top of an upturned surgical basin, like a grotesque hairpiece over a broken mask. He remembered noticing how the shocked expression of the frontalis muscles still wrinkled the detached forehead.

'Dennis gave it to me,' Ashley was saying. 'He makes them. He's got hundreds of them. Fairies, monsters, gargoyles, women, children. They've spilled out from his flat into the garage.'

Joss looked at the mask again, still thinking of the operation, of the way the scalp and half-face had flushed pink – the flush of life – once they'd stitched the graft to the right superficial artery and released the clamps. He was surprised at his strong reaction. He didn't like it in Ashley's bedroom at all. 'Do you think he's got a crush on you?' he asked, swinging his legs out of bed.

He heard her laugh from the kitchen and then she came back in.

'Would you care if he had?' He didn't answer and he saw that her eyes were sad.

She came and sat beside him and took his hand. She folded it gently and lifted it to her lips. 'Do you want a cup of something?'

'Coffee,' he said to be polite. Already, he wanted to be away. The temporary breathing space was going. Sybil's message filled his mind again. Ashley had unfolded his hand and was smoothing it with hers.

'I love the way you touch me, Joss. A lot of men are too rough. You have such beautiful, gentle hands. You could have been a healer.'

For a second he thought it might be right to say, I am – I was, but a terrible thing happened and I brought death to my family and here I am instead. He looked down at his hand, loose in hers. Ashley's were calloused and work-hardened from her garden, her pleasure ground that she was building outside.

She found a scar on his palm. 'Is this one from the accident too?' Joss nodded. Then she touched his face where tiny bits of shattered windscreen and shrapnel had embedded themselves in his flesh nearly three years ago.

'It must be terrible, losing your wife in such a shocking way,' Ashley said softly. He could only nod as the explosion erupted again in his memory; the crazy supernova of flame and deafening noise. His own shrieks. Sybil's. His ears seemed to ring again.

'Did you say something?' he said.

'No. I was just thinking what a terrible loss it was for you. All those years of marriage.'

Joss sat on the bed, staring at the red-robed Madonna. The expedient lie he'd told Ashley about Sybil being dead had lain quietly between them, uneventful, unimportant. In one sense, it was even a veiled truth; she had decided to leave his life permanently. But now Sybil was starting to stir like someone in premature burial. He noticed for the first time that all of the twelve stars around the head of the Madonna were tiny dancing people, their arms and legs spread wide, their hair flying.

'I'm going to take a shower,' said Ashley, and in a few minutes Joss could hear the water. He got dressed, turning his nakedness away from the hollow eyes of the mask. The rage against Sybil was easing, replaced by fear. It's not just Sybil who brings the demons with her, he was thinking as he pulled on his shirt. There are demons in me, too. This was such a surprising thought that he had to sit down again. He drew his trousers up over his legs, automatically careful of the indented section of his right groin where the ache never stopped. The doctors had decided against digging out the piece of metal lodged next to his pelvis.

The past is part of my structure, he thought. It's in my bones.


'How are you feeling now?' Ashley asked when he went into the kitchen a short while later. She stood in front of the kettle with her hair slicked back and a towel around her shoulders.

Joss shrugged. 'Okay,' he said.

She put her arms around him and looked into his eyes. 'No, really,' she said, the sherry-coloured eyes alert.

Joss chose his words carefully. 'I feel like I've been in a fight, died and then gone to heaven.' He kissed her head. 'And I feel awkward – stupid – that I can't tell you what the news was all about.'

'My mysterious lover,' she said, drawing back so that she could look into his eyes. 'You looked as if you'd just heard of a death.' No, he thought. Almost the reverse. A resurrection.

'How's Dennis doing with his anti-smoking therapy?' he asked, both curious and irritated at the thought of it.

She shook her head. 'You know I can't say anything about that.' And of course she was right. They both had secrets from each other. Once, he thought, I never would have asked that question.

'Well, how's work in general?' he asked, to give himself time. Ashley was checking canisters, looking for the tea to suit this time of afternoon. She had several.

'I need a break,' she said. 'It's hard to stay with so much pain without a holiday.'

'But surely you shut down all the time, steel yourself against the pain of other people,' Joss said, remembering his training, wondering what she could mean.

'There is no shutting down, no steeling against,' she said to him. 'There is only being with it and letting it flow through me. I grieve with those who are grieving. I rejoice with those who are rejoicing.' She decided on a sensible Ceylon. 'In this world,' she added drily, 'there's a great deal more of one than the other, although very few like to acknowledge that.'

'That mask,' he said, 'I don't like it. It's unnerving to think of a police officer making those.'

'Why on earth?' she asked.

Joss shrugged. 'It looks like someone's death mask. It unnerves me. I want you to put the Madonna painting back again.'

She laughed. 'You sound like one of those European men who have no time for religion themselves but insist that their women carry out the indispensable rites.' She poured boiling water into the teapot. 'I should warn you,' she said, 'there's another mask in the garden.' Lifting a heavy coat from a hook and putting it around her shoulders, she opened the back door. Joss followed her outside.

The westering sun cast low swathes of brilliant green across the small area of lawn Ashley tolerated. A stone path wound through bare European trees to a wooden summer house, covered in climbing roses. One of Ashley's larger sculptures leaned over the left-hand side of the path, a human figure androgynous and pleading. Behind this a square, classic pool edged with local granite blocks reflected the still sky, the black twisted boughs of a plum tree, the almost motionless clouds. To the right of the path was an enclosed garden with photinia, holly, tall rose bushes, garden seats and a wrought-iron table. Apart from several deciduous trees, this yard had been a flat, empty tract of paspalum and weeds when Ashley arrived here nine years ago with her sixteen-year-old son, Damian. Joss had seen photographs of the neglected yard. The garden was part of her heart's work, she said. And in this garden he always felt as if he could breathe more deeply.

Feeling cold he walked to a bare silver birch and leaned against it to draw the late winter sun through the dark wool of his trousers. Ashley reached up and pushed the hair away from his forehead, as if he were a child. Instinctively he pulled his head back.

'You're like a horse that's been mistreated,' she said. 'It's okay. I'm taking my hand away now.' And she did, dropping it to her side.

Sometimes her tenderness frightened him. Sybil had not been a tender woman. Sybil was quick and impatient and passionate.

'I wish you'd do some simple relaxation with me,' Ashley said. 'To help with the stress. The tension in your face gets deeper every day. And sometimes you're not even in there, behind the face. Where do you go to? Who are you with?' She brought her hands very slowly up to his shoulders. 'I worry about you. I *care* about you.'

He took one of her hands and folded it in his own. He felt the new callouses from the rock wall she was building behind the summer house. 'I know you do.'

'And you never say it back to me. You just stay safe and neutral.' She leaned closer to him and looked into his eyes. He turned away, shamed by her honesty. 'You are always perfectly charming and respectful. You accept my tributes graciously. But you never give me anything back.' She sighed and moved away from him. Several crowned calyces from the last of the roses jutted out from a bush and Ashley tweaked them off. She looked past the rose bushes down to her rock wall that ran along the back fence. The wall was now waist height. 'You have to let her go, Joss.'

Joss jumped at her words because Sybil was still haunting his mind. For some reason – it may have been the blackness of the water – Ashley's pool always reminded him of Sybil's mirrored eyes.

'She died three years ago,' said Ashley. 'You've got a life without her now.' She went to sit on the steps of her summer house and turned towards him. 'I think it's time you started to live it.'

Joss pushed away from the silver birch and walked down to where an old ironbark horse trough, now filled with the green spears of winter bulbs, divided the dark pool from the summer house. He balanced himself on one end of the trough. The late sun gold-dusted Ashley's strong tawny hair and eyelashes.

'Day after day,' she said, 'for who knows? Maybe another twenty, thirty, forty years?'

Forty years. It sounded like a life sentence. It was a life sentence, he realised. I am sentenced to live for the rest of my natural life. He had never seen it like that before. He looked away from her clear, direct eyes to see a stone face peering at him from above the rose lattice. She had warned him. It looked like someone's head up there.

'Do you remember,' he said to avoid thinking about the life sentence, 'a fairy tale about a horse's head that was nailed up over a gateway and that answered questions in riddles?'

'I do,' she said. 'But I'm not thinking about that now.' She stood up and walked back to the house, Joss following her. In the kitchen she poured very strong tea. She went to the fridge for milk, found sugar, and passed him a cup, all the while keeping her back to him, and when she finally spoke Joss thought he heard tears in her voice. 'Do you want to live all that time with a ghost?'

He couldn't answer her. He couldn't say anything, could only remember the time he'd used almost the same words to Sybil.

'Isn't there some room for me now?' Ashley had turned and was leaning against the sink looking at him, her face fragile with pain. 'I've been a friend of yours for a year and your lover for six months now. I've respected your decision not to talk about the past, but it's not just you who's affected by that. It's starting to hurt me too.' She went to pick up her tea then put it down again. 'There is something hard and unhealing in you. Defended. This isn't like any grief I know. I think you need help.' There was just a touch of 'there, I've said it' defiance in her voice.

Joss remained silent, drinking his tea slowly, knowing that what she had said was true. He put his cup down and went and collected his coat, leaving her in the kitchen. When he came back she was still standing against the sink. He stood in the doorway. This is too much, he was thinking. I can't deal with this now. He walked out again.

'Joss?' She stopped him at the front door, her face pleading. 'Joss, please. I had to say this. I've been needing to for a while now. Say something.'

He looked down into her face, her ardent eyes, her soft mouth. 'I'll consider what you said,' he told her in a level voice. Then he left. He didn't kiss her goodbye. Nor did he turn around, unable to bear the sight of her face.

Joss placed the torn page from the *Advocate* under the clock on a shelf in his study. He went upstairs to his bedroom and stood at the window. Tonight he didn't care if there were hidden knives behind him. He looked down at his overgrown front garden and the cypress drive that ran to the road. The mountains were dusted with moonlight, gleaming cold like skulls, part of the great indifference of a universe that sustained everything just as it was: love, rage, hatred, murder, birth, cruelty, compassion. Everything is of the same order to you, Joss thought. And we all come to the same end. The only difference is in the manner of it.

He knew the fear was coming closer to the surface. Ashley had touched it when she reminded him he had a whole sentence of life to live. Lately, he'd come to the understanding that being a doctor actually created more fear around the process of living. More fear, more horror. Always anticipating, somehow expecting the worst. Seeing horror where anyone else simply saw a child running happily along with a stick. Whereas I, he thought, would see the collapsed eye and destroyed brain tissue that I'd have to try to save next day through microscopes. The child lighting the family barbecue on a sunny Sunday afternoon became oozing burn tissue to be covered with paper-thin skin grafts. There was a horror in having a body, bones and flesh and organs, because the world was full of hideous injury. And being a doctor brought that horror close. He thought of the Christmas set of bow and arrows he'd taken away from Alan because he'd had to remove an arrow from the soft palate of a young girl. Always careful, always trying to keep his children safe in a world that offered, in the end, only their total destruction. He realised he had never thought of this before – that the death of his children was inevitable. It was considered morbid, he knew, to dwell on death. As if we didn't all dwell *in* death. Even without injury the body dies as we live; teeth decay, hair falls out, joints turn to calcified stiffness – turn to bones – skin breaks down, eyes fail. Until the worms of the graveyard or the blistering flames of the crematorium mercifully complete the job. Did I permeate my children with my fear?

He caught a whiff of Ashley's smell and thought of the countless lovers who'd joined briefly under the moon's cold light. Who now were ancient dust and bones. He remembered Ashley saying that all the unexpressed ghosts of parents take up haunts in their children, that she had found her secret ghosts living in Damian. But Polly won't even hear me, he thought. She won't even let me talk about the haunting.

Somehow, he thought, I brought the fear home. Somehow, I drew death to the garage, into the Mercedes. And then let Alan drive the car.

He remembered Lombard struggling as the court sheriffs tried to drag his bulk into the police van outside, the contempt in his voice. 'You fucking little piss-ant *doctor*!' The tears of rage running down his suffused face. 'You'll pay for this!' Lombard had never been to prison in his life. Joss had stood there, stunned and silent, wondering if Lombard was about to have a coronary on the spot, wishing that he'd just done his job like a good boy and never asked those questions.

Eventually he went to bed. He couldn't sleep for a long time.

# 4

Patrick and Cecily Sharp walked hand in hand to the pedestrian crossing. Roberto the lollypop man had put the 'Children Crossing' flags out and he sat there nodding approval as the cars slowed. Patrick and Cecily stood at the kerb, waiting. Cecily didn't like Roberto. She was aware of the way he stared slyly at her small breasts, just visible under her navy tunic. She had taken to hunching whenever she was around him. All the parents and teachers thought Roberto was just wonderful. Patrick had no such fears; he enjoyed the fact that the lollypop man often had a sweet for him and the other little ones. He did, however, pick up Cecily's shrinking and he knew there was something irky about Roberto.

From home to school the two youngsters had a walk of about a kilometre through the town's wide streets, where often there were more dogs than cars on the road. Their mother had wanted to walk with them this morning, considering the terrible thing that had happened to Jeremy Smiles, but after discussing it with her husband had decided it was probably healthier not to make a fuss. Business as usual was the best way to go.

At 8.30 in the morning some of the locals were out in their gardens, watering because of the continued drought, pruning because it was winter, or just idling in the early sun with a cup of tea, the perfect reward for a well-spent life. Cecily and Patrick passed people who knew them by sight, if not by name. Most of them, when they saw the little boy and his sister, were unable not to think of another little boy, Jeremy Smiles, who had used to pass their houses once and would do so no more. Neighbours shook their heads and wondered what it was all coming to. The town wasn't used to this sort of thing. Most insisted the murderer could not be a local. Locals were graced with the innocence that birth and life in a country town bestowed. It was bound to be someone from Sydney or elsewhere, an itinerant, a rough labourer, a farmhand full of alcohol and madness. A monster, not one of them. They knew through gossip that all the local sex offenders – 'their' offenders – had been able to account for themselves and were none of them under suspicion of child murder.

Cecily and Patrick were well known in the town because Mr Patrick Sharp senior was deputy headmaster at Kiangra South Primary as well as a leading force in Rotary. Mrs Patrick Sharp – Jennifer – was also a teacher, and the mother of two other children. The Sharps had made the decision to leave Melbourne and settle in Maroonga , not only for Patrick senior's career path and mortgage requirements, but also because country living was superior, they believed, for bringing up a family in safety. There were fewer temptations in the country. A slower pace. Smaller numbers, less stress.

Cecily loved Patrick in a possessive way because he adored her, and so she clutched his hand tightly even though they were on the crossing. Hunching against Roberto's horrible eyes, she hurried them across. They arrived at St Callistus quite safely a few minutes later with Patrick looking forward to the annual infants' picnic. Cecily took the tartan rug she'd brought and gave it to Mrs Hammersmith, Sarah's mother, who put it in her car with a pile of others. Then she ran to join her girlfriends.

Several hours later, Patrick Sharp and slender fair-haired Simon Prendergast sat on the tartan rug at the picnic grounds in their green and gold party hats. The children had made the hats in craft class earlier in the week and were now enjoying far too many chocolate crackles under the supervision of Sister Mary Matthew, who was studying towards a higher degree in mathematics, and Miss Crawford, who taught Second Class. Two of the mothers had come along to help supervise.

The Maroonga picnic grounds covered several flat, cleared acres along the steep-banked Maroonga River, where a number of the hundreds of ancient river gums that once graced the banks had been spared to provide a shady spot for campers and picnickers. Some ten or twelve metres above this spot was a rest area for drivers, with fixed wooden seats and tables and a brick barbecue. A toilet block with stainless-steel toilets and sinks was kept reasonably clean by the local council, whose cleaner scrubbed every few months at the curses, lovers' intials in hearts, the damning of sluts and the naming of spunks. In front of the toilet block were five parked cars, and in front of them was the wire fence that gave on to the flights of stone and log steps leading down to the picnic grounds.

On the riverbank, Simon Prendergast stood up and approached Sister Mary.

'Yes, Simon?'

'Please Sister, I want to go to the toilet.'

Sister Mary Matthew looked around and called to one of the Second Class girls. 'Carmel, will you please take Simon up the steps to the toilets?'

The two children climbed the rustic steps until they'd reached the high ground. There they turned and looked down on the party of children in colourful millinery. Simon had an urge to throw a handful of stones but he restrained himself, and sighing at his own goodness he went into the the toilet marked 'Gents'. He walked into the darkness and blinked his eyes into adjustment.

'Come here,' said a voice. Simon peered into the darkness. He managed to see a man looking over the top of the furthest cubicle, where it was darkest. 'I've got a game for you.'

Simon stood his ground. He came from a family where even small members were treated with respect and so he had not been dazed into automatic obedience to adult commands. He didn't like the sound of the voice. It had a false note that warned him. Simon thought he saw eyes glittering.

'Come here,' the man repeated.

But Simon stayed where he was. 'I don't want to,' he said. He was feeling bad about this. He wanted to go to the toilet, yet he knew there was danger in that cubicle and he didn't dare go into one of the others because the man with the lying voice might come in and get him. Simon stood still, holding his breath.

'Come here,' the man said again, and this time Simon could hear the anger. 'There's a really good game here. It's just for you. I'm a friend of Patrick's.'

Simon was confused. This person said he knew Patrick. But Simon didn't feel this was right. In just the same way that people who are trained to discern counterfeit currency only ever work with the genuine article, Simon immediately recognised the wrong tones.

'You are not,' he said.

'Come here!' The man's anger was barely concealed now.

'No,' said Simon. 'I won't.' And he turned and ran from the toilets to join Carmel, who was standing further along the fence waving to one of her friends below.

'Finished?' Carmel asked.

Simon shook his head. 'No.'

'Why? Are they all full?'

Simon shook his head again. 'I didn't even go because there was someone in there and he was real weird.'

'Who?'

'I don't know. Come and see.' Simon took Carmel's hand.

But Carmel pulled away, sensing danger. 'Let's tell Sister,' she suggested, and the two children ran down the steps calling out. As they reached the bottom and ran over to Sister Mary, there was the sound of a car pulling out.

A few minutes later Miss Crawford and the two mothers, with Sister Mary Matthew minding the little ones below, made a thorough search of the toilets and the surrounding area. It was quite deserted.

Joss sat in his study under the Leonardo drawings. The malachite desk set still declared it to be July the sixth. In front of him was Eddie Chandler's autopsy report and copies of the notes taken by Dennis during his interviews with the parents of Jeremy Smiles. He stared at them and then put his head in his hands. If only I could find some peace, he said to himself. He was quite unable to concentrate, haunted by the message from Sybil, and unable to think yet what he ought do about it. He pushed the report away and went into the lounge room to stand at the large bay window.

Late sun on winter paddocks filled with long dry feed spread up to the foothills where erosion gullies, hooped by blackberry canes, split the slopes. Lower down, ten-cent sheep dotted the river flats, picking at whatever they could find. The brown river had sunk out of sight. This winter was so cold and dry. Like me, Joss thought. He went restlessly back to his study and from among the books on his shelves pulled out a text on homicide. He skimmed down the index until he found what he was looking for: child murder. The most common form of homicide. In most cases of child killing, he read, the perpetrator was one of the parents. Boys were more at risk than girls, up to the age of eight, after which more girls than boys were killed. In almost 80 percent of cases the killers were men. Newborn babies were particularly at risk.

Joss turned back to the police notes. Jeremy Smiles was eight and his mother had been juicing oranges on the food processor for his afternoon tea during the few minutes that he had vanished. Mr Smiles had been at work at the garage where he was an auto-electrician. There was no question of parental guilt in this case.

Jeremy always walked home from school with his friend Daniel Hammersmith. On Monday Daniel had gone into the milk bar in Addison Street, where they both lived. Jeremy, having no disposable income, did not follow him in; he waited outside. In the less than two minutes that it took Daniel to complete his transaction involving bubble-gum with football transfers, Jeremy Smiles had vanished.

There were only two directions he could have gone: on down Addison Street towards his home, or back the way he'd come. But he hadn't gone back, because Marjorie McManus, the elderly woman who lived in the house on the corner, had seen and heard the two boys go past her garden towards the milk bar, and neither of them had come back. And he'd never made it home. The shopkeeper remembered glancing up at the mirror over the doorway as he gave Daniel his change, and he didn't see anyone outside. The two boys were very familiar to him, with Daniel coming in almost every day. Nor did the shopkeeper, Daniel nor anyone else hear or see a car. When Daniel came out of the shop and looked down the street to see where his friend was, Jeremy had vanished.

Addison Street was one of the better streets in town, home to a large number of retired people. Opposite the milk bar was the high cyclone-netting fence planted with vines and flowering shrubs that ran along the parking lot to the shopping mall. On the side of the street where Jeremy lived were houses full of people and dogs. No one had heard or seen anything out of the ordinary. No one had seen Jeremy after the two boys reached the shop. The only possibilities were impossible to believe: someone had taken the child, either struggling or unconscious, through the front garden and down the side to the backyard of one of those trim houses – filled with headmasters' widows having afternoon tea in the winter sun, or gardening – then somehow climbed over a back fence with his burden, straight into the backyard of one of the adjoining houses of parallel Kimberly Street, similarly populated, and worked his way silent and unnoticed, out of the front garden and onto Kimberly Street. Or he had somehow negotiated the three-metre cyclone fence opposite the milk bar – difficult enough for an adult to climb alone – at peak shopping hour without being seen by anyone in the car park.

Every house in the area had been checked and searched with the owners' utmost cooperation. Not one shred of physical evidence had been found to indicate that a man and a boy had crossed over two properties back to back. No garden beds had been trampled. No dogs had barked. No one had seen or heard anything, least of all Daniel. People were adamant there had been no car.

Mrs Smiles had become worried when Jeremy was ten minutes late. The rule was that he always come straight home, then he could go out again and play. He had never broken this rule. Mr Smiles used to thrash his children if they broke any rules, Mrs Smiles told the police. Jeremy had not yet had one of his father's thrashings, but as the youngest child he had witnessed many assaults on his two older brothers and his sister. Mr and Mrs Smiles prided themselves on the obedience of their little son. Mrs Smiles knew something terrible had happened to her son when she went out looking for him and heard what Daniel had to say.

Joss laid the notes aside and his heart was heavy. With the routine violent assaults they called discipline or child-raising, the Smiles had trained their little boy to become a killer's prey. Jeremy would not have been capable of saying no to an adult, particularly not to one he sensed was capable of violence like his father. Joss hoped the Smiles never became aware of this, because the pain of it would be too terrible to bear. He remembered the training tape from the FBI he'd watched in his fast course in criminology, the interview with the murderer of seven little boys in New York. 'I hang out where the little kids go,' the killer said. 'And I watch them. I watch for the most obedient little boy. He's the one I start talking to. From there on, it's child's play.'

Joss couldn't concentrate. Thrashings. Obedience. He rubbed at his aching eyes as facts about the deaths of children kept rushing into his mind. As if that wasn't enough, bronze and gold images of Sybil were haunting him. Her sherbet smell, her infuriating ways, the mirrored eyes that seemed to open onto a history so ancient he often felt naïve and raw in comparison. Their lovers' game. How he would lift her chin up, amazed in the early days that such a vivid and beautiful woman could love him. '*Sivilla, ti thelis?* What do you want?' he would say, using the famous question and answer routine to the ancient Sybil. 'I want to be kissed,' she might say. And he would. Or, 'I want to be fed.' And they would walk hand in hand down Victoria Street looking for the right place to eat. Or, 'I want to be held.' And he would take her in his arms. Or, 'I want to be left alone,' and he remembered her snarl, her cruelty and her sharp teeth. Her falseness. How she could turn into Medea in an instant, screaming and vicious. Go away, he told the images. It was a long time ago and things were very different now.

Deliberately he leafed through Eddie's report, trying to bring his mind back to little dead Jeremy Smiles, noting the photographs of the crosshatched markings. Thrashings and a belt. Something started moving in his belly and then in his mind. A flashing image – it exploded in his imagination – shocked the entire landscape of his mind. The image was cold and jerky, as if caught in a strobe flash, stark and very terrible: a child being beaten with an odd, short strap. He felt the symptoms of shock collapse his physical system. His mind raced and spun. He thought he was about to faint. He leaned back in his chair and tried to breathe more deeply. Then just as suddenly the image vanished, leaving his mind plunged in confusion. This wasn't the usual torment, the memory of the explosion. This came from another place, a deeper, older stratum. *What is happening to me?* he screamed in silent terror.

Joss sat still for a few seconds then stood up shakily and went back out to the lounge room. He felt he wanted a drink or a cigarette, yet he hadn't smoked in years. He couldn't be still. He walked from room to room, looking in each one as if the thing that would bring him peace was lying around somewhere just waiting for him to pick it up. He stopped pacing and willed himself to turn around and go back to the study, to his reading. The phone rang. Joss snatched it up, pleased at the distraction. 'Yes?'

'Another kid's gone missing.' It was Dennis. 'A boy. Patrick Sharp. Seven years old.'

'I'm on my way,' said Joss, putting down the phone.

He drove straight to the police station. Dennis was sitting at his desk under a wall clock that said 4.58.

'It looks bad, mate,' Dennis said as Joss came into the room. 'Real bad. He's the same age group, the same uniform. It's the same MO as far as the disappearance goes. Mr Invisible again. The kid's sister was a bit late picking him up from the infant school. When she gets there, there's no baby brother. She gets hysterical and runs away and hides. Neither of them show up at home and the mother comes down here screaming. In the meantime the sister's gone home, told the father, he comes down here and I've had the father, mother and the girl to deal with. And an aunt.'

Dennis stood up and walked around his desk to the grey metal filing cabinets against the wall. He opened a drawer roughly and started patting through the files until he came to one towards the back. He opened it and found the cigarette. When he had lit up he hunched forward, pulling a chair out for Joss to sit on. 'I've got the worst feeling about this,' he said. 'I'm praying the little bugger's gone to a mate's place or run away. But all my instincts tell me it's the second killing.'

Joss nodded. 'It's fast,' he said. 'Two in five days.'

'It's fast,' Dennis agreed. 'This guy's way out of control.' He stood up. 'The doorknock's been extended to a wider area.' He indicated a semicircle on the map. 'All the streets around where young Jeremy Smiles lived. And Patrick's vicinity. The school grounds are being searched. Next door,' Dennis jerked his thumb towards the incident room, 'they're checking records nationwide, releases from jails, psych hospitals. See if any crazies are out and about.' He sighed. 'We've pulled in all our sex offenders. I'm asking around to see if there's anyone new in town.' He picked up a photocopy of the herringbone marks and threw it down in irritation. 'How come nobody sees anything? I'm just praying young Patrick's sniffing glue safely somewhere with a few little mates.' It was a bitter joke and the two men looked at each other. 'I'm going round to talk to the sister again when she's calmed down a bit. I think you should be there.'

Twelve-year-old Cecily Sharp was calmer now. Her pale, pretty face was swollen from crying and Joss could see she'd been sedated. He sat silent while Dennis leaned back in the comfortable leather lounge. Good art work and ceramics and shelves of books made the room pleasant. Beside Cecily sat her Aunt Harriet, the adult witness the law required when a minor was interviewed. Cecily's mother was completely incapable of being interviewed and her father was on his way back to the family house, after leaving his wife in the care of relatives.

'I was with Scottie near the fountain in the park,' Cecily was saying. 'We were just talking and stuff and then I looked at my watch and I got a terrible fright because I was late to meet Patrick. I was meant to get him earlier than usual because they'd been on the picnic.'

'And then?' Dennis asked.

'I ran all the way. He wasn't there.' The girl started crying in hopeless, low sobs. Her aunt's arm tightened around her. 'Come on, darling. You've got to tell the police officer everything you can remember.'

'When you're ready,' Dennis said, taking out his notebook. 'When you can, Cecily. I want you to tell us everything. At the moment your brother's only missing.'

'No he's not,' cried the distressed child. 'He's dead, like Jeremy. And I killed him. Mum said.'

'That's not so, Cecily. That's not so.' Joss spoke without meaning to, and was aware of Dennis's quick eyes turning to him, surprised and a little annoyed.

'Come on, dear,' said white-faced Aunt Harriet. 'It won't do any good going on like that.' She patted her niece's knee in a vain attempt to stop the sobs that were racking the girl.

'I didn't notice anything,' Cecily finally said, lifting a despairing face to the two men. 'I was too frightened when

I saw he wasn't there. I ran back to the park and I just sat there. I didn't know what to do.'

'How long were you there, in the park?' Dennis asked.

'Half an hour or so,' Cecily answered. 'I just didn't know what to do.'

'You were in shock, Cecily. It's common, that feeling of not knowing what to do,' Joss said, remembering. The girl's eyes fixed on his and her voice became stronger.

'I ran back to the school and looked around for him again. But he wasn't there. Then I went to his friend Simon's place. He wasn't there, either. Then I went home and Dad was there. I told him. Dad hit me across the face.' Her voice choked with crying. She was too distressed for further words.

Dennis stood up. 'Thanks, Cecily. If you remember anything else, no matter how small or silly it might seem to you, will you contact me?' Dennis pulled his card out of his pocket. The aunt put her hand out to take it on her niece's behalf but Dennis deftly slipped past her and put it in Cecily's outstretched hand. 'Promise me you'll ring me?' he said. 'Any time of the day or night? I don't sleep,' he added.

The girl nodded. She looked up at him, her face stricken and swollen. 'Please find him,' she said. 'Please.'

'We'll do everything possible,' Dennis reassured her. 'I promise we'll do everything.'

In the hall, they met the returning father, silent and stooped with worry. He handed over more photographs of his missing child.

'That was only three weeks ago,' said Mr Sharp, pointing to a snap taken on school sports day. 'He would've come first except he'd hurt his ankle training the week before.' Joss saw a smiling child holding a trophy. Mr Sharp let them out the front door.

The cost of murder, Joss was thinking as they stepped into the cool air of the Sharp's garden. The distraught, heavily sedated mother; the despairing, repressed father; the errant older sister who slipped up in her responsibility and missed picking up her brother, *once*. One mistake, that's all it takes. Joss shivered. One deviation from the usual way of doing things and a crack opens up and something from hell slips through like smoke. Did he really believe that? That adhering to the formula keeps you safe? Surely not. That was the place where magic grows and Joss thought of himself as a rationalist.

They got into the Commodore and Dennis started the engine. Joss stared ahead at the pleasant street, with its wintering European trees and khaki eucalypts along the nature strip. One mistake is all it took and I am here and Alan is not.

Dennis and Joss found three people waiting to see them at the station: Miss Crawford from St Callistus school, and Mrs Prendergast and her little boy Simon. Miss Crawford apologised for Sister Mary Matthew, who was at that moment sitting an end-of-semester exam at the Protestant Presbytery. Simon had something to tell them and he was not interrupted while he gave his account.

'Do you think you could tell us what that man looked like, Simon?' Dennis asked when the little boy had finished his story.

Simon shook his head. 'I couldn't really see his face. It was too dark.'

'Could you see what colour hair he had?'

'Sort of brownie coloured, I think.'

'Like mine?' Dennis said, indicating his head.

'No. More like his,' said the boy, looking at Joss.

Dennis swung around to look at Joss then turned to the boy's mother.

'Mrs Prendergast, can you please come with us to the picnic area before it gets too dark?'

With two other police officers following in a second car they returned to the picnic ground, where a mist was starting to gather over the brown river and the bare willow tangles and eucalypts were very still in the cold air.

Simon stood just inside the entrance of the toilet block, while Dennis, Joss, Miss Crawford and the two police officers went in turns into the last cubicle, closed the door and looked over. 'He was about that tall,' Simon said, pointing to Joss, who was the tallest and cleared the top of the door by a good half-head.

'What's your height, Joss?' Dennis asked. 'Six foot two?'

'And a half,' Joss added drily and Dennis jotted it down in his notebook. 'What about his voice, Simon? What sort of a voice?'

Simon thought. 'It was an ordinary voice,' he said. 'Just an ordinary man's voice.'

'Do you know what an accent is?' Dennis asked him. Simon did because they had several children from other countries in his class. 'Did he have any accent?'

'No,' Simon said. 'He didn't have an accent. But he sounded angry.'

The group walked slowly along the fence where the cars had been. 'What about the vehicles parked here?' Joss said, looking down at the hard rock and dust. It was not an area for tyre marks.

'There were several,' said Miss Crawford. 'About half a dozen, I think.'

'Could you describe them for us?'

Miss Crawford looked dejected. 'There was Mrs Hammersmith's car. That's a red Toyota. She and Mrs Lamb were helping us with the children. The other cars... I don't know. There was a white one. Or a light colour – fawn perhaps.' She frowned, trying to recall. 'I've got an idea there was a blue one. Maybe another red one. I really don't remember. I was mainly making sure we didn't leave anyone or anything on the bus.'

Dennis nodded. 'Will you and the, ah – Sister and the other mothers please get together on this? Try and remember the cars. Ask the kids, too. Any other details. And if you could ask the children in a quiet sort of way if any of them have been approached by anyone at all lately. I'll come and talk to you all on Monday. See what you've remembered.' He handed them his card and ushered them into the car with the officers.

'Let me know straight away. Ring any time,' he said. 'I don't sleep.' Dennis put his hand out to the boy. 'Thanks, Simon,' he said. 'For helping us.'

'That's all right,' said Simon.

'I wish young Daniel Hammersmith was like this lad,' said Dennis as he and Joss drove away. 'Some kids are there. They're observant. Some kids are away with the fairies.'

And some kids are gone with the angels, thought Joss.

Back in Dennis's office, Joss tried to loosen a contracted muscle in his neck. Dennis opened a drawer and took out a carved Indonesian box with a lonely cigarette. He lit it with relief, then swung round in his chair to face Joss.

'At about one o'clock this so-called friend of Patrick's talks to Simon Prendergast about Patrick Sharp in the toilet block at the picnic ground. And in less than three hours, Patrick is missing. If it's our killer, he's high-risk yet very organised.'

He stood up and went to a whiteboard and wrote the last four words he'd spoken. 'And bloody invisible. If it's not a copycat and this is the second killing, we're dealing with a very bold offender. Anyone could have come into that toilet block. Anyone could have turned a corner and found him grabbing the child. Someone passing in a car. But nobody sees anything. No one hears anything. It doesn't add up. People notice things. They come forward. But we haven't got a thing.' He shook his head. 'High-risk but premeditated. Maybe he watches, sees where the weak link is and then moves. Maybe he's always ready and just moves when it's safe. Like a guerilla operation. Is it just coincidental that these boys are so similar? Or does he do a careful selection? Has he already got a list?'

Joss shuddered at the thought: a list in a child killer's pocket of little fair boys and their names, where they went to school and where they lived.

Dennis picked up his phone and pushed three buttons. 'Get someone down to the Prendergast house right away,' he said. 'That boy shouldn't be left alone.'

Joss ran his eyes down the whiteboard where the physical details of Jeremy Smiles were listed. Age: eight. Height: three foot, six inches. Weight: four stone, twelve pounds. Colouring: sandy hair, blue eyes. Slight build, last seen wearing the St Callistus school uniform of blue shirt, grey winter trousers, maroon woollen tie, maroon jumper, maroon blazer. Black school shoes, size six. Scar on the left knee. The word 'uncircumcised' completed the list of details.

'We'll need to check everyone who works at the school,' said Dennis. On a second board, under the heading 'Missing', he started copying Patrick's details from his notebook. 'Look at this,' he said. 'Age seven, but almost exactly the same height and weight. A bare three and a half feet tall. And neither kid was ever away from home like this before. It looks bad,' he muttered. 'What are your feelings?'

Joss glanced down at the occurrence sheet on Patrick Sharp and saw the routine phrase, 'Fears are held for his safety.' He stared at the details of the two boys. He considered. 'We've got two little boys, similar colouring, similar size. One dead, one missing. Both attend St Callistus school, both wear distinctive maroon blazers and long grey winter trousers.' He picked up the picture of little Patrick smiling with his trophy and attached it to the whiteboard that carried his name.

Dennis looked at him and shrugged. 'Maybe he's offended by the names, Smiles and Sharp. They're unusual,' he said. 'They're short. They both start with S.' He underlined the two names on each of the boards, underscoring the capital S's heavily.

There was a knock at the door and the probationary constable Graham Parke came in. 'Um,' he said, half in the door, half out.

'Yes Graham?' asked Dennis impatiently. 'What is it?'

'There's a driver from Marshall's at the front desk,' said the young man hesitantly.

'And?' said Dennis, his voice becoming irritated.

'He's had some of his load pinched.'

'He's what?' repeated Dennis, looking at the young man as if he suspected all of the probationary constable's load was missing.

'He's had some of his load pinched,' repeated the young man, awkward and unbalanced in the doorway.

'Constable,' said Dennis in a parody of exaggerated patience, 'what exactly do you want me to do about it?'

The young man stared back at him. 'Um. It's the report. I'm not sure how to set it out on the report, sir. It wasn't the whole load. It was just the mirrors.'

'What the hell are you on about?' snapped Dennis.

'The driver left the truck to have some lunch, and when he came back all his mirrors had been pinched off the furniture he was delivering. Like screwed off the dressing-tables? And off the vanities? But the furniture wasn't pinched.'

Dennis rolled his eyes to heaven. 'Constable, go and get Kylie and ask her to show you how to set out exactly what you've just told me. Okay?'

Graham Parke backed out and closed the door. Dennis shook his head. 'Don't know where they get them from these days.'

'So what do we do now?' asked Joss.

'We wait,' said Dennis and put his marker pen down.

This was one of the big differences between them. All Joss's training lay in action, interference: diagnosing the problem, discussing procedures, deciding to cut. 'But surely,' he said. 'I mean we've got a missing boy, presumably in great danger. Don't we look for him? Turn the countryside upside down?'

'We're already doing a doorknock of the area with everyone we can dredge up,' said Dennis and his voice was harsh. 'We could search for a year and still not get anywhere near finding him.' He started patting his pockets, looking for something. 'We might fluke it. But without a lead it's slow and almost always useless.'

'So you're saying we do nothing?' Joss asked in a voice equally harsh.

'I'm not saying anything of the sort. This killer is highly premeditated, yet seems to act on impulse. Two very contradictory MOs. Nobody sees him. Yet he appears in the most public places: in a main road outside a school, in a residential street next to a shop. He's taking children from under our noses. How does he do it? How come he's invisible? His methods don't fit any profile I know, any theory I know.' Dennis picked up his lighter from the shelf at the bottom of the Jeremy Smiles whiteboard. He drew a single cigarette out of his top pocket. He put it to his lips and lit up, dropping his hostile eyes in a frown against the smoke, raising them narrowed again. 'A theory is a box of lead, in which to hide a heart that's dead,' he said unexpectedly.

For a second Joss thought he was reciting a nonsense poem. Then he realised what the words meant, and he remembered Ashley saying them, teasing him with them some time ago.

'And I didn't say we do nothing,' said Dennis, pocketing the lighter. 'I said we wait.'

Joss took his leave and drove down the emptying streets. He passed the mobile field unit sent over from Tamworth that had been set up near the school. He couldn't help admiring the way Dennis worked.

It didn't take him long to find the Smiles family home: a bungalow in a block of ten houses that fronted a wide country street lined with birches. Bare trees behind the house formed a lace against the silver sky. There were no lights on and the house looked uninhabited. He remembered hearing that Mrs Smiles had collapsed completely and was in hospital.

He remembered Sybil at the hospital dressed in black with her nose running and tears spilling from her eyes, how she had looked the moment she told him she wouldn't be coming with him, that she could never forgive him for the death of her son, couldn't change her life and her whole identity. That she'd take her chances as they came.

And that there was someone else. The shock, the terrible shock of that phrase, thrown almost carelessly into all the other anguish. *There's someone else.* Those words that change the world.

He focussed again on the neat cottage and wondered where Mr Smiles was and what he was doing. A tyre swung from a camphor laurel tree in the front yard. This house in South Maroonga seemed unearthly.

Joss restarted the car and drove home through the too quiet streets of town.

# 5

He felt the familiar surge of relief as his lights picked up his daughter's white Celica near the old shed. The shadows in the cypress drive seemed darker than they had ever been as he switched his headlights off. He sat there for a while with the engine off. Why did I come back to this house, he wondered to himself. This town? Because it is the only place that holds some sense of home for me. He had taken the job created for him at the University of Western Australia, was there for a few months, but couldn't stop watching his back. If the protectors know, someone else can know, he kept telling himself. It's not safe here. He was reading through the positions vacant when he saw that this university in the country town where he'd once lived with his grandmother needed someone with his skills. His new skills. And it had been sheer accident that the old house had come onto the market around the same time. But there are no accidents, Freud had once remarked, and Joss shivered.

He thought of the mask over Ashley's bed. He thought of the twenty-year-old woman who had been missing half her head and face. What was the last thing Alan had seen before the explosion stopped his seeing forever?

His mind turned to the killer. Who are you? A loner, in your twenties or thirties, ill-educated, unemployed, with a criminal history like the common profile of violent killers? Or are you fifty-nine, Joss thought, and the father of six children? Employed in a bank. An honoured citizen of this community with a devoted wife. A man who steals towels from cheap hotels. A family man who picks up boys to kill on his way back from Rotary meetings? Where is your house, Joss wondered, staring out the window of the car at the dark hills.

He made a mental note to find out what had been happening in town at the time the boys disappeared. What places of work knock off before four o'clock round here? You might be a technician, employed by the university, driving home after setting up the lab for the last ag-science lecture. It's perfectly feasible that you might be someone like me, an academic. Professor Murderer, PhD.

Joss got out of the car, shivering in the cold air, and let himself into the house. He called his daughter's name. There was no answer. He went upstairs but she wasn't there. His heart froze until the sound of an axe took him to the window of his bedroom and he could just make out her figure, splitting firewood. The terror drained from him and he switched on the radio to hear the last of the local news. At the end of it came an advertisement for number nine chooks, on special at the supermarket. He wondered why the announcer was suddenly screaming and then he realised it was Polly shouting downstairs. Joss spun around, snatched the iron poker from the fireplace and almost fell down the stairs, two at a time.

'What is it? *Who is it?*' he yelled as he reached the lounge room. He raced to where Polly was standing quite alone, holding the piece of paper torn from the *Advocate*. Her face was hollow, white with rage.

'How dare she!' she screamed. 'How dare she do this, the damn bitch!'

Joss felt the poker fall from his hand. He went to take the paper from her hand but she crushed it and threw it down. 'You weren't supposed to see that,' he said weakly, picking it up and taking it back to his study. He saw where Polly had dropped a small pile of neat kindling in front of the fireplace. She must have seen the edge of the paper sticking out from under the clock when she straightened up. Curious, observant Poll.

'No way is she going to come back into our lives!' Polly was screaming as she followed him into the study. 'She made her fucking decision. Let her stick with it. We've both had to.'

Joss went to place a hand on her arm but she shook him off. He looked into her scared, hard young face. He saw that her whole body was shaking with anger. 'You're not going to let her, are you Dad? You're not going to respond to this. You're not. You couldn't be.'

I have to find a way to deal with my daughter, Joss thought. Somehow, I keep hurting both of us. To gain a few moments for himself he went out to the kitchen where the kettle was rattling. He tipped the old tea out into a garden bucket and heated the pot. He could hear Polly crying now and blowing her nose. He emptied the hot water out of the pot and spooned in tea. He poured the boiling water, put the lid on the teapot and found the grubby teacosy that he'd been meaning to wash for months now. Gripping the bench top and bending his head, he squeezed his eyes shut briefly against the whole terrible mess. Then he blinked a couple of times and took two cups and saucers out of the cupboard and a carton of milk out of the refrigerator. When he finally carried the tray in, Polly was sitting in the bay window with the mountains behind her. She was wearing her hair in two long tails above her ears and she looked about fourteen, a forlorn spaniel.

He set the tea things on the table and she turned her pale face to him.

'How did this happen?' she asked, pointing to the piece of paper.

'Dennis gave me a message about there being something in the *Advocate*. He got a call from Malcolm.' He watched his daughter stiffen.

'That creep,' she hissed. 'Him and his video security.'

'He probably saved our lives, Poll. He organised everything for us.'

Polly shrugged. 'That's his job,' she said. Then her face crumpled, the spaniel ears fell forward as she hung her head and covered her face with her hands. 'He didn't save Alan,' she whispered.

'No,' Joss said. 'He didn't save Alan.'

He went to comfort her but again she pushed him away.

Finally, he felt, he was starting to understand her anger with his heart. Yet here he was again, still playing the protector. 'Do you want a cuppa?' he asked.

She nodded, sniffing. He could see the anger in the stiffness of her shoulders, the set of her head on her neck. He poured a cup of tea and passed it to her. She let it sit there, steaming.

'You don't know what it's like,' she said. 'Lying all the time. Telling my friends and Ignatius all this phoney bullshit. I'd just got settled in Perth and we had to leave. I'm not blaming you for that. I think it was a good decision. But I hate all the lying. About what I did when you were supposedly studying at Strathclyde. And Mum being dead, killed. Although that doesn't worry me too much, she's dead to me. And Alan never existing – that hurts me.' Her voice wobbled, then grew strong again. 'It's disgusting. It is insulting to Alan. It dishonours all of us.'

It's true, he was thinking. We are all dishonoured, diminished by this false life.

'And anyway,' Polly went on, 'Ignatius knows there's something weird. Something going on. He asks questions because things just aren't quite right. He's an intelligent man. I've got to look into his eyes and lie to this man. And to everyone.'

'I'll bring some wood in,' Joss said, getting up.

'No. You stay here,' she commanded. 'Don't run out on me. Listen to what I'm saying. How am I ever going to have a real relationship with another human being if my whole life, *my whole self*, is built on a lie? Built on these secrets? How can I ever be real?'

Joss stood there in front of her feeling helpless. 'We went over it, remember? We're not doing it to defraud anyone, Polly, we had to do it. You didn't see Lombard's face that day. I did. I know the lying is hard. You have Ignatius Ho, I have Dennis Johnson. And Ashley Smith. But you know what the alternative is. The alternative is what happened to Alan.' He paused. 'Poll. The lying comes with the territory.'

She started to cry then and despair welled up in him like nausea. 'Polly, listen to me. Since Alan died, I've come to see things differently. I used to have rigid ideas about what was good and what was bad. Now I know it's not that simple. I'm not so sure what's good and bad these days.' He realised the truth of the words as he said them. 'My old belief structures are changing. All I know is that some things are worse than others.'

She hadn't heard him. She was preoccupied. 'You're not contacting her, are you.' Her voice was hard and it was more a command than a question. Joss realised that, for a moment, he'd forgotten the inital subject of their discussion. 'You're not to, Dad.'

'I don't know,' he said. 'I was as shocked as you.'

'Yes,' she said, 'but the thing is, I hate her. You don't.'

It hurt him to hear her words. 'Do you really hate her, Poll?'

His daughter's face was white with pain and she was unable to speak. 'She wouldn't come with us,' she said at last. 'She rejected us. Just because she was having some stupid affair.'

'Poll. She was forty-six. She said she couldn't do it. Couldn't have her life made over again. It wasn't the affair.' Joss closed his eyes briefly against the pain, all their pain.

'*Bull*shit! She didn't want to be where she was. She was always restless. Always discontented. Always wanting something else. She was never happy with how anything was.'

'Poll, she was an unhappy woman who never really made the adjustment to living in this country.'

'Why couldn't she? Millions of others have. She never tried. And you didn't help. You just sedated her so you wouldn't have to deal with her. And now the new relationship hasn't worked out and she wants to come home. She wants to come back to us. For a while, maybe. Till the next enthusiasm. Well, fuck her.' She slurped angrily at her tea.

'I didn't know you knew about – about the affair,' Joss said, feeling worse than awkward. It felt wrong, talking like this with Polly.

'Parents are so dumb,' she said and her contempt was bitter. 'They think kids don't know. Don't you think we've got ears? We heard you both. Night after night the same damn fight. On and on. Don't you think we can see and think and hear for ourselves? Just because neither of you had the guts to say, Look, this is what's going on, you think we didn't know.' She jumped up and ran upstairs. Just before she got to her bedroom door, she yelled back down. 'If she comes back, I'm going. I'm going back to the old life. I don't care how dangerous it is. I won't care any more about anything. If she comes back, I go and the bastards can blow me up too if they want to.'

He heard her door slam. Wearily he picked up his tea. He had no doubt about the seriousness of his daughter's intentions. He remembered the futility of trying to persuade her to retain the new name she'd used in Western Australia. But she had insisted on reverting to Polly when they'd moved to Maroonga.

The phone started ringing. He picked it up. It was Dennis, who had just been speaking to Sister Mary Matthew. She hadn't been able to tell him anything about the makes of the cars parked at the picnic ground, she couldn't recall the colours, she couldn't even tell if they were late or older models. But she did have a mathematical memory and keen eyesight, and because she'd practised mental arithmetic using the figures from the number plates while the children were eating their lunches, she was able to give him the five registration numbers.

'Sometimes,' said Dennis, 'the guardian angel of detectives gives us a sweet one like this. I'm checking it through now.'

When Joss put the phone down he noticed his hand was shaking badly. He stood, stooped over, observing it. Too much, his mind was saying. Too much is happening too fast.

He went and found the torn-out newsprint with Sybil's message written in their old question and answer routine, their lovers' game. Surely no one else in the world knew about that. Then the box number.

Almost in the same instant that he thought of it, Polly was running downstairs expressing the fearful question that had just seized him. 'What if it's not her, Dad? What if they're using her name to flush you out? Please Dad. Don't you see? Either way you mustn't, *mustn't* answer that ad.' And she ran into his arms and he held her. He rocked her.

As he held his daughter's shaking body, there suddenly came images of a child being beaten with that terrible short strap. Then just as quickly the images vanished, leaving him stranded and panting. Polly stepped back to pull out a tissue and noticed his face.

'What's wrong?' she said.

Joss sank into the nearest chair. There was no strength left in the bones of his legs. 'It's my head. It aches.' They looked at each other, she much stronger than him at that moment.

'Either way,' said Polly in a softer voice, 'you mustn't respond to this.' Her eyes were full of despair and grief and the pain of locking her mother out of her heart. She stood there for a few moments then went slowly back upstairs.

He remained sitting, too drained to move, and soon he could hear the strains of the *Dies Ira* being chanted by monks. *Salva me, salva me, fons pietatis.* He managed to get to his feet again and went to the tea tray. He poured himself a cup, not caring that it was cool. I need help, he thought to himself, if it's Sybil. And if it isn't, they know I'm living in Maroonga. They've found me. I've got to get Polly out of here. I can't do it alone any more. I've got to get help.

He put his cup down and went up to his bedroom. At the back of his wardrobe in a locked box under a pile of shoe boxes, he kept a Smith & Wesson .38. He drew it out, along with ammunition. He went to Polly's door and knocked gently.

'Yes?' Her voice still tight.

'Can I come in?'

Polly had switched on her bedside lamp and was sitting up in bed. He walked over and she made room for him to sit. She looked at the gun and then at his face.

'Poll,' he said. 'I want you to take this and grab a few things and I'll drive you over to Ashley's place. I want you to stay with her.'

She sat up, holding the doona around her neck. 'What?' she asked with irritation. 'Right now?'

'If they're on to us, it won't take them long to get this address. I'm going to Sydney to try and contact Malcolm. I don't want to make any phone calls to him from this house – not even from this town.' And he wanted the freedom of the air, he thought, the illusion it brought of detachment and superiority. The pure night skies of the tableland. 'I want you to keep this with you.' He indicated the gun. 'You know how to use it.' She nodded. She'd learned two years ago. 'Maybe take it out tomorrow and have a practice, loading and firing.'

His mind raced. As their case officer, Malcolm was supposed to be the only person who knew where Joss was located. But Joss had not stayed in Perth. Perhaps Malcolm had given Joss's last known whereabouts to Sybil. But why would he do that? Unless someone had traced him from Perth. Or maybe someone had rung Dennis using Malcolm's name, and it was just coincidental that Sybil had advertised the same day? No, that was too impossible. Maybe it was Dennis who was in up to his neck with Lombard? Maybe there never had been a phone call and Dennis was watching him now to see whether, and how high, he jumped. *But no one could know about the Sybil game.* Could they? There is no one out there I can trust, Joss thought. Not a soul.

Polly watched while he placed the gun on her bedside table. He put six bullets in the top drawer, where they rolled heavily. 'You're going to meet *her*, aren't you?'

He winced at the loading on the pronoun. 'Poll. Be reasonable. I can't meet her. There's only a box number. I'm going to see a man about a dog.' It was a stupid phrase and he regretted it immediately.

'A bitch, you mean.' The word stung him but he remained silent. Polly settled back down in bed. 'I'm not going anywhere. I've got the gun and I'm not leaving this bed. What would you tell Ashley anyway? That I'm scared of the dark?'

'She wouldn't ask questions if I asked her not to,' he said.

'We can't trust anyone,' Polly reminded him. 'Anyway, this place is like Fort Knox. It's safer than anywhere else in town. No one could get in here.'

Joss looked at the grilles on her windows, the almost invisible electric wire that ran across the wall to the door, and in the corner the winking red eye that never slept. Could electronic devices protect them against Lombard's rage and his curse? Nothing had been able to protect them against the crater under the garage at Woollahra.

'Please, Poll, do as I ask. Get dressed now and come to Ashley's. They want to make an example of us.'

'Then what's the point of running?' Polly was looking at the ceiling, a slight frown on her face as if she were just now coming to this realisation. 'Can't you see? If they've broken through this whole bloody story that you and I learnt off by heart, this big set-up, then it's all been done for nothing.' She sat up again. 'The state has wasted its investment rather badly.' Leaning over she picked up the gun and the weight of it pulled down her narrow wrist. 'I'm a very light sleeper. Anyone getting in here would have to use a D-12 caterpillar and gelignite. I think I'd wake up,' she added drily, although fear had sharpened her face. 'I could just pick them off.' She pointed the barrel of the gun at first one, then another imaginary figure near the window. 'I think I'd enjoy killing them after what they've done,' she said.

He looked at the slight form of his daughter, her pale

face and neck, the fragile collarbone, the twin tails of hair shiny on her shoulders, the gun gleaming in her white hand. None of this should have happened, he couldn't stop thinking. This is beyond terrible.

'Poll,' he said stricken. 'I'm so sorry about everything. About all of this. I'd do anything to undo it, anything at all.' She stared at him, willing the tears to stay out of her wide eyes. 'I didn't know it would be like this, Polly-Wal-the-Doodle.' They were both surprised by his sudden reversion to her old pet name. 'I took that position at Farnesworth in good faith. It seemed perfect. Your mother and I were going through a rough time. When I found out about some of the transplants they were doing at the clinic,' he gestured and his hands made a huge shadow on the ceiling, 'I did what I thought I had to. I believed I was bound by an oath. I didn't know what I was lifting the lid off. If I'd known then what was going to happen to all of us, I wouldn't have said anything. Perhaps that might disgust you, but I'm not a hero. I didn't know Alan would have to die. That your mother wouldn't be on our side. I didn't know about the lies we'd have to live. I didn't know the first thing about myself. I thought I had all the answers. But the truth was that I was fifty and I had no wisdom.' As he said the words, he recognised their truth. 'Forgive me.'

Polly looked at him steadily but her eyes had softened; she was touched by his frankness. 'Of course I do, Dad. It's just that you haven't really changed. You still think you've got all the answers.' She knelt up in the bed and kissed his cheek. 'I'd like to go back home just once,' she said, 'to get one thing.'

'What's that?'

'My little girl diary. The blue one with the gold clasp on it. Malcolm said under no circumstances could I take any personal papers that might reveal anthing, and I did what I was told. Wasn't I the good little Vegemite?'

'We both were, Poll.' Joss remembered the fat little book, clamped together like a missal, in which Polly had written her secrets when she was small.

'I'd like to have that book,' she went on. 'Read through it, remember being a little girl again. How life was like before all this.' Joss found he couldn't remember. It all seemed so lost, the old life, in this new place where every minute was sharpened by terror.

Polly wiggled the gun then put it in the drawer. She pulled the doona up and he leaned down and kissed her. In spite of everything, it was the closest she'd been with him in years and he felt humble and absurdly pleased. He could feel a smile pulling on some of the tiny pits and scars on the surface of his face.

'Thanks, Dad,' she said. 'You're starting to sound like a human.'

Joss realised he knew very little about this young woman who was his daughter. He left the room wondering if it was too late to start learning.

An hour later he was ready to go. He left the lamp on in the upstairs hall and stepped quietly downstairs, avoiding the creaks. In the dark lounge room he looked at the pattern of bars on the moonlight-silvered carpet. He pocketed the newsprint with the Sybil message, left a note to Polly telling her to be very careful and then tore it up, knowing how much it would anger her. I'm going to get someone to mind her, he decided. He double checked all the locks on the doors and windows and the winking red eyes in all the rooms. Then he went outside and activated the alarm. The stillness of the clear, cold night and a rising three-quarter moon vindicated the Civil Aviation Authority forecast. A bull trumpeted from the river flats as Joss got into the car and let the brake off, rolling it down the drive, not engaging second gear until he was almost on the road so as not to disturb Polly.

The airfield was deserted as he did the pre-flight check on the Piper Navajo he leased from Airtrax. From time to time he glanced uneasily over at the low amenities block where several hooded lights made haloes in the frosty air.

He climbed into the Navajo and found the frequency for the weather report, switched on first one engine then the other. He had decided against phoning through a flight plan. The coded runway lights lit up at his signal and he taxied out, warming up.

Joss opened the throttle full on and the aircraft shuddered as the revs built up. He could feel the Navajo straining to be airborne, dipping along faster and faster past the lights. His heart felt lighter in spite of himself as he eased the stick up. The moon climbed onto the Navajo's nose.

An hour and fifty minutes later Joss parked on the grass behind Canterbury airport. He switched everything off and climbed out. The cold felt softer here down south, but his breath still steamed as he crossed to the airport. There was one cab on the rank and he was booked into a room at the Regent in just over an hour.

The death threats had started as soon as Joss told the authorities the provenance of some of the organs used at the clinic. Even before the trial, Malcolm would collect him from the hospital and brief him, sometimes taking him to a bar where the noise level kept their conversations safe. Then Malcolm would drive him home to Woollahra, check in with the man from the federal police protective services who sat outside all day, then check the house and gardens. He'd go inside and let Joss in. He'd check the logging tapes, check the internal security of their house. It was strange having another man almost living in the house. Joss remembered arguing with Sybil while Malcolm was in the next room, how unsatisfying it was to fight in whispers.

Now, from the fourteenth floor of the Regent Hotel, Joss looked out over the stunning lights of Sydney Harbour. It was a view like nowhere else and he had missed it. Behind him the room was international hotel style, first class, pink and grey, with watercolours of flannel flowers on the walls. He took out his little book and used the phone number he hadn't dialled in two years. A guarded voice answered. 'Yes? Who's speaking?'

'Malcolm, please. I need to speak to Malcolm Guest.'

'I'm afraid Malcolm left us some time ago. Who is this?'

'Doctor Ross Pascall.'

There was a silence. Then, 'Perhaps I can help?'

'I doubt it,' said Joss. 'Where did he go? Was he transferred?'

'I can't really say,' said the other. 'He no longer works for this department.'

'Where can I find him? It's urgent,' said Joss. 'I need to speak to Malcolm.'

'I've told you he doesn't work here any more. Ring again in the morning, my supervisor will be here then. Maybe he'll be able to help you.'

Joss hung up. He stood by the phone feeling abandoned and even more afraid. He only needed Malcom to check out a simple fact. Had Malcolm rung Dennis as part of a ring-around to university towns? He needed to talk with him. He needed to know what to do next. He needed strategy and he needed help. He sat on the bed and looked around, wondering what he was doing, why he was in Sydney. This is paranoia, he told himself as he felt the pressure building up. He pulled out Sybil's message and went over to the writing desk. She had used the phonetic English spelling of the classic pronunciation of her pre-Christian name, given her by her Cretan mother in defiance of the priests. It was safer; it no longer looked like the name people recognised. 'Sivilla,' he read in the grubby newsprint, 'what do you want?' And then the answer: 'I want to come home.' God, thought Joss. Home. So do I. He was hit with longing for a home he'd never had, never known. He remembered his childhood dream of the island of Samsura, how he'd believed that there were wonderful wild animals there, and possibly treasure. His special island where his father had helped put down the surface for the aircraft that flew in men and arms and supplies during the battle of the South China Sea.

He pulled out some Regent notepaper and picked up the narrow hotel pen. He stared at the wall and tried to think intelligently. What if I do nothing? What if I just pretend it hasn't happened or that I didn't see it in the paper? What if Dennis hadn't bothered to pass on the message? I wouldn't be sitting here. Nothing need happen unless I act. What would Dennis do? he found himself wondering.

He got up again and walked to the window, leaning his forehead against the cool glass. Navigation lights winked in the channels of the black harbour. His head was thick with tiredness. And what if Sybil wants to come home? How do I feel about that? I've had two and a half years without her. Sometimes I can almost believe Sybil is dead, that she died in a car accident.

I'm almost used to being a widower with just a daughter, he thought as he went to the courtesy bar and pulled out a toy bottle of scotch. He poured it into a glass and drank it quickly. If this is real, I need to meet her, to decide if I want to see her again. And if I meet her, I need to set it up in a place that's safe for me. A place I can check out thoroughly beforehand. See who comes and goes. Where is that place? Somewhere only she and I would know? He thought he knew now what Dennis would do. Dennis would wait to see what happened next. Polly's threats came into his mind. If Sybil comes back, I go, she'd said. Back to the old life. That was like suicide.

'They think they've got you,' Malcolm had said to him in the hospital. 'They'll be looking for a woman and two adolescents now. That's good. They'll be looking for the wrong configuration.' And then it was even better, Malcolm had thought, for Joss and Polly when Sybil had refused to go with them. They wouldn't be looking for a widower and his daughter.

My son. Joss closed his eyes. That I have to say I never had. *Stop that noise, you two. Run outside. Run away.* Joss bowed his head as the pain intensified. Al, I didn't mean you to run that far. He leaned against the desk. How else could I have done it? he asked himself for the millionth time. He thought of the trial, himself in the witness box giving his damning evidence about the transplants. He saw Lombard's eyes again, with murder in them, opposite him in the court room.

'You're a fool,' Mr Barker the head surgeon said to him later at the clinic. 'We're *saving* lives here – thousands of your fellow Australians die every year because they can't get transplants, and you blow the whistle on this hospital. You throw away thirty years of my hard work building this place up. Just because a tiny percentage of the organs – less than 5 percent – come from a source that our laws choose to deem illegal, for the time being. No one knows how to handle this sort of thing. The laws are changing all the time. No one was harmed. The only law that was broken was some unimportant clause in the Immigration Act, for god's sake. These people were paid very well. Everything was done with first-class medical supervision. If people can say how their organs are to be disposed of after they're dead, surely they can do the same when they're alive? Doctors weren't even allowed cadavers to dissect not so very long ago. The law is an ass and you're a self-righteous fool. Look at Lombard's sentence. He'll be out in six months. Men like him come in one size – international. He's too big for policing anywhere. Fighting him is like fighting City Hall. You were mad to even think of it.'

Joss closed his eyes. If I could just pay the fine and go home, he thought. Just be finished with this pain. He remembered trying to tell Barker that established criminals like Lombard were not the sort of people he wanted as business partners, but it had sounded pompous and pathetic.

He looked down at the traffic lights, changing uselessly in the deserted streets. I could jump, he thought, and that would be the end of it. They could cross off another of their symbolic figures. It was always a choice, that one. And it was his to make. No it wasn't, because there was still Polly. She needed him, the little protection he still offered, the buffer between herself and the evil that would wipe her out to terrify other people into silence.

But I have to meet Sybil, he decided. The custodian of my past, my lost history. My wife, the mother of my children. And he knew suddenly the place to meet her – the pyramid of slipped volcanic rock that rose from the sea, covered with seagulls and their droppings, the water in the bay the same colour as the sea off Cyprus, the purple and red pea vines trailing over native rosemary and banksias. The lighthouse, the sand dunes sliding down to the wild long Pacific beach. He turned back to the desk and wrote quickly. 'I'll meet you at the place where we first made love.' He added a time and date but didn't sign the note.

He addressed the envelope care of the newspaper box number and put it in his pocket. Until I send this, he thought to himself, nothing changes. But once I arrange delivery the universe swings around into another gear. It might mean they will move in closer, stake me out, kill me. Or Sybil could return, making my life turn upside down with her energy and her demands. Or both. He felt himself shiver with fear and excitement. Ashley, he thought, I will have to say something to Ashley.

He fell onto the bed and was amazed to wake again three hours later. He rang room service and ordered a knock-out macchiato and then he ordered a cab to the airport. Downstairs at reception he ordered a security courier to deliver the letter. It's done, he thought. Then he flew the Navajo through the dawn back to Maroonga.

He was back home by 9.45 to find a note from Polly saying she'd be late that night and reminding him to take the chicken out of the freezer if he wanted a casserole. He went upstairs, set his alarm and pulled the phone out. He woke an hour later, blinking and frightened at the buzzing of the alarm, not knowing whether it was still the same day or the next that he'd blundered into. He showered, made coffee and sat down in the lounge room, where the mountains glowed through the bars in the late morning light.

There were several phone messages on his machine. Ignatius for Polly, Brian Edgeworth inviting him to a faculty picnic at the weekend, then Dennis's voice, increasingly angry by the third call.

'Where in hell are you? We've found Patrick Sharp. Dead. I'm at the crime scene now. Used to be the Maitland Hotel. The old Maroonga Road where it meets Macquarie Street. Get here quick.'

Then the click. To Joss's overloaded mind, Dennis's voice sounded accusatory, as if he believed Joss was somehow responsible for the death of Patrick Sharp.

Joss parked the Niva near the blue-and-white checked police tape that cordoned off the old pub. He saw Barry Armstrong from the *Advocate* talking to Dennis and another detective. Dennis looked up and gestured him over.

'Three juveniles broke into the premises during the night. They saw Patrick Sharp and they freaked. They didn't tell us until hours later. They say they didn't touch anything. We're about to send him over to Eddie. The guys from the hospital morgue have just arrived. I've been trying to contact you since five this morning.'

'I was out.'

Dennis's eyebrow lifted enquiringly.

'Personal business,' Joss added. 'I was out until about two hours ago.'

Dennis stood looking at him, waiting for more, but Joss said nothing. 'I'd appreciate it if you'd let me know in future where you can be contacted,' Dennis said coldly. 'You signed a contract. You're part of this team now. It's hard sometimes for academics to think like that.'

Joss followed Dennis into the interior of the old hotel. He found himself in the saloon bar where a beam of powerful light cut upwards through the dusty air from a trapdoor in the floor. At the open well of light he put his hand up to shield his eyes from the glare. He turned to descend backwards down the narrow ladder until his foot touched the ground. Turning round he saw that he was standing in an underground room about four metres by three with two barred windows on the right-hand wall, high up where it met the ceiling, just on ground level. Every surface was iced with white fingerprint powder and was harsh in the brilliance of the police lighting.

In the right-hand corner was a big old-fashioned sink with a cold tap over it. Three dented beer barrels stood in a line down the centre of the room, dividing the space into two narrower areas. On one side of the barrels was a long, narrow bench of the sort children used to sit on in schoolyards to eat their lunch. The floor was wet in patches and small pools formed in its uneven sections. The video filming was finished and the photographic people were packing up. Dennis Johnson stood as still as someone under a spell, only his pencil and his keen eyes moving as he sketched in his notebook.

And there on the ground, just near the bench, lay the small and wretched body of murdered Patrick Sharp.

# 6

The body was wrapped in a damp sheet. Joss walked over and stood looking at it. Death has an atmosphere, he remembered, and the underground room was filled with it. The child lay on his right side, hunched round in the foetal position he'd left only seven years before. His still-agonised face was partly visible where the sheet had fallen away from his head, like a monk's cowl. Joss looked at the face and the half-closed eyes of the dead boy.

Alan's body had had no eyes. His face had gone. And most of his head. The blast had tornadoed up through the Mercedes' floor, its epicentre in the gear box under the console. Alan had been blown inside out. Then redistributed in shocking pieces.

Joss stared hard at Patrick Sharp, whose face seemed to be changing as he watched. He looked again. He had observed that some of the faces of the dead show expressions of great sweetness and peace. But not the violently dead. The rolled-up towel that was under the child's head was muddied on one corner where it touched the dirty floor. There it was again, the kindness towel under the murdered head. Halfway down the body the sheet had fallen away, revealing Patrick's naked right hip, and Joss found himself staring at the familiar crosshatching. He seemed to be hypnotised by them. At the edge of his vision, the bars on the high windows that cut the outside light into stripes on the cellar floor bent and wavered like sea grass. He felt his mind waver with them. He groped towards the bench and sat down heavily, shaking his head to clear it. A startling idea had started to form in his mind but nausea took its place, and for a moment he thought he was going to be sick.

'You right?' Dennis was asking.

Joss grasped the bench and nodded. 'I didn't get much sleep last night,' he said. He saw Dennis take that in. He saw Dennis draw a wrong conclusion, and the death-filled air of the cellar was suddenly charged with male hostility.

'Tell me what you make of this,' Dennis said curtly.

Joss looked around at the cellar, the bars, the dead child at his feet. He tried to compose himself. The nausea had eased and he was able to bring his mind to bear on the work he had to do here. 'I think,' he said, 'it's remarkable – they could have been brothers. Same size, same colouring, same school.' He looked harder at the squashed face. 'I think they even look alike.'

Dennis paced away then looked back at Joss and the pathetic little body on the ground. 'It's him again,' he said, lighting up a cigarette that, this time, he hadn't bothered to hide. His voice was thick with anger and frustration. 'Almost certainly. Mr Invisible. Same set-up. No clothes. The damn sheet. The kindness towel. The water. Eddie was here earlier and took his temperature. Reckoned he'd been dead around sixteen hours. He was killed quite soon after he was taken.' Dennis ashed the cigarette into the palm of his left hand, then walked around, wondering what he was was going to do with it, too well trained to contaminate the crime scene. 'He's used the same belt to hit the poor little bugger.'

Upstairs, they could hear voices and occasional bursts of laughter. It reminded Joss of being outside church after a funeral, when people gather on the steps to have a cigarette and a few words before following the coffin to the cemetery.

Dennis found an envelope in his pocket and tipped his cigarette ash into it. 'What were you doing at the picnic grounds yesterday morning?' he asked suddenly.

Joss, staring at a smear of mud on the dead boy's cheek, looked up shocked to encounter Dennis's tired, watchful eyes.

'Picnic grounds?' he repeated stupidly. 'What picnic grounds?'

Dennis growled and opened his notebook. 'A vehicle registered in your name was at the picnic grounds at the time Simon Prendergast was approached by the man in the toilets.'

Joss shook his head. 'It's simply not possible. Not possible.' He stared in disbelief. The dismal sound of the tap dripping filled the garishly lit cellar. 'I wasn't there. Except for when we all went out together later. I haven't been out there for ages. What are you saying?'

Dennis shut his notebook and walked over to the bottom of the steps. 'Baz!' he yelled upstairs. 'Have you got all the pictures you want?'

Barry Armstrong yelled back and the morgue contractors, who had been waiting for Dennis's nod, lifted the humble little body in the sheet onto the bag, open ready to receive him. The bag was zipped and the contractors carried their slight burden up the steps.

Dennis came back to where Joss was sitting and stood over him. 'A white 1987 Celica, registered in your name, was one of five cars parked there yesterday.'

Sudden relief coursed through Joss. 'Polly,' he said. 'That's my daughter's car. It's registered in my name.' He saw something shift in Dennis's face. Relief? Curiosity? Disappointment?

'That explains it then. Will you ask her to drop in and have a word with me as soon as possible? She may have seen something helpful.'

'Sure,' said Joss, wondering at the weird coincidence. The feeling of nausea rolled through him again. This cellar. This place.

Dennis lifted his head and looked down his nose at his notes, frowning. You're getting long-sighted, Joss thought. The muscles of focussing are loosening.

'All up,' said Dennis, 'yesterday was a busy day for bad guys in this town.' He flicked back a few pages to another batch of notes. 'We were honoured by a visit from a big dealer from Sydney.'

'What was he doing?' Joss asked.

'Doing what dealers do,' said Dennis.

'And?'

'And then he left town. I wouldn't have known except the new eager beaver at the station recognised him.'

Joss stood up and pulled out his own notebook. How curious that Polly should have been out there and not mentioned it. Maybe she and Ignatius were doing some parking. He didn't like to think of that. He deliberately turned his mind to something that had been teasing him. With careful strides he stepped out the approximate dimensions of the cellar, length and breadth. He jotted the measurements down: four metres by three and a half. He noted the position of the two barred windows, jotting down their positions on his sketch, the position of the sink almost in the right-hand corner. He sketched the way the three barrels had been set up to divide the room; he drew in the position of the bench on the near side of the barrels. He drew a small figure to represent Patrick. 'Look,' he said to Dennis, peering down at the floor. 'These barrels have been dragged out from the wall over there.'

Dennis looked up and down, frowning. Three furrows ran in a curve through the dirt of the cellar floor from the wall to where the barrels now stood. 'You're right. That's odd,' he said. 'We'll check with the kids who found him, see if they did it. Those marks are quite new. I'll make sure Baz got photos of that.' He went to call the photographer back.

Joss put his notebook away. Something was stirring in him, very deeply. He wanted to drive out to Spring Caves again, he wanted another look at that first place.

'I need to pick up a relative for identification,' Dennis was saying as he came back. 'There'll be a briefing at my office. Four o'clock. For us and the homicide people. I'll go over what we've got so far. Eddie should be finished by then.'

The cellar was suddenly filled with flashes of light as the photographer recorded the drag marks. Joss followed Dennis and Barry Armstrong up the cellar steps into the dusty world of the disused bar, and then outside into natural light. A dog was curled up in the middle of the road as Joss swung the Niva out and made a U-turn. The dog lifted its head, tucked its snout back under, and slept.

Spring Caves was deserted now and the place seemed desolate despite the bright light of day. Joss walked through the upper cavern and easily pushed past the re-established masonry that blocked the narrow corridor leading to the lower cave. He flashed his powerful light down the sloping way, taking it carefully. Did the child walk in terror with his killer down this dark calvary? Or was he already unconscious and carried by his murderer? The place was too dark to see properly without light, and Joss wondered how the killer could have carried the boy, his implements and a torch. He stood at the bottom of the slope and swept his flashlight over the length and breadth of the murder cave, feeling its dimensions. Weird shadows sprang up onto the roof and walls. He started pacing out, measuring. He pulled out his notebook, and settling the flashlight against a rock he squatted down and sketched an impression of the cave.

Outside once more he stood for a few moments enjoying the light. The sun was in its mid-afternoon position, directly above and opposite the cave's mouth. It was a relief to be out in the open again, away from those subterranean killing grounds. He went back to the Niva and drove into town.

At four o'clock Dennis and the two homicide detectives who had been seconded from Sydney the previous night were sitting with cups of coffee in the incident room at the station. An unlit cigarette lay waiting on the ashtray in front of Dennis. Constable Kylie Philips was sitting up straight in her chair with her notebook open. Behind Dennis two whiteboards headed 'Crime Scene 1' and 'Crime Scene 2' stood each side of a map of the city. Dennis introduced Joss to the two men from Sydney: Detective Sergeants Neil McCabe and Ian Bannock. Then he went to the first of the whiteboards, which held the details of Jeremy Smiles. He turned to face the room.

'For the benefit of Neil and Ian,' he nodded to them, 'and for our own revision, I'll go over what we've got so far. The first victim, Jeremy,' he moved his hand to indicate a little red flag on the map marking the spot where he said goodbye forever, 'was taken somewhere here. At approximately 3.40 in the afternoon. Right outside the milk bar in which his little friend was buying bubblegum. The friend, Daniel Hammersmith, has told us that Jeremy said he'd wait for him. That was the usual scenario. When Daniel came out of the shop, he looked up and down the road and Jeremy was gone.' Dennis underlined the time '3.40 pm' and put a question mark beside it. 'We got the time from the shopkeeper, who says the Hammersmith boy was in the shop for less than two minutes.'

He cleared his throat. 'Nobody saw anything. Jeremy didn't go back the way he'd come and he didn't go on, either. Nobody saw or heard a car – they had to be on foot. There's a three-metre wire fence to a car park directly across the road. Let's say somehow the offender grabbed the boy, scaled the fence with him – which is almost impossible to believe – he'd then have to make his way, still holding the boy, through the mall car park at the busiest time of day. It just doesn't seem possible. Jeremy's family is very well known in town. All the people in the mall shops know the boy. Nobody saw him.' He paused. 'And the only other way they could've gone is down the side of one of the houses on Addison Street. That's almost as difficult to accept. See here on the map? Addison and Kimberly have two rows of houses between them, back to back. It's the same between Addison and Walker.' He pointed with his pen to the street running parallel to Addison in the opposite direction. 'Taking a kidnapped child through the backyards of suburban houses at that hour is about as plausible as taking him through the mall.'

'He might live there,' said Ian Bannock. 'In one of those houses on Addison Street.'

Dennis nodded. 'That of course was our first bet. But it gets less and less likely every minute. Addison Street is mostly retired professionals and one or two younger families on higher than average salaries. Everyone knows everyone's business. We've gone through those households very thoroughly. There's no evidence, nothing out of order in any of them. A sunny winter's afternoon and everyone's out gardening or having their afternoon tea in the sun. No one saw anything.' The room was silent, thinking of the puzzle of Mr Invisible. 'But we're continuing to question the residents of both Addison and Kimberly, because nothing else makes sense.'

He put his pen down. 'The second boy, Patrick Sharp, was probably taken from the school grounds or right outside them just after school hours. There's about twenty-five minutes between when he was last seen waiting at the school gate after the excursion bus had dropped the kids off and when his sister arrived to find him gone.' Dennis pointed to the second whiteboard. Beside Patrick's name was the time, 3.20 pm–3.45 pm. 'Notice the times,' he said. 'So far, no one's come forward to say they saw or heard anything. Roberto Cardoza, the lollypop man who takes care of the pedestrian crossing near the school, didn't see or hear anything out of order. The other school gates are kept locked and never used except for emergency services.'

Dennis moved away from the boards and picked up his notes from the table but he didn't look at them. 'He checks out okay, by the way,' he said, anticipating suspicion about the lollypop man. 'So far.' He put his notes down again. 'The kids were both taken about the same time. You know that they're from the same school. You'll notice they're the same colouring,' he continued, pointing like a teacher down the boards to each detail as he named it, 'same height and weight approximately, although they were in different classes. Jeremy was small for his age. Both light-eyed.

Both slight build. They were both uncircumcised. Both Australian. The way they were beaten and killed is almost identical. As Joss has noted,' Dennis nodded briefly at Joss, 'they could be brothers, twins almost. Looks like he goes for a certain type of boy: thin, slight, sandy colouring. We don't know at this stage what that indicates, but it means something. They've even got similar surnames. Both short, both start with S. We've got a mannequin dressed up outside the civic centre and I've been on radio this morning appealing to the public. The first crime scene is a cave – a sort of double-decker cave – about eleven kilometres out of town. The top cave is a fairly popular camping and picnic place. Underneath that is where we found the body. It had been boarded up by the council but the killer or some other party made a hole through the boards. I'll arrange for you two blokes to go out there.' Dennis nodded at the Sydney detectives. 'The second crime scene is this cellar that you've all seen. It's interesting that he goes underground.'

Underground, thought Joss. Underground is safe. A lair. Hidden.

'We don't know yet,' Dennis continued, 'whether that means anything more than a natural tendency for him to select places that are out of the way so he can take his time.' He stopped and scratched the back of his head. 'We don't know whether the kids are conscious or unconscious when he beats them and kills them, but he certainly doesn't want to be anywhere where he can be disturbed. So far we've got a cellar and a cave. Joss here suggested it may have been the Gold of Egypt exhibition that triggered off something in the killer. Apparently there's a fourteen-year-old boy-king from three thousand years ago. Glad we don't have to do the physical on him. There's just possibly some link between the mummy in the exhibition and the way the sheets are wound around the dead boys.'

'And the darkness of the exhibition is like the darkness of the cave and the cellar,' said Joss, thinking aloud.

'That's something,' said Dennis, writing 'darkness' on both boards.

'But presumably he's got a light source with him,' said Neil McCabe. 'He's got to see what he's doing. There was no power on at the old Maitland pub cellar until your men got there. He's got to have a torch or something.'

'That's right,' said Dennis. 'He'd have to have a light of some sort. He's got the boy with him and he has to carry the things he brings. Unless he sets it up earlier somehow and takes the boys there later – that's a possibility.'

Joss remembered standing in the mid-afternoon sun and a thought suddenly struck him. 'Spring Caves faces due west,' he said. 'Once he pulled that masonry down, he'd have the sun shining straight in at sunset. For the rest of the day the overhang would keep the lower cave dark.'

'It's possible he could use natural light. That's one less thing he's got to carry.' Dennis drew a big sun with rays all around it on each whiteboard and added a question mark.

'We've got the Queen's birthday coming up. Maybe that's stirred him up somehow,' Neil said.

'Maybe he's a royalist?' suggested Ian. 'Hates Catholics?'

'Like you, mate?' Neil suggested.

'At this stage, it's possible,' said Dennis. 'He didn't take boys from any of the public schools.'

'What about this lollypop bloke?' Neil asked. 'You're sure he's all right?'

Dennis nodded. 'He's clean. The deputy was there, doing some marking, and he saw Cardoza going about his business and then go into the staff room for his cuppa.'

'What about the deputy?'

Joss looked at the men around the table and the young woman taking notes. No one was presumed innocent.

'His wife picked him up. He's all right.'

'Don't know how you can say that,' said Ian. 'All my teachers were paedophiles.'

'You've got a black outlook on life, Ian. And you went to a private school. It's affected you.' Neil slapped his colleague on the back.

'Known offenders?' asked Ian, taking no notice.

'Nothing doing there so far,' said Dennis. 'We've been round to the bars and parlours and checked out all of them. The gay hang-outs, too. The ones we know of. This kind of killing is completely unheard of in this town. No one we know has a history of this sort of thing. Might be someone new in town. That's what we're checking out now. Camping grounds, hotels, motels, service stations. There were two cars at the picnic grounds yesterday that we haven't –'

The phone rang. Dennis snatched it up. 'Yeah?' he said. 'Right.' He pulled out his pen. 'How do I spell that?' he asked the caller. He scribbled a sentence, going back to check the spelling of one of the words. '*Cladophera*,' he said as if he were copying the pronunciation. Thanks, Eddie.' He hung up and looked around. 'Eddie's just had a phone report back from the botanist. That greenish stuff on the edge of the sheet Jeremy Smiles was wrapped in? It's called *cladophera*,' he said, reading from his notes, frowning at his hurried writing, 'and it's a –' he pulled his head further away from the word to see it better, 'a filamentous algae found growing in drains and damp places. It doesn't grow anywhere near the cave area. It looks like it came from a boot, trodden onto the corner of the sheet. It couldn't have been the girls who found him, so it was brought to the crime scene either by the killer or Jeremy Smiles himself.' He wrote the algae's name on the first board.

There was a pause. 'How does he do it?' Neil wondered aloud. 'How does he just grab a kid like that and not be seen by someone? Talk about the luck of the devil.'

'I suppose a woman isn't entirely out of the question,' said Dennis. 'Could be a couple working together, but it'd be unusual.' Then he turned to Joss. 'Have you got anything you want to tell us?'

For a moment, Joss thought Dennis was accusing him of child murder. Then he realised what was meant. 'We've got a few things,' he said finally. He didn't need to refer to any notes. He knew this stuff by heart. 'In this sort of murder it's almost certainly a man. He takes the kids between school and home, the weak spot. Between three and four in the afternoons of the fourth and the eighth.' He paused. 'It was nearly one o'clock when we think he was in the toilet cubicle at the picnic grounds. That's lunchtime, so he could be employed and duck out during lunch break. Maybe he's got the sort of job where he doesn't have to clock on. Maybe self-employed. Maybe he's a tradesman. By the way, the weather on both days was very clear. Perfect sunshiny winter afternoons.' Dennis was scribbling on the boards in abbreviated form as Joss spoke. 'Possibly unemployed and under twenty-five, but once again that's only a statistic. Don't get blinded by these profiles. They're only outlines. He could be on holiday from work. He could be on sickness benefit. He's what we call an organised killer, rather than a disorganised one.' Joss had his audience's complete attention. Murder is riveting, he thought. 'By organised, I mean he brings his own gear with him. In this case, the sheets that he wraps the boys in, the strap that he uses. Three barrels had been moved in the cellar – from the wall to the centre.'

He glanced over at Dennis, who said, 'I checked with the kids who found the body. They say they didn't touch them.'

Joss continued. 'It's possible the killer arranged them in that way. Then he takes the strap away with him. And the clothes. We haven't recovered any of the clothing. He might keep that for re-enactments. We're finding that re-enactments are common in this sort of killing – if the killer can't find another suitable victim, or things are too hot to take another one. The FBI have caught several murderers when they've come back to re-enact the crime. Our man is not just acting on impulse – he plans the killing. He could be homosexual, but don't count on it. He keeps his victims quiet, probably by threats. Maybe he makes them climb into a sack. There's no evidence he knocks them out physically or drugs them. "Shut up or I'll kill you" is possibly all that's needed with a terrified child. FBI information indicates that often these sorts of killers deliberately watch playgrounds before they make their selection. To make sure they get the most obedient children.'

Joss blinked his eyes several times to dispel the gathering tension across his brow. He picked up a photograph of the crosshatching on Jeremy Smiles. 'He's cruised public toilets once that we know of. But he'd already made his selection. He beats them severely. He uses something that leaves this mark.' He pushed the photographs around the table.

'What makes those marks?' asked Ian. 'I've never seen anything like that.'

'A belt, a strap of some sort. We don't know at this stage,' said Dennis. 'We've circulated the photos in the *Advocate*. We're hoping someone will know something. It's very distinctive, the crosshatching.'

'We had a few phone calls,' said Kylie, looking away when the two Sydney detectives stared at her pretty face. 'But nothing helpful.'

Dennis said, 'The second child, Patrick, is covered in these marks too, although we haven't got the photographs back yet. And then there's the towel. The kindness towel that he puts under their heads so that they're comfortable.'

'While he beats them and strangles them he wants them to be comfortable?' Kylie voiced the disbelief of the group. Her young face still showed the painful distaste that her older colleagues had long ago learned not to feel.

'It's the sort of inconsistency often found in these sorts of killings,' said Dennis. 'It's done to show us the killer is human, according to the experts. Well, at least that's what the blokes in the United States reckon. That's the theory.'

Joss tried to remember the strange little couplet that Dennis had quoted earlier about theory and lead boxes and hearts, but could not bring it to mind.

'We already know the killer is human,' said Neil. 'Animals don't behave like this.'

'We know from the conversation at the picnic grounds toilet that he knew of Patrick before he took him,' Joss continued.

'And yet,' interrupted Dennis, 'he was trying to get Simon Prendergast too. Simon has the same characteristics as the other two. He's a couple of years younger but very tall for his age.'

'Does he have sex with them?' Neil asked looking up from the black and white pictures of the dead bodies.

Joss shook his head. 'No. He just beats them and strangles them.' He heard his words, their matter-of-fact tone, as though they were a long way off. The feeling of nausea was swelling again from the pit of his stomach and he swallowed. 'I'll have more when we get the PM report on the second boy, Patrick Sharp,' he said. 'I'm building up the database and I'll be fine-tuning as much as I can, but just for now, that's all I can say. It could be anyone – male most likely – in this town. Eddie says he holds them around the throat with one hand and hits them with the other.' Joss felt a circle of pain around his own neck as he spoke that moved up to his brow. 'There's just one thing I should point out,' he said, blinking. 'Just because a sex offender doesn't have a previous history of violence doesn't rule him out. Recent research from the addiction models tends to suggest that this sort of crime is the last part of an escalation. It might be that he's been able to contain the pressure for a long time before he breaks out. So his record might only show things like peeping, snow-dropping, exhibitionism. But something will suddenly happen in his life – the death of a parent, or the anniversary of a death, some other stressful event like that – and he could find himself acting in ways that he's never needed to before. Keep that in mind, will you?'

His voice was coming in an odd, detached sort of way from somewhere other than his own throat. He coughed and struggled on. 'Even something like the Gold of Egypt exhibition might have triggered his particular psychopathology. Maybe he was locked up in a dark place as a kid. Maybe the mix of gold and death sets him going.' In the darkness of his mind, a golden light blazed. He seemed to be in darkness, then his head was filled with an agonising radiance. He just had time to wonder if this was an aura and he was about to have a *grand mal* seizure when his headache exploded. The pain soared through his brain and bulged at the top of his skull like a hideous jack-in-the-box. *Sheets, beating, pressure*. He put a hand up to his head and leaned his elbow on the table, taking some of the weight from his neck. God, he thought, this must be an aneurism. I've got to get out of here. He was aware of the silence from the others in the room and their curious eyes. His own eyes were blind with shock and tears. An aneurism, a cerebral haemorrhage? He thought of the lecturer who'd died in front of the theatre full of medical students. I'm not ready. There are things I have to do. Polly. Sybil. He staggered towards Dennis.

'What is it?' Dennis was asking.

'My head,' Joss managed to gasp. 'Something's happening. I can't think.' He was aware of Dennis reaching for the phone. 'Get an ambulance,' he heard him say. Joss groped his way out of the briefing room to the front counter. He fumbled at the buttons of the phone and managed to reach Ashley's number. Her recording started to tell him she was currently unavailable and he despaired. He wanted to bang his head against the wall to kill the pain. Then her voice cut in.

'Hullo? I'm here.'

'Pick me up,' he managed to say to her. 'I'm at the police station.' Dennis came out. 'No,' Joss added quickly. 'The Seven Sisters instead. I'll wait for you there. Pick up twenty Nembudeine from Bloomdales. Tell them I'll drop the – ' He was about to say 'script' and stopped. Dennis was listening. 'Never mind.'

'Joss, what *is it*?' Her voice. Loving, concerned.

'Please,' he said. He hung up. He didn't know what he was going to say to Ashley. He just had to get out of there. I can't die, he thought. Not just now. He needed to make contact with someone who cared about him. Someone who could drive him home. Someone who would touch him with loving hands.

He managed to focus on Dennis. With massive effort of will he was able to think past the pain in his head, turn to Dennis and compose a sentence. 'I'll ring you,' he said. 'I need to get something for this.' He was holding his forehead blindly.

Dennis looked at him. 'The ambulance is on its way,' he said.

'Ambulance?' Joss couldn't understand the words. He started sliding down the counter. He grabbed it and supported himself.

Dennis's steady voice. 'You need medical attention.'

Joss pulled himself up and stood shakily. 'I'll be all right. I'll get it.' He walked carefully away, robbed of the strength in his muscles and his bones, leaving the other man staring after him. The pain seemed to be both light- and movement-sensitive, so he kept his eyes half closed and his head as still as possible.

He felt his way down the side of the wall of steps onto the footpath outside. He couldn't tell if it was getting dark or if his vision was failing. The pain hovered in and over his field of consciousness, a huge and blazing UFO waiting to land. He walked like a very old man, hardly lifting his feet, until he came to the café and went inside to wait for Ashley. She arrived in less than ten minutes. The pressure in his head had eased somewhat and was now pulsing with his blood.

'God, what is it?' she said, sliding in beside him. 'You're in pain.'

He nodded. 'Can you drive me home?'

'I think I should take you to Casualty. Come on. You look as if you're about to collapse.'

'No. No hospitals. Please. I'll be all right.'

'How on earth can you know that?' she said.

'Just do as I ask you. *Please.*'

Ashley gave in and took him to her car.

Joss carefully leaned his head back while she drove in silence, turning to look at him from time to time. She took the road to his place. He found that if he closed his eyes and kept his head in a certain position, the pain was manageable.

'What's wrong with you?' she asked finally. 'What's happened?'

'I'm not entirely sure,' he got out 'The symptoms are those of migraine.' He was still conscious, but it could yet be a cerebral haemorrhage.

'Something's going on.' He sensed Ashley turning to look at him again as if he were mad. *Of course something's going on*, he felt her saying inwardly. 'Tell me,' said Ashley. 'Tell me what's going on.'

But he couldn't speak. He needed everything he had just to keep his head balanced. The lid on the jack-in-the-box eased closed again.

They reached his place, where the scent from the cypresses seemed to increase his headache. A wind stirred the pines. The coffin-wood pines, he thought, shivering. And the Celica wasn't there yet, he saw. 'What day is it?' he asked Ashley as they walked to the door.

She turned to look at him. 'It's Saturday.'

Saturday. She has an orchestral rehearsal till six, he was able to recall. He pulled out a handkerchief and wiped a tear away from his right eye. He blew his nose.

He seemed to take a long time to disarm the security system. Inside Joss hobbled over to put the lamps on. He remembered the young surgeon who had dropped dead from a cerebral haemorrhage, scalpel still in hand, opposite Joss at the operating table. He wondered if he were about to do the same.

The house was warm from the combustion stove in the lounge room. He held his head and tried to bend over to pick up a log, but Ashley gently pushed him away. 'I'll do that,' she said, taking the log from him, sliding it into the stove and turning the draught up.

Joss felt agitated, despite the pain. He went to the kitchen and put the kettle on. He remembered his grandmother saying, 'Just put the kettle on.' If someone had just died, if someone had just had a baby, it was always the right thing to do. When the news of his mother's death had come, his grandmother had put the kettle on. Then the memory of his grandmother disintegrated and a screaming child took her place and Joss sank to his knees, pressing his hands against his forehead, stupid with pain.

Ashley came into the kitchen and squatted down beside him. 'It's hard for me,' she said, 'to see you in such pain. Can't I ring a doctor?'

'No,' he said. 'Don't. I don't want a doctor.' He was aware of her close to him. The images receded and the screaming in his mind quietened, so that with her help he was able to stand up and move again. 'It's easing a bit,' he said with relief.

He followed her into the lounge with the tea things. The pain in his head now pulsed only with each heartbeat and it was rolling back from his eyebrows towards the top and back of his head. 'For a moment I thought I was having a cerebral haemhorrage.' He felt guilty then that he had not thought of her at all, his lover of six months, in that moment of fear and anguish when he thought he was going to die. He put the tea down on the low table near the bay window, drawing the heavy old curtains against the coldness of evening. One day, he thought, when all of this is over and Polly is safe, I'll pack some books of poetry and philosophy and fill the tanks of a sleek twin-engine aircraft and I'll fly to one of those deserted islands. I'll learn to meditate. I'll develop wisdom. The old, dead dream. On the top of the mantel, his models of the Flying Fortress, Dornier, Mig, Mirage, Sea Fury and Hurricane locked wings.

'You've made this place like a fortress,' Ashley remarked. It was the first time she'd been inside his place, because of his feelings of loyalty to Polly. 'What is it you're keeping out? Nothing or nobody could get in here.' She looked out at the mauve sky through the bars on the window.

'Ashley,' he said, not knowing how to begin. He went to sit near her in the bay window. She needs to know some things to be able to help me, he was thinking as he poured the tea. He tried to sort out the truth and the untruth, but there were areas now in his mind where they blurred together.

'This investigation,' he began.

'Yes?' she said.

'It's brought up things in me – unresolved grief, I suppose you would call it. I need your help.' He realised he had never used this phrase about himself, only about his work. He felt her warm presence in her silence. 'There's no one I can confide in,' he said. 'It wouldn't be appropriate with Polly. She's not with me in this, anyway.' He nearly said, 'She's against me in this,' realising fully the depth of his daughter's hostility towards him. 'So there is no one I can talk to except you.' He looked at the sky through the bars. Somewhere, he thought, is freedom. But I don't know what that means yet.

'If I were asked to explain what's been happening to me, I'd explain it as some sort of mental strain. Perhaps even something a bit like a psychosis.' She looked at him with interest, nodding her head slowly. 'It's like being in solitary, how I am. How I've had to be for some time. I'm – ' There was a tremendous resistance to what he wanted to say next but he knew he must, otherwise he might well collapse entirely. If that happened, Polly and he would be in even greater danger. He groped for other words, but they weren't truthful. He would have to say it as it was.

'I'm hallucinating,' he said.

He watched her carefully for any sign of fear or recoil. There was neither. She simply put down her cup. 'Tell me.'

He poured her more tea. A bull bellowed in a nearby paddock. 'I get images in my mind of a child being beaten. Like flashbacks in a movie. First there's a sort of golden radiance. Like an aura.'

'Who is it?' Ashley asked. 'The child in the flashbacks?'

Joss shrugged. 'I don't know. He ... I can't see his face.'

'Do you have any idea who it might be?'

He shook his head.

'When do they come, these images?'

'There doesn't seem to be a pattern. I think they're connected to the investigation,' he said hopefully. She said nothing. 'Lately they've started to come up when I'm in the middle of something important. Like just then when I was talking to the task force. The nausea, the aura, the pain in my head, and the pictures in my mind of this beaten child.'

There was a silence until Ashley spoke in a matter-of-fact voice. 'What were you talking about when the pain happened?'

Joss tried to recall. 'Something. I don't know. I just can't think ...'

'Don't worry about it now.' There was a pause before she spoke again. 'Were you beaten, Joss, when you were a child?'

He didn't know who she was talking to for a moment. 'What? No,' he said. 'No, of course I wasn't. I was brought up by my grandmother. She was a dear.'

'What about your parents? Where were they?'

Suddenly he felt intensely sleepy, as if he were about to keel over. He yawned widely. His eyes were threatening to close.

'What's happening?' she asked.

'Nothing,' he said. 'I just feel exhausted.'

'You were speaking about your parents,' she said.

'Yes. My father was an engineer who worked with the Americans in the last year or two of the war. He helped build airfields in the Pacific, in the South China Sea.' He gestured behind him to the WAC chart. 'The sort that were laid down like a huge metal carpet.'

She nodded to show she knew what he meant.

'He came back and he was different. He never spoke about it. But he had some sort of nervous disorder. I suppose it was a breakdown of some sort. No one ever knew what he'd endured during the war. In those days there was no debriefing. A soldier returned home from hell and was expected to just get on with it. Of course, nobody ever spoke about it. It was all secret and somehow shameful.'

'And your mother?'

'She had her hands full coping with him. I can't remember much, except that she seemed to be entirely taken up with him.'

'How was that for you?'

Joss looked at her. He frowned. 'What do you mean?'

Ashley opened her hands in an expressive gesture. 'You've told me about two people who were involved with each other. But those two people had a little boy. Were they involved with him too? Did they care for him?'

'I was always well cared for.'

'I didn't actually mean that,' she said.

'There were housekeepers. I really can't tell you much more. Then my father died and my mother couldn't cope. I went to live with my grandmother.'

He sighed and closed his eyes and the pain in his head moved back behind his lids. He felt her take his two hands and sit with them in hers. In a while he opened his eyes. She was getting up to go. Joss cleared his head and stood up. 'Are you leaving already?'

Ashley looked at her watch. 'I've got a couple of things to do. You're exhausted. You need a bath and an early night.'

'Is that all?' he said, feeling dismissed.

She came over to him and squatted in front of him and put her hands on his knees, looking into his eyes. 'No,' she said. 'It's not all. But you've been through the wringer and you need to rest. I'll call you in the morning.'

He was too tired to do anything but agree with her.


Of course I was never beaten, he thought to himself after Ashley had gone. What a strange question. I was brought up by my grandmother. My father went to war and came back damaged. My depressed mother couldn't cope with that and a little boy as well.

He was lying on the banquette that ran the length and shape of the bay window. Polly still wasn't home. The headache had all but gone and he felt hung over, depleted.

He was dozing when he heard the Celica pull up outside and Polly come in going 'Brrrrrrr' with cold. He heard her slapping her folders and bag on the kitchen table.

'Dad?' she called and his heart filled with love for her.

'I'm out here, darling. It's been a hard day.'

She came out and the sight of her face gladdened him further.

'When did you get back?'

'Early this morning. I didn't stay in Sydney. I had a coffee and flew back.'

She stood in silence for a moment. 'Did you go to our house?'

He shook his head. 'I stayed at the Regent.'

Polly softened. 'You look awful,' she said. 'Where's your car? I didn't see it outside.'

'I got a migraine. Ashley drove me home.'

'A migraine?'

He nodded. Carefully.

'Ashley,' said Polly. 'You like her, don't you.'

'Yes, I do. What do you think of her?'

'I like what I see. She treats me like a real person. She doesn't put on a big act of "I must be very nice to the daughter" stuff.'

Joss laughed. 'There's no doubt about you, Poll. You know how to talk straight.'

'It's important to me. She's real. She doesn't try to be nice. She's not ratty.' She didn't add 'like Mum is'. But Joss thought he could sense it. 'Anyway, what's this about a migraine? You don't get migraines.'

'I do now. It's nearly gone.'

Polly looked guilty now. 'Dad, I said some hard things to you last night. I feel bad about that, and I'm sorry if I upset you. But,' she continued, her determined expression creeping back, 'I want you to know I did mean what I said. If she comes back, I'm going.'

Joss nodded, stood up and went into the kitchen. He suddenly felt absolutely starving. He pulled out the chopping board and chopped onion, celery, capsicum. He crushed garlic and sealed chicken pieces in a pan. Polly went upstairs and he heard the shower going. He was careful not to use the taps until she'd finished.

When she came back down the chicken was quietly simmering in red wine with a bay-leaf. Joss decided against his pre-dinner brandy. He still felt completely enervated. He served up and carried the meal into the lounge room where Polly had set the table. She'd picked some red berries at the university and they glowed in the middle of the table. A Bach partita filled the room.

'Why did you really go to Sydney then?' she asked at the end of the meal.

'I was trying to contact Malcolm, like I said.'

'Why?'

'I wanted to find out if the message from your mother was genuine.'

'Even if it was, it wouldn't be,' said Polly, sweeping her knife and fork together and leaving the table with her plate.

'Poll?'

'Yes?' she called from the kitchen.

'Your car.' He felt awkward, accusatory even asking her. 'The Celica showed up in a rego check as one of the cars at the picnic ground yesterday. I told Dennis I'd confirm it with you. Will you give him a ring and tell him you were there?'

'But I wasn't,' she said, coming out with an apple in her hand. 'I haven't been out that way for a year or more.'

Joss stared at her. 'But the Celica was there. The registration number was given to the police.' The headache knocked over one eye, reminding him it could always come back in again.

Polly shook her head. 'Nup. Not me. ' She flopped down on the old brown couch and bit into the apple. 'Let's see, on Friday I was up at the library for a while, then I spent a couple of hours trying to get a handle on the *Hammerklavier* in the music department.'

He told her the story of the mathematical nun and she smiled. 'Well, she's got it wrong. Just one digit would make all the difference.'

Joss nodded. 'I'll tell Dennis.'

'He's cute, Dennis,' said Poll looking up at him. 'Let me tell him.'

Joss grunted. He went into his study, closed the door and phoned Wallis Island to book a boat to pick him up there the following day.

'I'm going to bed,' he said when he came back out. 'Good night, darling.' He pecked her on the cheek.

Polly watched him as he made his way, holding the banister. 'Is your head okay?' she asked.

He nodded. It was almost the truth.

Joss lay on his back, eyes open in the dim light. He could hear Andras Schiff playing the *Hammerklavier* downstairs. He suddenly felt wide awake again. Now that the migraine had eased, the thought that had been troubling him before its eruption returned in full force. He remembered the overwhelming excitement from years ago that had accompanied a seemingly impossible diagnosis. Not here, he had been thinking as he examined a patient in the teaching hospital. You just don't have it in sophisticated Sydney, Australia. It's not possible. But I've seen this before, he'd kept thinking. These symptoms, this concatenation of suffering. This distorted tendon. And he remembered the only other occasion he'd seen a leprosy case, in medical school thirty-two years previously, and in so doing, made the correct diagnosis.

Ever since he'd measured out and roughly sketched the cellar where Patrick Sharp's swaddled body had lain, this same strange notion of impossibility had assailed him. It was the reason he'd gone back to the earlier crime scene at Spring Caves to compare proportions. He sat up, wishing he still smoked. There is something in these situations that I've seen before. He got out of bed and went to the window, throwing his dressing-gown over his shoulders. It was cold in his room. He recalled the derelict baths at the cave where Jeremy had been murdered, the way their walls made a sort of division down the centre of the open area, the position the boy had lain relative to the baths.

In the cellar where Patrick Sharp died, someone had dragged three barrels down the centre of the cellar to make a rough room divider. The windows had been high up on the right-hand wall. In the death cave too, the bluish source of light from the upper cave had been high up on the right-hand side. The set-up in the two places was remarkably similar. Extraordinarily so. He considered this for a moment, feeling its awfulness, its mystery. But it wasn't only this that teased and frightened him. There was another feeling that wouldn't leave him alone with its frightening insistence. It's not possible, he told himself. It's just some sort of déjà vu experience – perception looping back on itself. But he had no peace. The feeling grew stronger the more he battled its impossibility.

He dragged a chair over to the window and sat in it with the doona over him, unable to settle down. In both crime scenes, the killer had made a crude scenario, a coarse theatrical set. He had set things up to resemble some other place, some chamber of horrors that only he knew about.

And the thought that was unsettling Joss, that kept him up half the night until the moon sank behind the bald mountains and his head fell forward as he collapsed into exhaustion, the thought that would not leave him alone was this: *I know this place. I've been there too.*

# 7

On Monday morning at nine, Joss was in the incident room at the police station with Neil McCabe and Ian Bannock. Eddie Chandler's report on the second killing lay on the table. On the drive into and through town, Joss noticed the increased traffic on the roads as parents drove their children to school, not trusting them to the bus. As he cruised past St Callistus he saw that Citadel Security had two uniformed men at the front gates. There seemed to be more teachers than pupils at the school. Parents must be keeping their children home, he thought.

Outside the police station, a Channel Three van nudged the kerb. Dennis was being interviewed in the next room and his voice could be heard through the thin partition.

'Finally, Detective Sergeant, do you have anything you'd like to say to the people of Maroonga?'

'I'd like to tell the kids this: don't go anywhere with anyone you don't know, no matter what the story. Mum and Dad only, kids. Or a very close relative with prior arrangements in place. Okay? If anyone approaches you, run like mad and make a lot of noise. Teachers, tell your classes where the Safe Houses are and make sure every kid knows where the closest one is. We've got a killer in this town like we've never had before. And we are of the opinion that this person will almost definitely attack again.'

In a moment, Dennis was back in the incident room, wiping his face. 'I don't know why, I always sweat in front of cameras.' He nodded at Joss, who greeted him back.

'I've gone through Eddie's report,' Joss told him. 'It's almost identical to Jeremy's. Cause of death: asphyxiation, strangulation. Severe beating with that short belt or strap again. Body wrapped in a sheet. Face covered. Kindness towel in position. Here are the photos.' He handed them around the table and the pictures of little Patrick Sharp's defiled body were compared with those of Jeremy Smiles. In both cases, the crosshatching could clearly be seen.

'There's also the same coarse fibres,' Joss continued. 'The same hair, thought to be canine. Eddie's sent that away for definite identification. Shouldn't be too long. And we've got traces of *cladophera* again, too. Eddie thinks it's pretty specific in its habitats. He'll get back to us.'

Dennis took over. 'We've got to find this damn strap. I want every shop that sells any sort of belts or saddlery checked out.' He handed round photocopies of details of the strap, its stitching and measurements.

'There was also a piece of a condom wrapper caught in the sheet,' Joss added.

'If he jerks off, he doesn't want to leave us anything interesting,' said Dennis. 'Or maybe it's just a fragment from some other party occasion. You guys got anything interesting to tell us?' He looked across at the men who'd been working most of the night, asking questions and going over pubs, clubs, motels, caravan parks and toilets.

'Not much,' said Neil. 'One thing though, the local gays are pretty angry about the whole thing.'

'Yes,' said Dennis, 'I know. The boss told me I've got a meeting with someone from the gay lobby this morning. They took exception to something I said in yesterday's paper. They want me to make it clear that gay men don't go round beating children to death as a rule. Want me to run a list of statistics to show that it's heterosexual men who kill their children. They've got a point, although this is not a family killing we're dealing with.' He looked tired. 'Anything else?'

He was interrupted by Graham Parke putting his head round the door. 'Um, Dennis, there's a bloke here from the council. Wants to see you about some dead puppies. Thinks it might have something to do with the case.'

'Tell him to ask for his money back, mate,' said Neil.

Dennis and Joss went together to the reception area. Near

the front desk a small man waited. 'You wanted to see me?' Dennis asked, introducing himself.

The man was flustered and shamefaced. 'I saw you on the telly the other night,' he said. 'You said you wanted to hear anything, no matter if it seemed a bit, you know ...' he shrugged.

'Yes please,' said Dennis.

'I work with the engineers at the council. My job is to inspect the drains. I go round all the drains, the culverts, especially after any big rain.'

'Yes,' said Dennis again.

'Well, I found these two puppies. Not in the same place. Not even the same day. But I thought they might have something to do with those little boys.'

'Canine hairs,' said Joss.

'Yes,' said Dennis. 'Go on.'

'They were both dead,' the council worker continued. 'Maybe their necks were broken. I don't know. But one was in the culvert not far from where the first little boy disappeared. And then yesterday I find this other little puppy. I thought, that's strange, that's the second one and it looks the same as the other one that I found the day before. Like his brother.'

'Where was the second puppy?' Joss asked.

'In a culvert near the side gate to St Callistus school. In Raglan Street.' The man shrugged. 'It's funny, I said to the wife, two puppies both dead like the little boys, both looking alike like the little boys. Both near where they disappeared.'

Dennis was nodding. He kept on nodding. 'Yup,' he said to himself a couple of times. 'That *is* funny. Can we have your name, please? Just for our records. We might need to check a few things with you.' The man gave his details to the desk sergeant and Joss and Dennis walked back to the incident room.

'What do you make of that?' Dennis asked.

Joss shrugged. 'I'm not sure. Dead puppies in drains. Maybe the bitch has a litter in a drain and then there's some rain and the puppies are swept away and drowned. Or ...?' he questioned.

Dennis gave him a hard look. 'Dead puppies in drains near where two little boys are taken. Eddie finds coarse fibres, maybe from sacking. Use your imagination.' Joss felt himself stiffen against the tone in his voice.

'When you've been on the job as long as I have,' Dennis was saying, 'you get used to throwing a few what-ifs around. Like molesters often use animals to lure kids.' 'Grab your coat,' he said to Joss. 'We're going out to look at some drains.'

A man mowing his front lawn in Addison Street looked at them, made the correct assumption and then went back to work as Dennis squatted beside the entrance to the culvert, a pipe about a metre in diameter.

He pulled out his notebook. He looked back at the shop further down the road, then the other way down the street towards Jeremy's house. Currawongs called overhead in the leather jacket eucalypts. Several shrunken black apples hung on a bare tree nearby. Dennis walked for some distance, paused and then walked back, jotting notes.

'Just say I'm the killer,' he said, 'and I'm down here,' he scrambled down the kerb again, 'out of sight of the shop'. The excitement in his voice was new. 'And I've pushed this puppy some way into the culvert. The kid's been warned all about stranger danger but he hears the puppy yelping and here's this man, maybe waving up at him, very upset, saying, "Can you go down there and get my puppy out for me? I'm too big to fit in there." '

Joss nodded. 'It's good,' he said. 'It's good.' Dennis's enthusiasm caught him. 'I could wait for the kid to crawl in and then I'd just grab him from behind and drop this hessian bag over him and heave him up onto the footpath and then straight into my stationwagon, and if anyone saw me, they'd think I was just lifting a bag into the back. Tools, rocks, spuds. Anything. Just a man lifting a sack into the back of a working vehicle.'

'What about the puppy?' Dennis asked.

'I'd just leave it there. Or kill it,' said Joss. 'Nothing to it.'

'And did you do it that way?' Joss heard Dennis say.

'What?' said Joss. There was a sudden flash of golden light in his head and a spasm of headache.

'Did he do it that way?' Dennis repeated. 'It certainly explains how he picks them up without any upset.'

The two of them stared at the drain in silence for a few moments and then climbed back into the car. Joss sat with his hands motionless in mid-air, halfway to buckling up his seatbelt, stilled by thought.

'No,' he said. 'It doesn't work.'

'Why not?' asked Dennis, faking his seatbelt across his lap. 'I like it.' He leaned forward and started the car.

'Don't get too attached to it. It doesn't work because it takes too long. The shopkeeper reckons less than two minutes elapsed, remember. He saw the two boys outside. Daniel comes in, Jeremy waits outside. Daniel does his business, goes outside again and there's no Jeremy. What you've just described would need more time.' Dennis grunted. 'And then he's still got to lift the kid into a vehicle, sack or no sack. It's too long-winded. And no one saw a vehicle nearby.'

Dennis grunted again. It was true. He pulled away from the kerb and drove the several blocks to St Callistus.

The Raglan Street culvert near St Callistus was even bigger. It was in a quiet spot with the children's playground on one side of the street and a piece of vacant land, which had been known as the Common for years, on the other. Four real-estate agents' boards declared the land for sale. Dennis stood near the culvert, notebook in hand, and looked around. 'There are no houses opposite. The playground would have been empty. All the kids were gone.' He jumped down into the culvert. 'I can almost stand up in this one.' Joss heard Dennis's voice echoing through the ground.

'How does he do it? He's got to use a vehicle,' Joss said as Dennis climbed back up onto the bank.

'Let's think about how he might do it without a vehicle,' said Dennis. They stood together in silence.

'Hey, Dad!' a youth yelled and Joss swung round, his mouth almost shaping Alan's name. The boy was about fourteen, darker than Alan, heavier. But the voice had been almost the same; the enthusiasm, the excitement. The youngster cycled by and a man in a car on the other side of the road tooted his horn in response. Joss looked away, but as he was getting back into the car he saw Dennis regarding him very closely across the roof. Joss did up his seatbelt with fingers that weren't working too well.

'If the killer knows the culverts,' said Dennis, turning the ignition, 'maybe he works for the council. Or used to. A maintenance person can move around freely during the day. We should have a closer look at that man who reported the puppies.'


Joss stopped Dennis in the hall outside the incident room shortly after lunch. 'Any news?' he asked.

'Only that the council worker checks out okay. At the time of both disappearances, he was working in the office with several technical officers.'

'What about response to the piece in the *Advocate*? On the strap?'

Dennis took a sip from the mug of coffee he was holding and rolled his eyes. 'The usual. Phones haven't stopped ringing but none of it's useful.'

'You should know,' Joss said quickly, 'that I'll be out of town for twenty-four hours.'

'Oh?' Dennis raised his eyebrows.

'Personal reasons.'

'Yeah?' There was no doubt about the hostility in Dennis's voice.

'Look Dennis, say what's on your mind.'

'You, mate. You're on my mind. You're supposed to be

part of this team, not just pissing off whenever you feel like it. Where's the profile I'm expecting?'

'I'm doing it.' This wasn't entirely true. He had made a start on it but the surges in his own life had distracted him in the last couple of days. 'It'll be ready in ... ' he grabbed a time out of the air, 'forty-eight hours. I'm waiting for the analysis of those hairs. And the habitat of *cladophera*.'

Dennis spoke fast and angrily. 'You could've given me something before this – something just on the profile of the killer, without reference to the physical aspects of the crime scene.'

'I could,' Joss agreed, standing his ground. 'And I think I've given you quite a lot already in the briefing sessions. But I still have to leave town for about twenty-four hours.'

Dennis stared at him and was about to speak when he suddenly turned and swung away down the hall. He tripped on an uneven piece of floor covering near his door and swore viciously. He kicked it flat again. Then he turned and called back to Joss. 'I get a feeling about you, mate. I get the feeling that you're not too fussed over this case. And that makes me very interested, because I want to know why that might be. Why I get the feeling that you're not 100 percent behind getting this murderous bastard.'

Joss stood silent for a moment. The distance between them was difficult. He didn't want to raise his voice. He moved closer, aware of his own racing heart and the way his nails were biting into the clenched flesh of his fists. When he was close enough to speak quietly he said, 'I want to stop this person as much as you do. And I can't help you understand the workings of your own fears and feelings.' He couldn't stop himself saying the next bit, even though he regretted it as he said it. 'Maybe you could ask Ashley about it.'

There was the flash of male edge between them, and in that nanosecond Joss knew that Dennis knew. They glared at each other for a full fifteen seconds before Dennis walked away.

Joss left a message on the kitchen table telling Polly to remember what was in her bedside drawer. 'If you want me, contact me through the pager,' he wrote. Then he called Hamish Alabone from Citadel Security.

They met half an hour later in the underground car park behind the mall shopping village where Citadel ran its office. The stink of exhaust gases didn't seem to do Hamish any harm. He was a solid, ruddy ginger man, ex-army, and had worked with Joss before. His small golden-fringed eyes narrowed as Joss pulled a couple of photos out of his pocket. Joss wrote down Ignatius Ho's address; Hamish already knew Joss's.

'I want this address and this young woman kept under constant surveillance,' he said, handing over a photo of Polly.

'That's your daughter, isn't it?' Hamish asked.

Joss nodded. 'I want you to be her guardian angel while I'm out of town for a little while. There's her university timetable. This is her boyfriend.' He handed Hamish the second photograph. 'Sometimes she stays overnight with him. He might stay at my house while I'm gone.' Something made Joss feel very uneasy at that idea. 'I don't care how many people you have to use, but they've got to be the best. I want her watched twenty-five hours a day. If anything happens that's even a little bit different from the timetable, grab her and buzz me on this immediately.' He gave Hamish his pager number. 'Here's a key to my security system and the house. If I haven't phoned you by eight o'clock tomorrow night, open this.' He handed Hamish an envelope. 'My solicitor has a duplicate in his safe.'

Hamish looked impressed. 'Where the bodies are hidden?' he said with the grunt he used as a laugh.

'Could be,' said Joss.

'Is she in some kind of trouble?'

'You're here to make sure she's not.'

'I'll never leave her side. Promise,' said Hamish without the shadow of a smirk. Hamish was very tough, very efficient and very gay.

The two men shook hands. Hamish pocketed the photographs. 'Look after yourself.' He was frowning.

Joss patted him on the upper arm. 'I will,' he said. 'Just look after her for me.'

It was a hundred and thirteen nautical miles from Maroonga to his destination. Joss sat in the cabin of the Navajo warming up. His heart seemed high in his chest, from fear or love, or both – he couldn't tell. He taxied onto the runway, checked the weather report, built up to full throttle and rumbled down the airfield. Lifting off he banked and turned, then headed south-east, passing Mt Enmore and then Mt Baynes.

Cold, clear winter skies with a little high cirrus and the world seemed a long way off. Impossible to believe up here that malevolence, or even benevolence, existed. Things just *were*, up here. The perfection of detachment, he thought. The Navajo's engines throbbed heartily. Blue and white above with the wind bumping in gusts, and the rush of air; while down there, glimpsed between scattered low cloud, was the brown and khaki and green, the camouflage colours of north-eastern New South Wales in winter. The rivers fanned out like brown corals, their branches wriggling across the low country, or corroding the surface of wrinkled mountains and valleys.

In a little over half an hour he was flying directly above the township of Yarrowitch, and then the navy-blue of the Pacific. He had to fly along the coastal corridor at about five hundred feet so as not to be shot down by the F-18s from Williamtown. 'They'd miss, anyway,' Wal had said bitterly when he'd flown this way with his student, telling Joss about the Auster that had somehow flown itself off the runway and into the air, never to be seen again, despite Air

Force attempts to shoot it down. But that had been a long time ago. Joss didn't want to test this. Wal had been one of the few pilots whose licence was endorsed to fly single-engine fighters.

Below him, the sea crashed in glacial fountains against the black volcanic rock of the coast. The odd four-wheel-drive had left its tracks on the long, deserted beaches to his left. Beside him, a white-tipped sea eagle hardly seemed to move, quivering on a thermal.

Out of the coastal corridor, he took the Navajo higher. The lighthouse at Seal Rocks swung underneath him, and the rocks themselves, almost hidden in the sea, were frilled with white today. He turned north-west towards Wallis Island. He checked the diagram of the airfield and did another fly-over. It hadn't improved a bit, he thought, as he made his final approach. Wallis Island and its airfield was very flat, almost sea level, and on his approach, on top of the usual safety margin, he added the cautious flyer's extra hundred feet for Sybil, another hundred for Polly, and then another for Alan out of habit.

Forty-nine minutes after taking off at Maroonga, starboard wing edged into the gusty wind, he was rounding out, altering the attitude of the Navajo to place the mains on the rugged airstrip in the middle of Wallis Lake. He taxied across to the grass and switched everything off. He climbed out of the rocking craft and went over to the green fibro house and the peeling sign that welcomed him to Forster Airfield.

After paying the landing fee he went down to the jetty, walking through banksias and mosquitoes. Joss hoped the outboard heading in his direction was the one he'd ordered the day before. Beneath him, at the end of the jetty, the water was shallow and clear. Fat mullet, a plate-sized bream and several good-sized taylor swam past the piers. Island life, he thought, could be very peaceful.

It was his boat and it didn't take long for him to be in Forster, where he organised a car to drive south to Seal Rocks. 'I'll wait there for twenty-four hours,' he'd said in his message, 'from seventeen hundred hours on the twelfth.' He'd given himself an hour's grace. Time to set himself up quietly and then retire to the higher ground from where he would have a good view of the headland.

Joss drove carefully, listening to the radio. The world remained the same, he thought. War, murder, sport, Lotto and politics. He remembered a world that he'd once thought important, of reading newspapers, staying abreast of current events so that he could have opinions about everything.

He arrived at the caravan park across the road from the long beach. It was very quiet, with just a few of the permanents going about their business. No one took any notice of Joss. He booked a van and set off along the dirt road, heading for the lighthouse he'd seen from the air. The sea was on his left, dark blue and aquamarine, its winter colours much deeper and colder than summer's. The wind whipped tears up in his eyes and he wiped at them. He wrapped his parka more closely around him and remembered this place as it had been in January twenty years ago. His mind was full of Sybil. Her bronzed face and coppery hair as she ran ahead of him, turning to pelt him with seaweed, and him taking off after her and chasing her down the beach while she yelled and ducked and thrashed out into the water, screaming back at him in incomprehensible Greek. He had raced into the low surf after her and grabbed her and stopped her from splashing him and fought her strength until she was weak from laughing and kissing. She was so very strong, in spite of the smoking. Those narrow brown arms and fists.

At the shop he stopped and bought a packet of biscuits and the one old apple that was sitting on the counter. The shop's cat sat next to the cardboard boxes of sweets, intent on fishing out a jelly baby for itself with a delicate paw.

'He likes the green ones best,' said the old woman serving him. The shop seemed so safe, so normal, that Joss felt the depth of his alienation from that ordinary world. I have never been there, he realised. I have always had to be extraordinary.

He stepped outside and looked at the sea through the dark Norfolk pines where birds murmured, and a shiver of terror reached his heart. How good to be ordinary, running a shop, feeding a cat. He wished he had a weapon with him. He went back inside and bought a cheap fishing knife, then he walked down the hill to the lighthouse.

He passed the little faded fibro cottage up on the hillside to his right and remembered their time there. Daytime lovemaking; blowflies in summer buzzing against the glaring blue glass and him kissing Sybil's agonised mouth as she came under him. The jade vein that ran from the corner of her left eye, her hairline pulsing with her cries. Joss stopped walking, aroused and shaken by these hard-edged memories. He stared up at the cottage, so different now, so removed from him. Across from that house of memories was the fault-slipped igneous outcrop, whitened with seagulls' droppings. Gulls stood in ranks on its slopes, groups of them picked along the water's edge.

He kept going. A cold wind from the unsheltered Pacific beach hit him once he'd left the leeward side of the headland and he wished he'd brought a scarf. He could hear the roar of the waves on Lighthouse Beach. Breaking through the scrubby coastal trees, he found himself looking down the coastline to the misty cones of Port Stephens, just visible off the southern coast. He went to the rock wall that formed the northern end of the beach and leaned there against its prehistoric wave pattern, wiping tears as the wind blinded him and flattened his clothes.

Turning, he climbed up the rough trail behind him until he found a spot to wait in. He squatted down. Perfect. He could see every part of the beach along its three-kilometre length. And he could see the paler marks of the many tracks that led onto it. No matter which way she came – if she came – even if she walked round the dangerous rocks so as to come up behind him, she would have to pass the slip-fault wall below him to get onto the beach.

The sun was moving west over the sand dunes. Joss settled down and bit into the apple. It was soft. He threw it away. He waited.

He was roused from his trancelike state by the sound of someone thudding down the sandslide path nearest the black wall under him and onto the beach below.

It was her. A little heavier, hair a little darker. She was standing looking around, pulling her jacket tighter. He imagined her expression – the frown lines above her jutting nose, the luminous dark eyes as she shaded them with her hand. Joss got to his feet. He could see up the path behind her, and further behind that to the bush track she'd come along. It wound back to the edge of the reserve and it was deserted. He stood still, waiting until she turned away from him and headed down the beach. She followed the water's edge, head down, mahogany hair flying red in the sun, hands tucked into her pockets. Her tread left footprints in the glistening sand.

He let her go about half a kilometre before he set off after her, calling her name in Greek as he caught up. She turned in fear and stood stock-still, her mouth open, tears running from her eyes. He walked slowly up to her and they stood in silence, staring at each other.

# 8

They did not touch. He looked at her and observed what grief and two and a half years of fear had done to her burnished skin. Her face was just starting to show the stigmata of heavy drinking: pouchiness around the glands of the jaw and cheeks, a further heaviness under the beautiful Cretan eyes, now soft and tired. He remembered her eyes as remote, mirrored, but today they seemed lustrous with an ancient light.

She stared back at him, taking him in, then she reached out a hand and touched his cheek. Quickly she pulled it away and he wondered if he'd flinched. '*Agapi mou*,' she said in a whisper. '*Tho eisai*. Here you are.'

He nodded dumbly. He wasn't sure if he could speak.

'You look so different,' she said. 'Your face.' Her hand lifted and dropped again. Last time she'd seen him his face was bandaged like a mummy's. But she was referring to the subtle differences, the changed features. He ran his fingers over the rough surface of his skin, trying to feel the difference she'd noticed. Tiny bits of metal and glass still sometimes worked their way through his pores. His heart was beating all through his body.

'Are you well?' she asked, a slight frown over her intense eyes.

He nodded again and on an unspoken cue they started to walk along together. His tongue unlocked.

'And you?' he finally said. She shrugged.

'You're crying,' she said a moment later, and stopped. He pulled his handkerchief out and wiped the tear away.

'It's nothing,' he said. 'It's sinus damage. My tear ducts don't drain properly. It just looks like I'm crying.'

'We have good reasons to cry, the two of us,' she said,

and her voice sounded hard to him. Three crows jeered around something dead on the slight rise where the dune grass met the beach. The wind was icy.

'How are you?' he asked her again.

'Unhappy.' Her voice was matter-of-fact. 'I think of Linos all the time. He's in the house sometimes. It's true,' she said looking at him. 'I often turn and there he is – or was. As if he's just left the room.' The lustrous eyes filled. 'I run after him. I even call him in English. You know how he hates me speaking Greek to him.' There was a pause. 'He can't rest, I know that. I went to the priest and I told him that *Linos mou* couldn't rest and he talked to me about forgiveness.' From the tone of her voice, Joss knew that if she'd been a man she'd have spat on the sand. Joss remembered that, until she died in Crete only ten years ago, Sybil's mother threw rocks at all passing German cars. Cretans never forgot. And never forgave. 'Please tell me about my girl. *Panayota mou.*' His wife's voice was tough again with its hard smoker's rasp.

Joss remembered what Polly had said about her mother. 'She's very hurt,' he said. 'About you. She seems unable to forgive you for abandoning us.' He imagined his wife's usual defensiveness, explanations, excuses welling up. Sybil could never be wrong. Instead, he felt her nod beside him. This was very different, he thought.

'Yes, I imagine she would be. I thought at sixteen she was old enough to do without me. I was wrong. I've come to see a lot of things, Joss. A lot of things about myself that I didn't know. I used to blame you and the kids for the things I couldn't do, or didn't do. Then when you'd all gone and I was entirely alone and free and I still didn't do them, I was forced to realise some hard truths about myself.'

He looked at her. This was indeed a new Sybil. She pointed at a dead fish whose empty eye socket was filled with blood. 'They're terrible birds,' she said, pointing to the gulls. 'When the fish are stranded they just go along and pick the eye out, then move onto the next fish. Imagine lying there, watching out of your fish eye that you can never close, and seeing the gull coming down closer and closer. Then the stabbing and the pain and then blackness. Poor fish.' She turned it over with her toe and the underside eye stared up at her through the sand on its glassy surface. 'I was forced to see that I'd always hidden behind you and the kids,' she went on. 'Used you as an excuse not to live life fully. I tried to live through you but I know now it can't be done. I have to make a life of my own. I've been forced to do that over the last two years, but I find it very hard.' She stooped to pick up a bivalve shell with iridescent lining inside, like pau shell. She examined it and let it fall.

'So you see, I had to see you again,' she said. 'To tell you how I've come to know these things about myself. That my life was really empty, that I didn't notice because I had three other people filling it up. And when those people left, there was only my own terrible ... *monaxia.*' She searched for the word in English. 'Loneliness. Emptiness. I had no one to blame. Even if I tell you nothing else, I had to tell you this.' She stopped. 'And the other thing – I had to have your forgiveness. And Poll's. But that may not be possible. *Agapi mou,*' she added in a softer voice, 'you've no idea how I've missed you both.' And she began to sob, pushing tears away from her face and chin, half laughing at herself.

Joss forced himself not to touch her.

'Did you think to bring photographs?' she asked. He shook his head. He hadn't taken any personal photographs in two and a half years. He was feeling estranged from himself. This is Sybil, he told himself. The abandoner. The unloving mother, the faithless wife. And yet he felt a smile trying to express itself on his face. Because something was also saying, This is Sybil, *Sivilla mou. Agapi mou.* She is coming to see things that I am just beginning to glimpse, too.

They walked on and he told her almost everything about Polly and almost everything about himself. He didn't mention Ashley because the time was not right.

Sybil scooped up a stranded medusa and pushed it back

into a wave. 'Sometimes I save them and sometimes I don't,' she said. 'And sometimes I wonder if the act of putting them back in the water finally drives the last little bit of life out of them.' She straightened up and faced him. '*Thelo na yiriso sto spiti mas*,' she said.

It was really no surprise to him. And he suddenly felt how deep was the desire in him, too. To come home.

'I know,' he said.

'Do you want me back? Do you think it's possible?' She stopped in front of him, looking at him. Her voice was humble and sad. He felt around his heart for the answer but there was nothing there, just a dark heaviness. He shook his head.

'I just don't know, *Sivilla mou*,' he said. 'I don't know. What about your lover?' Something reared up in his guts. 'Who is this man, by the way?' he asked, hating himself for wanting to know. 'Angstrom?'

Sybil coughed. He felt a sudden jealous hatred blaze across his back. 'What does it matter?' she asked, looking at him with eyes that seemed to open onto centuries of passion and pain. 'It was just something to fill up the terrible aloneness. I was mad with the pain of Alan's death.' She choked on the last two words. 'I wanted to hurt you as much as I was hurting. The son of my heart. I felt you'd killed him.' Joss closed his eyes. Guilty as charged, he thought to himself. 'I hated you because you weren't him,' she was saying. 'I hated you because you were alive and my son wasn't. I hated you for not driving the car that day. Stiff neck! Of course you have a stiff neck. All of you is a stiff neck.' She started crying, deep sobs shaking her whole body.

He stood and watched her. He felt a huge stillness in him. He knew if he put his arms around her and she moved against his heart and neck, he would hold her and everything would be different from how it was just at this awesome, arrested moment, mysterious and contained. Instead, he watched her body shaking and then looked away over the dunes to where a sea eagle circled on a thermal, moving higher with each lazy curve. A cloud obscuring the sun helped him recall the facts.

'Sybil. This is not entirely the truth. You were involved elsewhere before Alan died.' He remembered his jealousy over her attention to Rod Angstrom and Angstrom's comments about her new Cleopatra fringe, the way he'd lifted the coppery strands with his polished gynaecologist's little finger and allowed them to fan down over her black eyebrows. He brought his attention back through the years to the present moment. Sybil was shrugging as if that didn't make any real difference and looking down at her feet. She was writing something in Greek with the point of her left toe. 'What I'm saying,' he said, 'is that you were already having an affair, and that was not a result of the state of mind you were in after Alan. And it's dishonest to imply that.'

'Okay,' she conceded.

He glanced down at the script in the sand. '*I love you, Joss,*' she'd written. There was still plenty of the old Sybil there, he thought. He looked away, distracted and angry at her.

'But it only became *serious* after Alan. Don't you see?' Her voice was anguished. 'I couldn't go to you for comfort, or Poll. You were injured, locked away in your own suffering. Your guilt. Poll was – well you remember what she was like. This person – I felt safe with him.'

'Was that your only affair?' he asked, wondering why he wanted to know now.

Sybil looked sideways at him. 'That is a question I might answer later,' she said. 'If we can get back together again.'

They walked on again and the sun disappeared behind a bank of clouds that was building up in the south-west, towards the misty cones of Port Stephens.

'You should know that I've become involved with someone else,' he said finally, and sighed, wishing for the moment that it wasn't so. Things were so messy in his world already.

'Is it serious?' she asked and he could feel the weight of her question.

'I don't know,' he said. 'Yet.' It was even colder without the sun.

'Then it's not. If you don't know, it's not serious. There seem to be a lot of things you don't know.'

He could hear the old anger. He looked away from the coastline and back at her and saw the reflected sea moving in her eyes, the jade vein throbbing in her temple near a strand of sticky hair. He reached out and pulled the hair away from where it had attached itself in a straight line to the corner of her mouth, tucking it behind her ear. It was such a familiar gesture. It brought him in closer to her and he stepped back to put some distance between them.

'Surely,' he said, 'you don't think you can just come back and move in again, into our lives, just like . . . ' He made a gesture with his hands and then dropped them at his sides.

She shivered and shook her head. 'No, I don't. Of course I don't. But I believe I can start building towards you and our daughter. In time. If you both want me. I could perhaps visit. There's no hurry. We can all take it very gently. Joss, forgive me. I've made a terrible mess, but I think I had to do it like this to find out the truth about myself. Let me come back and love you and Polly again. I locked you out of my heart when Alan died. I never came home from the funeral. I've spent the last two and a half years years grieving and regretting. I know I did a terrible thing, not coming with you at that time. Linos is dead, but he's just further down the road. We'll be dead so soon. Let's not waste the rest of our lives.' She pulled a handkerchief out and blew her nose. 'That's if you want to try again,' she said, and her voice was tired.

Joss spoke. 'You're forgetting that if you do come back to us and they're watching you, you'll bring them straight to us. To Poll.'

'I'm not forgetting,' she said. 'But surely they've got better things to do with with their time. We're no threat to them any more. No one's watching me. I'd know it. You know what I'm like. I am the Sybil. And –' She stopped, about to say somebody's name. She edited herself and went on. 'And he was crazy about discretion. We never went anywhere where we'd be seen together. We always met separately at big hotels. Different times. Different rooms.' There was a silence and then she said, 'We could all leave Australia. Live overseas. Live on Crete.'

They had turned around and walked back past the lighthouse above the black volcanic wall against which they'd first made love in the dusk of a spring night. Sybil joined him in his thoughts. 'That's where Poll was conceived,' she said and turned to him smiling. 'That's Poll's wall.'

'I was just thinking of that.'

'No you weren't. You were thinking of the lovemaking, I'll bet.'

He couldn't deny it, although at that moment his penis felt as if it would never move again, shrunken by the events of this moment and the wind that blew steadily from the north. He hunched against it as towering cumulo-nimbus toppled overhead. As they reached the sheltered side of the headland and the road that led back to the caravan park, purple lightning over Forster became magnesium. The storm was moving closer. They ran the last of the way to the van in preternaturally still and stormy darkness, struck in the face by huge infrequent drops of rain, and were scrambling up the steps as the torrent hurtled down. Inside, they sat close together, shivering. He put his arm around her, a familiar automatic gesture.

'Ella, ella 'tho,' she whispered, pulling him closer, sliding her arm under his coat.

The close air of the van seemed suddenly charged with old adulteries and they kissed each other, shaking with cold and desire, familiar and yet excitingly strange. Sybil's own smell, musky and bitter, came to him under the floral perfume she always used. He could see past her cheekbone to her sinewy ear and the tiny gold disc coiled on her lobe. Her hands slid under his clothes until they touched his back and he was electrified with their cold and their strength. Within seconds, it seemed, they were snaking over his back and buttocks. He put his hand under her skirt, pushing her pants aside. 'I'm bleeding,' she whispered, and he kissed her again. They took off their clothes and huddled naked together under the blankets of the caravan's bunk. He stroked her body and kissed her, rediscovering her tawny skin, the purplish nipples, and the darker lion shades towards her armpits and groin. Sybil rolled away from him, grunted and pulled the tampon out of her body, wrapping it in a handkerchief and tossing it onto the floor. She turned back, fitting her body around him, her hands around his neck smelling of her blood, pressing her belly against him, opening her thighs against his erection, kissing him open-mouthed, her body moving in slow waves against him so that he didn't really know at exactly what stage he'd been absorbed when he found himself hard inside her. It was such an accustomed place for him, so effortless. They pressed sideways together and she was pulsing in waves against him, her eyes wide, desperate even, her hair still wet from the rain spreading across her face and the uncovered pillow. 'It's so good to have you home again,' she whispered, and she lunged against his pelvis, slippery with blood, repeating 'home again' and calling his name in broken cries until she was quite incoherent. He sighed as his orgasm spilled into hers.

   He lay beside her, panting, while she propped herself up on the bed and leaned over to find some tissues and cigarettes in her bag. She shoved the tissues between her legs and lit a cigarette in silence, and for a little while he could believe that Polly and Alan were both doing their homework somewhere close by, that Sybil would shortly put the cigarette out, stretch and say, 'I'd better have a shower and think about what's for dinner.' That he would say, 'When are you going to give up that suicidal habit?' She would make a rude noise at him and vanish naked into the bathroom, and soon he would have to ring the hospital to finalise tomorrow morning's list. He dozed for a while, and woke to Sybil rooting through her bag for another cigarette.

In the amenities block, because there was no one there, Joss washed her and himself, their bloody pubes and thighs, then they ran back shivering through the rain to get dressed.

They had dinner an hour later in Forster, where it was still raining. There was only one other couple in the fish restaurant. Sybil looked quite beautiful in the candlelight, her burnished skin transparent and her hair coiled in a chignon. She smoked one cigarette after the other and drank her wine too quickly. The skin of her neck and arms was damaged by years of sunburn, and the newer lines round her eyes and mouth were poignant to him. There were smoker's clefts in her top lip but her cunning lipstick outlined only her full mouth. He had forgotten her solemn beauty. Her eyes gleamed fierce and golden, like an eagle's.

'How did you know where to contact me?' he asked as their grilled bream were placed on the table.

There seemed to be a long pause. Was she concocting a lie? Syblil looked at her fish and then up at him again.

'Malcolm told me.'

Joss looked straight into her eyes. 'Malcolm doesn't know where I am, Sybil. I'm supposed to be at the University of Western Australia.'

There was another pause. Joss felt distrust grow and swell to fill the gap between them.

'Malcolm suggested I should start by looking at places where criminology is taught,' she said, talking too fast. 'Institutions, universities, colleges. He thought it likely that you'd build on what they'd given you, even if you ran away from them.'

'It's a damn good thing I did,' said Joss, feeling very angry. 'I wonder who else he's advised?'

'Don't be silly, darling,' she said in a proprietorial way that sounded odd to him. She picked up her knife. 'He was our case officer, after all. He knew talking to me would hardly be a security breach. I'm your *wife*.' She laughed. 'I know what you're thinking. You've got that "look out for my Cretan wife" look on your face.' She touched his cheek with a warm hand, then drew a finger lightly across his lips. 'Joss. I had nearly twenty years where I could've murdered you, and I didn't.'

She was still smiling but Joss had a strong intuition that she was uncomfortable about something. 'I wish you'd thought to bring a picture of Polly. How does she do her hair now? How much taller is she?' He told her everything she asked and when they finished the bottle of wine she ordered another, and Joss found himself wishing the old wish that she would not. He told her about the case he was working on, about Dennis.

'What makes them do it?' she said. 'Why do people want to kill children?'

Joss shrugged. 'Why do people want to kill at all? Hate. People kill out of hate. Rage. Hurt.' He was thinking of Sybil going to the priest and the priest talking about forgiveness.

Her thoughts must have been there with him; she often knew what he was thinking. 'I would kill the person who killed Linos. Just like that.' She snapped her fingers. Joss remembered Medea's revenge and shuddered. Lombard's action was revenge, but also something else, contrived and chilling. To discourage the others. It was the action of a terrorist. Lombard had given the order, in custody as he was, and someone had accepted the job, got through to the garage during the storm that night, using his brain and his expertise and his fingers, fixing the transmission so that selection of reverse gear set off the detonation. Who was worse? The man who gave the order? Or the mercenary who did the job? Or the naïve fool who blew the whistle and started the whole murderous thing?

Later, Joss drove them in silence back to the caravan. The night was dark, though the rain had eased. Sybil stretched out along the bunk, feeling in her bag. 'Do you want a nightcap?' she asked as she pulled out a flask of brandy. He shook his head.

'Stop giving me that disapproving look,' she said, and all the familiar angers gripped him. He thought how impossible it always had been with Sybil and she felt it and was immediately contrite.

'I'm only drinking like this because I'm nervous,' she said. 'I hardly drink at all these days.'

Joss sighed. 'You don't have to justify yourself to me.'

'Oh yes, I do,' she yelled. 'Always, always, *always*!'

'Listen to us,' he said, 'just like the old days.'

Sybil seemed about to shout something back, but quite as suddenly she started laughing and pulled him down beside her. Joss felt drained. 'I know I'm impossible,' she whispered in his ear. 'But I love you, and have loved you for twenty years.' He felt her tongue moving near his ear and neck and the warm wetness made him tighten his hold on her, guilty and excited, thinking suddenly of Ashley, of how he was caught between two women who desired him. And how he was caught as well by the past and the fear.

'Do you still dream about the island of Samsura?' she asked.

He nodded into her neck. 'Only the other day, I was wanting to fly away there with some books of poetry.'

'Poetry?' she said, drawing back from him in surprise. 'Do you read poetry now?'

He shook his head. 'Not so much now. But there was a time after Alan died. I read some old ballads.'

Sybil began to recite a poem in Greek about an island the Turks had razed, murdering everyone, killing all the animals so that nothing moved except the wind in the grass. Then she rolled over to face him. 'One day,' she said, dreamily and half-drunk, recalling the old dream as he sheltered in her arms, 'when your life is finally in order, you'll fill the tanks of a big twin-engine aircraft ... ' She paused, swigging on the brandy flask. Joss was enjoying the fumes, the story-telling, the old dream. 'Something like a Piper Navajo,' she resumed, 'maybe something fancier, I don't know.'

He shook his head. 'No,' he said. 'Nothing fancy. What I'd really like is a DC3, but that's a bit unrealistic.'

Sybil kissed his hair. 'And you'll climb into it and you'll take one last look around your world. Because you'll be ready to go. The holy island of Samsura, where peace is found and all struggle ceases.' Her voice was pleasantly blurred. 'Me ...' He felt her shrug. 'I end up in Hades, unfortunately, because that's where people like me go. Probably next to poor old Tantalus. Or chained on the rock next to Prometheus. But you, *agapi mou*, my warrior, you will have come to the end of all your battles and all your loves and all your hatreds. I'll be dead – '

'Don't say that,' he interrupted. But she took no notice of him.

'And everything in your life will be in order. Settled. Linos in heaven. Polly safe and happy. Now there is just you and God. You take off. You don't bother with a flight plan because this is the last flight you'll ever make.'

'Hang on,' he said. 'I don't remember the story quite like that. I can't go until everything's in order, that bit's right. But why are you dead and everything else sounding like it's ground to a halt?'

'Because,' she said, considering, 'this sort of voyage to that sort of island is always done at the end of things. So don't interrupt me any more, please,' she said. 'Just listen.' Her voice was stern and final and he looked up past the bones of her jaw and cheek to the shadowed eyes hidden under her brow. The lines of her face, her edges and curves, were very clear. The chignon had fallen undone around her ears and she looked like Medea with the golden snakes in her ears and the drunkenness around her eyes and smeared mouth. The Sybil, he thought.

'You'll fly and you'll fly,' she continued, 'with your father's maps spread out, and finally you'll come to Samsura, a tiny speck in the South China Sea. You'll make your descent and you'll land on your father's airfield. It will be a perfect landing, the best one you've ever made and not a soul to notice. Just a few palm trees and a rotting bamboo control tower. Maybe a pool of fresh water. Maybe not. Maybe some stores left there by the Yanks.' She looked at him and laughed. 'Hey! Maybe there'll be some crazy old Japanese soldier still fighting for the emperor. And you'll climb out of the airplane and you'll stand there in the warm breeze. I wonder what sort of sounds there will be? Will there be any birds? Gulls? Pelicans? Maybe some little white *fokia*? How do I say them?' She frowned, looking to him for the English.

Joss laughed. 'You don't say them at all. Not there.' Sybil's general knowledge of geography and biology had always been vague. 'You don't have seals there, for godsake.'

Having Sybil in his arms, listening to the story about his childhood island, the familiarity of it all was bringing something in him undone. And another thing was happening. He was recognising seduction and he knew now it was impossible. He moved away from her slightly and sat up on his elbow, newly alert. She felt the distance open up between them and her face became instinctively more beautiful, more vulnerable, more poignant. He looked down at his faithless wife. No, he said to himself. It is all finished now. The life with Sybil and the children. Finished. Gone forever.

Sybil's voice intruded on his thoughts. 'Maybe some exotic Asian birds will be disturbed by the first aircraft to land there since 1954.' She paused. 'And what will you do then?' He was silent. 'Come on,' she said, prompting him. 'You know the rest of it. Say it. The bit about the temple. You start pacing out ... '

But he shook his head, gathering himself.

'Come on,' she was saying. 'Your temple. You know.'

'No,' he said. 'I don't know. That dream is dead. That was in another life. Another man's life that's finished now.'

'Go *on*,' she said, desperate for him to pick up their old story. Knowing that her future depended on his usual entry. 'You *must* tell me. You must tell me what you do next. You have to. You can't spoil the story.'

He pushed away from her and stood up awkwardly in the narrow space. 'The story has already been spoiled,' he said. 'Come on. I think I'd better take you back to your car.'

She was looking at him with her luminous, suffering eyes. 'I can't come back, can I?' she said, knowing the truth, having felt the ending of it too. Outside, the wind had come up again and was howling in the telegraph wires, and in the cables that attached tents and tarpaulins around the park. She started to cry then, long heartbroken sobs, and he took her in his arms as she stood up.

'I just don't know.' He softened it a bit for her, although he did know. You can't come home, he was thinking. Her sobs eased and she drew back, turning to find a hankie in her bag, blowing her nose, settling her face into its stern lines, straightening her courageous shoulders. She gathered up her things and followed him as he stepped down out of the van, turning to help her negotiate the steps. The wind knocked and gusted.

'My car is just down the road a bit,' she said. 'I can manage.' It was dark and cold. She turned her face up to kiss him and her eyes glinted in the electric light. He touched her cheek with his lips and her skin was cold. 'Goodbye, Joss.'

'I'd like to walk with you to your car,' he said, but she shook her head.

'No,' she said, quite definite. 'I don't want that. From here, I go on alone.' He heard the finality in her voice, and he watched her as she walked away from the sad pools of light around the caravan park, out the ill-lit gateway onto the road beyond, where her carefully stepping figure vanished into darkness. Then there was nothing except the wind lashing the tarps until, some time later, he thought he heard a car start against the crash of night surf.

He couldn't sleep. He left money under the door of the caravan park office and drove back to Forster. It cost him triple to get the boatman to go to Wallis Island at that hour.

The flight back to the tablelands was uneventful. As soon as he'd parked the Navajo, he rang Hamish from the public phone at the Maroonga airfield.

'Everything's fine, mate,' said a grumpy voice when Hamish finally answered. 'What's the time?'

'Where is she right now?' Joss asked.

'At his place. The boyfriend picked her up after the last lecture. They had tea at the Golden Wok and went back to his place. That's where I left them about five hours ago. I've got another bloke sitting outside, okay?'

Joss made Hamish describe Ignatius and the house he shared with another student. 'Okay, okay,' said Joss. 'That's all right.'

'Well, maybe you should you know this, ' Hamish's voice continued, more alert now. 'Konrad Muller dropped around for about an hour last night at Ho's place. I don't know whether he was there to visit Ho or his flatmate. As far as I know, Muller only deals in dope. Check with Dennis.'

Joss didn't like hearing that at all. 'First thing in the morning, Hamish, I want you to do a security check on Ignatius Ho. He's a Filipino, here doing post-grad research. Go through Immigration. Find out exactly what sort of visa he's out here on. What his family does back home. Everything. I'll pay whatever's needed. You might have to get into the AFP files somehow.'

'I'll see what I can do,' said Hamish.

Joss rang off and found the door to the aeroclub lounge unlocked. He went to the drinks machine. He selected a mineral water; his tongue was furred with exhaustion. It was a streaky grey morning, bitterly cold. He flopped down at a table and swigged on the cold drink. Someone had left the previous afternoon's paper open at the sporting pages and he pulled it towards him without interest.

Then he turned it over and saw the photo on the the front page: George Lombard's jowled face waving to the press as he walked a free man beside his lawyer. Just behind them were the two Japanese men who had been released at the same time. Joss remembered them from the trial, especially the younger one with the odd greenish birthmark on the side of his face. Joss's blood froze; the whole world reduced itself to the newsprint eyes of the man who'd murdered his son.

Somehow he made his way to his car. He got in and sat there. He remembered the conversation with Barker, Barker's contempt for him. He realised that what Barker had said was true: he'd lain his life on the line, endangered his family, lost his son, all on account of a criminal who'd been convicted only of several relatively minor offences against the Immigration Act. Who now was out of prison. Wanting revenge. He tried to think of how this changed things, but his mind was not functioning properly. All he knew was that Lombard on the loose was infinitely more dangerous than Lombard in a cell. He tried to be rational. He would have to step up security. Keep Hamish on Polly all the time. Send her overseas. He realised he still had the newspaper clutched in his hand. He threw it to the floor. He covered his face with his hands. What do I need to do? An immense tiredness enveloped him; weird lights throbbed behind his strained eyes like hallucinations, and strobic images of Sybil filled his mind. Then the murderous eyes of George Lombard. He leaned his head against the steering wheel and closed his flickering eyelids. His body shook with emotion and exhaustion.

A tear ran down his cheek as he lifted his head. Nausea, combined with physical tiredness and a lack of food and sleep, threatened to overwhelm him. Beneath his feet, a crumple in the newspaper made Lombard appear to smirk up at him. Joss kicked the face, treading it into the floor of the car. He was too exhausted to work out the new implications. He started the drive home.

The dark mass of the Boys' Home loomed in front of the steel grey sky as he drove the last few kilometres, longing for a hot bath and a good sleep. When it first started happening he thought it was something outside the car, a fire, an explosion. Then the nausea and the radiant light, and a torrent of images flooded his mind. The beaten boy seemed to rise up before him in front of the windscreen and Joss instinctively swerved the car, swinging the wheel widely, then overcorrecting hard. Wildly out of control, the car plunged and bucked to smack hard into the ditch beside the road. Joss snapped back against his seatbelt, yelling in fright. The vehicle stalled against the steep angle.

He sat there shocked, panting in the stillness that was filled with the smell of petrol and the shrieking of plovers. Now the images had stabilised and he saw very clearly what was happening. A small boy was at work in a laundry, standing on tiptoe, lifting heavy wet steaming sheets from an old copper with a stick, then lowering them into a sink full of water. Other young boys were loading sheets into another copper, looking fearfully behind them from time to time. The boy at the sink had almost finished transferring the steaming linen when Joss saw in his mind's eye that a man in a cassock was coming up behind him wielding some sort of weapon. As the boy leaned over the sink, the cleric bashed at him. The child's scream filled Joss's head.

Then the vision was gone. Only the dim paddocks and the mist rising from the river as it wound its hidden way among the foothills and flatlands were visible in the dawn. Joss realised he was gripping the steering wheel with both hands. He blinked and leaned back in his seat. This is psychosis, he thought to himself. This is breakdown. Visual and auditory hallucinations, schizophrenia. I nearly killed myself just now. His pulse was racing and sweat chilled his underarms, making him shiver. Lombard's loose. The beast is out of its cage. Then another thought: I've got to get help. Because if I crack up, who will keep Polly safe?

He leaned his damp forehead against the hardness of the wheel. Help me, he prayed to nowhere. Help me.

Joss closed his eyes and slept.

He woke about half an hour later, cold and stiff, and drove carefully home without further incident. He let himself in, read the note from Polly saying she was staying over at Ignatius's place and would be home later today. She'd heard the news about the escape, she wrote, and it didn't change anything as far as she was concerned – this was defiantly underlined several times. Joss listened to the answering machine and heard the botanist Owen Duckworth saying he'd put together a list of places where *cladophera* grew in town. He had also taken photographs, as requested by Eddie Chandler. Could Joss contact him, please. He went into Polly's bedroom, checked her bedside table and saw that the gun had gone. He went to his own room, fell onto his bed and into a deep unconsciousness.

When he woke, he rang Ashley.

# 9

'I think I'm having some sort of breakdown,' he said when she had let him in. He gave her an edited version of his wild swerve off the road.

'Well, it's been clear to me you're just not coping.'

He looked at her. He knew it was true, but he didn't know how she knew that.

'Can you help me?' he asked her. 'Perhaps some ... I don't know ... relaxation?'

She nodded. 'That might help. Or do you want someone to help you work with the images of the boy who nearly caused your death this morning?'

Joss thought about what she'd said. Finally he nodded. 'Yes,' he sighed. 'I suppose I do.' He looked closely at her. 'I've never really asked about your work, hypnosis I mean. It's never been part of our relationship. I've never talked to you about what happens.'

'I've noticed that,' she said. 'There are a lot of misbeliefs about hypnosis, that it has something to do with the power of the hypnotist over the other person. The reverse in fact is the truth. A person comes to me already wanting something. Wanting to be hypnotised. Wanting whatever result she thinks hypnosis will bring her. Just about all the work has been done by that person's mind a long time before they even ring me up. All I do is join in and help them do what they have already made a deep decision to do. That's all. Two minds joining for the one purpose creates the possibility for deep change. But the person being hypnotised has to be willing. It happens sometimes that deep down someone doesn't really want to change, although in their conscious mind they honestly believe they do. In that case, the facilitating hypnotist has no effect at all.'

'What happens in those sessions?' asked Joss.

Ashley shrugged. 'They sometimes come out of the trance. More often they just go to sleep. I understand that as a deep defence system and I respect it.' She laughed. 'Apart from that, it's just not possible to go past another person's unwilling mind. Mind is the most powerful part of a person.'

'Tell me about trance.'

'Again, nothing mysterious. We move in and out of trance states all day. Different states of awareness. Different degrees of consciousness. That's all trance is – complete focus, deep absorption. Watch people at work and see how often they gaze into space. You know that they're just not there. I often look down when I'm gardening and find I've cut myself without feeling anything. It's because I've been so focussed on what I'm doing. Writers are in deep trance in another world. People move into trance watching television. That's why they can tune out, that's why they find it relaxing – they're in a hypnotic state. A cinema full of people watching a movie is a cinema full of people in trance. They know with their conscious mind that they're really watching nothing but the play of light on a screen. They've just paid ten or twelve dollars to do this. They're willing before they sit down. Within seconds, in their trance state, they have entered the hearts and minds of non-existent people and are living in a story that has no reality in the physical world. Yet they feel the fear, joy and suffering of non-existent people. This is deep absorption. Hypnosis.'

'The physical world,' said Joss, 'is the only world I know. Although I understand that there is a mind-body connection, the only world I've worked in, studied closely, operated on, is this physical plane. Not the mental. What if I don't believe it'll work?'

'Then it won't work,' she said.

'What if my conscious mind wants to believe it'll work, but all my training and experience have set up a deep, unconscious resistance in me?'

Ashley shook her head. 'Training and experience don't

set up the unconscious,' she said. 'They can only sit on top.'

'Why do I get these flashbacks? Is this repression?'

Ashley shrugged. 'Repression,' she said, 'is a word. I'm not sure why some memories are clear and unhidden and others seem to make themselves known in this way, as if they're somehow breaking out of a secret box. There's a lot we don't know about mind.'

Joss considered. 'I used to put hypnosis in the same bag as astrology, crystal balls and snake-oil cures. I can't believe I'm even thinking about doing this,' he said.

'You're only thinking about deep concentration. Hypnosis isn't magic. It isn't a therapy. It's just a tool. You want to clarify certain incidents? An absorbed state may help. And it depends on how much you want to live,' she added.

'What?'

'There's a very real chance that if you neglect the boy who took you off the road and into a ditch this morning, you'll end up killing yourself. In my experience, images like those you've described to me need to be dealt with. It could be extremely dangerous not to check them out.'

He looked at her. Her face was grave. 'It is very serious,' she said. 'I've had clients die rather than face the truth of what has happened to them. Indirect suicide. One client who was just starting to come into the feelings around his early childhood stopped his car at the level crossing out at Abercrombie and was reading something, not noticing that the car was rolling forward. He was so engrossed he didn't even hear the 3.15 until it was too late.'

Ashley's words were very real to Joss after this morning. His mangled body would be freed from the vehicle, and the other driver, if not dead as well, or seriously injured, would say that the Niva appeared to swerve onto the wrong side of the road, that there was nothing he could have done.

'Why did you say I'd need someone to work with? Are you saying you won't take me on as a client?'

'But you're not a client,' she said. 'You're my lover. And I certainly don't want to cross the boundaries around that.

It would be too much of a muddle for me. For you, too.'

Joss nodded. He knew Ashley's opinion about therapists who developed a sexual relationship with people who had come to them for help. 'But we're in a different category,' he argued. 'The emotional, sexual aspect of our relationship has been in place for six months. You'd hardly be abusing my trust,' he said. 'I really need your help. There's absolutely no one else I can ask.'

She walked over to the other side of her lounge room and leant against the wall, looking back at him. 'Ten years ago,' she said, 'I'd have refused outright. But I don't think human relationships can be constrained by rigid rules.' She sighed, making her decision. 'Okay, I'll do a little bit with you, so you get the feel of it. But that's all I can do at this stage.'

Joss grinned with relief. 'What do I do?' he asked, feeling self-conscious.

She came back and sat opposite him. 'Are you comfortable sitting there?'

He nodded.

'Okay. Lean back and relax and when you feel ready, just let your eyes close.'

He did. 'What now?' he asked.

'Let the feeling of relaxation move through your whole body. I'll explain every step for you. There is nothing to fear. You are always in complete control of the situation. You needn't fear you'll tell me anything you don't want me to know just because you're in a deep state of absorption. A person is as discreet in this deeply absorbed state as he is in the normal state. You will notice by now that you are becoming very interested in my words. Part of you is becoming deeply focussed on the experience you are having, and part of you is listening with interest to my voice. Meanwhile, you just lean back and listen and ponder.' Her voice was low and soothing. 'And if you get worried or frightened, any time, you can tell me and I'll stop.'

'I'm already worried and frightened,' he tried to say, but

found he could barely get the words out.

He lay back in Ashley's leather recliner, while she took him through a long process of relaxing his tense muscles, the holding in his body, the tightness of his ligaments and tendons. He followed her voice down the dark corridors she was describing, catacombs under the earth, down, down, down to deeper levels, deeper floors. Her voice was a shadowy figure he trailed, turning with it down steeper flights, until he was very still, in a deep part of his mind where darkness swirled and restfulness surrounded him. He stayed there for a while until the shadow of her voice continued from the soft darkness nearby.

'You are perfectly safe,' she was saying. 'Completely safe. If you should feel any anxiety, all you have to do is wake up. You are in absolute control at all times. I want you to allow yourself to visit that laundry you saw this morning. But it will be like watching a video. You are separate from the events. You can stop the frame any time. You can rewind it, you can switch it off altogether. Nothing can frighten you or hurt you there. You are only watching something on a video screen. Do you understand? You are completely safe. Are you ready?'

As if from a long way away, Joss heard his voice, slow and soft, agreeing that he was.

'You're watching the video now. It's a film about what you saw this morning in the car before you swerved to miss the boy. Where was the boy? Tell me where he is.'

There was a pause while Joss mustered his drowsy strength to speak. He sighed deeply. He was hardly aware of Ashley at all, just a voice in the distance.

'He seems to be in this laundry. Or washroom.'

'Describe it to me.'

'It's a large high-ceilinged room. There are no proper windows. Just a barred one high up on the wall. I think this laundry is in a basement somewhere. It feels subterranean. The walls are mouldy and streaky with condensation from the steam.'

'Where's the steam coming from?'

'There are these big old-fashioned coppers. Full of boiling clothes. Linen. Sheets.'

'Sheets?' Ashley's voice remained even.

'The boys are lifting them out of the coppers into the big tubs to rinse. They're using sticks. Dowelling, like broom handles. The wet sheets are very heavy.' He was aware of his body floating nearby, weightless like some sea fan, his mind dropping even deeper every time Ashley's distant voice resounded. It was an effort to speak.

'Can you tell me anything else about this place?' she asked. He sighed deeply again. For a while, he couldn't reply.

'It's not a good place. The boys are unhappy here. They're frightened. They keep looking around. There is someone here that . . .' Something loomed up in his mind – huge, terrifying; an immense loop of cruelty curling around him, very close.

'Are *you* there? In the laundry with the other boys?'

Joss didn't answer.

'Are *you* there?' Ashley repeated. But again there was no answer.

'Joss? Are you there? In that place? Joss?' She looked across at him and noticed the complete collapse of his head onto his chest, his heavy breathing. He had fallen asleep.

He was aware of her shaking him. 'I must have fallen asleep,' he said. 'How long?' He struggled to regain control of the present.

'A few minutes. Not long. Do you want to continue?'

'Yes,' he said.

'Then I wonder why it is,' she said smiling, 'that you are shaking your head no?'

'Am I really shaking my head?' he asked, surprised to find that he was.

'Do you remember what I was asking you when you suddenly went to sleep?' Joss shook his head.

'I was asking you if you were there,' she said, 'in that laundry.'

He was silent awhile. 'And I went to sleep,' he said, 'as soon as you asked me that?'

Ashley nodded. 'It's not unusual. Are you sure you're all right to go on?'

'I'm sure,' he said, suddenly very weary. He followed her voice again, down the escalators, further, deeper, until the laundry filled his mind – the fearful children, the huge tubs, the steam condensing and running in tears down the wall.

'Remember it's just a video,' she said. 'You can watch what happens in that laundry with perfect safety. You can stop it whenever you want.' Joss murmured that he understood.

'What are the children wearing?' Ashley asked.

He looked around in his mind at them. 'Grey shorts. Grey uniforms. They're only little boys.'

'How old, do you think?'

'Seven. Maybe eight. Some are older. There's one who's only about five or six, I think.'

'What's he doing?'

'I don't know. I can't see him.'

'Why can't you see him?'

No answer.

'How do you know he's there if you can't see him?' she rephrased.

But there was still no answer and Ashley saw that again Joss was slumped in deep sleep.

'Look,' she said later, passing him a cup of coffee, 'this is not at all what I'd normally do.' Joss still felt sleepy, yet the cruel force that he remembered looping itself around him seemed to have seeped into his body, lay deep within him under the calm post-hypnotic state. 'Normally, I'd respect your defence system. If we had time.'

He saw the seriousness of her face. He smelt her perfume and closed his eyes. Perversely, it was Sybil who sprang into his mind, laughing and bloody. He opened his eyes to look at Ashley.

'What do you mean? I just got tired. I'm exhausted, that's all.'

'Do you think there are things in your mind that you are aware of and things you are not aware of?'

He reflected for a moment. 'It's something I've never really thought about.' The world I lived in, until *then*, was so different, he was thinking. It was a world of externals; of study, of surgery, of problems to be solved through operating microscopes, of interference in the human body. The mechanics of mending broken bodies. Torn and bleeding tissues and pipelines that needed to be debrided and rebuilt, so that another human body could heal.

'As you say,' Ashley said, 'you've never had to think about it very much. Let me describe an ocean to you. On the surface of it, waves move and small fish dart around. The water is clear and transparent in the sunlight for a depth of a few feet. At ten feet things are bluish, the water filters out the red tones. At twenty feet it's even dimmer, bluer. At a hundred feet it's almost dark. At five thousand feet it's black. At twenty thousand feet, it's darker than we can imagine. At thirty thousand feet – that's around the cruising height of an average airliner – huge things stir. Down there, creatures so ancient they were thought to be extinct for millions of years are still occasionally found. That ocean is your mind. Any human mind. Most people swim in the top few inches. They never want to look below because they think there are monsters down there. They swim in fear all their lives. Because of the fear of the monsters they never live fully. They build elaborate floating palaces on the surface and hope that nothing comes up in the night, that the tidal wave doesn't hit them.'

He considered this.

'What do you know about yourself?' she was asking him. Once he would have had a ready answer. He thought for a while.

'I don't know very much at all,' he said finally, leaning his head back against the chair. Then a truth that he couldn't deny forced itself from his lips. 'But there *is* a monster in me,' he said, almost whispering. 'I've experienced it. That's why I'm here.'

'Yes,' nodded Ashley. 'Yours has made a rare trip to the surface. Everyone is terrified of their own sea monsters. They live in shallow water, but somewhere they know they have avoided themselves. They find another distraction, something new. They get married, build a house, take a tranquilliser, a lover, a new job. Have a baby. Create a new anxiety. Have renovations done to the floating palace – anything to keep busy so as not to have to go diving. In the last part of their lives, they become engrossed in their own illnesses. Then they're dead. It's sad that they choose to live like that, but that is their choice.' She paused. 'However, in some cases, and I think yours is one of them, I believe that if the work that's waiting in the ocean isn't done, you will die. You, Joss. Not later, but sooner. Like you could have this morning.' She looked straight at him, unflinching. 'Or,' she continued, 'you could have a complete breakdown and have to be taken into care. And then you could end up doing the rounds of the latest medications and institutions. Your truth – the truth which would set you free – could be lost forever and you'd be another chronic psych patient.'

Only a few months ago, weeks even, he would have been insulted by her words. But the anguish of the last week and this morning's near miss had humbled him. He listened. 'What can I do? If this is an unconscious defence, there's nothing I can really do.'

'You can make a conscious decision to allow things up. You can say to yourself that you're willing to look within. You can find out as much as you can about your earliest life. You know how to investigate. Start getting evidence. Is there anyone you can talk to who would know about the events of your childhood?'

Joss shook his head. 'No one,' he said. Ashley's diploma

and one of her paintings blurred as his eye teared.

'If I told you,' she said, 'that you'll find your worst monster curled around your greatest treasure, would that help you?'

He pulled his handkerchief out and wiped his eye. 'I don't think so,' he said.

'To do this is deep and sacred work,' Ashley was saying. 'This is your soul we're touching. You'll have to go to the very best practitioner.'

Something in him, his forgotten soul perhaps, recognised the truth of her words. 'Because I can't work with you on this,' she added.

He raised his head to look at her. Everything was shifting around him. Sybil wanting to come home, Lombard out and running, Ashley pulling away. It seemed that he was balancing on a piece of theatrical machinery sinking in a surreal ocean. 'Ashley,' he whispered. 'You *have* to work with me on this. I can't take this stuff to anyone else.'

'You'll build up rapport with someone else,' she said. 'It just takes some time.'

'That's not what I mean,' he said. 'I can't trust anyone else. There are other considerations. I am – ' He hesitated. 'I am not what I seem,' he said. 'And I really can't say any more than that. Except to ask you to trust me with my little mystery.' He tried to play it down.

'I already know that you're not what you seem,' she said. 'And I do trust you. But I don't believe the mystery is little. I believe it is about your life. And Polly's life.'

'What makes you say that?'

'A life lived in terror is obvious,' she said. 'Why is your house fortified like the maximum security wing of a prison? And why is your daughter even more haunted than you are?'

Joss was shocked. 'What makes you say all that?' There was an edge of anger in his voice.

Ashley stood up and went to the window. Outside, someone walked past on the footpath. She turned to face him. 'These,' she said, pointing to her eyes. 'And these,' she repeated, indicating her ears. 'And most of all, here.' She placed a hand over her heart.

He stood up and came to her. 'I think I'd better tell you a few things.'

The stove flickered low. The room had been silent for some time now.

'Sybil thinks they'll leave us alone now,' Joss finally said. 'But I can't believe that. Especially now that Lombard is out of jail.'

'Wouldn't he just get out of the country?' said Ashley.

Joss shook his head. 'He might. But men like him can reach a long way. He was already in jail when Alan was killed. I can't forget that card they sent. It said very clearly, "One down and three to go."' He looked down at his hands, the strong fingers, the scrubbed and fine-trimmed nails. Ashley touched his arm and he continued. 'I still have nightmares that Alan's alive and I can't find anything to help him with. I'm trying to clean him up, stop the bleeding, hold his body together with my bare hands. The clamps melt like treacle. The sutures dissolve as I pull them through. Nothing holds.' He looked at her. 'That's why I've got the fortress out along Long Swamp Road. I believe they will never let up. The federal people took it seriously enough to organise a completely new life for me and Polly.'

'I remember reading about that clinic,' Ashley said. 'People were prepared to pay hundreds of thousands of dollars for an immediate transplant and not have to wait for a suitable donor.'

'Lombard's people were recruiting and matching donors all through South-East Asia and bringing them into Australia,' said Joss. 'People in Manila and Singapore could make relatively good money selling a kidney or a lung or even a limb. Hearts were flown in from China. They were supposed to be from executed criminals, but I had the feeling that having a heart that matched a wealthy American or Australian businessman could be seen as criminal in itself. I'm quite sure there was – is – a lot of murder involved. These people aren't bound by any code.'

'Wasn't there some business college involved?' Ashley asked.

Joss nodded. 'Yes,' he said. 'Most of the people who worked there were ordinary teachers, teaching English and business studies. There were some quite legitimate students enrolled, too. Even the principal didn't know that it was a shopfront for international criminals. The selected donors were flown into Australia on student visas. But they never attended classes. Once they'd donated the organs, they were paid and flown home. It was alleged there were several deaths from post-operative complications.'

'So you were the surgeon who started it all off. Doctor Ross Pascall. I never forgot the name.'

'Yes,' he said. 'And I wish I'd never said a word. I wish I'd just kept my mouth shut and got on with my job. I had no idea what I was coming up against. If I had, I'd have just turned a blind eye. Alan would still be alive. My family might still be together.'

'So Sybil is very much alive,' said Ashley.

'Very much so,' said Joss. 'I spent most of the day before yesterday with her.'

Ashley was silent. 'It's a beautiful name,' she said finally.

'Yes,' Joss nodded. 'And she's beautiful. Very discontented. Restless, irritable. And sometimes wise and surprisingly generous. I loved her very much.'

'And you still do.'

Joss nodded again. 'It's true, Ashley. Twenty years is a long time to be with someone. But it's not possible to go back to that life, that marriage, any more. I can love her at a distance now. Too many things have happened. Too much pain. Change. Too much betrayal.'

'What an awesome journey your life has been in the last few years,' Ashley said.

'Awesome?' He sounded suddenly angry. 'Terrible is the word I'd use. Terrible and painful and terrifying.'

'Yes,' she agreed. 'All of those things.'

Joss stood up. His legs would barely hold him. 'I have to go home,' he said.

'I'll run you,' she said. He nodded, grateful.

'This is very difficult for me,' he said as they were leaving, 'putting myself in your hands like this. I'm a doctor. A surgeon. We are great believers in *matter*. All our training reinforces that. I trained and worked with human *bodies*. With flesh and bones and sinews and tendons. With this dense fabric. Not with this, the mind.' He touched his temple.

'I'll tell you something I've never told another soul, not even my wife. The first time I cut into human flesh, I felt, among many other confusing things, *furtive*. Because it is such a shocking and extraordinary thing to do. It proves that matter is real, somehow. That this stuff,' he tugged at the flesh of his arm, 'is more real than anything else. To do it to a corpse on a dissecting table is real enough. To cut into living, responsive, bleeding human flesh is quite extraordinary. That's only come to me since I'm not doing it any more. While I was working, it didn't seem like that. And it brings more and more conviction with it of the reality, the rightness, of the material world.' He dropped his hands helplessly between his knees and looked up at her. 'This mental world that you work with – well, it somehow doesn't seem real. I don't know any neurosurgeon, even the most experienced, who doesn't find opening the skull and the brain the most awesome act of surgery.'

She nodded. 'Is that how you're seeing me? As someone who is opening your brain?'

He thought about that. 'I suppose I must be,' he said, surprised that she'd seen what he meant before he had.

She considered a moment. 'Joss.' She was looking for words. 'It must be very hard for a doctor. You're going to have to let go of a huge belief structure in your mind. Because this is *not* about brain, which doubtless you do know a lot about. This is about *mind*. Not just mind, but *your* mind. This is about *you*.'

He realised he was afraid. Afraid of himself, of the things he didn't know. Ashley saw it. She put a hand on his arm. 'I'm familiar with the depths,' she said. 'I've done a lot of deep-sea diving. It's always done in pairs, so there's always someone there.' She saw that his face remained tight and frightened. 'I know the monsters very well,' she added. Her eyes were clear. 'I know them by their names.'

They didn't kiss. They didn't even touch. And he knew that she was speaking the truth. For the first time in over two years, and even though it was still a long way away, Joss thought he could discern, even through the fear, a glimmer of hope. Perhaps there was a way home.

He woke on Wednesday morning before the alarm to the phone ringing. He snatched it up, suddenly wide awake, looking round for a weapon. Lombard – I want a gun, he thought. It was Dennis.

'Some bones were found early this morning,' he said. 'Out near Spring Caves. Eddie's putting them back together, he's already found a few interesting things. He wants to tell us what he's got. Come straight down, will you? It might have something to do with something.'

Joss got up, showered, breakfasted, and arrived at the police station fifty minutes later. He parked his car just behind two police vehicles and nodded through the windscreen at Graham, who was returning from the bread shop with breakfast. Dennis came out to the front desk just as Joss was walking in the door and the two men went down the corridor together.

'We've got bones. Adult,' said Dennis. 'Almost a full skeleton. The cocky out at Narrabeen, old Charlie Darling, found him.' Joss knew the big property, the white-painted four-gallon drum for the mail and the bread, the cattle grid and double gates a few kilometres along the Spring Caves road. 'Old Charlie was ripping stumps out of his back paddock when this fellow pops up, dragged up by the ripper. At first he thought he might have disturbed

Aboriginal bones. But not wearing a black suit and beads.'

'Black suit and *beads*?' Joss asked.

'Yeah. Some of the young blokes are still out there with Charlie and his grandsons looking for anything else we might have missed.' They were nearly at the door of the incident room and Dennis suddenly changed tack. 'My profile ready yet?'

Joss inhaled. He could lie. He didn't. 'I'm finishing the last of it today. You'll have it tomorrow.' He suddenly remembered the botanist's message and put his hand in his coat pocket to make sure he had the phone number with him. 'I'll have it on your desk in the morning.'

'Do that,' said Dennis in his most relaxed voice. Joss wasn't fooled. 'By the way,' Dennis added, with his hand on the doorknob, 'your daughter has no explanation as to how the vehicle registered in your name happened to be at the picnic ground that morning. I had a word with her.'

'You have no right to drag her into this,' snapped Joss without thinking.

'Mate,' said Dennis deliberately, taking his hand off the door knob, 'I have every right. I'm investigating two very serious and horrible crimes. And I'm not getting any help from you at all. And for what it's worth, your daughter rang me.'

Joss lowered his voice. 'Look,' he said to the younger man, 'I'm under a lot of strain lately. My personal life – '

'Even a cop has a personal life,' Dennis interrupted. 'Can you believe it?'

'I'm not making excuses,' said Joss, 'I'm describing facts. It's been unrelenting lately, the pressure.'

'I'm sorry to hear that, Doctor Haskell, because I need to press you to answer a few questions myself.'

'Like what?' asked Joss, feeling oddly panicked.

'Like where you've been for the last twenty-four hours when you're supposed to be part of the homicide team. Like why you flew to Sydney the other day and made a phone call to the federal people's dog squad in the middle of the night.' Joss found himself wide-eyed in surprise.

'Yes,' said Dennis. 'I got a mate to check your account at the Regent, and the number you rang came up as silent and unlisted. Turns out it's a number used by the federal dog squad.'

Joss's mind was racing. Federal dog squad. Danger very close. Reaching backwards, forwards. *What does this mean?* He couldn't contain his shock. 'How did you find that out? How could you get that sort of information?'

Dennis smiled. 'I've got contacts around the place. Seems like you have, too.'

I can't trust anyone, Joss was thinking. He tried to keep his voice mild. Did Witness Protection share phone numbers with another department? He tried to sort through the new information. 'What do you mean, dog squad?'

'You know quite well what I mean,' said Dennis, the watchfulness cold behind his narrowed eyes. Suddenly he was smiling, as if enjoying some secret they shared. 'You know the dog squad. The blokes who do the odd jobs. Bunch of pervs, if you ask me. I want to know why you rang them, and I still want to know how your Celica came to be at the picnic grounds the morning the killer spoke to Simon Prendergast in the toilet block. Your daughter says she was at lectures all morning.'

'Maybe someone borrowed it?' suggested Joss.

'I think your daughter would have noticed when she came out at lunchtime, don't you?' said Dennis drily.

'And *put it back*,' said Joss, furious. He forced himself to calm down, and continued in what he hoped was a reasonable tone. 'It's none of your business, but in the interests of cooperation I'll tell you what happened. I made a phone call from the hotel. To a friend. And he was no longer at that number. The simple explanation is that the number's been reallocated to your dog squad.'

'Not my dog squad,' said Dennis, finally turning the handle of the door.

Eddie Chandler looked up from in front of the two whiteboards as they walked in. Neil and Ian and other members of the investigative team turned to look too, from where they sat around the table.

'Like I was just saying, I found this,' Eddie said, picking up a bag, 'when I started to put this fellow back together at the morgue. He was mostly in a hessian bag, except for the bits and pieces that the ripper dislodged. This was with him. Maybe it's just one of those weird coincidences, but I wanted to bring it down myself.' He undid the plastic bag and carefully removed several other smaller ones, placing the contents on the table. In one bag Joss could see a pile of black beads, in another a silver ring. But it was the third bag that drew everyone's attention. In it was a commemorative medallion in silver and enamel, its colours still bright. Joss picked it up and looked at it through the clear plastic. There was a shield design of heraldic style, and very clearly round the edge he could read 'St Callistus School Centenary', and a date.

'I haven't established identity or cause of death yet,' Eddie continued. 'But I can tell you now that this fellow is most definitely a mature adult, elderly, so I don't know whether this means anything or not in terms of the two recent murders.'

Dennis and Joss and the other people around the table stared at Eddie. 'He's been dead a long time,' Eddie was saying, gathering up a folder and putting it in his bag. He looked at his watch and started towards the door. 'I should be at the courthouse. But it looks like we've got another dead St Callistus boy.'


When Joss got back to the university he rang Hamish Alabone again. 'What have you found on Ignatius Ho?' he said, bringing his mind back from elderly St Callistus boys to student visas and academia.

'Steady on.' Hamish sounded peevish. 'Don't rush me. It's not easy getting into some files. I've got a few little things. Just relax. He's okay. How long's your daughter been going out with this man?'

Joss considered. 'They met last year, I remember. I know he's doing post-grad research, but to be honest, I'm not sure what area he's in.'

'Let me tell you,' said Hamish, and Joss imagined his grin over the phone. 'Immunology.'

'That'd be right,' said Joss. 'I know he finished medicine the year before last.'

'I'm double checking with a few contacts over there. Waiting on a fax. But you'll be pleased to know he comes from a very highly regarded family in Manila. Very well connected. Very Catholic.'

'So was Marcos,' Joss couldn't help saying.

Hamish laughed. 'It's not like that. You can relax. He's on a research visa and it's all straight down the line. He checks out clean as a whistle.'

Joss felt an immense relief. 'Good. Now, will you do something else for me?'

'I'll do anything for you as long as you pay your bill,' said Hamish.

'Will you do a bit of work on Dennis Johnson?'

'You mean Dennis? Our friendly detective?' Hamish's voice sounded bewildered.

'I mean Dennis. I want his CV. Relations are a bit strained between us at the moment.'

'That's easy.'

'And Hamish, keep on with Doctor Ho. Anything. Everything.'

'Okay, okay. I get the message. Is she wanting to marry this man? He's rather cute.'

Joss hung up and rang Owen Duckworth, arranging to meet him on the other side of the university. He decided to walk. He wanted to think, now that his mind was clearer. It was a cold morning and he felt steady and grounded.

There was nothing he could do about Lombard except wait. Just like Dennis would say. Keep security tight, and wait. Wait for the right moment. The Tao of waiting. But this time Joss had something for Lombard that he hadn't known was in him before – hatred. And this hatred gave him a new edge. I know how to help with healing, how to create the conditions that go to make a human body whole. I know how to put someone together again, he was thinking.

And I also know how to do the reverse.

# 10

'*Cladophera*'s pretty choosy round this area because of the cold winters,' Owen Duckworth was saying. He was a slight man with a pointed beard and khaki trousers. 'But it grows very well in the deeper, more sheltered drains.' His office was tidy, its walls covered with posters exhorting care of the environment. He passed Joss a photograph of a canal with a floor that sloped to a central, shallow V. A stained green streak ran down the middle. 'It grows in strands, filaments. This is where I found the best example of it.' He passed another shot that looked directly into the canal. The green weed was growing vigorously along the bottom of a channel that was at least three metres deep and more than four metres across.

Joss looked closely at a long shot of the back fences of houses that backed onto the weed-covered banks of the canal. 'Where's that?' he asked. 'Isn't that the old abattoirs building in Nightingale Street?'

'That's right,' said the other. 'That's where you'll find a lot of this stuff. Kids are always slipping in it, twisting their ankles. This one'll give you a better idea of the location of the canal.'

Joss looked at a picture showing the backs of the houses in more detail.

'It grows all the way along the canal until it meets the entrance of the drain system that goes under the city.'

'And what happens then?' asked Joss.

Duckworth shrugged. 'It stops, I should think. It needs sunlight.'

Of course, Joss was thinking. His spirits booted up, his mind processed fast. Green indicates the presence of chlorophyll. Chlorophyll indicates the presence of sunlight. The greenish stain on the edge of a sheet. The culverts. The stormwater canal ran to join the drains under the city where *cladophera* could not grow. Joss's mind raced. 'Where else have you found it?'

'There're a few other locations, but this is the best example. There's some along Long Swamp Road actually,' said Duckworth, 'in one of the culverts.'

'Can I use your phone?' said Joss, picking up the handset even before the other had agreed. He rang Dennis, but learnt from Graham that his colleague was in court.

'Get someone to go over to the council engineer's office, will you?' Joss told Graham. 'Get a copy of the layout of the stormwater canals and the drains under the city. I'll be back in the incident room in – ' He glanced at his watch. 'Thirty minutes. When Dennis comes back, tell him to wait for me there.'

Driving back to the police station, Joss studied the photographs of the houses in Nightingale Street whenever a break in the traffic allowed. He was thinking fast.

He made an impromptu detour to the council engineer's office himself, then drove the short distance to the station and pulled up too fast. He hurried inside clutching the photos and strode down the corridor to the incident room, where he found Dennis back from yet another adjournment. Joss leaned over the table where Graham had spread out the plans of the stormwater system under the city.

Dennis pulled a photocopy towards him, resisting the unlit cigarette resting on the ashtray. 'What you got?' he asked, peering at the photocopy.

'Take a look at this first,' said Joss, pulling out the photographs Owen Duckworth had given him and passing them to Dennis. 'This is *cladophera*, the green stain on the sheet. And this is one of the places where *cladophera* grows. Now look at this canal and look how those houses back onto it.'

Dennis scanned the pictures, reading them fast, shoving

one behind the other as he finished, looking again at the shot that showed the back of Nightingale Street with its row of fences along the banks of the stormwater canal.

'Now look at this,' said Joss, passing the plan of the city's drains to his colleague. Dennis put the photographs down and turned his attention to the map, tracing a finger along the stormwater canal in Nightingale Street to where it joined the grids of drains under the city. Together they formed an identical underground road system, even posted with the same familiar street names, the shadow of the sunlit roads above.

Dennis looked up. 'Where else do you get drains like this?' he asked Joss. 'Exactly like this – next to houses?'

Joss shook his head. 'You don't. I've just come from speaking to the engineer. This canal was put in after the '89 flood. This is the only street that has this sort of set-up. The others are the older sort, crawling space only and completely enclosed. No sunlight. No chlorophyll.'

'So no *cladophera*,' said Dennis.

The two men stared at each other. There were low comments from the others. 'He could jump down into the canal,' Dennis said, his voice getting quicker, 'follow it along a bit, and then he reaches the entrance to the underground system under the city.'

Joss was nodding, his mind picturing a figure intent on the murder of a child, scuttling in the darkness through the drains.

'He could pop up anywhere. That's why no one ever sees him.' Dennis jumped to his feet. 'He just pops up out of the ground where there's a large opening to the drain system, like a culvert, does the puppy routine, the kid goes down to help the puppy, and our bloke grabs him and scurries away with him through his private underground, along the canal and up into his own backyard! What a set-up! No wonder no one ever sees him.' He was grabbing his jacket from the back of a chair, stowing the unlit cigarette in his top pocket.

Joss pulled on his coat and followed Dennis down the

corridor. 'I've got to get back to the university,' he said.

'I'll take a look at Nightingale Street,' Dennis said. Then he looked at his watch. 'Fuck it. I've got to be back in court. The boss'll have my arse otherwise.'

'No way,' said Kylie, coming out of her office. 'It's too ugly and hairy.'

'Not what you said last time, sweetheart,' leered Dennis. He went back to speak with Neil and Ian. 'I want Nightingale Street checked out again. Every single household. Someone's got to have seen something.'

As he was winding up his lecture, Joss saw Polly slip into a back seat in the theatre. The class was larger than usual because word had got around that Dr Haskell's lecture was to be on criminal policy and its impact on women. And, more importantly, that he was going to give some hints on what might be in the exam.

'Okay,' said Joss, packing up his notes and looking around. 'It's good to see the interest here. It's good to see people from other disciplines. These are important issues for our times.'

He walked with Polly to the staff bistro for an early dinner. 'Do you think someone could have taken the Celica to the picnic grounds that day, while you were at lectures?' he asked her as their meals were served.

She frowned. 'I suppose it's possible. But wouldn't I have noticed something? Like some damage to the lock? And why would a thief return it? Why not just dump it?'

Joss tried to concentrate his energies. But Lombard was always in the back of his mind, and the new excitement about the killer's use of the drains under the city kept distracting him.

'Are you serious about Ignatius Ho?' Joss asked. 'If you are, I should get to know him a bit.'

'Oh Dad,' she said. 'Give it a break.' Then she saw his face and softened. 'Look. He's a nice man. But I don't know.' Then she lowered her voice. 'I'm thinking of calling it off after we get back from this camping weekend. He works too hard. He's too anxious. He's always worried. He's not learning to deal with things. I don't need another man like that in my life. I want someone who's fun.'

He remembered her mixture of anger and resignation the night she'd talked about her little girl diary. 'Oh Poll,' he said. 'You deserve some fun.'

She looked straight at him with her mother's eyes, with the question she hadn't had the chance to ask him yet. 'You saw her, didn't you. When you were away.' There was no question mark at the end of it. Joss nodded.

'Well?' his daughter demanded. 'What did you say?'

Joss looked away. He longed to tell his daughter that it wouldn't work, this toughness. Not indefinitely and not in regard to her mother. 'I think we both realised too much had happened. Too much change.' His voice cracked. 'Too much suffering.'

'And whose fault was that?' Polly's mouth was like a bitter woman of seventy's, lipless and downturned.

'I don't think fault's a very good word here, Poll. I've come to see that things just happen.'

'You bet things happen! Grown-ups fuck up their own lives good and proper and everyone else around them has to pay. That's what happens. Do you know what it was like for me and Alan growing up with you two? It was horrible. We hated it. He was terrified of you. All you ever did was yell at us. And now he's dead. And I'm here with you, trying to live my life – this pathetic half-life, full of lies and bullshit. Creeping around waiting for those bastards to come after us. Just waiting.'

Her voice had risen and people were turning to look at them. Furious, Polly lowered her voice and hissed, 'I went out yesterday to the back of the O'Donnell's place and practised with the .38 and it felt *great*. I really liked it. There was no one there but Tim had left some proper targets in the shed – the man-shaped ones that the cops use, with the bullseye in the middle of the heart. And I stuck that picture of Lombard up, the one from the newspaper. I shot him right between those dead eyes of his.' She looked away. 'I realised something yesterday. I really want to kill him. That came as a bit of a shock.'

She had torn her bread into bits and was now rolling it into little grey balls. 'So that's what I discovered about myself yesterday. That I might be scared, but I'm not running any more. There's no point, anyway. I decided I'm going to face whatever is in front of me. What about you? What's happened to *you*?' The distress in her voice was awful to hear. 'Once, you used to at least know what you were doing. Once you were strong even if you were a bully. Now you're – ' She stopped, aware of having said too much.

'Now I'm what?' he asked, wanting to hear. Even though what she had said hurt him very deeply, he recognised its truth. He remembered Alan's silence, the downcast eyes when Joss would yell at him to pull his socks up, start working at school. He remembered the last time he had looked into his son's eyes, as he stood near the Mercedes' door. He remembered the fear in them, behind the eagerness to help. He could hardly bear to think of that now.

Polly stood up. She had tears in her eyes. She pushed her chair in and tiny pills of bread scattered over the table. The people who had just been listening now sat back in their seats, awaiting the rest of the drama. Polly no longer cared. 'I hate to say this, Dad, but you're just not dealing with what's happened. You think you are because we don't talk about it. You think you can push your fear under the carpet. But it spills out sideways. The way you're always checking up on me. Always *leaning* on me. It's like you want me to make it all better for you somehow. Help you hide from your own grief. You never talk about it honestly. You never deal with it. And I have to bear the whole unspoken weight of your refusal to face things. I can't do it, Dad. I've got my own stuff. And I can't turn to you because you're so full of denial of your own pain. You're supposed to be the father. You're supposed to be my parent. But you're using me. You're – ' she whispered the last word through tears, 'pathetic.' Then she turned and ran out of the bistro.

'Polly!' he called after her. 'Come back. Please.' He followed her out. She was getting into the car, slamming the door and taking off too fast. He watched the lights of the Celica vanish down the long driveway. He stood there in shock and realised he was shaking all over. He went back to the bistro and paid for the meal, trying to ignore the looks of the diners and the manager's coolness.

On automatic pilot he walked back through the grounds they'd just covered on their way to dinner. Polly's words crowded the thin chill air of the tableland. Pathetic. A user. Leaving her to deal with the weight of an unspoken burden. Leaning on his daughter with his unresolved fear and anxiety. Yes, he thought. She's right. There was a time when I thought I was strong and capable. But deep down, I must have suspected I wasn't. I hid my own lack of competence. I hid my suspicions even from myself. I covered my fear with intensive studying that left no time for doubts, until I had almost fooled myself.

He saw himself as he had been, the busy surgeon striding through the hospital past deferential nurses and patients, almost waiting for the applause. Then he saw himself revealed as he always was, a fearful, unsure man who pretended to be otherwise. Just another man trying to lead his life in nice, precise patterns, trying to draft out his life so that it would be ordered and controllable.

I tolerated things in Sybil I should have spoken out about, he thought. I knew she was getting involved with someone and I said nothing. I never went back to study music after she graduated, the way we'd agreed. I hid behind duty to avoid the uncertainty of real life. And he could see now what all this had done to his surviving child. Polly had been forced into adulthood in a classic reversal. She seemed to him now more like a middle-aged woman than a young girl. She must feel it, too. It was poignant that she wanted only her little girl diary from the old life. As if that might somehow remind her of how things were for the young, since she could never be young again. His immaturity had forced her to grow into a depth and breadth that he himself seemed not to have.

He went into the law building. In his office he closed the door and remembered why he'd come here. The profile. He'd promised it to Dennis in the morning. He should collect what he'd done and take it home. But Polly's words still stung him. He picked up the phone and rang Ignatius Ho's number. She answered.

'Poll?'

'Yes?' Her voice guarded, wondering what he might say.

'Look. What you said is right. And wrong. I used to believe I was right and competent. But it was never true. It was an image and I was deluded and thought it was true. I was never able to voice my anxiety.'

She didn't say anything for a moment. When she spoke her voice was soft, in a way he hadn't heard since before Alan's death. 'I'm not sure I understand what you're saying, Dad. But thanks for ringing me. You seem so ... I don't know ... dead, or something these days. And I think I've been at fault, too, thinking I could put it all behind me and just stick a lid on it and get on with life. I've been denying things, too. And I didn't see that until I accused you.'

He didn't know what to say. He had no words. He remained silent.

'Can we have a good talk when I get back?' his daughter was saying. 'I've never had a good talk with you in my life.' She didn't say, And soon it might be too late, but Joss heard it anyway.

'Yes, Polly-Wal-the-Doodle. Let's talk. I'd like that.' There were so many things he wanted to clear up, but this wasn't the moment.

'Dad. I've got to go now. I've got to make sure everything's packed up tonight – we're supposed to be leaving straight after class tomorrow. We're having Friday off. I'll be home some time on Sunday night. Goodbye, Dad. Please don't worry.'

Joss put the phone down. There were many questions he wanted to ask. Later. Perhaps when he knew more about himself. He rang Ashley.

'Hullo?' Her warm, low voice.

'What are you doing at the moment?'

'I'm painting some japonica blossoms. I just got back from being called out to a sexual assault.'

'Was it awful?'

'Yes,' she said. 'It was awful.' He realised he'd asked a stupid question.

'Is it appropriate for a visit tonight? I want to do some more work with you.' He felt exposed. 'Some hypnosis. Should I bring a snorkel and flippers?' He tried to joke, but her answer didn't allow it.

'I don't think they'll be very helpful. Nothing from the surface can help down there.'

He felt a chill of fear and rang off. He gathered up the papers he needed for his profile, packed them into his briefcase and left the office. He thought he heard whispering from the bushes near where his car was parked, but when he turned on the headlights he saw that the heathlike shrubs were too low to hide anyone. He drove to Ashley's place.

She let him in without touching him, led him into the kitchen and made them both blackcurrant tea. The interrupted japonica painting lay on the table, while the original, its blossom sparse amid the glossy dark stems and thorns, arched from a glass container nearby.

'Are you all right?' she asked, observing him.

'I had a row with Polly. She said something that hurt me.'

'Oh?'

'I think because it was true.'

'Yes, that's usually the case.'

'Why is that?' he asked, wondering. 'Why does the truth always hurt?'

Ashley smiled. 'It's never the truth that hurts. The truth is always innocent. What hurts is the death of the illusion about yourself. The death of another self-image.'

'It ended on a hopeful note,' he added. 'We're going to have a talk when she gets back from her camping trip.'

'Good,' said Ashley. 'You need to listen to each other.'

Joss looked at her. 'I need to know more about myself,' he said. 'I need to do the deep-sea fishing. And I think it has to be done now or I may never be brave enough, or hurt enough, to do it.'

Ashley's office was a warm earthy-toned room with her art work on the walls, a blue and white tiled stove, and a vase of poppies. Joss sat in the armchair and Ashley curled up in a nest of cushions against the opposite wall. He settled back, then looked up. 'Bloody hell. What's he doing up there?' he asked in a harsh voice, pointing to the mask above the desk.

Ashley turned to look up at the blind face. 'You said you didn't like him in the bedroom, Joss. So I put him in here.'

'I don't like him here either. Take him down, please.'

'What, now?'

'Yes. Please.'

'I'm no longer working with Dennis. He says he wants to go it alone. Cold turkey.' She smiled. He was relieved to hear that. He didn't want another man here, especially not Dennis, in the work Ashley and he were doing. He was surprised at the depth of his antagonism towards the other man.

Ashley got up and took down the mask, placing it on her desk. She resettled herself on her cushions. Joss leaned back and listened to her voice softening his body, softly helping him down, down, down in body and mind, to the place below top-mind. He followed the familiar voice, experiencing the shifting focus and wavy distortions of time and body until he was finally down to the laundry. There it was: the grimy walls, the steam, the coppers, the tubs, the dripping taps.

'Tell me what's happening,' he heard her say from a long

way away. Joss found it hard to speak. The images filled his mind until they stretched so wide that he could step into them, into this other world, so deep, so real. Finally his voice came, slow and heavy, from that deep place.

'The boys are working there, sorting and stacking sheets and towels. They are frightened all the time. They work fast. They never speak. Speaking is forbidden. This place is run in silence. The men who run it use wooden signals to gain the boys' attention. They issue commands with clicks. As if the boys are animals they have to train. They don't use human speech.'

'Tell me about the men. The men who run this place.'

Joss looked around until he saw one of them. An immense fear gripped him. 'I can't talk about them,' he whispered.

'Remember,' Ashley's firm voice came through to him, 'these are just images you're watching. You're safe and comfortable, as if you're watching a video. You can alter the focus and the size any time you want. You can switch the whole thing off if it gets too uncomfortable. There is nothing to fear. You are perfectly safe.'

'*No!*'

'You are perfectly safe,' her voice repeated. But Joss was fighting the effects of her voice because a terrible idea was occurring to him from another part of his mind. What if Ashley were part of *them*? The organisation that had killed Alan? 'Wherever you are, I'll find you,' Lombard had threatened. And Lombard was on the loose, coming after him even now. He fought his way through and sat bolt upright. Ashley moved nearer and touched him on the arm.

'You're safe. It's okay. You're here with me. Breathe deeply.'

He was finding it hard to breathe at all. Then he looked at her concerned face and wondered how he could possibly have believed his earlier thought. 'For a minute I thought you were part of them,' he got out. 'Alan's killers.' He felt suffocated, he loosened his collar. Then he had to take off his jumper. 'Is it very hot in here?' he asked irritably.

Ashley shook her head. 'I'm not sure you should be doing this right now,' she said.

'I want to do it now. But I think I might be sick,' he said. His voice sounded pitiful to his ears, and about six years old.

'You might be sick,' she agreed and pulled a covered bowl out from under her desk. She put it beside him on the floor. 'Use that. It's there for that.'

Joss looked at the bowl and then at her. 'Do people often vomit here?' he asked.

She nodded. 'Quite often. The truth can be sickening. Especially if it has never been faced.'

He leaned back again, and soon she took him down there to the laundry with steam and misery in the air, the children fearful and the men in black. 'Are you there?' she asked, 'with the other children?'

Joss looked and nodded. This time, the images were safely on the video screen. 'He is just arriving,' he answered, seeing a little boy come to the entrance of the laundry.

'And what is he doing?' Ashley's distant voice.

'He's just waiting in the doorway. No one's seen him yet. He's very frightened.'

'Why?'

'Because he's been brought back here.'

'Where did he come from?'

'Home,' answered Joss.

'Why is he here?'

'He has to be.'

'How old is he?'

'Six,' said Joss.

'Where is his mother then?'

'She brought him here.'

'His mother brought him here? Why?'

'Because he has to stay here.'

'Why?'

'Because they can't manage with him at home.'

'Why can't they manage with him at home?'

'Because his father is sick from the war and his mother has to mind him all the time and she can't look after a little boy as well.'

'Why can't she manage to look after a little boy?'

'Because the little boy is too much trouble.'

'Why is he too much trouble?'

'Little boys make too much work for their mothers.' Joss suddenly pulled up in his chair, yanking his head backwards.

'Go back to the video screen.' Ashley's quick voice. 'Look at the little boy on the screen now. What's happening?'

'One of the brothers has seen him.'

'Are they his brothers, the men?' Joss shook his head. 'No no. That's just their name. The brothers, like "the pictures" or "the paddocks".'

'I see. So what's happening now that one of the brothers has seen him?'

'The little boy is trying to run after his mother but she's nearly gone. The brothers pretend to be nice when she's there. Once she's gone they're cruel. They are sly and they are cowards.' Joss started writhing in his chair.

'It's okay, it's okay. You're just watching a screen. Nothing can hurt you.'

But her voice was no defence against the huge man who was towering over him, roaring at him out of his purple face, slicing the air with a strap, slapping him. The strap was burning where it hit. *Slap*, across his chest. *Slap*, around his legs. *Slap*, curling around his arm and chest. Joss tried to fight him off, but this only made the madman worse. 'Insubordination,' he yelled, striking out again. Joss screamed.

'Joss!' Ashley's voice, sharp with command. 'Turn off the video! Now!' But her voice was lost to him in his terror.

'No, Brother, no!' Joss was screaming, straining forward, almost out of his chair.

'Joss! Turn off the video! *Now*!'

He became aware of Ashley holding him. He became aware of a huge beating in his ears. He realised it was his heart. His chest was heaving. His breathing was wild.

'You're all right,' she was saying, repeating it softly. 'You're safe here with me, Joss. It's all right.' He was back from the laundry. He panted with relief. He closed his eyes and slumped back in the chair, heart still racing, the sweat turning cold in his armpits. Ashley's hands were still on him, warm and comforting.

And now he could feel something else. It was as if the blows from the belting still stung on his body, his chest, his back and around the backs of his legs. Even though he was out of the hypnotic trance, he was sure he could still feel a stinging sensation, like nettle burns, over his body. He opened his eyes and shook his head. He sat up straight. The pain on his skin grew. He tore his shirt open.

He heard Ashley's gasp, and felt her shock. 'Oh my god,' she said.

She was staring down at his chest, where the shirt had fallen open. He looked down to follow her stare. There on his breast was an angry red weal. It seemed to be getting redder and angrier as he watched. He looked at his forearm, pushing his shirt sleeve back. Sweat crowded into his eyes and they blurred and stung. He jumped to his feet, gasping for air. Another red mark was starting to form on his arm. He pulled at the shirt, ripping it off him. He ran to the bathroom and switched on the light. Turning his back to the mirror he craned his neck around to see over his shoulder. In the mirror he saw Ashley come to the doorway and he turned to face her.

'What is it?' he said. 'What's happening to me?' She was looking at his chest and then over his shoulder at the reflection of his back. Scarlet weals stood out on his skin. Joss pulled up his right trouser leg. The crimson marks curved around his shin and calf muscles like a tattoo. He lifted the other trouser leg, saw what was there, and let it drop. He straightened up, terrified. 'What does it mean?'

They looked at each other in silence then back at the marks, which were just starting to lose their clearcut intensity.

But they were still well defined enough to show a familiar shape: a crosshatched pattern identical to that on the bruised bodies of the two little dead boys.

# 11

Joss slept exhausted in Ashley's spare room until he woke suddenly in terror. He got up. The house was in darkness. He made tea and went with it into the lounge room where firelight flickered in the stove window.

Now he remembered everything.

He sat and stared into the fire, going over it again. He found paper and a pen and started writing. He wrote for nearly an hour and then he put the pages in his pocket, left a note for Ashley, and drove home through the night.

He woke very early and went to the window of his bedroom. The morning was still and frozen. Winter sunrise was lighting the cold tips of the trees and a wreath of mist curled over the invisible river. A plover screamed from the flats, iced with frost.

He remembered being taught about repression and finding it a curious, somehow not quite believable, phenomenon. Something that happened to other people, never to a clever, ambitious man who knew what he wanted out of life and how to get it. But somehow it had happened in him. In *his* mind. This extraordinary defence against the terror of his childhood abandonment. All those months lost – how many? – unremembered. Dropped from his early childhood life. Rage and grief mixed in him like the physical expressions of heat and chill he'd experienced the night before. A white heron rose over the river, origami wings unfolding and spreading. What a mystery it all is, he thought. If that whole chunk of time has been lost to me, what other things might I have lost on the way? How much of me is left? How much of me can I trust? What can I know about myself?

He turned away from the window and went downstairs

to his desk to work on his report for Dennis. He found it difficult to concentrate; he needed time to process this new development, to understand where it all fitted. Some time later he heard a car coming up the drive and looked out the window to see Ashley. He went downstairs to disarm the security system and she came in, bringing the fresh new morning with her.

'I was concerned for you,' she said. 'I came with breakfast. Look.' She showed him fresh bread that she'd picked up from the bakery and some fancy jam with a gingham mobcap on its lid.

She went into his kitchen and started finding things from the cupboards. 'How did you sleep?' she asked.

He shrugged. 'I didn't much. This is very big. To just lose time like that. It's rocked me.'

'It'll take a while,' she said, 'for it to settle into you.' She started slicing the bread. 'Have those weals gone down?' Joss nodded. He pushed his sleeve up to show her.

They sat together in the kitchen but Joss was too angry to eat. Angry at the memories of what had been done to him. Angry at everything in the recent past and present. Lombard. His faithless wife. Angry at Dennis Johnson on his back. He pushed his plate away from him, as a child would. 'And somehow,' he said, 'with all this going on inside me, I still have to come up with the goods for Dennis. The profile I'm supposed to be doing on the killer.' He stood up, and paced around.

'Tell me about profiles,' Ashley said, chewing.

'They started in the United States,' he told her. 'The profile of a killer starts with an attempt to read the murder scene, to try to build up a picture from what happened there. Whether the killing was simply an efficient termination of a person, as in a professional hit, or whether it was a savaging. How the victim is lying, whether the body has been touched after death. Whether it's a sexual killing. Whether the victim knew the killer. In some cases, the face has been virtually removed.' He saw her wince. 'Or the eyes mutilated – that almost always indicates that the killer and the victim knew each other very well.'

'How?' she asked.

'Something vicious like that points to personal involvement.' He laughed shortly. 'The end of the love affair. Every little detail is fed into a database. And I mean everything. Time of day, day of the week, month, weather, how the body was found, where the clothes were, colours of the clothing, what sort of area it was. Inside, outside. Nothing is considered unimportant or irrelevant. The crime scene itself can extend very widely, like it did out at Spring Caves. The paddock around the caves was searched, as you may remember. We've got this information from the FBI and other agencies around the world. And from the killers themselves. Certain sorts of killers like to talk about their work.' He picked up a piece of bread and jam and put it down again. 'Most people like to talk about their jobs,' he remarked bitterly.

'There's been some resistance and criticism of profiles here in Australia,' he said, coming to sit opposite her again. 'But that was often because the profiles were using American, rather than local, data. And sometimes the information was misapplied. This is why Dennis Johnson and I have been working to build up a local bank. Profiles are more helpful in certain sorts of crimes than others. They're especially helpful in this sort of thing. The sort of crime we have here points to major psychological disturbances. The so-called motiveless crime.'

'There's a motive all right,' Ashley said. 'Human beings don't do things without good reason. There'd be a motive. It's just that an outsider doesn't know what it is.'

'What do you think it is?' he asked, interested.

'I think it's revenge,' she said. 'But he – I suppose it's a he, isn't it – probably isn't aware of that.'

'Revenge for what?' said Joss.

'For what was done to him,' she said. She cut some more bread. 'Where's your toaster?' she asked. 'I feel like some toast.'

He lifted it down from the cupboard and Ashley put a

slice of bread in it. Crows were calling outside and the windows were running with condensation. The kitchen looked dark and soft, and he remembered sitting there while his grandmother let him make toast on a fork in front of the old range. In the silence while Ashley waited for the toast, Joss thought over what she had just said. It made no sense.

'What on earth could those little boys have done to him?' he asked. Ashley brought the toast to the table and he realised he was hungry, very hungry.

'You used the phrase "major psychological disturbances",' she said. 'Hasn't someone else often paid the price of *your* anger? It's a very common human sin. The boss who screams at his employee, who then goes home and yells at his wife, who then beats the kid, who runs outside and kicks the cat. Displacement. That's what we call ordinary psychological disturbance. Normal people do it all the time. I think the killing of the little boys is the result of the killer's displacement. Not just ordinary disturbances like I've just described to you – like we all live with. It's even more complicated than that.' She paused. 'Those two little dead boys were practically identical, weren't they?'

'Yes,' said Joss. 'They were. They could have been brothers. And they both wore the same uniform.'

'You know what I think?' Ashley said.

'Tell me,' said Joss, intrigued. 'Sounds like the police force has lost a great detective in you.'

'I think you'll find that the killer used to wear a uniform like that. A little grey and maroon uniform just like that.'

He looked at her. She was carefully spreading strawberry jam right to the edges of her toast.

'Tell me what you've got so far,' she asked. 'What you've come up with, you and Dennis.'

Joss brought his notes out from the study and spread them on the table, moving aside the breakfast things. 'Right,' he said. 'This is what we think.' He realised he was enjoying this. He'd been too much the suppliant lately in his relationship with Ashley. This was his area of expertise – one of them. 'We've got a mature man,' he said.

'Not an adolescent. The crime scenes are too ordered to be the work of an adolescent.' He picked up a graph from the floor. 'For both crime scenes, the killer has selected a place that is underground. Not only that, but both of them have the light source high up on the right-hand side. In both, the area is divided into two sections. I went back and checked. There is a division down the centre of the space in both crime scenes. At Spring Caves, I noticed that the low walls from the old mineral baths made a divider down the centre. At the pub, he'd dragged three old barrels and a bench to form a sort of room divider. He's tried to recreate some place, like a theatrical set.' He stopped. He didn't say, And I feel I know that place, too. It is set up to look like a place that I am familiar with.

Instead he cleared his throat and teased a couple of sheets of paper apart with his fingers. 'He's a very organised killer. We think he finds the crime scene first, takes his time to set it up and then stalks the right boy. He brings his own equipment along: the sheets, the strap or belt, or whatever the damn thing is that he uses to beat the children with. The rolled-up towel that he places under their heads. The kindness towel.'

'He makes them comfortable, this killer? While he beats them?' Ashley asked.

Joss nodded. 'It's thought to be something to do with killers like this not wanting to be thought of as completely monstrous. They add little touches of kindness to show that they're human after all. That's what the American profilers have suggested, anyway. There are frequent inconsistencies in sadistic killings.'

'I have a quite different and completely simple explanation for that sort of so-called inconsistency,' she said.

'What?' he asked, interested.

She shook her head. 'No, go on. Tell me more. It can wait.'

Joss shrugged. 'He waits and he watches, and when he finds the boy that suits him he uses his knowledge of the drainage system under the city.'

He noticed her startled face. 'Oh yes. We think he uses the stormwater canal that runs past the old abattoirs in Nightingale Street to get into the drains under the city. He uses the underground drains just like a road system and he pops up in the culvert near where he knows his victim will be. We're pretty sure at this stage that he uses a puppy to lure the child down. We've found canine hairs and a greenish stain on the sheet, which turns out to be a filamentous weed that grows in the canal and a few other places.'

'A puppy? He uses a puppy?'

Joss nodded. 'Many of the drains are like long horizontal tunnels. Certainly the two culvert drains near where the boys were taken are of that type. We think he puts a puppy a fair way along the drain, then he climbs out and asks the child to help him get it. He probably says he can't fit, or he's got a crook leg, or something. The child climbs down and he jumps him. Then he takes the child back through the drains under the city to his canal. That's how he's the Invisible Man. We think he probably lives in Nightingale Street.' Joss lifted another sheet of paper. 'We've got the numbers of the vehicles that were at the picnic grounds the day Patrick was taken. There's one registration number unaccounted for – NHV 536.'

'When you say unaccounted for, what do you mean? Surely it's simple to trace registration?' Ashley asked.

'They've traced it back to the last owner in Sydney. She says it was stolen weeks ago. That checks out. The killer may have come on foot that day to the picnic grounds, of course. Polly's car was there, too.'

'What's so important about the picnic grounds?'

He realised she didn't know about the killer's visit to the grounds – Dennis had decided not to go public on that yet. Joss told her about the approach in the toilet. 'He'd already found out Patrick Sharp's name by then.'

'That doesn't fit in with the other two, does it?' she said.

'No,' Joss agreed. 'It's quite different. Maybe he cruises sometimes. Maybe an impulse hits and he has to try and approach a child. Maybe he wasn't going to kill Simon Prendergast. Maybe he was just going to expose himself, or something. Or try and make the boy touch him. Maybe,' he said heavily, 'it was his way of trying to make friends.'

They were silent a few moments, then Ashley said, 'Maybe there are two different people involved? And the man in the toilet is just an exhibitionist?'

Joss shook his head. 'No. Because he said he was a friend of Patrick's and Patrick goes missing a few hours later. And then is found dead under the old pub.'

'It's someone who plans everything out, isn't it,' said Ashley.

Joss nodded in agreement. 'And it's someone who knows this city well. Someone who uses his local knowledge to carry out the killings. Someone who grew up here. Perhaps he played in the drains when he was a kid. Someone who remembers the cellar behind the bar at the old hotel – maybe someone who used to drink there.' Joss picked up his tea and sipped it. He went to the cupboard and took out the Vegemite. 'And another thing, we've probably spoken to him already. I think just about all of the adult male population of Maroonga has been interviewed. Dennis tried to talk his boss into having both crime scenes watched all the time, because often the killer goes back and fantasises about it. The Yanks picked up a killer just like that. They watched the crime scene and approached anyone who parked there. A few weeks later – bingo. They interviewed a man who'd stopped there and whose car was full of pornography, and when they looked in the boot, there were the gloves and the ropes and the roll of masking tape he'd used to tie and gag his victims. They took him in and got a perfect match with the physical evidence. But it's not possible for us to do that, we don't have the manpower.' Joss spread Vegemite on his toast and bit into it. 'So that's basically what we've got. The person we're looking for, we think, is an organised, highly efficient, local-living male probably in his thirties, not older than middle forties, who either lives alone or with a parent, has a job which takes him out and about, or is on sickness or unemployment benefits.'

'How do you get to that?' she asked.

'Because of the hours he keeps.'

'And why do you say he's probably in his thirties? Not older than mid-forties?'

'Violent killers like this are the types who become homicide victims themselves. They live and breathe in violent worlds. They've either suicided, been killed one way or another – pub brawls, MVAs; sorry, car accidents – or they're in prison by that age. I should add that I'm personally convinced he grew up with violence and comes from a broken home.'

'Broken home?' said Ashley.

'You know the tag. The kid witnesses a lot of yelling, maybe beatings. Truancy. Juvenile offences. Foster homes. Maybe institutions. Brutality.'

'You're describing a broken child rather than a broken home.'

'A lot of things can break a child,' Joss said defensively, 'but that child doesn't necessarily grow up to be a child killer.'

'That's quite true,' she said. 'The way I see it, there has to be silencing for the hatching of a killer. No one to help the child witness what is happening to him. Complete silencing of the child at the time of the brutality. Suffocation.' He looked at her. Suffocation through the sheets, he thought. 'When there is no supporting witness to help the child experience what has happened to him, the child can't bear it. The terrible things that were done to him must be completely suppressed. This is how I understand the working of repression of memory. It's possible that, because memory is a construct, a brutal event during which the child is totally alone is stored somewhere else in the mind other than in memory. It has always puzzled us as to why some people have clear and terrible memories and others seem to forget completely until later in life.'

Joss stared at her. Like I did, he was thinking. Complete suppression of what was done to me.

'It's my understanding of these matters,' Ashley was saying, 'that if the child has nowhere to take the horror of his circumstances, no one who will hear him and agree with him that this is intolerable, he will create an impregnable defence system over the wound. The wound never heals. Quite the reverse, in fact. It grows bigger and more poisonous, creating a deep desire for vengeance, and the more it is resisted, the stronger the drive becomes. Until one day, that adult starts stalking another child.'

'But surely there are lots of abused children who don't grow up to be child killers,' Joss repeated. 'Otherwise we'd all be serial killers.'

'I think that in most cases such children have other ways of dealing with their pain.' Ashley sipped tea. 'Maybe they can go to a neighbour who will comfort them. Or a relative. Maybe they're clever enough to intellectualise it and go up into their heads. Maybe they disassociate from their bodies. I've worked with women and children who left their bodies while their father was raping them or beating them. They live life from the neck up, all in the head. Explaining away their pain, talking, talking, talking. They've talked so much: words against the pain. Many of them spend endless years in psychoanalysis.

'I had a client recently who'd spent years talking to a male therapist who wouldn't even engage her eyes. She talked to the back of a man's head for eleven years. She thinks her condition has worsened considerably.' Ashley squared up the papers in front of her. 'I start to work with them in a way other than talking. Then they have to come back to the feelings. Eventually. It's terrible for them, but the alternative is perhaps more terrible – the unlived life. Lots of children grow up to find acceptable outlets. They become writers who kill people horribly in their stories. They become arms dealers, designers of nerve gas. Maybe they go into the army where they can legitimately unleash their hatred in war. The ranks of the SAS and the Green

Berets are filled with the children of brutal parents. And less commonly, they do what is happening in this town now. The man who drags children down into the drains.'

Joss picked up the photograph of the crosshatched marks on the boys' skin. He hardly dared look at it now, knowing that somehow the same cruelty was stored in him.

'I think,' said Ashley, taking the photograph from his hand and studying it a while, 'that he's re-enacting the beatings he used to get. And I think you'll find he's doing it very specifically. If we could only translate it – I mean the sheets, the strap, the kindness towel, all those things. The suffocation. I think all these things actually happened to him in some way.' She put down the photo and looked directly into Joss's eyes. 'Your images, your visions, of little boys in a laundry with sheets are quite astonishing, given the circumstances of what you're investigating. These murders serve the killer well, otherwise he would have to identify with the victim he once was. A person with this psychic set-up would rather kill another human being than ever experience again those unbearable feelings of shame and helplessness.'

Joss felt a shiver go down the length of his spine. He thought of the marks he had seen on the two dead children, and last night on his own middle-aged flesh. 'Are you suggesting,' he asked her, 'that if we could decipher the story he's telling in these two murders, it might be possible to work backwards? To track him down that way?'

She nodded. 'Yes, I am,' she said. 'I've got quite a lot already. Do you want me to tell you what I think I've been able to hear so far?'

'Please,' he said. 'We need all the help we can get. The local shrink is talking about narcissistic personality disorder, or our old friend the humourless, pitiless psychopath.'

'Oh, he's all of those things, if you want to call him names,' she said, getting up and refilling the kettle. She turned and leaned against the sink. 'I've come to see that these sorts of murders are act three in a horrible drama. The world never sees act one or act two. But they happen, just as surely and horribly as act three. Remember that case in England a couple of years ago where a toddler was murdered by two ten-year-old boys? That was act three. Acts one and two happened in the hidden, earlier lives of those two older boys.' She hugged her arms across her breast. 'I'm getting cold,' she said. 'How's the fire?'

They left the kitchen and Joss stoked up the stove. It blazed up quickly. Outside, the wind had come up, but it was cosy here, in his fortress. Ashley sat on the floor.

'This is the story he's telling us,' she said. 'Once upon a time there was a baby boy. This baby was born with all the astonishing and wonderful attributes of a human being. He had the potential to be a warm and loving person. Let's suppose he was raised by his parents. The father was probably a very brutal man who beat the child. Or maybe there was a stepfather or a lover involved. The mother, if she didn't beat the child herself, certainly did not defend him when he was attacked. Many times, perhaps, the child witnessed his father beating and raping his mother. That's act one in this horror show. Millions of children grow up in act one. It's hard for people like us who've had more run-of-the-mill upbringings to grasp that – I mean, really know it, in our hearts and guts. Parents have at their disposal, to love or to destroy, the most exquisitely sensitive being.

'The child whose story I'm conjecturing was never allowed to express the pain and suffering of his life. He had to turn it in on himself and deny it. He had to stop feeling. You are looking for a person who cannot feel sorrow or remorse. Not because he was born that way, but because he had to learn not to feel or he would have died of grief. He is incapable of pity and compassion because he never saw it, never felt it, never experienced it. And he can only learn what he sees and hears and experiences around him, in the same way that he learns to speak English and not Urdu. But the rage and the hatred build and build and we come to act two. He probably took it out on animals, torturing them, finding some relief in that from the pressure of his hatred. Hurting smaller children. I think he grew up somewhere where there were a lot of sheets. A hospital? Or was it a hotel? Perhaps his mother was a nurse? Or did his mother take in washing? Did she beat him if he dropped the washing? Did she use to tie him up in the sheets if he was bad? Anyway, I'm certain, that's how he was abused. Beaten and half-suffocated through sheets. And if he was put in an institution, there's no limit to the abuse that could have befallen him there, an unprotected child. I think you'll find that he spent time in an institution, like a boarding school or an orphanage.'

Joss felt the shiver go through him again. Like me, he thought, as the memories that had suddenly emerged last night filled his mind.

'Look for someone with an expressionless face.' Ashley stopped, considering. 'Although if you know what to look for,' she added, 'it's not expressionless at all. It's really a fixed expression of frozen horror. I've seen it in the faces of abused babies.'

Joss wondered what his expression was like when he wasn't in front of the mirror, posturing.

'And it will be someone who by now will be freaked out by the doorknock, who knows that you know about the puppies and probably the drains.'

Joss looked at her with admiration. 'That's exactly what Dennis said. Where did you learn all this? I'm a doctor, and then I studied criminology. I could never have seen this.'

She laughed. 'No. It's easy to become dazzled by theories. Often it's the experts who have long since stopped doing simple things like looking and listening and hearing. They prefer to look for the gene that makes someone a mass murderer. People learn cruelty in the same way they learn to speak.'

There was a silence while Joss added to his notes, then he suddenly looked up. 'You said you had some ideas about the kindness towel,' he said.

'Oh that,' she said, 'seems very obvious to me. Once again, he's just doing what was done to him. What I've noticed is that in mad households, everyday normal actions mix in with sadistic insanity. Even though there might be a knife fight at the dinner table, or Dad might nearly kill someone during the washing up, the normal little things go on. Vegetables are peeled with the same knife that was held at the daughter's throat. Meals are prepared. Even if dinner ends up on the walls and ceiling, the table is set. Maybe your bed gets made by the same woman who ties you to it from time to time. In your killer's case, I imagine that years ago, after Mum or Dad's half suffocated him in the sheet, beaten him senseless, he cries himself into exhaustion. Just before he falls asleep, in comes the mad parent, asks him if he's sorry, makes him promise he'll be a good little boy in future, says how it's all his fault, how he's got to learn not to drive Mum mad, and it's all for his own good.'

'And?' asked Joss, following the scene in his mind.

'And fixes the pillow under his head.'

After Ashley had left, he worked until he finally had the profile in some sort of order. He found an envelope for it and put his overcoat on. He was thinking of Ashley when he remembered that Dennis Johnson was no longer a client of hers, but his pleasure in that was short-lived. Ashley wouldn't get involved with a client. Was she free now?

He got into the Niva. On his way into town he stopped below the Boys' Home. It was built on a hill that rose steeply from the roadside, from where he could see the top storey of the building and even the tufts of grass growing in the eaves. He suddenly remembered the sickening feeling as his mother's car engaged first gear to make this final climb, how he had shrunk back into the leather and walnut smell of the car, his body tensing against the fear while his voice chattered on so that she would not feel his terror and be distressed. The lost time of his life.

He didn't want to drive up there so he got out of the Niva and walked up the rise to where the gates stood crookedly open, rusted and overgrown with creepers, sulking on their hinges. He walked through them, along the weedy pathway that used to be the drive, up to the portals of the squat, granite building. The huge double doors, paint now peeling, were set under a square portico. Only the ghostly outlines of the original iron hinges, shaped liked spears, and the black iron lock could be seen. A cheap padlock replaced them now. Over the portico the Latin legend 'Suffer little children' and the date '18—' the last two numerals unreadable, were carved on a smooth block of granite. This was a place where that injunction used to be taken quite literally, he thought grimly.

Most of the ground-floor windows were boarded up. Joss walked around the building until he came to the northern side. A long verandah, enclosed in dirty and mostly broken louvres, ran along the length of it. This had been a dormitory, he remembered. A hot box in summer and freezing in winter. He remembered running with jugs and basins and trying not to flinch from the freezing water on winter mornings. But the place didn't feel familiar to him, it looked far too small and harmless. Through the dirty glass he could see that vines had got inside and were luxuriating in the makeshift glasshouse. They were flattened pale against the glass like snails, and Joss could see the filaments of white root that glued them to the louvres. He walked through the yard, fighting his way through nut grass, English broom and creepers that had taken over completely. A derelict fence sagged under the weight of unrestrained vegetation. The handball courts were rubbish tips; the old dairy had collapsed into grey slabs of ironbark cobbled together with vines. He remembered being forced to stand outside in the freezing night in his pyjamas as a punishment, just here, and the feeling of desolation that he had been forever forgotten by anyone who cared about him welled up in him again. Good, he thought, looking around. Let it all decay and rot. This place of suffering and cruelty.

He pushed the back gate open against a wall of kikuyu and stepped over what had been the old woodpile. He walked on until he came to the playing fields, now almost indistinguishable from the surrounding bush. He stood there a few moments and realised something: the tearing of his eyes had stopped. He hadn't felt a tear run down his face at all this morning. Usually by this time, he'd have dealt with two or three. Interesting, he thought. He kept walking, down to the quarry – now mostly filled in with rubbishy weeds and saplings although here and there lay boulders of granite. This place, too, seemed much smaller than he remembered it.

The air was cold and filled with ghosts. He thought he heard crying, but it was only frogs. A thin mist hung over the stagnant pool at the bottom of the quarry. Joss skidded down the slopes, silencing the frogs with his approach. Two hawks cruising their circuits made him look up. He clambered up the far side of the quarry and came to a low and rusted iron fence, barely visible through undergrowth and scrub. He stepped over it, catching his trouser leg on thorns and having to tug the fabric free. He knocked his hand on some hidden wire as he swung his other leg over and looked down at the scratch over his knuckles. He thought of the chilblains of his childhood, the festering, itching sores on his fingers in this place where a child could never be warm. He looked around to see that he was in the private cemetery attached to the Boys' Home, filled with the graves of unloved children and the forgotton religious. Some of the graves were in good repair; some were sunken with lichen and erosion, the names of their dead smeared. Joss wandered through the plots, studying the headstones. Judging from the dates of their deaths, a group of children must have died during the great influenza epidemic after the First World War. Suddenly he stopped and frowned.

Heaped up in a far corner, a pile of freshly dug earth was just visible above the tall grasses and weeds. A new grave? Joss made his way over to it and stood looking down. The hole contained nothing but what he thought might be the tip of a tarnished silver cross, or perhaps the handle from an old coffin. He had the impression from the surrounding soil that something had been removed, that the hole, rather than waiting to be filled, had been recently emptied.

He moved to where he could see a corner of the granite headstone under a pile of soil. With his shoes he kicked and smoothed the dirt away until he could read the name. There it was, under a plain, carved cross. Joss stared, transfixed. *You*, he thought, suddenly recalling the purple face suffused with rage.

A noise behind him made him jump and swing around. An old wombat was lumbering towards him, head down, broad nose sniffing the trail. It caught the smell of human and stopped. It's not your time to be out, Joss thought, then he saw the opaque, blind eyes. He stepped aside to get out of the creature's path as it panicked and ran, blundered into a headstone and staggered to one side from the force of the collision.

Joss stood there, thinking again of a place with bars on the window and the light source high up on the right-hand side; he was thinking of act one.

The wombat snuffled out of sight, and Joss turned and strode back to the car.

The grave is open now, he thought, and the bones are on the move.


Dennis looked up from his desk as Joss came in and placed a manila folder in front of him.

'The profile you've been requesting.'

Dennis went to say something, then changed his mind. He stood up and retrieved a crooked cigarette from his filing cabinet. 'Some very weird things are going on in this town,' he said, putting the cigarette in his mouth and lighting it. Nothing happened. 'Fuck this,' he said, throwing down the broken stick. He stalked out of the room and stuck his head in Graham's office.

'Graham, get me a carton of cigarettes, will you,' Joss heard him say.

Graham looked up. 'What, now, do you mean?'

'That was my intention,' said Dennis, passing him two twenty-dollar bills.

'What sort?'

'I don't care as long as they're strong. Twelves at least.'

'I thought you were giving up.'

'Just get them.'

Dennis came back into his office, walked past Joss to his chair and picked up the manila folder. He sat flicking through the pages, nodding and saying, 'Yep, yep,' under his breath. When Graham returned with the cigarettes Dennis took them from him with a grunt. He lit up the moment Graham had left the room, smoking in greedy inhalations, and continued skimming until he reached the last page. Then he put down the folder. He turned his attention back to Joss.

'First things first. You know Mr Bones that turned up at Charlie Darling's place? Black suit and beads?' Joss nodded. 'Well, seems he's been buried elsewhere for a long time, then dug up quite recently and reburied out at Charlie's. There're two separate soil types, plus fragments of coffin wood and lining. Looks like he was a legitimate burial and then he walked. Looks like desecration. But nothing's been touched at the cemetery. What do you make of that?'

Joss took a deep breath. 'I know where he came from and I even know who he is. Was,' he said. 'Those beads,' he continued, 'are rosary beads, aren't they?'

Dennis nodded. 'As a matter of fact,' he said. 'Have you been talking to Eddie, or is this the result of a conversion experience?'

'No,' said Joss, ignoring the sarcasm. 'But I know where his original resting place is. In fact, I've just come from there.'

Dennis was looking curiously at Joss. 'I'd like to know how you got to this,' he said.

'Come out with me now,' said Joss, 'and I'll show you. I want to get into the premises.' He gestured at the manila folder. 'I think you'll find this exhumation is connected to the murders we're investigating.' We don't come into the picture until act three, he was thinking, we investigators. 'I think the Boys' Home is where parts of act one and act two happened.'

Dennis snorted. 'Act one and act two of what? What the hell are you talking about?'

'Just what I said. The murders of two small boys from St Callistus school. Two small boys who wore grey and maroon uniforms and were beaten and suffocated through sheets.'

Dennis shook his head and stood up. Joss could see he was disturbed from the way he ground out his cigarette. 'You reckon this character we found on Charlie Darling's place has some bearing on Mr Invisible?'

'Come with me and I'll show you something,' said Joss. 'I'll show you a place that will remind you of two other places we've seen.'

Dennis stared at him and Joss thought he saw suspicion in his face. 'All right,' he said eventually, moving to the door.

Joss followed him out into the corridor. 'Anything happen overnight?' he asked.

'Bloomdales was broken into. Some drugs taken. There's a big piece on profiling coming out in this Saturday's *Australian* because of this case and we've been allocated extra people from Newcastle and Sydney. We've done another doorknock of Nightingale Street and didn't get a thing, not a damn thing. There's also a piece in this morning's *Advocate* that's designed to make our man very jumpy. Saying how we're closing in on him, that it's only a matter of time. That's what's happened overnight.'

'Is that safe?' asked Joss as they went outside and down the few steps to the footpath. They stood near Dennis's car. 'I mean mightn't it push him over the edge saying we're onto him?'

He watched while Dennis lit another cigarette and slipped the lighter back in his pocket. 'Dr Rumble, our old mate the narcissistic personality disorder, was on the air-waves this morning,' Dennis's voice was tired, 'saying that I'd be responsible for the killer's suicide if what I said pushed him over the edge.' The detective's face was pale with anger. 'This killer's been over the fucking edge ever since the day he started stalking little Jeremy Smiles.'

Dennis climbed into the car and pulled his belt on. 'Whose side are these academics on anyway?' he asked, starting the engine. 'If he so much as scratches his arse, we jump.'

The Commodore pulled out fast, narrowly missing the back of the Niva. Then Dennis braked. 'Hang on. What am I doing? Where are we going?'

Joss told him.

Dennis drove them out of town, past the disused pub where Patrick Sharp had been murdered and took the road that led out to the Boys' Home.

'Tell me what I need to know,' said Dennis.

'The brothers used to board children,' Joss began. 'Actually most of them weren't orphans, but kids whose parents didn't want them at home for one reason or another. They were taught over at the convent when they were in primary school – '

'St Callistus?' Dennis interrupted and Joss nodded.

'And in secondary school, the brothers taught them. They were tough schools in those days, with a brief to educate smart kids from the Catholic working classes so they could get up and into positions of influence in the public service and other areas of government. The children were pushed and driven by the ambitions of an institution that perceived itself as embattled – the children were the storm-troops. They did lessons during school hours and worked afterwards.'

'You seem to know an awful lot about this. Where did you find out about it?' Dennis lit another cigarette.

Joss looked across at his colleague. He suddenly saw that Dennis was in fact a very good-looking man. And seven years younger than he was. Ashley's age. Joss coughed at the smoke in the car. 'Why did you discontinue hypnosis for those things?' he asked, waving away smoke with irritation.

'Because I wanted to smoke,' said Dennis shortly. Because, thought Joss, you know her rules. 'Stick to the point,' said Dennis.

'There was a quarry where the boys used to work after school hours, because this place was always needing new buildings. They also cut stone for other builders and masons in the area.'

Dennis swung the car up the rise to where the Boys' Home squatted and headed for the rusted gates.

'There was also a laundry,' said Joss, 'which was set up to bring income to the institution. The boarders wore little grey and maroon suits, just like the ones St Callistus still wears.'

Dennis dropped the car back to first gear and lurched up the steep drive through the gates. He parked the car on the side of the overgrown driveway. They both got out, looking around at the gloomy portico and the ugly granite building. It looked like a nineteenth-century jail.

'Give you the creeps, this joint,' Dennis shuddered, dropping and crushing another cigarette in the dirt. Joss saw that he was staring with narrowed eyes. 'Fancy being dropped off here when you were a little fellow.'

Joss remembered the sinking despair, the hopelessness. He led Dennis round to the back, past the old louvred enclosure on the northern side, past the overgrown dairy at the back and over the playing fields towards the cemetery. They took the long way, around the quarry.

'What's this?' Dennis asked, once he was over the low iron fence.

'The home had its own cemetery,' said Joss, leading him through the wilderness of blackberry and long grasses to the corner of the graveyard and the open grave.

'Crikey,' said Dennis. His pace picked up. He reached the edge of the gaping hole and stood looking down. 'So this is where Mr Bones came from.' He squatted and studied the headstone. 'Kevin Kelty, Compassionate Companions, RIP 1961.' He stood up and looked at Joss, frowning.

'Who's he? Who is this Kelty? And how do you think he fits in with Mr Invisible?' He glanced around at the derelict tombs and back again at the opened grave. 'This has taken a lot of work,' he said, indicating the hole. 'A lot of energy. Why?' He stood facing Joss with his legs apart, arms folded against his chest. 'A person doesn't do this sort of hard work unless there's a very good reason. Or he's a dedicated loony.' He paused for a second, looking hard at Joss. 'Okay,' he said finally, 'here I am. I've done what you asked me. Spit it out. Tell me why I'm here.'

Joss took a deep breath. 'I believe that the person who killed Jeremy and Patrick was the same person who dug this man up.'

Dennis looked across at him in amazement. Then he slowly unfolded his arms, until they were hanging loosely near his hips, but ready. There was a tone in his voice that Joss had never heard before. 'Why?' said Dennis. 'Why do you believe that? How the fuck do you arrive at that?' Joss remembered that Dennis was a fighter and automatically stepped backwards. 'Might I remind you,' Dennis continued in a low, angry voice, 'we're looking for a bloke who murders little kids? Eight-year-old boys? Got that? Not some loony who digs up old priests.'

'First of all, he's not a priest. He's a brother.'

Dennis lifted his shoulders in irritation.

'I believe the killer grew up in this orphanage,' Joss went on quickly. 'I believe he was abused by this man. And I believe he dug this man's bones up because he has to do *something* about the forces that drive him, but at the moment, because of the manhunt and the doorknock of Nightingale Street, it's too dangerous for him to move, to use his drain system. You said yourself he'd switch MO. And he has.'

Dennis gasped at him, then he shook his head hard, as if to clear it. He shoved his hands in the pockets of his jacket. 'Dug up some old bones, eh? Switched MO. I think it's past time for you and me to have a straight talk. There's too much about this business here that just doesn't add up. And there's too much about you that doesn't add up either,' he said, his eyes narrowing.

Joss was surprised that he'd never noticed before how cold Dennis Johnson's eyes were.

'I've been doing some checking up on you,' Dennis was saying. 'You never were at Strathclyde.'

Joss froze. He'd always known Dennis was the sort of man who did his job properly.

'You might have a piece of paper saying you studied criminology with that institution, but you – ' Dennis jabbed a finger at him, 'personally were never there. I sent your picture to a contact of mine, a bloke who *was* there on staff at the same time that *you* weren't.'

# 12

There was utter silence as the two men faced each other across the grave, Joss at the foot of it, Dennis at the head. Joss knew he was finished with lies and silence. Last night with Ashley the deceit had been breached forever.

'You're quite right, Dennis,' he said quietly. 'I'm not who I appear to be.' It sounded absurd, like a line from a Gilbert and Sullivan operetta. 'I'm Doctor Ross Pascall, I'm a surgeon, and I've been made over – not very well, as you've discovered – by the Witness Protection people. My daughter and I. I was the witness in a very big trial – you may remember it – the Lombard trial in Sydney a couple of years ago. The Barker Clinic at Farnesworth. Illegal organ donors from all over South-East Asia.' Joss felt completely calm. He almost enjoyed the look of surprise that came across Dennis's face.

'Yeah, I do remember it.' His voice was angry. Angry at being duped. He swung away from the grave and set off towards the cemetery fence. He stopped and turned. 'This is great,' he spat. 'Just fucking great! Now I find I've been working with a phoney for the last two years. I was right about that, at least. I always knew there was something crooked about you.'

Joss moved towards him. 'Dennis, I can understand you must be feeling very angry at being deceived like this but – '

Dennis interrupted with a snarl. 'Don't give me that social worker shit talk! You've made a fool of me and this whole operation. I've been working this case, this very important murder case with the national press on my back, the boss giving me shit, the fucking gay lobby and the public all yelling at me to do something, and I've been relying on *you*. Now I find I'm stuck with someone who isn't what he says he is. Where do you think that leaves me? Do you know the first fucking thing about investigative procedures? Do you? You've been stringing us all along with your fancy degree and your bodgie brass plate. Wasting my time! Wasting the time of this town. Not to mention two grieving families. I've got to tell the boss and the boys from Sydney that we're nowhere.'

Joss heard him out, waited till he was finished with him. When he spoke it was in low, urgent tones. 'Dennis, listen. I mightn't have the degree, but I've put in the work and I believe I'm better educated than most criminologists. And I don't believe I've been wasting your time at all. Quite the reverse. I'm onto something that you'd never have got onto here except for having me on the case.' He pointed back towards the open grave. 'The link here.'

'That,' said Dennis, jerking his head, 'is the work of a loony. A desecrating loony. A crazy. This is no link! What the hell makes you think that this and those two little dead kids have the slightest connection?'

'A lot of reasons,' said Joss. 'Just do one thing. Please. One small thing. Come inside the building with me, I've got something to show you. Once you've seen this, you'll be convinced. Just give me two minutes of your time.'

Dennis exhaled heavily. He put his hands in his pockets. The day was warming up but beads of dew still shone on the webs in the undergrowth. Crows jeered overhead. Dennis kicked at a clod and then looked up at Joss. 'No way in the world. Fuck you, mate. I don't know what's going on with you. As far as I'm concerned, you're off this case. Your contract is void as of now. I don't want your help.'

He strode off out of the cemetery, head down, fumbling furiously in his pockets for cigarettes. Joss followed him, catching his curses as the cigarette failed to ignite in the wind-rush of his angry stride. He caught up with him. He felt cool and very determined.

'Dennis. This place is part of the investigation. This place *formed* the killer. You saw the profile – the killer has a history of institutions or fostering or both. This is the place. This place structured him first, and then his murders.'

Dennis stopped and bowed his head, cupping his hand against the wind. He put the lighter away. Acrid smoke filled the space between them. Joss talked fast. At least he had the younger man's attention again. 'The killer spent years here. I know it. I can prove it.'

Dennis stood, legs astride, not wanting to stay, but not going either. 'Why didn't you tell me?' he said to Joss as if he hadn't been listening. 'About your real identity? How could you work in with me and not tell me that?'

Joss shook his head. 'Would it have made any difference to this investigation what my name was? I couldn't tell anyone. I had my daughter as well as myself to protect. They murdered my son.' His voice broke.

Dennis looked at him. 'You said you never had a son.'

'Lombard gave orders and my son died instead of me.'

Dennis shifted awkwardly and when he spoke, his voice had lost some of its hard edge. 'I'm sorry about your son, but that's not my affair. As far as I'm concerned, you've hardly involved yourself at all in this investigation. That's been fucking obvious to me from the start. And I've got more important things to worry about at the moment. Like two child murders. He was silent for a moment. 'And how do I know that what you're saying is true? I read that you were killed in an explosion. Your car blew up in the garage. I remember the photographs in the Sydney papers.' He looked accusingly at Joss, as if he should be dead.

'They thought they got me – and the police gave the story to the media.'

Dennis grunted and kept walking. Joss followed a few paces behind, and when they reached the front portico he stopped at the double doors, with their flaking paint and the marks where the huge hinges and old box lock had been prised off and replaced with a padlocked bolt, and made one last appeal.

'If you'd only take a minute to look in here, everything will fall into place. You'll be convinced.'

Dennis threw his cigarette away. He stood for a minute in the sunlight, undecided. Then in silence he continued towards the car and Joss slumped in defeat. Dennis was leaving. He was about to go after him when he saw that Dennis was opening the boot and pulling out a torch, the jack lever and some tin snips. Joss breathed again. Dennis went up to the door, studying the timber, the cheap replacement hinges and the housing of the padlock. It was screwed across both doors with a connecting bolt. Dennis put the torch in his back pocket and dropped the tools he was carrying. He took a few steps backwards and made a running jump at the door, kicking out with all his weight just beside the lock. The hundred-year-old timber shivered and one side of the bolt housing lifted away from the door. Dennis bullied the rest of it with the jack lever so that he was able to push one of the double doors open. It resisted, jamming on the floor. He bashed until there was enough space to walk inside. 'Why the fuck am I doing this?' Dennis muttered, looking around.

The air was chill, rank and heavy with damp. Sunlight fell in behind them and hung in solid blocks over filthy floors covered in rat droppings and old bottles. A long corridor lay ahead of them.

Dennis kicked aside a pile of rubbish and they walked in silence through the filth. Fungus and graffiti covered the walls. To Joss the air was ghostly with the unabsolved, hopeless misery of unwanted children.

'Okay,' said Dennis when they'd reached the dark end of the long hall. 'Show me something.'

'Down here,' said Joss, pointing to a rubbish-strewn stairwell.

'The dormitories were upstairs,' he added, remembering never being able to get properly warm, crying himself to sleep in that long cold room full of the snores and weeping of others. 'Down here is where I believe it all began.'

Dennis pulled the torch out of his back pocket and shone it down the stairs. Joss was already on his way down. The steps were solid right until the last one, where his right foot crashed through the timber and sent him staggering into the wall. He hopped in pain. His shin felt like it had been stripped of flesh.

Dennis remained where he was, halfway down the stairs. 'What are we looking for?' he asked in an irritated voice. He shone the torchlight over Joss, who was stooping and rubbing at his shin. 'What am I here to see?'

Joss regained himself. As he straightened he looked down to see his hands smeared with black streaks of fungus. There was a second or two when last night's hypnosis memories of the fungus fused with the black streaks now on his hands. Joss felt his mind waver like a curtain. He wondered if there were anything solid at all in this world. Wiping his hands slowly on a handkerchief he nodded at Dennis's question. 'Come and see for yourself.'

Dennis descended slowly, watchful. He kept his eyes on Joss until he stood at the bottom of the steps. Then he flashed his torch around, noting the size and layout of the place, the barred window high up on the right-hand side of the wall, the old coppers down the centre dividing the room in two, the tubs in the corner under the barred light source. The two men looked at each other.

'Holy shit,' said Dennis softly, 'this is the place! This is it!' His voice rose in excitement. 'It's the same as Spring Caves. And the cellar under the Maitland. It's all here.' He flashed his torch again. 'The underground space, the division down the middle. The light source on the right-hand side and high up.'

His face had lost its angry, set look and was now as alive as a child's. He pulled out his notebook, propped the torch on one of the steps and scribbled away madly. 'How did you work this out?' he asked Joss, looking up.

'While I was checking out Spring Caves, I had this strange feeling. And then in the cellar, at the Maitland, I had the strongest sensation that I somehow knew the place, that the killer was creating a scene that I knew too. I became very afraid. I'd been having these terrible flashbacks about a beaten child. I thought there was some possibility of my being connected somehow.' He stopped, and was aware of Dennis waiting for him to speak again, the pressure of silence.

'And just recently,' he said, feeling very awkward, 'I've been doing some work with Ashley.'

'Oh yes?' said Dennis in an odd, casual tone, putting his notebook and torch aside, pulling his cigarettes out. The torch threw a bright circle on the wall opposite, highlighting some indecipherable letters scratched into the plaster. Joss thought how weird this moment was: the two of them standing in this filthy disused laundry, just out of the spotlight, and the unspoken edge between them about Ashley.

'What sort of work? Hypnosis?' Dennis flicked his lighter.

Was there an ironic loading on the question? It was impossible for Joss to say. 'As you can imagine, I've been under a lot of pressure lately. I hadn't been dealing with things in my life – a lot of grief about Alan's death. One of the things that came up for me during a session last night was a lost period of my life. A period that I spent here, in this Boys' Home, when I was six. I had no conscious memory of it at all.'

'You were here?' Dennis was incredulous. 'In this town? In this home?' His brow furrowed.

Joss nodded. 'Here. In this place. When I was six.'

'Were you an orphan?'

'No.'

'What were you doing here then?'

'I was put here to board because things were difficult for my parents.'

'And you only just found out about this recently, working with Ashley?' Dennis looked hard at his colleague.

Joss considered. 'I only found out last night. My body knew about it, but my mind was hiding it from me, until the flashbacks. Then it came up during hypnosis.'

'It's hard for me to believe that a person can just lose an experience like that,' Dennis finally said. 'And it's very weird, isn't it, that you end up back here, investigating a place you once spent time in? I find that an extraordinary coincidence. I find this whole story just too much to cope with, too much coincidence.'

'It's not quite like that,' Joss said. 'When I went through the process of identity change, I was set up in a university in Perth. But I only stayed a few months. I didn't want *anyone* to know where Polly and I were. Not even the people who set it all up, particularly not them. If they knew, so could Lombard. Polly and I decided to come here when I heard about the vacancy. I realised that moving to Maroonga wasn't entirely safe, given that it was a link with my real past, but I didn't think the risk was too great – it was forty-seven years ago. If you really want coincidence, the house I'm living in with Polly was once owned by my grandparents.'

Dennis glanced around the bleak and chilly underground room. He looked uneasy, restless. He shoved his notebook in his pocket. It occurred to Joss that Dennis could easily be part of them. And here he was alone with him in an underground room in a derelict building.

'Your wife,' Dennis's voice made Joss jump. 'Where is she now?'

'She stayed on in Sydney. She didn't come with us.'

The beam of the torch caught the edge of the ceiling where dusty spiderwebs hung down like black stalactites.

'God,' said Dennis. 'What a dreadful place.' He fished about for another smoke. 'I've learned a bit about the mind since ...' he looked guiltily down at the cigarette in his hand, 'I did that work with Ashley. But I'm still inclined to say bollocks to some of this. I can just accept why a kid might take that horrific experience out of his mind – but I'm more interested in what else you might have denied and repressed.' He studied Joss very carefully.

'Like what?' asked Joss, feeling his throat tighten.

'Like if you've been able to lose entire months from all those years ago, isn't it possible that you might have lost a few hours here and there more recently? Let's have a look at this, shall we? Let's take a good look at you, *Doctor*

Haskell. You've lost your son, your wife, your fancy career as a top surgeon, all that fuss and admiration. The prestige, the honour, the power. The trips. The fancy cars. You've lost your name. You don't exist any more. Now you're just another middle-aged bloke who's pretty well had the Richard. The world's full of them. Now you're just another academic in the sheltered workshop for emotional cripples. I know enough from the work I did with Ashley to know that psychosomatic symptoms don't just happen for no reason. Remember the day of your headache? Your skull was practically breaking open that day in the incident room. I presume we're both in agreement that your conscious mind only knows what it's allowed to know? Do you remember what you were saying when your head nearly lifted off during the briefing session? You were saying that just because a suspect had no previous history of violence, there was no reason to assume that this would always remain the case. Remember how we used to think they were all harmless, the flashers? And how we're learning different these days? You said that recent data suggests the sort of murder we're dealing with is the last stop on an escalating scale of cruelty. You used the addictive model – the last stop. Did you get that blinding headache because you started to recognise yourself in your own description? By the way, you blew your cover that day. I heard you ordering a Schedule Six drug over the phone. We mortals can't do that. You were so distressed, you'd even forgotten you weren't supposed to be the great doctor any more.'

Joss was reminded again of the alertness of this man, the way he put things together.

Dennis flicked his spent cigarette onto the floor and stamped on it. 'Let's play around with this idea: just say a man with your history goes to the Gold of Egypt exhibition. You see a dead fourteen-year-old, same age as your son, all wrapped up in sheets. This rocks you. You think of your boy, forgotten, denied even. Then you see kids walking around alive and well and you start thinking about your dead boy. How come those kids are alive and well when your boy's dead?' Dennis stood quite still opposite Joss in the filthy laundry. Outside, a long way away, a crow mocked. 'Tell me you haven't thought that. Tell me you haven't felt that. Go on.'

Joss shook his head. 'Of course I've thought that. Everyone who loses someone thinks that.'

Dennis refused to be deflected. 'Let's say your secret suffering is demanding relief. In deepest blackout you find yourself cruising around in your daughter's Celica, looking at little kids. Little *alive* kids in grey and maroon uniforms like you used to wear when you were incarcerated in this dump.'

Joss could only shake his head. It isn't true, he kept thinking. It isn't true.

'We've got a result back from those hairs on the sheets – the animal ones Eddie had to send away. Turns out they're from a treated pelt. Kangaroo. I've seen you wearing gloves with a fur trim.'

'So does half the population of Maroonga in winter,' Joss couldn't help saying.

'One of the places *cladophera* grows,' Dennis continued, 'Owen Duckworth tells me, is in the culvert near your place out at Long Swamp Road. You black out, and next thing you know another child is dead. Then, when I start moving in on you, you don't dare grab a kid, you come out here and you dig up this old bastard who used to beat the shit out of you. And it brings you some relief. That's how come you know about Mr Bones and the laundry set-up here. That's how come you know so much about these crimes. Not because of some damn hypnosis session with Ashley Smith, which doesn't damn well work,' he said as he pulled another cigarette from the packet. Now Joss could feel the other man's anger and jealousy. 'What do you say to that? What do you think of that, Doctor bloody Haskell?'

Joss found he'd almost stopped breathing. He sat down on a bench and leaned his head in his hands. It reeled from Dennis's words. His own doubt and fear magnified.

'Don't think it hasn't crossed my mind in the last couple

of days,' he finally said. 'But I know I'm not the killer. I put the energy of my pain into caring for others. People admired me for that. In some cases it's undeniable that my slicing and excision saved life – whatever that might mean in the long run. But I've never killed anyone.' He paused. 'That's not entirely true,' he said. 'When I was a student, the professor of surgery told us to keep two little books, one to write up all our successful operations and a little black book to remind us of the people we killed. Of course, I didn't keep such books. But they're in my head, the ones I killed. I've never forgotten them.'

Dennis paced the laundry, puffing and exhaling. He turned under the barred window. 'Tell me then,' he finally said, jabbing his chest with a forefinger. 'Convince *me*. Give me some good reasons why I shouldn't suspect you.'

Joss considered. 'First of all, I didn't commit the crimes, and that's the best and most convincing reason for you not to suspect me.' Dennis looked anything but convinced. 'Second, you haven't got any evidence.'

'Simon Prendergast said you were the same size as the man in the toilet cubicle. He didn't say I was, or anyone else. He said *you* were.' Joss spread his hands to indicate that there were a lot of men his height. 'Then there's the *cladophera*. Grows in a culvert near you. It was you who cracked the secret of the drains. Hardly surprising if you're the killer.' Dennis's voice sounded muffled and menacing in the dark. The torchlight threw both men's grotesque shadows onto the filthy walls like some Gothic puppet show. 'But the big one is – how did you know about *this* place? Do you think people are going to believe that your knowledge about all this came from *hypnosis*? Do you think the *jury* will believe in hypnosis?'

There was a long silence. Joss knew Dennis had made a very strong point.

'Any good counsel could lead the jury to believe that you knew about this place not through some airy-fairy magician stuff, *but because you are the killer*. And that the whole hypnosis thing with Ashley is a very clever and devious way of covering the tracks of a clever and devious and *murderous* man. Who fits the psychological profile.'

'That's absurd,' said Joss, swallowing hard.

'Rejected by your mother,' Dennis continued. 'Sent away in early childhood. Abused in the Home. You grow up. Your success in the world keeps a lid on it for all those years. But take it all away – your identity, your family and, most of all, your little bone saw, and whammo!' He paused before he added, 'This town never had child killings until you came.'

'Or you,' said Joss desperately. 'You've been here the same amount of time.'

Dennis ignored him. 'No wonder you've been slow to deliver the profile. I'll be on the stand to say that not only were you able to explain to me the motivation, the how, why and when, the MO of these terrible crimes, it also turns out that you lived here as a child. Played in the drains, did you? When I tell the court that you told me you were having flashback images of a child being beaten with a very unique strap, I think they'll throw away the key.'

Dennis took out another cigarette. He was chain-smoking now. 'If I'm convinced you're the killer, I can get the evidence, believe me. I'm a very experienced investigator.' He moved in front of the torch and for a second the cavernous room was almost pitch black.

'Are you threatening to fit me out?' Joss's voice was barely audible.

'I wouldn't have to go to much trouble. The circumstantial case against you is bloody strong. You've probably already contaminated the physical evidence just by being at the morgue. All I have to add is an interpretation of the facts.'

Joss felt a new desperation. This couldn't happen. 'The beating was done to me, not by me,' said Joss. 'It's true I've had a surprisingly similar history to the killer. But that's not so odd when you come to understand how this sort of thing works.'

Dennis gestured impatiently. 'Come on. I do know how

it works. We did a three-day briefing on child abuse and the thing I really remember taking home is that victims end up as perpetrators. You were beaten, so you beat.'

'That's true,' said Joss. 'But it doesn't work symmetrically. Everyone who beats was beaten, sure. But not everyone who was beaten, beats. There are other ways of dealing with the suffering. And the form can change. You've got to know what to look for.'

'Like what?'

'Activities that are based in hate,' said Joss. 'There are other ways of beating people, and on a much bigger scale.'

'Like how?' At least Dennis was still listening.

'Like becoming a dictator and sending your people to war. That way you can kill tens of thousands of men, women and children. Your own as well as the enemy. Wonderful revenge.' He remembered Ashley's examples. 'Maybe you end up designing Stealth bombers, nerve gases. Or you go into the entertainment industry, making video cassettes about sadistic sex.'

'Maybe you become a surgeon,' said Dennis, looking very pointedly at him, 'and make a living cutting people up. But that would stop working when that life got blown up. You'd have to start expressing it in a new way.'

Joss felt suddenly claustrophobic in the underground room. 'I've got to get out of here,' he said. 'I need air.'

Dennis studied him, then shrugged. He let Joss walk ahead of him up the steps and back along the corridor. Spindly tendrils of vines grew in through crevices and spread along the walls.

At the end of the hall sunlight streamed in through the broken doors. Joss walked outside and breathed deeply. It was good to be out of that place.

Dennis hadn't finished with him. 'I still want to know how a vehicle registered in your name turns up at the picnic grounds while the killer is there,' he said.

Joss shook his head. 'I simply can't answer that,' he said. 'Either the nun with the photographic memory made a mistake or someone unknown borrowed it.' It sounded weak, he knew. He looked over towards town, this town in the foothills where their three lives had come together, his and Dennis's and a child killer's. It looked so safe with its huddle of roofs and comforting, smoking chimneys, yet it was stalked by an assassin who burrowed through its hidden arteries to surface and strike at its children.

'Listen to me, Dennis,' said Joss, feeling suddenly calmer. 'I am not the killer. But Ashley's convinced me we can work backwards and translate his actions. She believes that the killer is doomed to retell his story in the only way he can. Help me with this. This is your area of expertise. Help me look at what he's saying in his crime scenes, translate the language of his murder.'

Dennis stood at the car, framed by straggly self-seeded annuals, frost-withered and blackened, all that remained of the old front gardens. He unlocked his door but he didn't get inside. 'Ashley. So she's part of the investigation now, is she?' He yanked at the door handle in irritation. 'You see my position?'

A semitrailer made hard going of the rising corner beneath them and Dennis let it pass before he continued.

'I'm being assisted by a man whose identity is all bullshit and a woman who's listened to too much misery. You two get together and come up with this notion – you reckon the killer's telling us a story.' He shook his head wearily. 'Someone's telling a story, but how do I know who it is? I don't know what to make of all this,' he said. 'You're the theorist, I'm sure you can make it sound convincing. I'm a cop and I deal in facts.'

Dennis sighed in irritation. Then he seemed to come to a decision. 'If what you say is true, and this act of desecration is tied in with Mr Invisible, then I want to track down any of the staff who worked here in – when was it you were here? – who might still be alive. I want the rolls and records of this joint. And I want to get a bootmaker to make up something like that strap he uses.'

Thank god, Joss was thinking. He's back on track with me. He believes me. Dennis stared hard at Joss as if reading his thoughts. 'I don't know what I feel about you right now,' he said. 'I'm taking a punt on you, Doctor. That you know what you're talking about, although god only knows why I'd think that.'

Joss climbed into the passenger seat and turned to encounter Dennis's sad, tired eyes.

'I'll tell you why I'm taking a punt on you,' said Dennis. 'Because I've got fuck-all else to go on.' He started the car. The Commodore roared in the silent morning. 'And I'm going to talk to Ashley about all this.' He held Joss's gaze for a provocative second too long before letting off the brake and doing a dusty U-turn in the overgrown driveway.

When they were nearly back to town, Joss broke the silence. 'Maybe Sister Matthew at St Callistus will know about the records of the Boys' Home. Maybe they were amalgamated with the school when the Home was closed down. If they weren't destroyed.' Dennis grunted, then kept silent.

As they pulled up outside the station, Joss turned to Dennis. He had to speak, even though he realised it could go badly against him. 'There's one other thing I've got to tell you. It'll make your visit to the bootmaker a lot clearer.'

'Yes?' Dennis pushed in the cigarette lighter on the dashboard.

'Make what you like of it,' said Joss, 'but I know exactly what he used to beat them with – the mystery strap he used on Jeremy and Patrick. I know what it is.' He swallowed hard as he spoke, almost feeling again the burning sensation of the hypnosis session, the stinging pain of the strapping.

'Do you now?' said Dennis, turning to him, cigarette in one hand, lighter in mid-air in the other.

Joss stared at the red hot circle of the lighter. 'It was a strap. A special sort of strap. A Compassionate Companions brothers' strap to hit children with.'

'Who made them?'

'The local bootmaker, as I remember. I didn't realise until

years later when I was talking to some ex-Catholic boys at university that it was customary for the brothers to have them specially made. Different brothers had different specifications. Some of them had steel edges inserted into them, or a split put down the middle so that they'd pinch and tear the skin as they struck.'

Dennis got out of the car. 'Crikey,' he said, slamming the door. 'And here's me thinking it was all gentle Jesus.' He walked over to the kerb.

'And how do you know,' he said, 'about the strap?'

They stood facing each other. 'I was back there in a hypnosis session with Ashley – in that laundry we've just left. Kelty's had a surface that hurt more than the others. It had a herringbone pattern.'

'I don't suppose you just happen to have it lying around at home, do you?' Dennis asked bitterly. He tightened his mouth and lifted his chin. He started to walk away. Joss followed him.

'Dennis,' he called. The other turned. Joss saw the tension and anxiety in his face. The battle. Disbelief. Desperate hope? 'We're right on track with this one,' Joss said. 'Believe me.'

Dennis looked at him a long second. Then he turned away.

'Never heard of such a thing,' said the bootmaker. 'And I've been in business here for thirty years.'

'Where else could they have ordered them from?' said Joss, despairing. Then without waiting for a reply he asked, 'What's your name, sir?'

'Debenham,' the man answered.

'You're Protestant by upbringing?'

The man shrugged. 'My family was.'

'There was a bootmaker down at the end there,' said Joss, urgent to make the man remember, 'where the mall starts.'

'Well, I've never heard of it,' said the bootmaker, moving

back to his work, dismissing them. He picked up a pair of bright green high-heels.

Dennis leaned over, his elbow on the counter.

'Make me one,' he said to the surprised bootmaker. Something in Dennis's tone made the man put the shoes down and come back to them. 'Just like he's going to tell you.' And he shoved his notebook over at Joss. 'Show him what you want. Draw it.'

The unwilling bootmaker watched as Joss started to draw the short, thick strap, like a Roman short sword, with a narrower section for the handle.

'I'll bring down a picture of the crosshatching and that'll give you the exact dimensions. You see what you can come up with.' Dennis flashed one of his best, phoniest smiles. 'Think of it this way. It'll be good for business.'

'Leather doesn't come cheap,' said the bootmaker.

'We'll fix you up,' said Dennis. 'We're rolling in petty cash. Or we'll raid the lamington drive money.' Joss looked at his partner.

'I'm very busy at the moment,' the bootmaker said, still reluctant.

Dennis straightened up. 'I think you should drop everything and do this now, mate.' He pushed the drawing into the hands of the bootmaker. 'A strap identical to this was used to beat the two little boys who were killed. Now do you see why we want it?'

The bootmaker stared, at the drawing, at Dennis, and then back at the drawing. Finally he nodded.

'And I want it done today. I want a photo of it in the national papers tomorrow.'

# 13

Joss drove back out to Long Swamp Road and stopped the car in front of the house. Then he remembered the mail and walked back down the drive past the cypress trees to collect it. Bills, a newsletter from the Criminologists Association, a letter from the teachers' college inviting him to be their guest speaker at the annual Alexander Mackie dinner, and a plain card that had no stamp. He turned it over and his heart almost stopped in his breast.

Four crudely drawn figures: two male, one crossed out; two female, one heavily crossed out. *Two down and two to go*, it said. Joss's eyes went out of focus. He blinked hard. He felt the rest of the envelopes slip through his fingers. He gripped the fence, which seemed to be rocking. Shock made him blind. For a few seconds he didn't remember where he was, or what exactly it was that had just happened. Then, *Polly. They've got Polly*. This thought was all his screaming mind could hold in its whirling axis. He heard a noise like a wail, and it was a few seconds before he realised it was him. Then he saw the Greek script that was typed below the four stick figures, the question and answer of the Sybil game. *They knew the Sybil game. How could they know that?* It was not possible for them to know that – that was his and hers alone. He looked again in despair. *Sivilla, ti thelis:* Sybil, what do you want?

He looked harder at the script and frowned. This was not demotic Greek, this was the old language. And this Sybil game was the real thing, the ancient answer given to the questioner. His modern Greek was only fair, and the ancient language was sufficiently different for him to find that he could not make immediate sense of the answer.

*Apothanien thelo*, he read, and the script danced before his eyes. The phone was ringing inside. *Apothanien thelo.*

'I want,' he translated. 'I want – ' But he couldn't work out the rest of the verb structure. Was it the phone ringing? Or was it the tintination of shock filling his head? It was the phone. He rushed up to the house, stumbled inside and yanked it up. He was about to scream at the caller to get off the line so he could ring the police when he heard his daughter's voice.

'Dad? You all right?'

She's alive, he thought. My daughter is still alive. They haven't got her. 'Poll,' he said. 'Thank god. Poll.'

'Dad.' Her concerned voice. 'You okay? You sound weird.'

'I had to run up from the mailbox,' he was finally able to say. 'Just a moment till I catch my breath.' He nearly dropped the receiver as his legs collapsed and he fell down, hard, on the cushions of the window seat. He put his hand over his mouth. He felt like vomiting and even looked for the spot that would make least mess. He was still clutching the card tightly. Dear God, Poll's all right. The nausea ebbed and he was able to speak again.

'You'll have to start going to the gym,' Polly was laughing. 'You're turning into a decrepit old man.'

He made a noise that he hoped sounded like a laugh. 'Yes,' he agreed. 'I will.' He was staring at the card. They know where we live. What am I to do? There must be something I can do. The archaic Greek sentence was burning his eyes. How did they find out about this? Their lovers' game? How did they find all this out? *Sybil has betrayed us.*

'I'm just ringing to say bye before we leave.' Polly paused. 'And because things have been so awful between us for a long time and I feel sad about that. And I know I've got to attend to my 50 percent of the mess. I hope that when I get back we can – '

'Polly.' Then he stopped. He was about to say, 'Come straight home,' but he realised that wherever *he* was, was the bullseye. Wherever he was was the most perilous place in the world for his daughter. She'd be safer where she was going for the moment, camping in the remote, wild Barrington Tops, where aircraft went down and were never found again.

'Yes?' she was saying. 'Did you hear what I said, Dad?'

'Yes,' he was finally able to say. 'I did. And it's good to hear your voice. Have a lovely time, Polly-Wal. I hope you catch a trout.' And I'm going to do whatever is necessary to stop them before they get anywhere near you, darling, he said to himself.

'Okay, Dad. Better go now. The others are getting restless. Bye now.'

She rang off. Joss sat for a moment. And when his relief began to subside, a new and dreadful thought hit him. What did the card mean if Polly was safe? If they didn't have Polly, perhaps they had Sybil?

He walked heavily upstairs to his bedroom. He opened the bottom drawer of the chest of drawers and the laughing face of his son looked up at him. There was a card Alan had drawn for his father's birthday, copied from the Mustang model. 'Not bad,' Joss remembered saying to his son, 'but you need to get the way the wings sit. See? You haven't got it right here.' If his son had looked crestfallen, would he have even noticed? Perfection. If it wasn't perfect, it was no good. Nothing was ever good enough for me, was it, Al? If you got ninety in maths, I told you to aim for a hundred next time. You were never all right the way you were.

At the end of a long envelope was a bunch of house keys. Joss pocketed them. He swept the model aircraft to one side of the top of the chest and propped the picture of his dead son in the centre. I regret that I never had time for you, Al. I had you for such a short time and I could not value you. Achievement, performance, success were the things I valued. He looked into the awkward smile of his dead adolescent son and wished he knew something about prayer.

He went downstairs and picked up the phone. He

imagined two grinning Dobermanns sitting under his father's WAC chart and determined to drive out to the German who trained killer dogs as soon as he had the chance. Okay, Lombard, he said to himself, this hiding game is over. Here I come, ready or not.

He drove to the airport just in time to get a standby seat on the commercial flight to Sydney. He didn't trust his shocked nervous system to handle the Navajo.

He rang Dennis just before he boarded. 'I'm flying to Sydney. They know who I am and they know where we live. I've had another card in the mail.' He pulled the postcard out of his pocket as he spoke.

'Who knows? What do you mean another card in the mail?' Dennis's tired, irritated voice.

'Lombard. I think they've got my wife. My daughter is safe for the moment. She gets back from Barrington Tops on Sunday night. If I'm not back by then, I want you to pick her up from her boyfriend's place and keep her with you at all times.' Joss gave him Ignatius Ho's address. He was having difficulty making his voice function. 'I think they've killed Sybil.' He explained about the symbols.

There was a silence on the line while Dennis considered this. 'I'll check around the morgues,' he said finally, and Joss's heart stumbled as he saw his Sybil's body, faded, dead, bruised on ice.

'I suggest you sit tight till we know what's happened,' Dennis was saying.

'Don't be crazy. I can't sit still. I'm going back to our place.'

'I wouldn't advise it. Surely you can see the danger in that?'

'They already know everything. My daughter's right – there's no point in running or trying to hide any more. Just promise you'll take care of her for me.'

It took him as long to get from Sydney airport to Woollahra as it had to fly from Maroonga to the city. He paid the cab off two blocks from his old address and walked along the street fighting a flood of conflicting sensations. At the security door in the stone wall he rang the bell. He felt like a ghost, haunting his own life. No one answered. Joss looked from left to right. The lane was empty. He was overwhelmed with sadness and thought he might start crying. Using his old keys he quietly let himself in.

He stood for a moment, taken by surprise. The garden and the back of the house were so very different from how he remembered. This grounded him a little, eased the ghostly unreality he was feeling. He was different, the garden was different – this was how it should be. Where the garage had been was now a sunken lily pool surrounded by paving stones, and in the centre was a carved stone figure of a young boy holding a bird. Around the sculpture huge pink lotuses rested high on their lampstand calyces. Joss looked at the inscription on the statue. 'Linos,' it read. 'Beloved son of Sybil and Ross, 1977–1991.'

Now you exist again in my history, Al, thought Joss. No longer deleted like the dead non-persons in a Stalinist photograph. He went up to the kitchen door and cautiously unlocked it. He stepped inside, standing silent for a few minutes, reading the atmosphere of the house. It was entirely still. Empty.

Satisfied that he was the only person there, he stepped quietly around. It was no longer his house and he felt that very keenly. There were new paintings on the wall. All his painstakingly made model aircraft had been removed from the china cabinet and replaced with byzantine icons, painted eggs and the Venetian glass that Sybil loved. The place smelt of her – her musk and roses smell, as well as the stink of cigarettes. He went softly from room to room, noting the changes, feeling intrusive. And extremely detached as well.

He went upstairs and opened the door at the top of the landing: Alan's room. It had a locked-up smell. The curtains were fully drawn. Everything had been stripped off the walls – the posters, the photographs, the pennants. The bedspread was different. Just the desk and chair were achingly familiar, their transfers and stickers untouched. Joss closed the door behind him as he went out.

Polly's room was just as she'd left it. He walked over to her dressing-table and there it was, among the adolescent litter – the fat little book with the gold clasp. Joss picked it up and, feeling like a heel, opened it at random. '... never feel they're on my side. Always pushing me. They never ask me what I want. They always presume they know what's best for me ... It never occurs to them to ask me my feelings in any matter they decide for me ...' He closed the book. It was enough. He looked around for something to put the diary in and saw a little nylon carry bag in the corner. He emptied out the papers and textbooks and put the diary inside.

At the end of the hall, overlooking the back garden, was what had been his and Sybil's bedroom. Joss pushed the door open and looked in. He realised that, ever since coming into the house, he had been terrified of what he might see lying on the floor. But here, too, all was in order. Their tastes had always clashed, but he'd overruled her on the bedroom as he had not been able to in any other room. He had banned smoking in here and it seemed his rule still held – at least, no smell was discernible. But Sybil had made the Middle Eastern bordello she'd always threatened him with – there were mirrors and cushions and silk hangings everywhere, and he felt he could have been somewhere in the spiced city of Alexandria. There was far too much cream, gold and apricot, and he caught the whiff of incense.

Joss walked to the windows and looked down. From here he could see the front garden and courtyard, the wall, and over it, through the wintering trees, into the street. On a polished table under the window was a picture of the two of them with the children. He picked it up. It had been taken about a year before Alan's death. His son showed the unease, the gawkiness, of his thirteen years in his suddenly too-big jaw and and lengthening head.

Moving restlessly around the room he picked up books on erotica, poetry, art, and put them down again. He had never been able to match his wife, her yearning, her alienation, her wanting she knew not what. He opened her silk-draped and mirrored cupboards and smelt her clothes. Some of his old favourites were still there: the tweed suit with the black velvet trim, the dark red evening dress that she'd worn to a dinner at Farnesworth. He recalled the blazing fight they'd had on the way home. He closed the wardrobe. He pulled the postcard out of his pocket and stared at the ancient Greek again. *Apothanien thelo*. He had worked out the first part of the ancient Greek verb – 'to be dead' – but the full construction eluded him.

He shoved the card back in his pocket and sat on her bed. Lying open on the bedside table was a Greek edition of the old and new Testaments, open at the Psalms.

He struggled with a few paragraphs of text and suddenly it came to him. The second verb. *Apothanien thelo*: I want to be dead. He froze. He tried to fit various ideas around the words. There was a chance the card was from Sybil herself and was a genuine, bitter suicide note designed to cause him maximum pain. He tried to remember if she'd been alone with his wallet in the caravan; if she would have had a chance to open it, to find his address on something. He himself had told her that he'd flown up. His registration papers, driver's licence and unrestricted flying ticket all had his Long Swamp Road address.

On impulse Joss opened the bedside table. He felt like a spy. Cigarettes, condoms, a little packet of sweets, a novel. And right at the back, something wrapped in gift paper, about the size of a book. He was about to shut the drawer again when he saw Sybil's barbed-wire handwriting on a little card attached to the paper. Her writing had always been impossible, like sketches for wrought iron. She mixed bits of Cyrillic in with the English alphabet. '*O Mavro mou*:

For my *Mavro*,' she'd written in her idiosyncratic hand, 'a memento.'

*Mavro*. 'Black' in Greek, and because of the masculine ending, the black man. A keepsake to remember an affair? Then why was it here? Hadn't she given it to him yet? Joss pulled the parcel out of the drawer and tore off the wrapping. It was a video cassette. Before the trial, when the threats had started, Malcolm had had a video camera surveillance system installed. He'd even insisted on logging tapes, so that when the house was empty the rooms and grounds were continually monitored. Had Sybil and her black man recorded the two of them making love? Don't let it be that, he thought in a mixture of rage and grief. He wondered what he should do with it. He could stick the cassette back in her drawer and remain in ignorance, or he could take it with him and possibly hurt himself even more by watching it. He sat undecided, wishing he'd never seen the damn thing. But it was not possible for him to let it go now. He shoved it in the bag with Polly's diary and went downstairs.

On the table near the foot of the stairs sat the phone and answering machine. He pressed 'play'. Sybil's voice. He thought he could hear everything in those smoky, accented tones: her faithlessness, her irresponsibility, her refusal to grow up. Her voice breathless and burnt-out from scotch and chain-smoking: 'I'll be out of town for a day or two. Please leave me a message to come home to.' Surely she was referring to the Seal Rocks trip, Joss thought.

Through his wife's recorded voice, Joss heard voices in the front yard. He opened the answering machine and lifted out the little tape. He pocketed it, adjusted the phone and sprinted down the hall towards the back of the house, away from the male voices which were now quite definitely outside. He flattened himself against the wall and peered around the cornice to look up the hallway. He heard a key turning in the lock. Two men came in. He didn't know them and he didn't dare look at them too long. They were casually dressed in overalls and boots. Maybe they were cleaners. Who else would have copies of keys to a comfortable home? Relatives? Housesitters? There was no sign of Sybil.

Joss snaked along the kitchen wall and fumbled with the key to the back door. As he slipped through he heard them coming down the hallway. He pressed the kitchen door closed behind him, praying that it would be noiseless. It wasn't. There was a loud 'click' that made him jump away and keep low.

'You hear that?' he heard from inside. He bent over and crept past the kitchen windows, making his way past more new shrubs in pots and barking his bruised shin on unfamiliar outdoor furniture near the wall. He heard the back door open and didn't move, just stayed crouched behind a bench near the gate. He inched his head up and saw the two men standing and looking around. Joss recognised the thick plastic bag in one gloved hand as the sort the police used for physical evidence. It was possible they were police. Dennis had said he'd check the morgues.

When the men had returned inside Joss moved cautiously towards the gate in his back wall, unlocked it and was safely outside in the lane. He stood for a moment, gathering himself, breathing again. He still had the bag with the cassette in his hand. He walked to the end of the lane and peered round into the street his house fronted. A white Holden was parked there but it could just as easily have belonged to the house next door. He memorised the number plate and walked off in the other direction, away from his old house, under the bare trees in the encroaching dark, his only companion the ice in his heart.


Dennis had left a message for him at the airport and Joss drove straight to the station. He found Dennis in the incident room.

'There's nothing that looks like your wife,' he said. 'I've checked around.'

Joss shivered in double relief. There is a truce between

Dennis and me at the moment, he thought, while we bury the dead. But he knew that hostilities could break out any time.

'George Lombard got himself out of prison,' said Dennis. 'A man like that can buy his way out of anywhere.' He looked at Joss. 'Then he'll be out of the country. It would be easy for him to get a replacement for his surrendered passport.'

Joss was thinking of his wife. He remembered the square set of Sybil's narrow shoulders as she'd stepped into the darkness beyond the dim circle of light at the edge of the caravan park. Going back to face the aloneness, she'd said. Then another thought hit him. What if Sybil wanted him to think her dead? Out of the way? He almost groaned aloud. *What if she's set me up?* Part of her believes that I killed our son – her son. Revenge is an honourable Cretan tradition. Could she hate me so much she could endanger her own daughter by revealing my whereabouts to Lombard's people? He sat down suddenly, the strength gone from his knees.

'What is it?' said Dennis, ever vigilant. In front of him he had notes scribbled everywhere, measurements, distances, photographs of the crime scenes.

'It's not possible. Could a woman endanger the life of her own daughter just to get a husband removed from the scene?'

Dennis didn't blink. That tired and steady gaze from hidden eyes. He sighed and put down a photograph of Jeremy Smiles. 'You're not expecting me to say, "Dearie me no, of course not," are you?'

'She wouldn't. She couldn't.' Then the subtle treachery of, *Why would she*?

Dennis stood up and walked to one of the whiteboards. He picked up the felt-tipped pen and drew a big 'S' slashed vertically with two straight lines. 'That answer your question?' he asked. Joss sat and stared at the dollar sign. He remembered Sybil in the caravan, wayward and bloody. But surely not the betrayer and destroyer of her own child, the child who had been nurtured and delivered from out of that same sinewy body? Then he remembered the Medea earrings coiled near her gleaming hair, Jason's murdered bride and children.

'Here's another one,' said Dennis. He added two letters to the dollar sign. Joss now read '$ex'. Dennis threw the pen down. 'Young constable near Nundle was set up by his wife and the boyfriend. Called out late to a domestic. Remote farmhouse. The boyfriend was waiting for him with a shotgun.' Dennis shook his head. 'The boyfriend was another copper, too. Hard to believe, isn't it? She had hubby blown in half, just like that.' Dennis's face was defiant and resolute with an 'I've seen it all and cleaned up after it all and got convictions after it all' hardness.

'But not her children,' said Joss, impatient. 'Not her kids.'

Dennis looked at him closely; his eyes became harder. 'Young woman threw her two-year-old over a cliff because the child was not acceptable to her lover.' Dennis paused. 'Who, I might add, was another woman.' Joss swallowed.

Dennis pulled out a chair and sat down again. 'What I'm saying is, anyone is capable of anything.'

'Capable, maybe,' said Joss finally. 'But that doesn't mean they do it.'

'Real betrayal, first-class blue ribbon betrayal,' said Dennis finally, 'can only come from those you trust the most.'

There was a silence. Then Dennis said, 'Let's play around with some ideas about this. Maybe the deal your wife made – it's okay, it's okay,' he raised a hand to ward off Joss's half-voiced denial, 'I'm just saying *what if*. Maybe the deal is just about you. It's not a bad way to get control of your daughter again, when you think of it. Maybe she deals you, on the condition that the daughter is okay. She could have some lever we don't know about if she's dealing with Lombard. That way, you're out of the way while your daughter is fine.'

'I don't want to think like that!' Joss cried. 'That's horrible.'

'I *always* think like that,' said Dennis. 'It's essential. I've seen what people are capable of. I've seen what they do to one another. You've only dealt with people on operating tables, in surgeries, hospitals. They're all on the same side as you. I have to deal with the opposition. I was trained at Suspicion School. Graduated with Honours in Horrible Suspicion.' His voice became less tough. 'It's my job to think like that, Doctor. Don't take it personally.'

Joss's immobilisation came to an end. He shoved his hands in his pockets and walked around the room. The two whiteboards with the dead boys' names and characteristics irritated him. Like detailed headstones, he thought. He wished they weren't there to distract him from this.

'It doesn't matter,' he said finally. 'I suppose. It doesn't matter in the short run who has betrayed Polly and me. The facts remain the same. The danger is the same.'

He went back to the table and sat down. He put his head in his hands and rubbed his eyes. He thought about where all the players in this game were. He was here, with Dennis, in this country town's police station. He believed he was okay for the moment. Polly was safe somewhere in the wild country of Barrington Tops with Ignatius Ho, the man from an impeccable Filipino family. This left him free for the moment to move and plan. Sybil was – and the image rose in his mind without bidding – slumped in a car somewhere on a side road with two small holes in one side of her head and two bigger ones on the other. Or, and this image sprang to mind with equal facility, she was rubbing herself against some black Greek, shrieking with triumphant vengeance. He felt his heartrate increase with rage and jealousy. He gripped a pencil. I'd much rather have the first image in my head than the second, he thought. I want Sybil dead rather than with another man, betraying us. He closed his eyes to recover himself. Ain't love grand, said a little mocking voice somewhere as another self-deception died.

His mind was on a treadmill. If it wasn't Sybil who'd sent the card to his mailbox, it was *them*. The ones he'd been waiting for almost every moment of the last two and a half years. They could be anywhere. They could be sitting in a car across the road from the police station. They could be waiting in his bedroom for him now. Or among the cypress trees leading to his house. Waiting. *Why hadn't they moved already?* He didn't understand.

He got up from the table, unable to be still. 'My wife – Sybil – hasn't changed the message on her machine,' he said finally. 'Maybe she never came home from the coast.' He looked away at that, then he asked the question that had been puzzling him ever since he'd found the card in the mail. 'If they know exactly who and where I am, why haven't they tried to kill me yet?'

'Maybe they have,' said Dennis.

'What do you mean?'

'After you called from the airport, Wal Griffiths told me he'd disturbed two men near the second hangar who were taking a great deal of interest in an airplane out near the aero club. Sierra Victor Whiskey.'

'That's the Navajo I lease,' said Joss.

'Wal said he checked it out and it all seems to be in order,' Dennis continued. 'But I'd suggest a very careful pre-flight check next time you take her up.'

'Did Wal say what they looked like?'

Dennis shook his head. 'They cleared off as soon as he started coming towards them. He was in the clubhouse and you know it's a fair distance.'

Joss stood up. He was aware that right at this moment there was absolutely nothing he could do. Dennis was right about waiting – it was all he could do now, too. See what Lombard's next move might be. With enormous effort, he brought his mind back to the murder investigation. 'Is there anything we should be doing here?' he asked, pointing to the whiteboards.

Dennis shrugged. 'We're doing it. What else can we do?' He picked up a list of notes from the pile in front of him. 'Graham's trying to track down the old records from the Boys' Home. I'll give him a hand. I'll contact you if anything happens.'

Joss drove home with images of betrayal undermining him: Dennis and Ashley in this together, setting him up, moving closer to him, one of them with an invitation to assist in an investigation, the other with the oldest lure of all. Had Dennis been warning him back at the police station, when he'd spoken of betrayal? Had the country copper briefly taken pity on the first-class mug they were setting up? Given him a sporting chance? Ashley and Dennis learning his secret, moving closer and closer till he trusted them and revealed his true identity. Oh God, no. Please. Not blue ribbon betrayal. He imagined them in the bedroom, whispering and laughing at how they had entrapped him. Then entangled and sweating as they strained together in her bed.

This is paranoia, he reminded himself. Or was it? There was one blessing in this. If Ashley and Dennis were the betrayers, then Sybil was not. Please don't let it be Sybil, he prayed. Not her. Yet they knew the Sybil game, and only Sybil could have told them that. That was something neither Ashley nor Dennis could have discovered. He had to talk to Ashley.

Joss stood near the window, trying to regain control of himself. Ashley came back with two mugs of coffee.

'What's happened?' she said. 'What did you want to see me for?'

'I've been thinking,' he said. 'Terrible things about betrayal.'

'Tell me.'

So he did. About Sybil. About her and Dennis.

When he'd finished, Ashley leaned back on the carpet and did a back bend. 'You're not taking this seriously,' he said.

'I am,' she said, sitting up. 'Very seriously. It seems to me you're in a terrible way. There is no one you can trust. You suspect me. And Dennis. And your own wife.'

'She hasn't been my "own wife" for a while. I knew she

was capable of adultery. I just can't believe she would help to murder me. And her daughter.'

'It sounds very unlikely,' said Ashley. 'Especially now. After more than two years' absence. You didn't find her burning with rage and resentment last week, did you?'

Joss shook his head. 'On the contrary,' he said. 'She was very ... um ... loving.'

Then he saw how that had pricked Ashley. 'I'm sorry,' he said. 'I didn't mean to hurt you.'

'I know you didn't,' she said. 'I'm pleased for you that she was loving. And you also know my interest in you.' She shrugged. 'That puts me in a difficult position. I don't like talking about it much.' She looked at him with a new expression on her face. Joss thought she was about to say something and thought better of it.

'What were you going to say?' he asked.

She shook her head. 'It can wait. I've been thinking, too. But you first.'

'Ashley, I actually wanted Sybil dead a while ago. I saw her in my mind's eye, slumped dead in a car. And I was glad.'

'Dead, rather than betraying you and Polly?' Ashley asked.

He nodded.

'Sounds normal to me,' she said. 'I'd rather she were innocent and dead, too, than alive and betraying. But then I'm biased, and I am too direct sometimes.'

He needed to be direct, too. The fear was strong. 'I imagined you and Dennis in that bed making love,' he said. 'And his bloody mask smirking down on the pair of you.'

Ashley nodded. 'He's a very ... ' she searched for the right words, 'full-bodied sort of male.'

'And I wanted to kill you both.'

'Yes,' she said matter-of-factly.

'But I never used to be like this,' he cried. 'Full of suspicion, jealousy and murderousness.'

'Oh, yes you were. You just didn't know anything about yourself. You were living in delusion, like most people do.

You've just discovered a bit about what's in you. Sounds very ordinary to me.'

Her phone rang twice and then stopped. Joss was immediately suspicious.

'It might be Damian,' she said. 'He said he'd ring some time today.'

'May I use the phone?' he asked. He dialled Hamish's number. It rang and rang. Joss hung up. She was looking at him with her frank eyes, her half-smile. He went to her and took her in his arms. He touched her strong, springy hair. He looked into those clear, direct and honest eyes. He recalled how filmy Sybil's eyes were, veiled in melancholy and alcohol. He hoped this woman was true. He could not be at all sure about his wife. 'I want to stay with you tonight,' he said.

Ashley shook her head. 'No,' she said. 'I need to be alone.'

He thought of her last word, of his house without Polly and the stair that creaked. 'I don't want to be alone,' he said. Outside it had started to rain, a bleak, small early-evening rain that darkened the garden and ran mournfully into the freshwater tanks.

'What I was going to say earlier,' she said, 'and didn't, is this.' She walked to the window and looked out at the rain, putting up a hand to push the curtain back. 'This will come as something of a shock to you. It did to me, actually, when I first realised it.' She came back to him and stood simply in front of him. 'I want to end our sexual relationship,' she said.

Joss felt shock and pain flush his cheeks. 'No,' he cried. 'Why?' The words were out before he could stop them.

'It's not because I've changed in my feelings for you,' she continued. 'It's because you have so much to do in your life at the moment, things that don't concern me at all.' She paused. 'Maybe,' she continued, 'if things turn out in a while, and you become free from your past and present preoccupations, we can be together again. I can't say any more than that.'

'But surely,' said Joss, 'you can support me in this, care for me while all this is going on.'

'I do care for you,' she said. 'That hasn't changed. I will do anything helpful for you and Polly in this crisis. But not as your lover. That must stop, because I also care for me and I know that you are still involved with your wife – no, please let me finish. I know you're not physically living with her, but you are emotionally involved and I can feel that in my cells. When we're quiet together sometimes, I know she's there with us – but not acknowledged. When we make love I feel you thinking about her, comparing us. I see you looking at me and I start wondering where I fit in. Am I part of a triangle? It's not good for me, Joss. You're not free. You have a lot to do. And I have my life to live every day too. My work is demanding. Damian wants to come back and live here for a while – that's not going to be easy for either of us. My garden needs constant attention. I need time to think about this, about you and me. I can't be with you during this time.'

He recalled the phone that had rung and then stopped. A signal. She had made no attempt to pick it up. Without warning, he was furious. 'Someone else is coming, isn't he!' he yelled. 'You've got what you want from me, you and bloody Dennis. You've forced me to expose myself – risk myself. I trusted you! You've set me up for the death dealers. And now, of course, I'm off the invitation list.' He saw the pain in her face. She shook her head and lowered it. She said nothing in her defence. 'That's it, isn't it?' he yelled. 'That's it, isn't it?' The next few words burst out of him. 'You – ' he heard himself scream. 'You treacherous *bitch*!' He found he was shaking with shock. He couldn't believe he was behaving like this.

She walked away to the kitchen. 'Who are you really yelling at, Joss?' she called back. 'Who's the treacherous bitch? Me? Sybil? Your mother?'

His legs were shaking so badly he had to sit down. He put his head in his hands.

'I'm sorry,' he said in a while. 'That was unforgivable. I

don't know where that came from. I don't know what's happening to me.'

'It was great,' she said, coming out from the kitchen. He looked up and she wasn't being ironic. 'It was about time you dropped the mask. You're starting to get real. I never thought of you as even being human for a long time after I met you. You were so completely dead from the neck down. I used to wonder if you jerked a bit when you first started to move in the mornings, before the machine warmed up. But now you're starting to turn into an ordinary, messy human being.'

'But I just insulted you. Screamed at you!'

'Yes,' she said. 'You did.' She was actually smiling at him even though there were tears in her eyes. 'Now I'm sure you'll be able to do it, Joss, what you have to do next. Welcome to the human race.'

'I don't know how I'll manage without you,' he said, and it was the truth. Then he was suddenly angry again. 'You opened all this up, with your damn hypnosis.'

She shook her head. 'That's not so. *You* opened it up. You were ready to start knowing the truth about yourself.'

'And what am I supposed to do now,' he heard himself demand childishly, 'with this wonderful truth about myself?'

'If you like,' she said, and he wasn't sure if she was being ironic, 'I can close that door again in another hypnosis session and you will forget you ever knew.'

'That's crazy,' he said. 'I can't forget what I already know. I can't ignore the truth.'

'I had some budgies in a cage once,' she said, 'in the days when I did such things. And one morning I came out and found that I'd failed to shut the door of their cage the night before.'

'Poor things,' he said automatically, wondering what on earth she was talking about.

'Poor things is absolutely the right comment,' she said. 'Because there they still were, sitting huddled together on their perch with a whole, huge world of change and adventure and freedom a few inches away. They'd made no attempt to fly out of their cage. It's how I lived until the day my husband told me a few things that I'd known in my heart had been going on for a long time. Even then, I was tempted to stay. To compromise. My cage was very comfortable. I had a young child to consider. I was too proud to tell anyone about myself, so I had no real friends.'

He walked around the room, restless with pain. 'Why are you telling me this?' he asked.

'Two reasons. Firstly to assure you that the truth is the easiest thing in the world to ignore. And the other is that, even though you're pissed off with me for not being with you in the way you want right now, this is your big chance for real freedom.'

Freedom, he was thinking petulantly. I wasn't seeking freedom. My cage was blown up. 'You mean this, don't you,' he said, realising this was not the histrionics he'd been used to with Sybil. 'About us. About not being lovers any more?'

'I do,' she said. She blew her nose.

'But you said you know the monsters by their names!'

'Yes,' she said. 'But I went against myself by being your lover and moving into a therapeutic relationship as well. I only did it because of your peculiar circumstances – your double life, your need for secrecy. But now that you're out, it's no longer necessary. Or possible. I've got the name of another person who can be with you during this time if you want. He's very good.'

'I don't want another person. I want you!'

He saw what this was costing her and he didn't care. He was ruthless. He took her hands. 'Ashley. Please.' He drew her to him. She rested a moment against him, then pulled away. The rain was heavier now, beating against the windows. 'I still don't know,' he said, 'if you and Dennis have deceived me.'

She shook her head, then leant it against the glass of the window. 'I haven't. I want you to go now,' she said.

'I can't believe you're just ... dismissing me like this.'

She lifted her head and straightened up, turning to face

him. 'Make what you like of it,' she said. 'What am I dismissing? What is that? Who is that? A man who has no real idea about himself? A man without any self-knowledge? Is that what you offer me?'

She looked hard at him and Joss didn't like it. 'I give a lot,' she said. 'Because I *am* a lot. I've given you my wholeness, my depth and breadth. My self-knowledge. My attention, my love, my respect, my energy, my time. And you can't match me because you're still in the dark about yourself. You don't know yourself. And you're still attached to ghosts of dead relationships. You've used me as a safety net, because you're too scared to stand alone. You've been only half here while we've been together.'

The anger blazed in her eyes and she looked directly into his. 'Grow up,' she said. 'Do it without the safety net. Until you do that, what you're offering me is too small.'

Joss walked out of her house and he heard the door close behind him. His breath came in clouds of steam through the drizzle. A cold drop found its way under his collar and he thought he had never been so cold and alone in all his life.

## 14

Joss turned on the light in his study. He hesitated in the doorway, then walked in and went to his desk. He pulled out his keys and unlocked the drawer. Under several manila files he found and took out a pewter-coloured .45 automatic. Thank you, Malcolm, he remembered. Somewhere in the house at Woollahra, there was even a licence for it, and for Polly's Smith & Wesson.

He felt around at the back of the drawer and pulled out a box of ammunition. He snapped the magazine out and tipped a handful of bullets into the palm of his hand. He found he liked their hard, cold weight. The tools of death. How different they were, he thought, from the tools of surgery, the delicate utensils of microsurgery: the fine steel needles, almost invisible wires, jewellers' forceps, suture thread finer than hair. He rolled the blunt cartridges around in his palm. He understood how people could write names on them, how satisfying that must feel. He'd like to write 'Lombard' on half of them. And 'Lombard's dog' on the others, for whoever had set the bomb under the Mercedes. He fed them one by one into the magazine, pressing them into their springloaded housing, shoved the loaded clip back into position and felt it click into place. He pocketed the gun. It was a good feeling.

This is new territory for me, he thought. This rage. This desire for vengeance. I have never let myself be here before. And of course I have no maps. He sat down at his desk and picked up a pen. Why haven't they moved? Do they want me to run? Do they want me to lead them to Polly? Were they going to nobble my aircraft? Put a bomb in it, like the car? He jumped when the phone rang.

'Eight-year-old boy's been taken from his bed,' said

Dennis. 'Number 17 Latrobe Street. Meet me there soon as you can. I'm on my way now.'

Fifteen minutes later, Joss met Dennis outside the house of Mr and Mrs Arthur Munro.

'If it's Mr Invisible,' said Dennis as Joss got out of the Niva, 'he's going wild. Digging up old vicars, busting into houses.' Joss slammed and locked his car door. 'He's getting bolder, faster. More dangerous.'

The two men walked up to the front door and rang the bell. Behind them, they could hear the voices and see the lights of the street search.

'Could be a copycat,' said Joss, 'or it's our man.'

Mr Munro let them in and they followed him through the living room, down the hallway and into the bedroom that ten-year-old Andrew shared with Brendan, his stolen brother. Andrew was wrapped in his doona, eyes wide with fear, sitting on the edge of his bed with his mother beside him.

'I didn't hear anything,' he said. 'I didn't know until Mum put on the light and started screaming.'

'It's very different from our bloke's usual style,' said Dennis, looking at the empty bed, looking across at Joss.

'The flyscreen's been removed,' said Mr Munro. 'He's come in through the window.' Andrew shivered and looked at the window, now wide open, filled with blackness. Dennis walked over and shone his powerful flashlight around on the sill and the floor below.

'There's a mark here,' he said, 'on the carpet and here, on the wall.'

'They weren't there before,' said his weeping mother. 'I vacuumed this morning. Brendan had only been in bed for an hour and a half,' she sobbed. 'I went in because the boys' room gets so cold – Arthur's been going to put a heater in here – just to make sure they were well covered. And I couldn't believe it. His bed was empty.' She started crying inconsolably and her silent husband patted her hand. 'The window wasn't open wide like that. Brendan always wants the window open a little bit. He likes the cold on his face.'

Joss shivered at the phrase. He looked at the window, a sliding aluminium-tracked frame with the glass now pushed right back. He went over and looked outside. The window would be very easy to climb in through.

'Anything taken?' Dennis asked.

The distraught woman didn't answer. The husband looked around and shrugged, as if to say, Who knows? Who cares? Our boy's gone. Who cares about anything else being taken? 'I don't think so,' he finally said. 'Just what he stood up in. His pyjamas.'

'He'll be so cold,' sobbed his mother. 'It's nearly zero outside. I looked everywhere. I ran out the backyard calling his name. The dog's gone.'

'Yeah?' asked Dennis. 'You've got a dog?'

'Useless bloody thing.' Mr Munro was barely able to speak. 'When you need it.'

Dennis was writing in his notebook. 'Okay,' he said. 'We need everything. I know this is a terrible thing for you both. But if we're going to have a chance at getting your boy back safe and well, we need to know everything.'

'Oh please. Please bring him back.' Mrs Munro started crying again. Mr Munro, holding his wife's hand, gave the details.

'Brendan Vivian Munro, aged eight,' Dennis wrote in his notebook. 'Three foot, seven inches, fair hair, blue eyes. About five stone.' Dennis Johnson steadfastly refused to think in metric. He caught Joss's eye. It's the same boy again, his look said. Joss nodded.

'He did take something,' Andrew suddenly spoke. He pointed at the top of a chest of drawers. 'Brennie's ropes for Cubs,' he said. 'He was practising his knots and the ropes were there when we went to bed.'

Joss looked at Dennis. Not our man, Joss thought he saw in Dennis's face. Our man is prepared. Our man brings his own gear. Our man is an organised killer. This looks too impulsive.

'Don't touch anything,' Dennis said. 'The crime scene fellows will be down in a tick to look at this. Mr Munro can we have a photo of Brendan?'

He was brought a photo of a sensitive, angular child's face with alert blue eyes and fair lashes. Two front adult incisors in a mouth of milk teeth gave him that rabbity look common to children his age. Brendan could have been the brother of either Jeremy Smiles or Patrick Sharp. He was wearing the maroon blazer and grey trousers of St Callistus.

'May we take this for a while?' Dennis asked. He removed the photo from its frame and pocketed it, then beckoned Joss outside.

Carefully they examined the area outside the boys' bedroom window. It was easy to see where the soil had been compressed, shrubs and flowers damaged by someone walking through them to get inside. And then out again, awkward under the weight of a heavy and unconscious, or silenced and terrified child. There were no apparent marks on the path.

'Where's the bloody dog?' Dennis asked, straightening up and flashing his torch around the garden and the street beyond. 'We had a case in Kimberly Street where the guard dog came inside with the burglar and when the owner came downstairs to see what the rumpus was all about, his own damn dog bit him. You can't even trust a dog any more.'

Outside on the edge of the street, bare trees hung over the black roads. Joss's heart contracted in his chest. My killers could be out there, he thought. I am hunting the child killer while my killers hunt me. While I wait to strike Lombard. The wild hunt of the world.

'What do you think?' asked Dennis.

'It's different,' said Joss, 'but it's him.'

Dennis was tapping a cigarette on a box of matches. 'Tell me why you think it's him,' he said.

'It's the right sort of child. The right sex, age, size, colouring, school. He's never done this before, gone into a house like this, so it looks like he's suddenly gone disorganised on us, but I don't think so. I think he's had this boy in mind for a while. Remember how he already knew Patrick Sharp's name when he spoke to Simon in the toilets? I think he's been studying the children for a while. Not only for physical characteristics. He's been looking out for the most obedient, the most biddable. The children who are good. Who do what they're told. But because of all the increased security, it's not possible for him to take a child from the streets. So he's worked this out instead. The window is easy to get into, away from curious eyes. I think he dealt with the dog and then climbed in. He's practised with dogs, remember. Maybe the dog's carcase is lying in the back of his vehicle.' His mind turned these thoughts over and over. 'Dennis. I think we have some little hope here.'

'What do you mean?' Dennis inhaled and the tip of his cigarette glowed, throwing his face into reddish light – the eyes narrowed against the smoke, the grooves from nose to mouth already deep, the little sun cancer.

'He's changed MO so much. He wouldn't have taken the scout ropes to secure him if he was going to kill him straight away.'

Around them, in the street, they could hear the voices of people searching. The sound of cars pulling up and going away. The tumbling blue and red lights of a squad car flashing through the bare trees and along the fences. Joss was aware of the sound of Barry Armstrong, the photographer from the *Advocate*, laughing somewhere, and wondered what there was to laugh at in this world.

'I think he's going to take Brendan somewhere else and kill him,' he said.

'To a place that he's set up,' Dennis continued, slowly nodding, the grooves around his mouth becoming deeper, harder, as he picked up the scene. 'A place that he's already selected and set up like we know. Some place like a cave or a basement. And he's going to beat that little kid with that damn strap, wrap him up in a sheet and then he's going to strangle him.'

The two men moved silently back to their cars. Dennis's radio was calling. Joss heard him answer, listen and call off.

'Come on,' Dennis yelled. 'There's someone down at the station who's got old documents from the Boys' Home.'

Back at the station they met Mr Bruce Leonard, 71-year-old semi-retired cab driver and now president and acting secretary of the Maroonga and District Historical Society. Mr Leonard was handsome in a dark blue silk cravat and jacket.

'We got a lot of valuable material when they closed the Home in 1960,' he said after Dennis and Joss had introduced themselves. 'You could come down and have a look at it tomorrow. We're very excited about some recent acquisitions. Some wonderful documentation from the old abattoirs. Very lucky to get it. Come down tomorrow, why don't you?'

'No,' said Joss. 'We need to look at it now.'

Mr Leonard looked startled. 'But it's nearly eleven o'clock,' he said. 'The wife always makes tea and a little something on a Sao at ten-thirty. Smoked oyster, although recently I heard that they're not a good thing to have last thing at night. Too stimulating. So if you'll excuse me, I'll have to be getting along. I only came down because the wife's been nagging me and we were just down the road at the club and she made me come back and tell you. I gave her friend Margery a lift. I'm already very late.'

'Mr Leonard,' said Dennis. 'Another little boy has been taken.'

'Oh really?' said Mr Leonard. 'Terrible business. It's all those working mothers. Terrible, terrible.' He hardly paused so that Joss didn't know for a second what he was talking about. 'All in boxes,' said Mr Leonard. 'Apart from the things I've been able to put out on display. It's a real mess, the Boys' Home acquisition. I've been president and acting secretary for two years now. People don't have the

249

interest. It's hard to find volunteers who'll help us catalogue. We had Amy Alexander helping us out for a while, but then her daughter had the big op and she said she didn't have the time any more. People just come and they go.'

Joss didn't wonder that they went.

Mr Leonard finally agreed to open the musuem despite the hour, and he led Dennis and Joss there in his own car. The Historical Society was housed several blocks away in an old church, in a street that ran parallel to the main road. Mr Leonard, quite resigned now to showing them around, let them in through a Norman doorway and then past a series of sepia patriarchs hanging on the stone walls, past glass display cases of mining tools, panning dishes, bits of alluvial gold in jars, old harrows and hitching rails.

The church had been partitioned off into various areas and Mr Leonard's office was off to the right, past a display of convict brick marks. He switched the light on and walked through his office to a storeroom where uncatalogued documents piled and tumbled. Joss's heart sank. But Mr Leonard picked his way unerringly through dusty manuscripts, ancient and rotting sheet music, a poster advertising a visit by Nellie Melba and carrying her large autograph, a box of lace scraps and withered button boots, and a metal advertisement about venereal diseases. Finally he came to a carton in a corner, next to a rocking horse. He dusted it off and dragged it, puffing away, into the narrow corridor that led through the piles of musty history.

'Here,' said Dennis, grabbing a corner. 'Give you a hand.'

Joss backed away awkwardly as the two men and the box came towards him, finally to be shoved through the door into Mr Leonard's office. Inside the carton were old leather-bound account books and diaries. Dennis lifted them out.

'What years are we looking for?' he asked Joss.

'*What* are you looking for?' asked the puzzled and puffing Mr Leonard.

'I was there in 1947,' said Joss.

'You went to this establishment?' asked Mr Leonard. 'The

250

old Boys' Home? I'd like to get you to write something about it. We've got the *District Chronicle* coming out every four months. We're always looking for new talent.'

Dennis was pulling old attendance books out, checking the dates, closing them, discarding them and digging for more. 'Look at this!'

Joss looked up, alerted by the excitement in his colleague's voice. 'Kelty's signature,' said Dennis, passing an attendance book over to Joss. A scrawl across the bottom of the page certified that the roll had been kept in accordance with the regulations set down for non-state educational institutions.

'That's in the fifties,' said Joss. 'You're getting closer.'

'We couldn't pay you anything, of course,' Mr Leonard went on. 'But just a little something. Personal memories, the old school days, happiest days of my life – that sort of thing. Most people are so pleased to see their names in print. We've got a great issue coming out next month. The old abattoirs is the main feature. Do you know how many head of cattle they used to get through every week? We've got the stun gun down here now. Very pleased with that. And the old killing hammer they used before the stun gun.'

'Here's 1949,' said Dennis. 'And 1948.' He looked into the depths of the carton. 'Where are the other ones?' he said.

'That's it,' said Mr Leonard. 'That's all of them. Just the one box of books. That's definitely all of them. Don't you want to see the killing hammer? It's a most interesting old object.'

'Fuck it!' said Dennis, throwing the 1948 attendance register to the ground. 'That'd be right. It stops the year before the one we want.'

'Language, language,' Mr Leonard clucked. 'Dearie me. We can't have that sort of talk round here. This used to be a church.' He stooped and picked up the book from where it lay skewed on the floor. Joss felt a twinge of compassion for the old man, who seemed unable to be silent. 'Did I tell you that the old convent papers were all destroyed?

Someone sent them to the tip. I was devastated, I can tell you. Then we lost all that important local history to the Mitchell Library when Lady Driscoll died. And her daughter promised me –' He stopped when he saw Dennis digging a cigarette out of his pocket.

'Oh no, no, no. I'm afraid you can't smoke in here,' said Mr Leonard primly. 'Valuable documents here, we can't have the chance of a fire. We had a chap here who smoked and I made him go outside. Standards are standards and God knows, so many of them are slipping. They want a new flag. Men fought and died for that flag. I can't allow smoking.'

Joss felt his compassion vanish.

'Mr Leonard,' said Dennis, lighting his cigarette deliberately in front of the man, 'will you just bloody shut up?'

There was a stunned silence and Dennis used it to ask a question. 'You said you had some things in the display cases?'

'What's that?' said the other, sulking now.

'Display cases. You said you had some stuff from the Boys' Home on display. Can we see it?'

Dennis and Joss followed the old man out into the main body of the church and over to a long horizontal display case. Mr Leonard opened up the top and took out a framed picture. He passed it to Joss, who hadn't offended him as much as the swearing and smoking and silencing detective.

It was a photograph of the Boys' Home and its inmates. Joss stared at the picture in his hands and a wave of sorrow broke over him. He saw rows of miserable children, ranging in age from about four to fifteen, awkward in ill-fitting woollen suits, necks pulled in with fear, or heads and chins tilted in defiance. They stood around the portico and the double doors, where the long-since pilfered iron hinges could still be seen. Skinny shanks, knock knees, the famished faces of rejected children. He felt Dennis standing nearby, looking over his right shoulder. The detective jabbed his cigarette at the picture.

'That's just outside the front entrance,' he said. 'Where

we were this morning.' The two men looked at the rows of pale faces, the too-small blazers. 'Look at this joker.' Dennis indicated a heavy man wearing a cassock who stood a little apart from the boys, arms folded across his chest. 'He looks like he'd kill his granny for a bet.'

Joss stared at the heavy figure, whose brows were lowered over a grimace that could as well have been a snarl as a smile.

'That's him!' he said. 'That's Kelty. Late of the Boys' Home cemetery. Brother Kevin Kelty. Killer Kelty.'

Dennis peered closer. 'He's dropped off in form a lot,' he joked.

'Kelty? Did you say Kevin Kelty?' said Mr Leonard, forgetting his sulk. 'Fancy that. Had a chap of that name here only a couple of weeks ago.'

Joss and Dennis swung around to look at him. 'He was,' said Mr Leonard defensively to their amazed faces. 'That was the name. He even signed our visitors' book. I've got an excellent memory for names.'

Joss shook his head. 'It's not possible,' he said.

'Maybe a relative or something,' said Dennis. 'Big families often double up on names. Different generations.'

'Tell me about this Kelty,' said Joss. 'What did he want?'

Mr Leonard looked disapproving. 'He seemed to think I was running a second-hand shop.'

Now, when Mr Leonard's garrulousness would have been welcome, he was suddenly prudent.

'What made you think that?' asked Joss.

'Asked me if I had any mirrors. I ask you ... Mirrors.'

'Mirrors?' Dennis repeated. He took one last pull on his ciagarette and went to the door, looking for a place to throw the butt.

'Police corruption,' Joss heard Mr Leonard mutter as Dennis tossed the cigarette out into the night. 'Think they can do anything they like. This country's turning into a police state.'

Dennis ambled back to join them, looking very heavy and irritable. 'Got a problem with something, mate?' he asked. Mr Leonard frowned severely at him but said nothing.

'Bloody mirrors again,' said Dennis. 'First the lot that vanishes off the furniture truck and now this.' He looked down at the photograph. 'What've we got here? Something, and we don't know what it is.'

Joss picked up the photo and found himself staring at the face, the hard mouth, of the big man who had beaten them so cruelly years ago. Kelty's features seemed to have gathered together in the centre of his face, like a caricature of himself, the centre of the mouth pushing up towards the nose, the brows pushing down towards the eyes, as if two powerful fingers had clasped his chin and forehead and pinched them together. Joss could almost feel again the burning strap, and his whole body flushed with shame and anger. He remembered the worst thing was his submission, allowing the adult to do what he wanted without any fight or argument. Meekly turning around and bending over. Bending over for the bully. Any attempt at self-protection simply increased the abuse. Insubordination, defiance, dumb insolence: the abusers had a very special vocabulary.

He abruptly turned his attention to something else in the picture, the rear end of a car partly visible in the driveway. He suddenly remembered something. 'See the car?' he said. The bishop had a big old Packard. There it is. This photo must have been taken when the bishop gave us a holiday. It was some big jubilee, 1947. God, I'm probably in there somewhere.' He started searching along the rows of children's faces, searching for himself of some forty-seven years ago.

'What does it mean?' Dennis was thinking out loud. 'The signature of Kevin Kelty? The mirrors?'

'That's not him, anyway,' said Mr Leonard, looking over Joss's shoulder at the cassocked figure in the photograph. 'My Mr Kelty was a much taller man. I told him in no uncertain terms that this was an important historical society and not a junk shop.'

'What did he do then?' asked Dennis.

Mr Leonard wasn't sure if he'd forgiven Dennis yet for police brutality and corruption. But he capitulated. 'He seemed very interested in this picture. Not the people in it, he wanted to know about this.' The elderly man pointed to something on the photo.

Joss looked and so did Dennis. Mr Leonard's pale old finger touched the area near Kelty. 'This belt thing here that's hanging down. He asked me what they're worth these days. "What's what worth?" I asked him. I didn't know what he meant. Some old belt. As if I'd be interested. I told him to go to a second-hand place if he had old clothes to sell. I think he was a bit touched myself.'

'Mr Leonard, you see further than most people,' said Dennis. Mr Leonard looked at him warily, unsure if he were being teased. But Dennis was wearing his frank Australian boy-oh face. Joss looked closer and saw that in the folds of Kelty's cassock a broad strap could be seen.

'God,' he said. 'That's it. That's the strap he used on us. The one that leaves the crosshatching.'

Mr Leonard, with the self-absorption that has no interest in any conversation outside its own limits, had pottered away. 'I just hope you two aren't much longer,' he called back as he switched his office light off.

'We're going,' said Dennis. 'I'd like to borrow this picture.'

'I don't know about that.' The elderly man shuffled back.

Dennis put the picture under his arm. 'What did he look like, your Mr Kelty?'

Mr Leonard shrugged. 'I don't see so well, to tell you the truth. But I never forget a name.'

'Anything you remember about him would be helpful,' Joss added.

'He was a tallish chap, around your height, as I recall. That's about all I can remember.'

'I'd like you to come down to the station tomorrow, just the same,' said Dennis. 'Look through a few pictures. You never know, you might remember something.'

Mr Leonard jutted his chin out. 'Let's have a look at the

visitors' book,' said Dennis in his most amiable manner. 'We could sign it for you.'

Mr Leonard couldn't resist this. Back he went to his office and when he came out again he had a sheepish look on his face. 'Is this the one you wanted?' he asked, holding out a battered attendance book with the date they'd been looking for.

Dennis beamed. 'You little beauty! This is going to be invaluable. And is that the visitors' book?'

Mr Leonard nodded and handed over both volumes. Dennis flicked open the visitor's book and ran the lid of his pen down the names. Joss leaned over to see. 'Kevin Kelty' was written in loopy writing.

'Look at the date. Two days before Jeremy Smiles,' said Joss, glancing up. 'What do you make of that writing?'

'Not much to go on, but it doesn't look to me like the hand of someone who does a lot of writing.'

They straightened up. 'I'd like to take these away with with me,' he said to Mr Leonard.

Mr Leonard was shaking his head in firm refusal.

'Goodnight, sir,' said Dennis, refusing to notice. 'Thank you so much for your time. If we think of any items of an historical nature tucked away at the station, apart from the sergeant, we'll keep you in mind.'

Mr Leonard was open-mouthed.

'And you come down to the police station tomorrow any time you like, sir,' Dennis added, as if he were doing the old man a big favour. 'You name your own time. I realise you're a busy man.'

The two men walked down the stone steps and out into the car. Joss felt suddenly drained. It seemed to be an effort to close the door. He leaned back as Dennis gunned the motor and rubbed the back of his neck.

'That break-in at Bloomdaless,' Dennis said, taking off and swinging the wheel to corner. 'I keep thinking of that. It wasn't like a druggie's break-in. They take everything. They sell what they're not interested in. Whoever broke in only took hypnotics. And then only some. Why didn't they strip the shelves? That's got me thinking. Remind me to go over the report when we get back.'

When Dennis turned another corner, Joss frowned. They weren't going in the direction of the police station. He looked at his colleague, a question on his lips. But Dennis was speaking. 'You reckon he was one of Kelty's abused kids, don't you? What if he was there when you were there?'

Joss shook his head. 'Unlikely. He's too old to be doing this sort of killing. He'd have to be my age.'

'Remember you said the profiles are only possibilities – not prophecies. If you're right on the Kelty exhumation, he *must* have known him. He also signed Kelty's name. He also asked about mirrors. Kelty's name is only on the rolls of the Home for eleven years. Our boy may well have been there when you were. What if he's been in custody all these years? On hold? Some hypnosis might bring a few ideas into your mind.'

'I think I know what you're getting at. And I don't like it,' said Joss.

'That's irrelevant,' said Dennis. 'If there's a chance, we've got to take it. Personal feelings aside.' He swung the wheel again and they turned into Ashley's street.

Outside her house, Dennis stopped the car. 'What do you say?'

Joss swallowed. 'I don't know about this,' he said. 'Ashley and I aren't ... ' He hated saying this to Dennis. 'Well, things are delicate.' Joss wondered whether it was triumph he saw in his colleague's eyes.

'I don't know anything about your personal life,' Dennis said as he pulled the keys from the ignition. 'And I don't want to know, either. But I've thought over what you said, about looking at what he's telling us in his re-enactment – if that's what it is – of what was done to him. And about working backwards to find out who he is. Because if what you say is true, there's an outside chance that we can get to the identity of this joker.'

He got out of the car, taking the attendance book and

the photo with him. Joss reluctantly followed. 'And hanging on that outsider, is that if we work out who the killer is we might get there in time to save the life of that little Munro boy. That's why I'm taking this punt.' He rang the doorbell.

Ashley, surprised by the late hour and her two visitors, listened while Dennis explained what he wanted. She was wearing a too-big jumper and the bottom of a tracksuit. The stove had been stacked with wood and closed off for the night. She adjusted the heat and made them hot drinks.

Joss stood awkwardly, staring into the flames, hating being in this room after what had happened here those hours ago.

'I can agree to do this, if Joss is okay,' Ashley said, looking over at him. He could see where crying had softened her eyes and reddened her nose and chin. He felt maliciously pleased that she was suffering too. And was immediately ashamed of himself. And then confused by the changing weather of these turbulent new emotions.

'You've been smoking,' she said, turning to Dennis. 'I can smell it. You'd better come back for another session.'

'After all this,' he said, indicating the stress of the investigation with a shrug.

'Here,' she said, bringing him an ashtray. 'It's okay if you want one.' She turned to Joss. He could hardly bear to look at her. 'Are you happy to do it, Joss? With Dennis here?'

Joss nodded. He wasn't, but he wasn't going to admit it. Yet he was aware at the same time of feeling oddly comforted here, with this woman and his difficult colleague. It was a safe place with the warm fire and the cocoa, away from the terrors of the stalking killers out there, away from Sybil, perhaps mad and murderous as Medea.

Ashley picked up the photo Dennis had given her and scanned the rows of children. She looked up at Joss. 'This is the Boys' Home? The place of the laundry?' she said. 'Which one is you?'

Slowly, Joss took the stiff card from her hand. His eyes ran along the back row, the next row, then the front row of very young children. He thought he had seen his haunted face back at the old church, but had pushed the picture away. Right in the front row, and flinching from the whole world, was a little face like a miniature version of the horrified man in Munch's *The Scream*. Joss pointed. 'This little fellow,' he said. His forefinger looked huge and coarse against the small and frightened white face, half the size of his tiniest fingernail.

Ashley took the picture back and studied it. Then she put it down again, almost reverently. 'Are you ready, Joss?' she asked. He nodded.

Dennis settled back as Joss lay in the recliner and Ashley started reciting the words to relax Joss and take him back. As he sank down, his head supported by a pillow, Joss had one beautiful moment where he no longer cared that murderous men were stalking him. Following Ashley's voice, he drifted into a deeply relaxed state, like the floating tail of a kite follows the swooping of the cross-barred frame. He forgot about Sybil, about the postcard that indicated she was dead. He let go of the images of her lying in a drawer at the morgue, of her being involved with his enemies in planning his destruction. He forgot about Polly. He forgot about Alan. He even forgot that Ashley had dumped him, so strongly connected was he to her voice. He forgot that he hadn't contacted Hamish and that he still hadn't played the video cassette from his old Woollahra home.

All his thoughts and fears slipped away like silk on glass.


He was back watching the scenes in the laundry. He could see the dirty walls again, stronger and clearer now that he could add details from his visit to this place of his memories. He could see the fearful boys going about their work, stirring the sheets in seething coppers, struggling to lift them out, rinsing them in the tubs, looking behind them to see if *he* was on the prowl.

'I want you to sit back and watch now.' Ashley's steady voice. 'You are completely safe. I will not leave you alone. I want you to look at this video in complete safety and security. I want you to look at all the boys there. I want you to tell me what you know about them. In your own time, there's no rush. Watch the boys on the cassette, and when you're ready, tell me about each one.'

Joss drifted, watching. He floated up to one boy, a solid fourteen-year-old. Joss heard a six-year-old's voice when he answered, high and thin, a great distance away. 'There's Matthew,' he said. 'He's good to me and the little ones. He makes us boats to go on the dam. He makes them out of paperbark. When Killer isn't around, we play races.' He paused for a moment. 'And that one's William. I keep out of his way. He's cruel to us.'

'Tell me about William.'

'He goes home once a month and he tells on us. Us little kids hate him.'

He heard Dennis speak. 'That one's a possibility,' he said. There was a pause during which Joss drifted comfortably.

'I think I'll try a more direct method,' said Ashley in a moment. Joss heard her voice change as she brought her full attention back to him. 'Joss,' she said, 'I want you to look at all the boys that live at the Boys' Home with you. I want you to tell me about the one who has the worst time. The one who has no one to care for him. The one who is the most unloved and unwanted and most cruelly treated of all. I can tell you a few things about him already that might be helpful to you. Maybe he has a limp or holds one of his arms a bit crooked. He might be very stunted for his age, he can't grow because of the abuse. Or he might be grossly bloated if he's adolescent. Very bad acne on his face if he's in his teens. There is no one in the world who cares for him or loves him. Because of this, he is completely at the mercy of any violent, cruel older person. He is very stoic. He will never complain of the terrible treatment, because he has never known anything else. And by now he is emotionally numb.'

Joss moved around in the theatre of his mind, looking at the boys in the laundry. He was starting to think he knew the one she meant. He wasn't aware of Dennis leaning forward, intensely interested, watching him. He was aware of nothing except the images in his mind and Ashley's voice.

'Look for this boy,' Ashley repeated. Joss's trance mind started to move towards one of the boys in the scene. 'The boy we are looking for knows only cruelty. He tortures animals. He may even kill them. He tortures children that are smaller than he is. He would have hurt you a lot if you were littler than him. It is the only time he feels some relief from his world of suffering. But he doesn't feel pain in himself any more. In fact, you can tell from his face that there is no emotion left at all. Except when he is tormenting someone – then you may see a special gleam in his eyes that you hope never to see again in anyone. It is the only time something moves him. The pain and suffering of another powerless person – that is what he needs to keep himself shielded from the fathomless depths of his own suffering.' Joss was moving confidently towards the boy he now knew to be the one. 'His face will be the face of the abused. From earliest days, he will never have known whether he will be fed or burned with a cigarette. It's a face that court reporters will later say shows no emotion, that will prompt the judge to say he is incapable of remorse.'

Joss had nearly zoomed in on the boy, a gaunt, no-lips child of eleven whose permanently horrified eyes scanned about him constantly.

'Can you find me this boy?' Ashley's voice asked. 'He has sandy hair and light eyes and he looks about eight years old. Although he may be considerably older than that. You are quite safe from him because you are only watching him on the video and he can never harm you again, if he ever did.'

'Easy,' said six-year-old Joss. 'That's him there.' Joss watched Kelty swoop on one of the boys, beat him around the legs, the body, the chest. Then Kelty grabbed the sheet the child had dropped on the floor, wrapped it around his throat, half strangling him, all the time bashing him with the strap until he got tired.

'Who is it, Joss?' asked Ashley from a long way away.

'It's Fishy Fuller. His real name's Eric. He's got these poppy-out eyes. Fishy Fuller. He likes to strangle kittens and puppies. Killer broke his arm and no one did anything until the bishop noticed. He's been here longer than anyone. His mother put him in here and never got him out again. She does bondage to her customers. But she never comes to get him. Us little kids hate him worst of all.'

Dennis was running his finger down the attendance book, looking for the name. His finger stopped at one entry and he looked up at Ashley. He nodded.

'You got him,' he said. 'You got him, Ashley. Here he is.' And he passed the book to her with his finger still under the name for her to see: Eric Fuller.

# 15

One twenty-three in the morning and the back room of the Maroonga police station was very quiet, except for the occasional ringing of the phones and the chattering of the computers where Dennis and Joss sat searching files.

'That Ashley Smith,' Dennis said without looking away from his screen. 'She's something, isn't she?' Joss remained silent. 'The way she worked on you. The way she pulled Eric Fuller out for us.'

Joss thought about Dennis. He was in a position of having to trust the younger man. He wanted to know if Hamish had found anything on him. He got up and left the room, found a phone in an empty briefing room and dialled Hamish Alabone's number. The answering machine told him to leave a message. He hung up. He wanted to trust Dennis, but at the moment he wished his colleague would get a transfer to Albury Wodonga. This is jealousy, he diagnosed. He came back down the corridor. He heard Dennis's lighter click and felt a strong pang for something – anything – to ease his tension. He pulled himself a bitter coffee from the café bar and came back into the room. He felt drained. Suddenly Dennis's voice shocked him out of himself.

'Holy shit! Look at this. I've got him! Eric Fuller. He's here!'

'Fuller, Eric Merle.' He twisted around to look at Joss. 'Isn't Merle a woman's name?'

Joss blinked. His eyes were bleary and he found it hard to focus. 'Read it out to me,' he said and sat down at the end of the table.

Dennis looked up from the screen and across at him. 'Are you fucking interested in this or what?'

'Of course I'm fucking interested in it,' Joss snapped back. 'I'm tired, that's all.'

'Yeah. So am I.' Then Dennis gave a sudden grin. 'Mate, you swore.'

Joss grunted and Dennis went back to the screen.

'Eric Merle Fuller.' Dennis read. 'Born 1935. Let's see. Six feet tall – he didn't remain stunted then, I see. Juvenile offences, uncontrollable, ward of the state by the time he's fourteen. Mum's a whore who specialises in sadistic sexual services. She's got a file too. See Merle Aimee Fuller, née Starkl, date of birth 6.8.19. Fuller was convicted of assaulting a teenage boy 1956, did three years.'

'His mother was sixteen when he was born,' said Joss, working it out. 'Any details about that assault?'

Dennis shook his head. 'But it must have been nasty – more than a punch on the nose to be three years' worth.'

'Go on,' said Joss.

'More convictions. Jail terms for serious assaults.' Dennis ran his eyes down the screen. 'Joined the army.'

'Ashley was right again,' said Joss.

'Dishonourable discharge following a sadistic assault on a young boy. Then he lies low for a few years, or we don't hear about him at any rate. Here he is, living at Darlinghurst. Late sixties there's another jail sentence for attempted murder. Then he's out and straight into attempted kidnap. Tried to take an eight-year-old boy from a street in Bexley, but the child's sister saw what was happening and intervened.'

'It's him!' said Joss. Now he felt the blood pumping through his system, renewed with excitement. 'We've got him!' His tiredness evaporated. He felt more alive than he had for a long time. The adrenalin surge of the hunt. 'Keep going,' he commanded.

But Dennis stayed silent.

'Come *on*,' said Joss, eagerly. 'We've got him. Keep going.'

Dennis's fist thumped down hard on the table. 'No! No! Fuck no!' He jumped up, walked to the nearest whiteboard and bashed it to the floor. 'Fucking *hell.*'

'What is it?' said Joss, getting up to look at the screen.

'*Fucking* hell,' Dennis was yelling. He swung a kick at the whiteboard where it lay on the floor. 'It's not him! The fucker's gone and died on us. He's fucking well dead! Why the fuck is this file still in the fucking system? Fuller died in February 1982. Twelve years ago.'

'He can't have!' Joss was peering desperately at the screen, his eyes searching the entry. 'It's got to be him! He's attempted kidnap on a child before. You just read it. You heard the hypnosis session we've just been through. He *is* the right one, he fits it perfectly. He knows the laundry set-up. The sheets. The beating. It's *got* to be him.'

But then he saw what Dennis had seen, the last entry: deceased, February 1982.

Joss slowly straightened up, despair settling on him.

Dennis was collapsed across the table, his head on his arms. He lay there not moving. Then he slowly pulled himself up, pushing his fingers through his hair. He stared at Joss and his face was hard and bitter. 'We're nowhere. We're back where we started.' He fumbled for his cigarettes and lit one. The animosity in his face was awesome. 'No, we're worse than nowhere.' He jabbed his cigarette in Joss's direction. 'You and your bloody working backwards theory. You've led this whole investigation up shit creek. Fucking academics and theorists. Why don't I ever learn? Where the fuck does it leave me now? Fucking nowhere, that's where. I've got two kids murdered and another one about to be and I've been chasing a man who's been dead for twelve years!'

He went to the chair where his coat was hanging. 'I'm too tired and too angry to talk. I'm going home.' He picked up his coat, dropped it, swore, kicked it, picked it up again and walked out of the room, slamming the door so hard that the whole wall seemed to shudder.

Joss sat there stunned. The silence after Dennis was unbearable. He stared at the screen where the details of dead Eric Fuller shimmered. There it was, the inexorable fact. The profilers were right: violent men died violent deaths, early. But everything else pointed to Fishy Fuller. The laundry set-up. The visit to the Historical Society and the name of Kelty in the visitors' book, his interest in the strap in the photograph. The reference to mirrors. The desecration of the grave at the Boys' Home. And Joss had seen Fuller so clearly in the hypnosis session. It *had* to be Fuller. And yet, there it was, glowing on the screen. Dead as a doornail. Twelve years dead.

Was there some wild, mad coincidental possibility that there were two men with the same name and the same history? That idea lasted a half second. Dennis was right. They were up shit creek. This whole trail was not just cold, it was as dead as Eric Fuller.

Joss went down the corridor and pushed the front door open, shivering as the freezing night air hit him. What were they going to do now? He had no idea.

He got in his car and drove off. Passing the civic centre he saw men who'd been working through the night now loading the Gold of Egypt exhibition for transport.

The house sat brooding in the moonlight. Joss unlocked it and went inside. His answering machine was winking and he poured himself a scotch and listened to his messages. The law secretary, a student, Hamish Alabone, and someone wanting to interview him for a book. He tried phoning Hamish but all he got was his answering machine, which didn't surprise him, given the hour.

Joss had moved from exhaustion into the place where he knew sleep was out of the question. He went to his study and switched on his computer, calling up the cross-reference system. He found the file on Eric Fuller. I know it's you, he said. It's got to be you. I'm starting to hear your story. Part of your story is about digging up the dead. You must have risen from the dead. Nothing else makes sense. He put SHEETS through a cross-check. There were hundreds of references. People hanged with sheets, people buried in sheets, partly burned sheets around partly burned bodies. A case where a husband had strangled his wife with the sheet of the marital bed. He ran checks on anything that might be related. He got side-tracked on WATERBED and found an attempted killing where the husband had slit the waterbed with a knife and shoved his wife's head through to drown her. Family life, he thought bitterly, thinking of his vanished mother. He thought of Ashley's matter-of-fact understanding of how the horror and the domestic sat side by side, to show up again later in details that had the experts scratching around to explain. But it was easy for him to imagine a woman hanging out the sheets, bringing them in from the line, making the bed. Then having another fight with her husband, wherein the same sheet forces the life from her body and she dies by her own housework. He remembered the savagery of Killer Kelty and the green jubes he handed out on the feast days of the Irish saints. Cruelty and green jubes together.

He checked PILLOW and found dozens of references to suffocation by pillows, people found dead with pillowslips over their heads. Everywhere he looked the domestic became the murderous. The shift from kindness to killing. He went back to SHEETS and started rechecking every entry, trying to find something that would allow Eric Fuller to rise from the dead and be alive and active in this country town.

But Fishy Fuller stayed dead.


At 3.50 am he was still at it. His eyes were blurred from lack of sleep and staring too long at the screen. He got up and went to the window, shifting his focus onto distance to ease his stinging eyes.

Outside, the stillness was immense. A low, eroded moon shed gloomy light on the skulls of the mountains, and the dim shapes of cattle barely moved in the mist of the river flat. The frogs had long been silent. He looked at the bars he had installed in his house, the prison he lived in. He wished Lombard would make his move. If he was going to move at all. Maybe Sybil was right and Lombard was safely swanning around a palace in Manila.

He went back to the screen. He was scrolling each entry like a zombie when the suburb of Bexley caught his eye. Joss sat up. Fuller had attempted to abduct a child from Bexley. He studied the entry. The body of a man had been found under the verandah of an old house in Bexley, having been savagely beaten then strangled in a sheet. The name of the murdered man was Eric Fuller. And there was the date, February 1982. Joss stood up, his mind racing.

Someone had murdered Eric Fuller in the same way that their killer was murdering little boys. Joss's exhausted mind couldn't even begin to examine this. Every cell in his body screamed at him for sleep. He left the screen shining and went upstairs.

He was aware of the phone ringing and wondered why no one answered it. Finally he woke, looked around bewildered for a second and then grabbed the receiver. It was Dennis.

'We've got something,' he said. 'Something real. Sydney Homicide just rang to say they've been contacted by a retired bootmaker, name of Bill Halliday. He's been away and only just seen the papers. Says he made a strap like the one our man uses, to just those specifications before he left. He's coming up on the morning flight.' He slammed the phone down.

Joss dialled Hamish. 'I've been trying to get you for twenty-four hours,' he said. 'That's not good enough, Hamish.'

'I had to go off the air.'

'Not if you're working for me, you don't.'

'Listen,' said Hamish, 'I'm a human being. I have to sleep. I have to take a shit. I have to tiptoe through the tulips.'

'What have you got for me?' Joss snapped.

'I've made some inquiries. Looks like your mate the detective is straight up and down. An unremarkable career in the force – I mean, the *service*.' Joss could hear the leer down the line. 'He doesn't drink with the boys so he probably won't be promoted.'

'Anything more on Ignatius Ho?'

'Leave it with me.'

'I have, Hamish. I'm paying you. Don't do that again. Don't be out of reach.'

He was aware of the edge in his voice.


Bill Halliday sifted through the photographs. He winced at the shots of the marks of the strap on Patrick Sharp's narrow body and studied the replica made by the unwilling bootmaker in the mall.

'Well?' Dennis asked. Bill Halliday removed his reading spectacles and folded them neatly in their case.

'Very like that, it was. Said he wanted it for a play. There was something strange about him. His face was – he looked too hard at things and wouldn't look at me at all. Anyway, I made it for him and I charged him forty-eight dollars. It took me a while. He said he wanted something over the leather, an extra layer. He pointed to some old resin sole fabric I had. He said he wanted that added on.'

'Kelty had something like that on his weapon,' Joss said.

Mr Halliday looked first at Joss, then at Dennis, and when he spoke again, his voice was almost a whisper. 'I made that bloody thing for him, didn't I? That strap that he hits the little boys with. I made that.'

'When was this?' Dennis asked gently, notebook in hand.

'About six months ago,' said Mr Halliday.

'What did he look like, this fellow?' Dennis asked.

The bootmaker sighed. 'I haven't got a clear picture in my mind. Just that he was odd. It was an unusual bit of work, otherwise I'd never have remembered.'

'How did he know you, Mr Halliday?'

'He was living in a boarding house down the road and he found out I used to be a bootmaker. You know how things get around. I had a shop there for years.'

'Where?' asked Joss.

'Bexley,' said Mr Halliday.

'Bexley again,' said Joss. Dennis looked at him.

'Thank you very much for your help, Mr Halliday. I'm going to hand you over to my constable now, who'll take down the details. This way, please.'

'Dennis, listen', Joss said as soon as Dennis returned. 'Last night when I got home I went through our index. Eric Fuller was found dead under a verandah in Bexley – wrapped up and strangled in a sheet!' He felt Dennis tense beside him. 'I'd like to know,' Joss said, 'how long his body was under the verandah before he was found.'

Dennis frowned. His frustration was controlled but still very evident beneath the surface of his face. 'What are you thinking?' he asked.

It seemed to Joss that Dennis was gathering himself up like a fighter, ready to attack any weakness. Joss took a deep breath. He imagined the sunken mess of decomposing tissues and fabric under an old verandah, the liquefying heat of a Sydney February. He imagined the further destruction by seething maggots and the postmortem. City rats dragging bones away. Dennis waited, silent.

'I'm thinking,' said Joss finally, 'what if it wasn't Eric Fuller under the verandah? Just because Fuller lived there and then disappeared, maybe there were some assumptions made about identification?'

Dennis almost spat. 'You've been watching too many horror movies.'

'It's happened before,' Joss reminded him. 'Wrong identifications have happened. You've got to give me that.'

'Highly unlikely.' Dennis's voice was hard, but Joss knew that his colleague was a man who liked to play around with what-ifs. And there was just too much of Eric Fuller in these murders for him to be completely written off. When the impossible is the only explanation, the whole diagnosis needs to be examined again.

'But it's *possible*,' said Joss. 'And it fits the facts we've collected. I couldn't make sense of it last night, I was bushed. But this morning I thought how death would be the perfect alibi for a compulsive killer. He's completely hidden for the rest of his career. What if this dead person under the verandah's not Eric Fuller? What if the murdered man under the verandah was in fact one of his early victims?'

He paused, examining Dennis's face, the way he was listening, processing, evaluating. He knew he had a show. Dennis did not suffer from a closed mind. But there were other issues between them that clouded things.

'Dennis, it's the only way we can make sense of what's in front of us. It's the only explanation that fits the facts. I *saw* in the hypnosis session what happened. You were there!'

Dennis's face was tight with concentration but he was nodding, he was wanting to believe. 'Yeah. But what about that radiant light of yours? Where does that fit in? That aura of light you see, it's always been a problem for me. It makes me wonder whether what you experience really happened at all, or whether it's some sort of fit you take. And your imagination has created a whole series of incidents using material from this investigation. I don't have to remind you of false memory syndrome.' He shrugged. 'Look. I don't disbelieve you have these experiences. But what if you've been having some sort of epilepsy? You had that headache. That's a standard epilepsy symptom, even I know that. People hallucinate and they see auras. Angels. Bright lights. Little green men. They're taken by aliens and experimented on. They remember past lives, they say. All sorts of things. None of it can be verified. I'm a cop and I deal in facts.'

Joss pressed on. 'What I experienced were flashbacks to repressed memories, not false memory syndrome. Not *grand mal*, believe me. There's only one explanation that fits the facts we've got. Despite your records, Eric Fuller is alive and well and killing little boys in our town. Nothing else fits.'

Dennis gave a great heaving sigh. 'If it *is* Fuller –' he began.

'It is,' interrupted Joss. 'He's close by somewhere. He lives in Nightingale Street, on the canal. We've doorknocked him. We've spoken to him. Bloomdales is the closest pharmacy to Nightingale Street.'

'Let's say your idea is right,' said Dennis, 'and Fuller is alive.' Joss saw the doubts assail him again. 'It's too farfetched,' he said shaking his head. 'You know how stringent the requirements are. You know the chain of custody.'

Joss nodded. 'I do know. But it's still possible that a wrong identification was made. You know what getting fingerprints off a putrid corpse can be like.'

Dennis nodded slowly. 'Yes,' he said. 'I do. From the days the cops had to use the bolt cutters.'

'Just say then that they've got ID from the house, maybe a wallet on the body, and for good measure a few similar points on the fingerprints taken off sloughed and putrid skin. Can't you imagine even a very honourable doctor saying, That's him, going home and having a very long hot shower and then off to the club?'

Dennis flopped down in a chair. 'Okay. I'll grant you that as a possibility.' But his voice was very grudging.

'If he's got the boy and he's delaying, it means something.' Joss was reminded of his own position with Lombard. 'What do you think it might be?' he asked, interested for both reasons.

'Something isn't right for him yet.'

'I agree,' said Joss. 'But what isn't right?' He looked at his watch. It was two o'clock, he'd had only a few hours sleep and no food all day. Dennis stood up again, restless, and shoved his hands in his pockets. 'He's got the boy,' he said. 'That's if he's still alive.'

'He's drugged him,' said Joss.

'He's got the boy, but he hasn't got the right place.' Dennis swung around in his chair. 'Okay. 'Let's have a look at what he needs. Let's consider what other places in town might fit his scenario.'

Two hours later they still sat there. An overhead projector was sitting on a couple of books in the centre of the table, where coffee rings overlapped in a pattern of chains around the phones. The computer screen showed CRIME SCENE – DIMENSIONS. Joss's mouth was vile with bad coffee, little sleep and no food. Dennis had keyed in the information from both places, down to the smallest details, the dimensions of the cave and the cellar, the distances between where the bodies had lain, where the scenery had been put in place in the cellar, the naturally occurring low ramparts of the cave, the light source high up in the wall on the right. Dennis had painstakingly drawn on a transparency the outline and features of the scene at Spring Caves. On a second transparency he'd drawn the cellar of the old Maitland hotel, scaling each drawing from the data on the screen. He put both transparencies in the projector so that they appeared superimposed on the wall ahead of them. If the much bigger area of the underground cave were disregarded, and the beholder merely took the area where Jeremy had lain in his sheet near the ramparts, and compared this with the place where Patrick was found near the bench in the cellar, both crime scenes overlapped each other in an uncannily perfect match.

'How does he get it so accurate?' said Dennis.

Joss remembered the clarity of his hypnosis images, the steam, the stains on the wall, the herringbone weals that had reappeared on his skin after nearly half a century. 'Maybe most people just don't know what's in their archives,' he said. 'We stop remembering.'

Dennis dragged the last cigarette from his pack. He tapped it on the table and lit it. 'God,' he said, glancing at the clock that showed 4.35. 'Those boys were killed at around five in the afternoon. What if he's spent today finding the place? This town is full of cellars. Basements.

We've got Buckley's of ever finding where he might go. What if he's already set it up? If Brendan is still alive, he isn't going to be for much longer.'

The two of them sat in silence with this thought. Joss stared at the overlapping crime sites, their *exactness*. When the phone rang Dennis snatched it up.

'You the copper in charge of the little boys' murders?' the caller asked.

Dennis reached for his notebook and caught Joss's eye. Joss picked up the other extension.

'Yes,' said Dennis. 'Who am I speaking to, sir?'

'The name's Walker. I think you should know that I just saw a bloke with a kid near the sports ground out along the caves road. The kid was struggling with him. I was driving into town and I never thought much about it until just then.'

'What time was this?'

'About ten minutes ago. Maybe fifteen.' Dennis checked his watch.

'At the sports ground you say, Mr Walker?'

'Yup. Ugly looking bloke with a kid about seven, eight – something like that. Looked like he was taking the kid into that members' stand there. Looked like the kid didn't want to go.'

'I know the place,' said Dennis, jotting down the information. 'What make of vehicle?'

'Light coloured stationwagon. Ford maybe. Pretty dusty.'

'Mr Walker, can you meet me there in – ' Dennis glanced at his watch again. 'It's 4.39 now – in fifteen minutes?'

'Sure,' said the caller. 'No worries. I'm on me way.'

'Mr Walker, can I have your address and phone number? Mr Walker? Shit!' cursed Dennis as eager Mr Walker rang off. He dropped the phone into place and started out the door with Joss following.

A few minutes later they were at the T-junction leading out of town, where Long Swamp Road headed west and the caves road east. Dennis swung the wheel hard left and Joss swayed against the window. The sun was sitting on the hills, just about to slide behind them. Dennis adjusted the rear vision mirror to take the reflected glare of the sun from his eyes.

'How far is it to the sports ground?' Joss asked.

'Seven, eight kays,' said Dennis, his foot down hard on the accelerator. 'This is too good to be true. But God knows, we deserve a break.' Joss liked to hear him say 'we'. Dennis was okay, he thought.

The winter lucerne crops along the river flats were an unearthly green, brilliant emerald in the late sun. Something in Joss stirred uneasily as they headed past the first turn-off, driving fast towards the Abercrombie junction. At first he thought it was just motion sickness, but it grew stronger. It was dark and vague and it would not let him be. It was an old, old feeling; it brought with it the leather and walnut smell of his mother's car as the Riley made its way in first gear up the steep driveway to the Boys' Home.

'That sports ground,' he said to Dennis. 'I can't remember it. What does it look like?'

Dennis shrugged. 'Not much to remember. Fence all the way round, like a race track. There're a few public stands, pretty rough and ready, and the members' stand for the squatters, with a room behind where they used to prepare the lunches. They set the kegs up in front of that.'

'I remember now.' He'd been there once to the local races. 'Which direction does it face?'

'You mean the buildings?'

Joss nodded. 'The members' stand. What direction does that face?'

'It faces towards Abercrombie,' said Dennis, pointing ahead. 'East.' A faded signpost whipped past, showing the sports ground was five kilometres down the road.

Joss sat considering for another kilometre, his feeling of unease strong now. 'Walker said the man was taking the kid towards the members' stand?'

'That's right,' said Dennis.

'No,' said Joss. 'It's not right.'

'What are you talking about? What's not right?'

Joss shook his head. A knowing, deeper than consciousness, was surfacing. He looked across at the landscape on his right. A kurrajong tree in a paddock turned viridian by the sun threw a long vase-shaped shadow towards Abercrombie. Everything was enhanced by the late rosy light. He looked at the blunt profile of Dennis Johnson, the pushed-out jaw, the sun damage showing in the skin above his collar, the tiny cancer on the lip.

'It's not right,' he repeated.

'Bloody hell! What's not right? What do you mean?'

'The light source. The light is wrong. We're driving the wrong way.' He remembered the radiant light, the nausea.

Dennis looked across at his passenger, his face hard and his eyes showing angry anxiety. 'What wrong way, for Chrissake?' he said.

Joss suddenly saw that late sunlight split by bars high up on a wall. 'Remember we've been wondering how he could hold a torch as well as a child, then beat and strangle him? That cave was dark when I went down there. And that was in daylight. We had to set up lights at the cellar, too.

'Both places face due west,' Joss continued. 'It's 4.48 and the sun is directly behind us.' He was aware of Dennis staring at him in quick turns of the head, but Joss remained looking straight ahead, thinking out loud.

'It's shining into the back of the car. Like it would be now at the cave. It'd be shining straight through that hole he made in the council's masonry on his way down,' said Joss. 'The stadium stand faces due *east*. Towards Abercrombie. Its windows are on completely the wrong side for him.' He paused. 'And it's not underground.'

Dennis had slowed the car but he kept driving. He felt confused.

'That sun will be shining directly through the bars of the Maitland cellar,' Joss went on. 'Right now, both those places are flooded with sunlight. That's the light he needs. The sun has to be there. And there won't be any light flooding through the members' stand windows because they face east. It'll be nearly dark in there. The light that I see in the sessions, and sometimes with the nausea, the golden light – he's got to have that and he doesn't even know that he needs it to be there. All he knows is a right place. He's got to find a place that has its light source facing due west. Dennis, we're going absolutely the wrong way.'

'But the caller,' said Dennis, torn. 'We've got a report about a child in trouble just down the road. We've got to check that out. This is the time he does it. This is his kill time. And I have to act on information received.'

Joss put his hand on his colleague's arm. His voice was low and urgent. 'Dennis, turn around! You've got to believe me, I know the place. I know where he's gone with Brendan. You kicked the door in for him yesterday morning.'

Dennis swore. Joss could see beads of sweat appearing on his forehead and over the cancer on his lip. He remained undecided for another second. Then he braked hard, swung the vehicle round in a wheeling skid that threw clouds of dust into the air, and accelerated straight into the full blaze of the setting sun, back in the direction they'd just come. The landscape blurred beside them; telegraph poles whizzing past like fenceposts.

'Jeez, you better be right,' said Dennis, pulling his sunvisor down. His anguish was apparent. 'What about that caller?'

The same thought struck them together, so that their voices overlapped. 'It was *him*.'

'Bastard's set us up,' said Dennis. 'Sent us in the other direction while he takes Brendan to the Boys' Home. Mr Bloody Walker!'

'Mr Walker,' repeated Joss. 'Ghost who walks. Man who cannot die.'

Dennis hit the boards.

# 16

The sun was behind them again as they took the final turn into the drive up to the Boys' Home. Even in this sunset radiance, thought Joss, the place looked evil, full of pain and ghosts. The shadows lay preternaturally dark across the ruined flower gardens. They pulled up at the front of the building.

And there it was, NHV 536, parked near the the crooked doors under the stone portico, its tailgate hanging down as if something had been lifted out.

'That's his car!' said Dennis. They took the steps of the portico two at a time, raced through the double doors and along the corridor. Joss found his feet slipping on the filthy floors. He had moved ahead of Dennis when a muffled sound stopped them both in their tracks. Joss felt Dennis's heavy hand on his shoulder, forbidding him to move. There it was again. Dennis's hand lifted, and with fast cautious steps the two men made their way to the end of the hall where the stairs led down to the laundry. Again Joss heard the sound. A sound so low it might have been the blood pounding in his ears. He could see the soft golden light that even now must have been suffusing the subterranean room. The low cry again.

Joss was at the top of the stairs when he heard the blow strike the child's body. The leathery slap of the strap, custom made for the Compassionate Companion brothers for just one purpose: the assault of a child. The rage came up in him as the low wail changed to a scream, unbearable in its terror. He skidded into the handrails of the staircase, grabbed them and swung down, hardly touching the steps with his feet. For a split second he stood motionless in the laundry. There was the row of derelict tubs down the centre, and the old coppers, the filthy walls and floors flooded with the blaze of sunset split by the bars of the window. Forty-seven years fell away and Joss was a terrified child again, cowering under the rage of a madman. Breaking the brilliant light into shafts and shadows was the figure of a man crouched over a cocooned little figure on the floor, already wrapped in his winding sheet.

'No!' roared Joss as the strap was raised again. The killer stopped and turned round. The shaking parcel on the floor wriggled and screamed. Joss felt again the sting of the crosshatching on his body. He felt the powerless terror of the child as the monster towers over it. The light that filled the laundry seemed to expand into Joss's head and there was nothing in the world except the eyes of Killer Kelty staring at him. The face without pity or remorse; the eyes blazing with something he had forgotten, had hoped never to see again. Hard, pitiless eyes of igneous rock. Obsidian hardness fused by cruelty.

But this time, instead of dropping his eyes as a shamed and terrified child, Joss the man stared straight into the pit. Time and space wavered and swerved. Joss felt himself swell and grow huge with rage, soaring over the other man, pitiless like some monstrous djinn let loose from an ancient flask and intent on vengeance. How little and helpless the other now seemed. Rage seized him and it felt like a blessing. It brought relief, and the promise of peace. Joss found his gun in his hand. Their mutual gaze seemed to lock and twist: the eyes of the abused and the abuser. Joss fired once, twice, three times. He saw Killer Kelty's face crumble as his cheek and neck flowered red with bloody bones. Something warm stung his own face. He fired again, and again, and again.

There was a terrible roaring as reverberations shook the underground room into final silence. The world swung round and Joss could hear someone yelling behind him. He stood trembling and the gun slipped from his fingers. He made no attempt to pick it up. Dennis was holding the screaming child, pulling the sheet back from him, holding him to his chest and saying, 'It's all right now. You're safe now, Brendan. He can't hurt you again. It's okay.'

And then Joss saw that both Dennis and the white-faced child were staring at him. Slowly he walked over to the bench and sat down. He barely saw Dennis check the body on the floor and stare down at the gun.

Only then did Joss start to feel the itchiness, on his face, on the backs of his shaking hands, as the blood of Eric Fuller started drying on his skin.

Joss sat dazed in the rear seat of the car. He looked down at his hands and turned them over – his fine surgeon's hands, the backs of the fingers blotched with blood. He was vaguely aware of Dennis making a series of low urgent calls on his radio, then some time later the car going in the direction of the hospital, Dennis patting the boy in the passenger seat beside him and repeating over and over that he was safe.

As the Commodore swooped to the kerb at the hospital, cameras flashed. The Munro parents came running as ambulance officers supported their boy out of the car. Joss watched the mother fall to her knees and clutch her son, her face shining with tears.

'Later,' Dennis was saying to Barry Armstrong from the *Advocate* as he was jostled by a crowd of reporters on his way back to the car. 'I'll fill you in later.'

Joss had not moved. A camera flashed at him and he flinched. Dennis was getting back into the car. 'I can tell you this much, we got him. That's all I can say right now.'

Barry had to jump away from the car window when Dennis took off. They drove in silence for a minute, then Dennis turned to look at Joss and back at the road. 'Listen. Are you listening to me?'

Joss found it was an effort to listen.

'What?' he said. 'What is it?'

'You'll have to write down what happened,' Dennis told him.

Joss made no reply.

'I said, you'll have to write down what happened,' Dennis repeated.

'I heard you,' said Joss. Then, 'Give me back my gun.'

'I can't,' said Dennis. 'I have to take it in.'

'You must return it,' said Joss. 'Or provide me with another one. They know where I live. I must have it. I can't go home without it.'

Dennis swore. 'Doctor, are you aware of what's just happened? Are you aware that this weapon here has just featured in a homicide?' He turned to look at Joss. 'Are you aware that you just killed a man?'

'I did what had to be done,' Joss said in a hard voice. 'That's finished business. But I have something else to deal with. You know that, Dennis. You can't leave me unarmed with Lombard and his people loose. My daughter will be back soon. I must have that gun.'

Dennis tried again. 'We can take both you and your daughter into protective custody.'

'We've done that one already,' Joss spat. 'It doesn't fucking work. Now, give me my gun back.'

There was a long silence between them while Dennis drove furiously, taking corners roughly, too fast, too late. 'This is my arse you're talking about,' said Dennis.

'This is my life I'm talking about. And my daughter's life.'

Dennis drove.

'If you don't give me my gun back, I'm going to hit you over the head with this tyre lever and I'll take it. It's up to you.'

Dennis looked round at him again, saw the tyre lever, said something incomprehensible under his breath, and finally leaned down and picked up something from the floor. Without looking back, he dropped the bagged gun over to Joss.

Joss reloaded with the shells in his trousers, put the safety catch on and replaced the weapon in his pocket.

By the time they reached the station it was quite dark

and his symptoms of shock were starting to subside. His blood was pulsing normally through his veins and arteries, the muscles of his limbs began to flex and move. Dennis walked with him down the hall to an interview room and then left to get coffee. Joss was getting his thoughts in order. *I need to ring Hamish again. I need to watch that video.*

Dennis came back into the room with a typewriter. He put it down in front of Joss and stuck his head out of the door. 'Yeah, yeah. Okay, I'm coming.'

'I can't stay here,' he said to Joss. 'I have to write my own version of what happened out there. Separately.'

The door closed and Joss was left alone with the typewriter. He stared at the blank paper that was already in position. He typed his name, his date of birth and the day's date. Then he started putting down the facts of what happened in the laundry of the Boys' Home. He wrote as if he were describing something he'd seen in a film; a psychic wall still separated him from the events.

When he'd finished, he went outside with the closely typed paper. Dennis was nowhere to be be seen. Joss gave his report to the uniformed man at the desk. 'Can I go now?' he asked.

He walked through the park and ended up in the cathedral where he'd first read Sybil's message. He sat in the same pew with his head in his hands. The cathedral was quite dark except for the bank of candles burning on a brass stand: a vigil for the murdered boys. Joss slowly got up and walked over. The candles had guttered and many were dipping out as he watched. He pulled out a dollar and posted it in the chute for donations. He lit a candle for Alan and stuck it right up on the topmost level of the stand. Then he lit another for Jeremy Smiles and one for Patrick Sharp. He lit one for Eric Fuller. He dipped his hand into the candle box again and took out one last candle. He lit it for Brother Kevin Kelty.

He drove home almost hallucinating from exhaustion. The house looked secure and dark, untouched. He unlocked the front door and went into the lounge, found the video cassette and pushed it into the VCR. Then he fell into one of the armchairs.

It was a commercial travelogue about Alexandria, his wife's birthplace. It was about all Joss could do, in his dazed state, to keep his attention on the uninspired documentary and the clichés of the video camera: slow pans up and down buildings of architectural interest, crowded streets, bazaars, colourful people, the inevitable belly dancer, silks, tapestries, art. Then the desert, the heat, the blueness of the sky, brilliant red dates on palms, camels. The narrative over-explaining. Joss stared like a zombie. This is what Sybil had wrapped up as a present for her black man? Maybe she wanted her lover to know something of her background. Maybe he was another displaced Alexandrian. He thought about his wife. All those years together and he'd never really known her, never known what was important to her, what she wanted. They had always been too busy. There were always interruptions. There was never any time. Now it didn't matter. It was too late. There was immense sorrow somewhere, but it didn't seem to be in him. It was like music heard at a distance – sad, affecting. He couldn't quite locate it. He nodded off.

He woke suddenly in a state of fear, jerking upright. The travelogue had ended and the video now showed the split screen of the old logging tape Sybil had recorded over. He remembered the four camera frames well: the front hall, the lounge room, the staircase, and the master bedroom where he and Sybil slept and argued and rarely made love. Malcolm the Minder was in the lounge, walking over to the window. Sybil came in. Then the camera angles changed into four split scenes from outside the house: the kitchen yard, the left side, the front garden and the garage. The garage was still intact. Joss felt the pain of the past weaken his body. He didn't know if he could bear seeing Alan come home from school, his cap on back to front, shirt untucked as it had to be, school bag slung over his shoulder. He felt the distant music come closer. He felt the sorrow start to move towards him. Once he would have taken some sort of action to stop it, some distraction: work, painting the markings on a Mustang, reading a text. But there is no defence any more, he was thinking. My family is gone, and I myself am just another killer. My only choice is whether to deny this truth, excuse it, rationalise it, or simply stare steadily into the hell of it. And accept it.

The video was showing the inside of the house again. The bedroom was still, the area near the door empty. Sybil had vanished from the lounge and Malcolm was looking through the security hole in the front door. Maybe the black man was visiting. There was the houndstooth wrapping of a David Jones parcel on the front step.

Then Sybil appeared in their bedroom, tossing down an empty packet of cigarettes. How well he remembered her prowling around looking for nicotine, driving up to Kings Cross when she'd run out. The addict's drive to obtain supplies. He wasn't quite numb enough not to care that Sybil was wearing the silk shirt he'd bought her, the one he always loved to feel against her warm, dry skin. The terrible sorrow was firmly located in his heart now. The video switched again to exterior scenes, and then there was Sybil back in the lounge room, moving with her graceful gait to the big mirror over the fireplace, looking hopefully in the heavy silver cigarette box, dropping its lid in disappointment. Not even a stale one, thought Joss. Poor Sybil. Malcolm was standing near the window, well back and to one side, checking the front garden again. Was he waiting for someone to ring back on the bona fides of that parcel on the front step? Had he heard some odd noise? They were talking about something, the minder and the chatelaine of the big house. Sybil was shaking her head. Was she saying, No, I haven't ordered anything from David Jones, maybe my husband has?

It wasn't until he saw Malcolm walk from the window, pick up Sybil's handbag from where it lay on the floor, and, instead of passing it to her as he would have expected, do something quite different that Joss stiffened and sat up straight. Then he leaned forward with a new and terrible realisation in his heart. He watched intently while Malcolm quite comfortably opened Sybil's handbag, dug around in the depths until he found her cigarettes, held them up with a told-you-so air, and closed the bag again. Sybil took the packet and pulled one out, lighting it with relief. Joss saw her shake the match out and lean back on the fireplace. Malcolm resumed his position near the window. Joss tensed and gripped the arms of the chair he was sitting on, because now he knew who the man was.

Only a man who is a woman's lover feels free to rummage in her handbag like that, Joss knew. That's who his wife's lover had been – maybe still was – the one who'd organised the whole thing. The man who'd supervised their identity change. Malcolm Guest, their federal protector. *O Mavro mou*, she'd called him on the card. My dark man.

The tape finished and went into automatic rewind. Joss sat staring at the static on the screen, consumed by an unspeakable sense of betrayal. *How long had this been going on?* The question the betrayed feel they must ask, because they have to know how long they haven't known.

Malcolm Guest. Malcolm the minder. Joss stood up. He wanted to kick the TV screen in. *Malcolm.* Somehow, not knowing had been more merciful to his ego. There had even been a chance the whole thing was a just a romantic illusion, something Sybil had made up in bored mischief. It was so much worse now, the feeling of rage and hatred, now that he was sure.

Malcolm Guest was a biggish man with thick dark hair and a face that was closed and guarded, so that he seemed to squint at the world. He never smiled. Serious, diligent, Joss had thought. A good policeman. Not stupid, but not well educated. Dressed badly. Polite, even-tempered. But seeing Malcolm's hand in Sybil's bag was just as shocking as if he'd seen it thrust between her legs. And what a perfect partner for a vengeance-bent wife.

Joss could feel his heart jumping. Racing. He got up from his seat and found himself picking up the phone and dialling even before he'd thought about it. He could not face this alone.

'I know this is against the rules of separation,' he said when she answered. He was aware that his voice was shaking, that his breathing came in stablike sobs. 'But please can I see you? I shot a man dead. And I know who my wife's lover is. It's about as bad as it can be.'

There was hardly any pause. 'Come over,' she said.

Joss lay face-down on Ashley's bed and she kneeled across his back, massaging his shoulders, his neck, and down his spine. She ran her thumbs down the knobby vertebrae.

'Ashley, I don't know what to do. Talk to me. Tell me. Too much is happening.'

'Just lie still,' she said. 'Just feel my hands. Just breathe. Think only of your breathing.'

He did as she said, concentrating on the in breath, the out breath. In a while, she turned him over and worked on his arms and chest. His eyes were closed as he spoke.

'It was like I was back there again. It was like I was a terrified six-year-old. And then something happened. I became enormous.'

She eased the holding and the tension in his pectorals.

'I don't know what they'll make of my statement. I really have no excuse for killing that man. He was unarmed, except for the strap, and that was no defence against six cartridges. Dennis and I could easily have overpowered him. But it wasn't him I shot. It wasn't really Fuller. The face I saw was Kelty. It was Kelty I was shooting.'

Ashley worked down his arms.

'It sounds like a Hitchcock script,' he continued. 'How can I say I shot a man who's been dead since 1982? I expect I'll be charged with murder. Manslaughter at least.'

'I suppose that's possible,' she said.

'Yes, but what do you think?' he asked. 'About what I did?'

Ashley sat back on her heels. 'I think what you did

is extremely understandable under the circumstances. Not only understandable but unavoidable, I would say inevitable. Because I know you and I know some of your history. You were acting from the sequence and landscape of your whole life. No one will ever properly know or understand that, not even you. Maybe if you tell the truth the charges could be – I don't know how they do these things – put aside in some way. Because of the circumstances. In a lot of people's eyes, you're probably a hero.'

'Yes, yes,' he said, impatient with her, sitting up to be level with her eyes. 'But we don't see things like that. You and I don't see that I was a hero.'

'How *do* you see it?'

Joss thought. 'I can't say. I feel very exposed,' he said, 'and I need some clothes or a towel or something.' He couldn't tell her about Sybil and Malcolm, not just now.

But Ashley was undressing, taking off the tracksuit she'd been wearing while she massaged him. She stood naked in front of him, simply beautiful. 'Come here,' he said, reaching for her. She lay beside him. 'I thought we were finished,' he said.

'I did too, at the time,' she said. 'But now it's all different. There are too many things happening, to me and to you. I can't build a wall against life.'

He made love to her, all the time looking into her eyes so that it was almost unbearable for both of them. At times, the figures of Sybil and Malcolm rose in his mind, the intimate gesture of his hand in her bag, the sure knowledge of her betrayal. But Ashley's face, softening and changing close to him, brought him back to where he was and what was happening.

Then Ashley had to close her eyes and so did he, and the charge flowed between them. Her words were shapeless and full of love. His were full of sadness. I have done a terrible thing, was the thought in the back of his mind, behind the sweet connection with this woman. And I must requite it. The potency of his orgasm when it surged through him was like a testament to this knowledge, as deep as the marrow of his bones.

Ashley grunted as Joss leaned over her dozing form. He checked his watch: 11.30 pm. Pulling on her tracksuit pants for something to wear he went into the kitchen, picked up the phone and dialled.

'I was just about to ring you,' said Hamish in his bright, tough voice. 'I hear you solved a major crime earlier today. One way or another. And I hear you're in deep shit.'

'Yes,' said Joss. 'Something like that.'

'And I finally heard back from my contact in Manila.'

'What?' asked Joss, his heart stilling at the name of that city.

'Young Dr Ho. Your daughter's friend. Ignatious Ho.'

*'What about him?'*

'Hey. Easy. There's absolutely nothing criminal against him. It may not even mean anything. A lot of med students use them.'

'Use what? *Hamish, use what?*' Joss found he was holding the handpiece in a crushing grip.

'It's just that his name comes up in connection with amphetamine dealers in Manila and out here. He's not a dealer, so just stay calm. Like I say, a lot of students play with speed, particularly around exam time. Especially medical students. Got that?'

Joss's voice was hoarse when he spoke. 'What do you mean,' he said, 'his name comes up in connection with? What does that mean?'

'It means that our intelligence has noticed he has had meetings with drug dealers in Manila and has bought quantities of amphetamines from these people. He buys them in small quantities. Got that?' Hamish was calm and steady. 'There's no evidence at all that he does anything except buy them for his own use. It's about as naughty as driving without a seatbelt. Okay?'

Joss stood there. He could see himself reflected in the

glass of a cabinet across the room, stupidly comical in the too-small tracksuit pants.

'Okay?' Hamish repeated.

'Okay,' said Joss.

'Listen. You've been through a lot. Get something to calm you down, settle your nerves a bit. See a doctor.' Hamish was startled at Joss's harsh laugh. He rang off.

'What is it?' Ashley asked as he walked back into her bedroom.

'Polly's boyfriend uses amphetamines.'

'A lot of people use drugs,' said Ashley. 'That's what they're for. Damian went through a period when he smoked dope.'

'But Polly's boyfriend is a doctor. A post-grad research student.'

She stared at him. 'So? You think doctors don't use drugs? Come on.'

'I shudder every time I hear the word Manila,' said Joss. 'Manila is where it all started. The clinic. The phoney student visas. The trade in human organs.'

Ashley climbed out of bed and put on her robe. 'Won't Polly be home tomorrow night? You can talk about it then.'

'I'd better go home,' he said. 'They might want me. The police.'

'Dennis will know to look for you here. Take it easy.' She moved into the bathroom.

He couldn't help feeling good about that. About Dennis finding him here. He started dressing. 'Sybil was having an affair with Malcolm,' he called to her, 'the federal officer in charge of security. He was also in charge of the change of identity for me and Polly.'

'That's horrible,' said Ashley, coming to the bedroom door.

'Our hero,' he added bitterly, putting his watch on.

'The unsecured security agent,' said Ashley. 'How awful! Women used to fall in love with their gynaecologists. Maybe something like that happened with Sybil. Maybe she felt unloved.'

Suddenly, betrayal by the woman was all around him. His mother, his wife, and now his lover?

'Ashley,' he started. 'When this is over ...' He thought of how he'd be sitting up all night with his hand around the .45, listening for the slightest sound. First thing tomorrow he would buy the killer Dobermanns. 'When this is over,' he said again when a car came around the corner too fast and stopped outside Ashley's gate. It was the Commodore. Dennis raced to the front door.

'You've got to come and have a look at this,' he said to Joss when he opened the door. 'Before the others get to it. Fuller's place.'

'Why?' said Ashley, coming up behind Joss.

'The mirrors. Come and see where the mirrors fit in.'

'Mirrors?' Ashley looked at Joss.

'I'll tell you on the way,' he said.

She ran inside to pull on her tracksuit and coat and Joss went out to the Commodore. He held the back door open for her and they took the road towards Nightingale Street, through the silent, sleeping town.

'Keep your hands in your pockets.' The street lights silvered the side of Dennis's face as he spoke. 'Don't touch anything. This is certainly not standard procedure. But you've got to see this. We can only stay a minute. Neil and Ian are dropping by on their way to Sydney – they're delivering the physical evidence to forensics in person.'

The radio came to life and a patrol told Dennis they were finishing up at the Boys' Home and were about to leave for Nightingale Street. Dennis drove faster.

They pulled up outside a low bungalow set back off the road in a half-hearted garden. The three of them walked up the path by moonlight and down the side of the house.

Dennis flashed his torch around. 'That's the back fence down there. Just behind it is the big stormwater drain that he used to jump down into to get under the city.' Joss felt Ashley shudder beside him. At the back of the house, several bits of furniture stood along the wall – a couple of old chairs and a dressing-table that had no mirror.

'As far as we've been able to find out,' said Dennis, 'Fuller came back from Sydney just a few months ago to live here with his mum. She hasn't worked for years – in her trade. Maybe she contacted him. The neighbours said she'd been sick. Maybe she needed him at home.'

The horror and the domestic, Joss thought, shivering. Home is the place, he remembered from a poem, where when you knock they have to let you in. Even Eric Fuller had a home.

They stepped up onto the verandah and Dennis opened the back door. It was unlocked, and as he opened it the stench hit them. Someone human very dead, thought Joss, remembering the distinctive odour. Dennis stepped back to let the other two through.

'I want to know which slacker didn't check this place the two occasions they were supposed to,' he said. 'Anyone with half a nostril would have been suspicious.' Ashley had her handkerchief across the lower half of her face. 'You okay?' he said to her as her eyes engaged his over the hankie. She nodded.

'Go straight through the house to the front hall. You've got to start at the front to see the set-up.'

They moved through to the centre of the house, past the tidy, old-fashioned kitchen into a small dark dining room, letting the powerful beam of Dennis's torch behind them usher them through. In a large sitting room two doors opened into the hallway.

'Now just go out that door at the end of the room and turn around,' said Dennis. 'You'll be in the hall then, just inside the front door. I've got to get some light in the main bedroom.'

He shone the light to allow them to find the door and Joss and Ashley stepped through into the hallway. Before the torchlight vanished, Joss had a chance to see that the hall runner was worn and bare, the walls badly in need of painting. The smell of death was very strong in this narrow space. He took Ashley's hand in the dark and was wondering why Dennis didn't simply turn on the lights when he heard him call out.

'Okay, fasten your seatbelts.' They heard him move and then the click of a switch. A weird light appeared to float just above eye level in the hall. Joss and Ashley looked up. He felt her stiffen and stifle a scream. Even Joss jumped. Somehow, halfway up the wall, hanging in mid-air, was the collapsed face of an old dead woman, the skin stretched dry from eye socket to collapsed mandible, so that it hung open in a jaw-dropping, soundless scream.

Joss realised he was looking at the shocking image in a mirror hanging on the wall, angled away from the front door.

'My God.' Ashley's voice was barely a whisper.

The light came on in the lounge room and they saw the next mirror, angled on the wall to pick up the reflected image from yet another mirror further up the room, closer to the top door of the lounge. There was the terrible face again. And again. Each mirror had been placed to pick up the image from the previous one and project it to the next; a portrait in semaphore of the decaying woman. They walked back through the lounge room, going where the dreadful face led them, mirror after mirror, until they came to the opposite end of the hallway. A mirror, tilted so that it picked up the image from the dressing-table mirror in the bedroom, hung just above Ashley's head.

The three living faces looked at the dead face in the hall mirror and then at its duplicate in the dressing-table mirror. They walked into the bedroom and saw the body on the bed. Her head was propped on a rolled-up towel. Fluid had drained from the open mouth and thin strands of hair spread stickily across a collapsed cheek. The eyes were sunk behind lids spotted with fungal growth. Her face, Joss thought as he stared, was like a mask, discoloured and patched with decay.

'What do you think?' Joss asked Dennis.

Dennis shrugged. 'Hard to tell. Could be murder. Could

be natural causes. We'll know soon enough. I'd say that was what kicked him off. The death of the mother.'

On a chair near the dressing-table was a hessian sack and Joss could see part of the contents: the maroon blazers, the long grey trousers. The missing clothes of the murdered children. This is where the childhood pain and hatred ends up, he thought. In the bedroom of the terrible mother. And in the mindless re-enactments carried out on other children.

Ashley left the room and Joss followed her. 'See what he's done?' she said, standing in the lounge room with the three mirrors, haunted by three different aspects of the rotting face. 'Wherever you are, anywhere in the house, you can see her. He only had to look up from any point and there she was, his mother. Mirrors are so right here. He's still telling his story, even now. Her cruelty is repeated by him in a different way. Reflected.'

Joss was thinking to the collapsed face: I killed your son. You started the process with your madness and your cruelty and I ended his life just a little while ago. He shivered in the cold of the stinking place.

'Okay? We're out of here,' Dennis called from the bedroom. They heard the click of the light and the death heads vanished.


Dennis ran them back to Ashley's place and the three of them stood under the brilliant, frosty tableland stars, pleased to be in fresh air.

'I don't know how we're going to get you out of the mess you're in,' Dennis said to Joss. 'And I've got to come up with some bullshit about that missing weapon. But I want to say that no matter what happens, you did a great job.' His eyes were shadowed under his brow, but there was warmth in his voice.

'You should be thanking Ashley,' Joss said, turning to her. 'She knew he was telling us what was done to him. She worked out the kindness pillow.'

'Maybe everything makes sense if you only know what

to look for,' said Dennis, getting back into his car. 'Don't know what's to be done about you, though,' he said.

'I won't stand up to too much scrutiny. I mean, the non-existent Joss Haskell won't,' said Joss.

Dennis swung round to lock the back doors. 'It might be a case of letting the federals do their dirty stuff,' he said. 'Let the bastards come up with some fancy way out for you. They've got the form for it. They've got away with murder in the past.'

Joss was staring at the car, which looked silver-grey in the moonlight, like his old Mercedes. He thought of someone lying underneath it, taping the explosives into place under the driver's seat, wiring them up to reverse gear. Dennis started the ignition and took off, turning out of the street. The sound of his engine hung in the air.

Joss drove home himself, wondering when he'd start feeling different now that he had the mark of Cain on his forehead.

He stopped at the mailbox, realising he hadn't checked it since the day of the postcard. In the low moonlight he put his hand into the box and drew out a letter with Sybil's crazy wrought-iron script on it. For a minute he was immobilised. So she wasn't dead. But he hated her, he hated himself. He got back into the car and switched the interior light on. The envelope was postmarked two days earlier. You might be dead yet, he thought. He ripped the envelope away and pulled out the letter. Her script tumbled over the page in a mess of mixed Cyrillic and Roman, and as he started to read it he felt his whole body soften towards her, his anger dissolve.

> *Agapi mou,*
> I don't know if you can ever forgive me. But I've found out the truth. I can't describe to you how I feel. I've made a terrible mess of things, but I swear I didn't betray you.'

Then the scribble was in Greek again and Joss could barely understand it. It was obvious she had been under great stress when she wrote it. He concentrated hard. He translated that Lombard had bought Malcolm after Alan's death, during the time Joss and Polly had changed their identity under witness protection. Then the words became a hybrid English again.

> I only went to see him again because he was the one person who knew where you and Polly were. But you weren't where you were supposed to be. The ads in the newspapers and the phone calls were his suggestion. He made the calls, I ran the ads. He wanted to know what they meant and I told him about our Sybil game. I thought I knew about hate before, but this hate I feel for him ... And I fear him. Please take great care of yourself and our daughter. He said you wouldn't believe me. But I'm praying that you will. Forgive me. I am *infidela*, but I'm not a murderer.'

He let the letter fall to the floor and put the car in gear. He wanted a drink.

He drove up the driveway past the cypresses, and parked the car at the front of the house. He barely had his door open when he heard a voice he knew very well indeed.

'Don't move,' it said. 'Listen carefully. When I've finished speaking, you may slowly get out of the car. We need your assistance. Don't do anything stupid.'

Then came the words that Joss had waited over two and a half years to hear. 'We have your daughter.'

# 17

Joss sank back in his seat. They had Polly. This time the terror was real – not the terror of anticipation but the shock of reality.

'Where's my daughter?' He felt his throat constrict. 'What have you done with her?'

'She is safe and well,' continued the voice. 'And she will stay that way if you give us your fullest cooperation.'

'You have it,' Joss said with all his heart. 'Don't harm my other child.' He didn't know what to do with his fury, the powerful feelings of hate that engulfed him in this terrible submission to them. But I must do what they say, he thought as his heart thudded. Polly must live. 'I'll do anything to ensure her safety,' he said. He inched his head around and saw the narrow barrel of an automatic pistol snouting through the door. 'I have no interest in trying anything stupid,' he said in a dull voice.

'You may get out of the car and pull both pockets inside out,' said the man. 'Slowly.'

There was nothing he could do. He slowly got out, lifted the gun out of his pocket and passed it over. He didn't look up. He didn't want to see the man who stood beside the car, holding his weapon with the ease of a professional. He needed some time before he looked him in the face, he knew that right now he could not guarantee his behaviour. Joss straightened and looked past him. He heard the man slam the car door and was surprised at the lack of fear in him, now that this worst of all things had finally happened.

'Lombard's waiting for us on the other side of the house.'

Joss's mind raced in emergency mode, the fast-forward magnesium brilliance that he remembered from the early days of the surgical team, racing along hospital corridors, arguing over procedures on the way to theatre. They hadn't killed him yet. *Why*? Maybe it would happen now.

'Where's Polly?' he said. 'I demand to see her. I'll do whatever you want but I must see that she's safe.'

'She's perfectly safe, Doctor.' The voice still neutral. Professionally polite almost. 'She's with her young friend in a safe place. He's been helpfully disposed towards us ever since we pointed out how easy it would be to get him deported as undesirable. We know about his amphetamine habit.'

'What do you want from me?' Joss asked, knowing now that they must want something or he and Polly would both be dead.

'Come inside and we'll discuss all this. We need your cooperation to deactivate that very elaborate system of yours.'

Joss stepped carefully up to the house, the other very close behind him. 'I have to get my keys out,' he said, not wanting to be cut in half from behind.

'Yes, do that. Very slowly.'

Joss retrieved his keys, opened the door and deactivated the alarm.

'Okay, now move inside and turn on the lights immediately.'

Joss did as he was told, then finally turned to face the man. 'I know about you and my wife,' he said. He noticed that Malcolm's body stilled, even though the expression on his face and in his narrow eyes didn't alter. A professional minder. A professional killer. Screw the wife and kill the husband. 'Did Sybil know you helped murder her son? Or was she too damn stupid to work that out?' He felt the rage hit and his fists balled, ready to tear and rip.

'Just move through the house and let the others in the back,' said Malcolm in his dealing-with-the-public voice, refusing to engage. Joss wouldn't have been surprised if he'd added 'sir'.

Joss opened the back door, switched the light on, and there he was, getting out of a dark green Volvo. He was lighter from his time in jail, yet somehow heavier in the face and jowls, his look a mixture of rage and triumph. The two men stared at each other for a moment, then Lombard pushed past Joss into the house. Two Japanese men followed silently. Malcolm shoved Joss in front of him into the lounge room.

'What do you want with me, Lombard?' Joss asked.

'Tell him,' said Lombard without turning round, taking great interest in the fading WAC chart over the mantelpiece. 'Tell him what our requirements are.'

'There's a little problem with surrendered passports, pending an appeal,' said Malcolm in his agreeable voice. 'You're going to take us to the airport and fly us out of the country. These two,' he indicated the Japanese, 'checked out the Navajo the other day. It'll do the job.' Joss remembered Wal's report of the men at the airport near Sierra Victor Whiskey. 'You'll take the four of us,' Malcolm went on, 'plus some baggage that I've got out at the airport. If you want your daughter to live, you'll do exactly as we ask.'

'I will do exactly as you say,' said Joss.

'Good.' Lombard's voice was contemptuous. 'Now, I could do with a drink.'

Joss's mind was working hard, running through ways to get Polly safe. What sort of deal would men like this honour? He would have to bind them with something they couldn't escape. What would they do with him once his part was finished? A bullet in the back of the head and then another in the heart as he lay on the tarmac of an unmanned landing strip?

He forced himself to move deliberately. He went to the cabinet and pulled out a bottle of scotch and one of brandy. 'Here,' he said. He fetched glasses and stood near the stove, watching as three uninvited men drank his scotch. The Japanese man with the greenish mark on his face refused. No one spoke. Joss was interested to see how very clear he was feeling, in spite of the anger. It seemed that now they had finally done the thing he feared the most, there was nothing left to fear. There was only some very good planning required to make sure Polly was safe. I am used to coping with emergencies, he thought, and taking appropriate and decisive action. This is my area of expertise. This is the time for the knife. This is the time for an intentional, surgical wound through the mess.

Joss glanced at his father's WAC chart and the sacred island of his childhood. An extraordinary idea was starting to form in his mind, breathtaking in its simplicity and danger, demanding a courage from him that he didn't dare hope he had.

He became aware that the phone was ringing. Malcolm watched as the answering machine switched on Joss's recorded voice. '... not available to take your call at the moment. Please leave any messages after the tone.'

'Joss. Pick up the phone for Chrissake, will you. Joss? *Joss*?' Dennis's voice, hard, angry. There was a pause during which Malcolm seemed to dare him to pick it up. Joss stood quite still.

'Listen, if you don't pick up the goddamn phone right now, I'm coming out there. Now.'

Malcolm gestured with the gun. 'Deal with this,' he hissed. 'Get rid of him.'

Joss walked slowly to the phone, wishing Dennis would suddenly hang up and jump into the Commodore that he drove too fast. And be out here in seven minutes to help him out of the nightmare closing around Polly and himself. But Dennis was still yelling his name, saying, 'I know you're there!' He could delay no longer. He picked up the phone.

'Yes?' he asked in a neutral voice. He was aware of Lombard's eyes blazing with the same hatred that he'd seen during the trial, the sneer that men like Lombard reserve for men like me, he thought – self-righteous, naïve fools like Doctor Ross Pascall used to be, who didn't even know they were alive. But things had changed.

'Mate,' Dennis's voice came down the line as if he were in the next room, 'I've got some double bad news. You could be in deep shit. George Lombard. In the district. Heading this way. I want to send someone over to your house.' Joss glanced over at Lombard. He was leaning forward, his face darkening. 'And there's something else,' Dennis said. 'I don't feel good telling you this on the phone.'

'Yes,' said Joss. 'I think I know already.' He felt something stinging his eyes. Tears for the woman who had suffered so much and lashed out at him in her suffering.

'The body of a woman was found on a beach near Wollongong. Your wife's car was also found abandoned at a lookout about two kilometres north.'

*Sivilla mou*, thought Joss.

'We'll have to wait for the full report,' Dennis said. But there was no hope in his voice.

'Yes,' said Joss. He could just manage the monosyllable. Had Sybil never come home from Seal Rocks? Had Malcolm met her somewhere to try and find out Joss and Polly's new whereabouts? Did she get suspicious of him? Did she blaze out at Malcolm like she used to with him? She could be quite uncontained and violent, he knew – like the several occasions on which she'd hit him hard across the head. Had Malcolm finally had enough of her volatility, especially now that he had the information he needed? Had he told her everything then, before he killed her? Joss tried not to imagine the scene, but he couldn't help turning to look at his wife's killer, now listening intently, his glass frozen in his hand, his face and features tense, straining forward like a Dobermann at the end of its leash. Did you shoot her when she wasn't looking, so that death took her by surprise? Or did she see death coming from you? You owe me two of my people, Malcolm, thought Joss. You're still responsible for Alan, even if you didn't go over until after the explosion.

'Are you sure everything's okay out there?' Dennis's voice, concerned, tired.

No, Dennis. Everything is about as bad as it can be, Joss said silently. 'All quiet here,' said Joss carefully. Malcolm was jabbing in the direction of the phone, hissing, 'Get rid of him.'

'And Polly is safe,' said Joss, desperate to convey his situation to his colleague.

'What?' asked Dennis and Joss could hear the younger man's familiar irritation. Get irritated, Dennis. Get really irritated and get out here with four cars.

'I said I'm safe and Polly is safe and I'm very tired,' said Joss steadily. He prayed that Dennis was as smart as he'd always believed he was. 'She's camping at Barrington Tops with Ignatius Ho, her boyfriend.' Malcolm had put his drink down and was coming at him, but Joss knew he had the advantage here. He swung round to face Malcolm fully and added, *'Ring Hamish if you're worried.'* He gripped the phone, willing Dennis to get it, to ring Hamish. Malcolm hissed again, jerking the gun.

'It's been a long day, Dennis,' he said. 'Good night.' He hung up.

'Who was that?' asked Lombard.

Joss took some pleasure in his answer. 'The detective sergeant I've been working with on a recent investigation.'

Lombard snorted. 'That's right. You became a real crime fighter, didn't you, Doctor, in your new life.' He put down his drink and opened a briefcase. 'If the detective sergeant comes out here, we'll deal with him.' Then he pulled out another WAC chart and spread it on the table. 'This is where we're refuelling.' He jabbed at a place on the map. Joss looked at it: Northern Territory, remote. It would be.

'I need to get my flight bag,' he said. 'I need the airfield manual and my gear.'

Lombard nodded grudgingly and Malcolm followed him into the study. He went to the cupboard where his pilot's bag was stored, wishing he had a double-barrel shotgun standing in a dark corner. He pulled out his bag and came back to the others, aware of Malcolm treading close behind him. He shivered. It reminded him of the days in the house at Woollahra, when his family was twice as big as it was now. He put the bag down on the coffee table and dug out the book of airfield diagrams, flipping through them until he'd located the airfield. It was of course a private one, running north-south, situated about thirty kilometres out of Darwin.

'Belongs to a friend of mine,' Lombard was saying. He passed Joss another map with the rural airstrip marked in more detail. Malcolm was swirling the last of his scotch around in his glass, just prior to throwing it down his throat, perfectly relaxed again except for his eyes, dark and watchful over the brim.

'Okay,' said Lombard, looking around in satisfaction. 'We've obtained the service of our pilot. Let's get going.'

Joss interrupted. 'I think it would be a good idea for me to take my medical bag as well.' Lombard gave him a searching look, then finally relented.

Malcolm followed Joss upstairs. 'Don't be a hero, will you, Doctor,' he said as they reached the landing. 'You're no good at it, anyway,' he added and Joss felt the professional mask drop away from his rival.

Joss switched the bedroom light on and Alan's photograph looked straight at them from the top of the chest of drawers.

'You remember Alan, Malcolm. That's my son. That's the fourteen-year-old boy your boss murdered.'

'Get the bag.'

'If you didn't do it yourself. You sold yourself, Malcolm. To someone like George Lombard. I hope he paid you enough.'

'Just get the fucking bag.'

'You're an arse-licker, Malcolm. You bend over for Lombard.'

'Just get the bag, you fuck!'

Joss opened the end door of his wardrobe where his medical bag lay, unused in over two years. He lifted it out and straightened up. 'Tell me about Sybil,' he said. 'How did you kill my wife?'

Malcolm lifted his chin so that he looked down his nose at Joss. The neutral, careful, professional policeman's voice had completely gone. 'You,' he snarled, 'downstairs. Now.'

Twelve minutes later, they pulled up at the airport. A few lights on the corners of hangars and outbuildings created hemispheres of light beneath them, like the markings on a basketball court. The shadows they threw beyond the buildings and trees were darker than night. Joss thought of Wal. He prayed he was sleeping in his office. Then he prayed he wasn't, because he could imagine what would happen if Wal came stumbling out of his room.

Joss got out of the car and Malcolm was behind him before he could move. 'I want to check the office,' Joss said. 'There are some things I need.'

Malcolm shadowed him over to the low building which housed Wal's office. A night wind caused the halyards on the flagpole to tap out a meaningless code. Joss walked past the window. In the light of the caged lamp above the eaves he could see with relief that Wal's office was empty. 'Resist what feels right. Don't turn back,' declared a poster on the wall. No fear of that, thought Joss. Not now.

Malcolm used a piece of plastic on the locked aeroclub door and it opened easily. Joss turned to see Lombard and the man with the marked face coming inside behind them, carrying heavy baggage. He switched a light on, praying that someone would notice, would call the police. But everyone in town was used to Wal pottering around the airfield at night. Joss weighed the suitcases and did the fuel calculations. Then he checked the contents of his medical bag on automatic: bandages, paraffin gauze, swabs, Hibitane, Xylocaine, Valium, Lasix, pre-threaded needles, scalpel blades, scissors, forceps, needle holder, all wrapped in sterile towelling in a kidney dish. He seemed to have a lot of the tranquilliser, intravenous Prosac. He took a swig of Catovit, then closed the bag and placed it with the others. He didn't know how many hours he'd have to stay alert. He went to the bar area and picked up the phone.

'Weather,' he said to Malcolm, who was beside him in a flash, grabbing his forearm. Malcolm listened while he dialled. It was a good night for flying – except for the fact that the pilot was exhausted, despite the stimulant he'd just taken. Joss was running on adrenalin, the high-voltage nervous energy that had always carried him through impossibly long surgical procedures. He got out his charts, spread them on the table and pencilled in a flight plan to the airfield.

Malcolm seemed edgy now. Lombard was impatiently wiping his brow and Joss was pleased to see that his enemy was sweating, in spite of the cold. Lombard shoved his handkerchief into the pocket of his expensive suit: on the run and well dressed. There had been a subtle shift in the balance of power, thought Joss. Of course Lombard had him, because Lombard had Polly. But he, Joss, also had Lombard, with his unrestricted twin-engine endorsement and the leased Navajo only a few metres away. The two of them were locked together.

Lombard looked startled when Joss spoke. 'This is what I want you to do about my daughter Polly, or there's no deal. These are the only circumstances under which I fly for you people. Understand?' He felt he was standing on rock and the rock was in his belly as well. He was aware of their attention. 'Polly and Ignatius Ho must be waiting for us at that airport of yours, Lombard.' He jabbed the map with a finger. 'And if they're not there, I don't fly any further. There is no negotiation about that. That is my offer. I will do exactly as you say, but Polly and Ignatius Ho must be in Darwin. I want my daughter given into the care of someone I trust. I don't care if you shoot me. And if you harm Polly, do you think I'd fly for you then?'

These men, he was thinking, had come into his life and destroyed his family. He looked around at them: Lombard frowning, trying to move past the ultimatum, trying to find a way to outdeal; Malcolm intent, trying to find the weak spot, the place he could attack from.

'Who's the person you want in Darwin?' demanded Malcolm after a heavy silence.

Joss ignored the question for the moment. 'Polly is to be handed over to this person and the switch has to be done in a way that I can see is safe. With my own eyes. As soon as I see Polly and that person in the same car, driving away from this aircraft, and as soon as I have all you people on board, including Ho, I'll take off. These are the only circumstances under which I will fly you. If Ho objects in any way, deal with him. He is not staying in Australia to endanger my daughter further. That's the deal. You can shoot me, but you can't make me fly this aircraft.' He saw that the men were listening closely. 'Do these things and I'll cooperate in any way you want,' he added to sweeten the deal.

'Who is the other party?' Malcolm asked again.

'Ashley Smith,' said Joss. 'My friend in town.'

'Who's that?' Lombard wanted to know.

'The woman he's on with,' said Malcolm, who knew everything. 'She's some sort of counsellor. She won't give us any trouble.' Joss nearly smiled to hear the woman who knew the monsters by their names dismissed so lightly.

Malcolm and Lombard walked away to confer by the windows. Joss heard '... don't need her, she knows nothing,' and felt relief. But then he heard Lombard say something that ended '... can be dealt with later.'

Until now, different possibilities had stayed fluid in Joss's imagination. But those words made him realise that there was no end to this business, that Lombard and Malcolm and their foreign cohorts would never let up, would never relinquish any position from which they might continue to advance the cause of suffering in the world. That was how they were. Joss knew they would never let him go. They could have bought a dozen people to get them out of the country. There was only one reason they'd come for him.

'Yeah, yeah, we'll arrange that,' Lombard was saying to Malcolm. 'Telephone Ho, tell him to get to Darwin with the girl.'

As Malcolm reached for the telephone, Joss put out a hand. 'Let me speak to my daughter,' he said. 'I will not leave this building without speaking to her.' In his voice was the non-negotiable quality of the man who has nothing left to lose and thus is able to make his stand in the emptiness.

Lombard and Malcolm looked at each other. Joss saw Lombard's slight nod. Malcolm dialled and waited. Joss moved closer and heard Ignatius Ho's voice answer, scared when he heard who it was, then subservient, out of his depth. The spoon can never be long enough, Ignatius, Joss wished he could tell him. While ever the other end is in the devil's dish.

'Put the girl on,' Malcolm commanded. 'Her father wants to speak to her.'

He passed Joss the telephone.

'Dad? Dad? Oh Dad, are you all right?' He could not believe how good it was to hear his daughter's voice. His Polly.

'I'm fine, Polly. How about you?'

'I'm okay. I'm scared. Ignatius told me what's happening. He's just so vile I don't know what ...' Joss could hear the contempt in her voice, her loss for words not quite hiding the pain of betrayal. 'I can't believe he can do this! What's more, it was *him* who took the Celica that morning. To make a deal. A bloody deal.' Her voice had the pouncing quality he remembered from when she was very young and something struck her as most unfair. Darling, angry, brave Polly. 'They were going to tell his parents about the speed he uses. He's *pathetic*! He says his father would kill him if he found out. I wish he would!'

Joss held the phone hard against his face. 'Just do everything they tell you, Poll. I have to fly them out of the country. They say they'll let me go after that. Ashley will be at the airfield when I land in –' Malcolm was lunging to take the handpiece from him. Joss swung away.

'Oh Dad.' He heard the pain in her voice. 'They're not like that. They'll kill you.' Her voice cracked.

'Poll,' he added in a voice so neutral he wondered if she'd ever pick it up, '*Samsura*.'

'What?' she said.

Malcolm snatched the phone from him and cut him off.

Fear, sorrow and regret mixed with something hard and brilliant. 'I need to make another call,' he said to Malcolm, who stood with the phone in his hard. 'To Miss Smith.' He stood unmoving while Malcolm looked at Lombard again.

Malcolm handed back the phone, then addressed his boss. 'I'll go round there now and go to Darwin with her. I'll charter something first thing in the morning.'

Of course they wouldn't just let Ashley act alone. Malcolm would have to go with her, Joss realised. Malcolm the minder.

Lombard was furious at this change in their plans. It could be seen in the way the ridges of his face swelled and in the way he glared at Joss. But he was smart and his whirring brain could see no other way. 'You've never been anything but a bloody problem to me,' Lombard snarled. And Joss could see in his eyes that he was cherishing the moment when he would give Malcolm the command to kill the pilot.

Joss dialled Ashley's number. Although he knew he had woken her up, her voice was alert and she listened intently.

'I don't know how to say this,' he said. 'I know it will seem extraordinary, and it is. But I beg you to do as I ask. Just do it without understanding. My life and Polly's life and I suppose your own now, depend on this. Shortly a man I know, Malcolm,' she will be able to put a lot of this together now, Joss thought, 'will be arriving at your place and will take you north to Darwin.'

'Darwin?' Disbelief, shock. 'Joss, what's going on?'

'At Darwin you'll find me and some other people waiting. Polly will be there. Malcolm will leave a car for you and Polly. Then he'll join me and the others in the Navajo. You and Poll will be free to go home. I won't do what they want unless you and Poll are free to go.' He kept his voice low and ordinary, so that the shocking content of his words would not startle her further. 'Do you understand what I'm saying?'

307

'No,' she was saying, 'I don't. I don't understand. What's happening? Is it the people who sent the postcard?'

'Yes. I just need your agreement that you'll do this for me and Polly. Will you?'

She didn't reply. He prayed she would act for him, for Polly.

'Okay. That's enough.' Malcolm grabbed the phone and interrupted. 'I'll be at your place immediately,' he told Ashley. 'Stay talking to me or your boyfriend dies. Got it?'

There was a silence and Joss wondered what it was that Ashley had said.

'You'll find plenty of things to say, Miss Smith. You can sing to me.'

Joss looked into Malcolm's eyes. Was that triumph? Was that 'I've got your other woman now'? Those eyes had examined Joss's house in Woollahra, advising on security systems, assuring both the doctor and his wife of his protection, always there, always looking. Checking the doorbell, the deliveries, the phone calls, the mail. Malcolm, their minder, their saviour.

Then those eyes on Sybil. Her tawny body with the dark lion shadows near her armpits and groin. Those narrow lips had kissed Sybil's mouth, her breasts, between her legs. Joss noticed that Malcolm's eyes were unflinching. This is a killer who pretends that what he does is just a job. I might have had to live in your garage at one stage, Doctor, those hard eyes seemed to say, but I've fucked your wife and she was hot.

Malcolm left the clubhouse and Joss heard him drive off. Lombard had to go with Joss now, across the tarmac to where the Navajo gleamed. Joss pulled a powerful flashlight out of his bag and walked around the plane, tapping the fuel line, checking tyres and control wires. He unlocked the Navajo and stepped up inside. Usually he loved the smell of this aircraft, the fittings, the carpet, its faint unique perfume, but now it failed to register. He wondered whether Dennis had contacted Hamish as he'd suggested, had discovered Ignatius Ho's interest in amphetamines. He sat in the pilot's seat, thinking. Dennis was a good cop. He was curious. He liked making up what-ifs. Liked trying to fit things together. What if he found that his ex-hypnotherapist had vanished from town with a strange man who turned out to be an ex-federal police officer? Wouldn't his colleague Dennis, that honours graduate from suspicion school, start asking some of the right questions?

He prayed that Dennis was as good as he hoped he was.

He was aware of the heavy presence of Lombard and the Japanese men as he put the Navajo through the pre-flight checks. He looked out into the darkness that surrounded the aircraft. He wanted to pray, but it had been such a long time that he didn't remember how. He thought of his parents, his wounded father, the depressed mother who could not cope. He had a lot of dead that he must pray for. That was something I could have relearned, he thought, in the next little while – if they'd been the sort of men to let me go after they'd finished with me. I could have offered gifts to a Buddhist monk, made an offering to a priest, and the dead would be free to continue their mysterious journey. And I would be relieved.

'Tell your friends I have to get some sleep,' he said when he'd finished the routine. 'It's a long flight to Darwin. Pilot error is the largest single cause of aircraft crashes. Pilots make mistakes when they're exhausted.' He enjoyed saying this. He leaned back against the seat and dozed.

At 5.10 in the morning Joss woke and looked around. One of the Japanese was standing on the tarmac. Joss could just discern him against the slight lightening of the eastern sky. The other Japanese man lolled in the seat directly behind Joss, a semi-automatic pistol visible under his jacket. He woke as soon as Joss stirred. Lombard was still awkwardly asleep across two seats, an arm hanging down into the aisle as if he were a dead man. Joss pushed past him, enjoying Lombard's fright as he woke suddenly.

'Get back here,' he yelled and the Japanese man appeared behind him.

'Nature calls,' said Joss and he realised he was feeling almost cheerful. It was a cold, still morning. The moon was almost down in the west. He went into the clubhouse with the birthmarked man following him. In the bathroom he urinated and washed himself. He walked back to the aircraft where he could hear Lombard talking with Malcolm on his mobile.

When they had reboarded, Joss checked the door at the back of the plane – the Navajo's only door – and went up to the pilot's seat. He checked that his waterbottle was filled. He took a deep breath and pushed the key into the ignition. He wouldn't be ringing a flight plan through for this journey. He turned the first engine on, then the second, letting them warm up while he did a final cabin check. He listened to the weather report and finally taxied onto the runway. The windsock hung limp in the grey light. It was a pity there was no fog. That would have made his companions nervous, sitting here in the mist.

He brought the Navajo to a standstill again and did a final check on the time and weather. Fine and clear, said the recorded information, some cloud around the tablelands. He taxied out and down to the end of the airfield, turning and pointing into the north-west hills. This long first leg would bring them, according to his calculations and depending on the direction of the winds over the continent, to their destination at around 2 pm. Joss gave both engines full throttle and the plane surged forward.

Mid-morning and the Navajo flew steadily towards the centre of Australia. It was a clear winter's day and there was little turbulence. Joss was aware of the commercial airliners thousands of feet above him. He wondered which flight Malcolm and Ashley would take, and Polly and Ho. With the aircraft on autopilot, he leafed through the manual to refresh his memory. He checked the whereabouts of the master fuel switch. He traced the diagram of the radio and found the isolating switch. He would need the radio till shortly after taking off again. At the back of the manual was a list of emergency procedures. In the case of a sudden loss of power, he read, the Navajo had an approximate glide of six miles. He looked over the sequences of a deadstick landing. He'd made several unpowered landings in the single-engined Cherokee, but both times he'd had Wal in the seat beside him. Now he had Lombard. He had never landed the Navajo without power.

Joss put the aircraft down on a badly corrugated runway cut short by hazard markers and several stringy-looking bullocks who'd come through the fence of the adjoining paddock. He taxied to a halt a hundred metres from a small demountable building and switched off the ignition. He looked across at Lombard. There was a fine mist of sweat over the heavy features, despite the coolness of the cabin. Lombard was not travelling well. He did not like the shift of power. He did not like another man in the pilot's seat.

Behind him, Joss couldn't tell if the Japanese were asleep or awake.

'Stay here,' said Lombard, putting his jacket on over the automatic pistol. He eased himself out of his seat and walked down the aisle. He tried to open the door and failed. He didn't like that, either.

Joss came down and opened it for him. 'There's a trick to it,' he said to Lombard.

'You know that if you try anything stupid once we've done the switch – '

'Stupid like what?' asked Joss.

'Stupid like refusing to take off, or getting out of this plane and running – there are any number of stupid things you might consider. I want you to know that if you do any of them, I'll make it my personal business that your daughter dies in front of you. Either here or in Manila. That's all. Understand I can make radio contact with people all over.

I only have to give the word and your daughter is as good as dead. So nothing smart like putting this plane down somewhere else. Understand?'

Joss nodded. 'I understand,' he said.

'Good,' said Lombard. 'It's good that we understand each other.'

He got out of the Navajo and walked towards the demountable. Joss watched him step up to the front door and unlock it. The building looked like stockmen's quarters. Joss glanced around. The runway was in the centre of a huge paddock. About a kilometre away was a cottage on the dirt road that led down to the strip, and beyond that was a sealed road. But at 2.30 on a Saturday afternoon outside Darwin, not much was happening on it.

Lombard was walking out of the demountable, speaking on his mobile. 'They're on the way,' he said to his men through the door of the aircraft. He pointed at two tarpaulin-covered drums, a pump and lines. 'You can refuel here,' he grunted at Joss.

As he stood in the shadow cast by the Navajo, Joss had the impression of being in a mirage. Above, the sky was a thin blue. The demountable had the look of a hollow set from a film. Lombard was pacing anxiously, picking his teeth on a piece of grass, his expensive suit jacket open to reveal his gun. Joss felt disembodied standing in that strange landscape where thin cattle watched through a fence draped with the rotting inner tube of a tractor tyre; he felt that he would shortly find himself back in his real life. But then again, his real life seemed so unstable now that it couldn't possibly be any more real than this Salvador Dali airstrip.

As he was completing the refuelling he heard a car. He looked up and saw a white Jaguar lurching down the dirt track past the cottage, closely followed by a small red Nissan. Lombard moved off to take up position on the verandah of the demountable. 'I don't want any dialogue here,' he said. 'Just stay right back near the plane.' He put his hand on his gun.

The Jaguar came right up to the building and Joss strained to see through the tinted window. Malcolm climbed out. So that's where Ashley was. The Nissan came to a halt and Ignatius Ho got out of the driver's side. Then Joss's heart lifted to see the back door open and Polly step out, looking hesitantly around.

'Dad?' she cried when she caught sight of him. He hadn't heard that tone in fifteen years, he could hear the tears hiding in her voice.

Then she was off and running towards Joss before Ignatius Ho had a chance to stop her, but Malcolm was faster and Joss saw how Polly was jerked to a standstill, mid-step, her arms reaching out. Joss found himself tearing towards her, to where Malcolm's grasp on Polly's sleeve was crushing her arm. 'Don't touch me!' she yelled, his fierce, brave daughter. She struggled against Malcolm, who slid his hand down to her wrist. He grabbed the other one and pulled both of them behind her back.

'Stop right there, Pascall,' Lombard yelled. He had his gun, supported by both hands, directed at Joss. Ignatius Ho was running towards Polly and Malcolm. Joss stopped short a couple of metres from his daughter, where she struggled in Malcolm's grip.

'Get back,' Malcolm snarled at Joss. 'Get back to the aircraft.' Ignatius Ho was suddenly there, remonstrating with Malcolm, telling Polly to calm down.

'Dad!' Polly screamed in pain as Malcolm twisted both her wrists.

'I'll kill you!' Joss thundered, hurling himself at Malcolm, going for his neck. Polly broke away and flung herself around her father. Lombard screeched something from behind. The sharp crack of a pistol split the air. Ignatius Ho screamed. Joss stumbled as Malcolm tore his hands from his neck and was just able to push his head near his daughter's ear as the butt of a gun grazed his cheek. '*Samsura, the island,*' he said before Malcolm pushed the gun hard into his left kidney and yanked his arm up behind his back.

'Dad!'

'I'm all right. I'm all right, Poll,' he yelled as Malcolm frogmarched him to the Navajo.

When he swivelled back, pulling against Malcolm's brutal hold, he saw that Ashley had taken Polly's hand and was leading her away towards the Nissan. Ignatius Ho lay flung out on his stomach like a doll, his only movement a tremor in the lower body and a bright stream flooding out from underneath him. Joss saw Lombard looking at the two women as they scrambled into the car, then take a few steps towards them.

'Don't you touch them, Lombard!' Joss yelled. 'You touch them and there's no way this aircraft gets off the ground. Let them go!'

The Nissan kangarooed forward and screeched in a tight turn as Ashley gunned the motor. The last sight Joss had of his daughter was her stricken face pressed hard against the window, tears streaming down, still calling after him.

Then there was a new sound. A car had appeared on the main road and was approaching the cottage. Joss mentally urged it to move faster. Was this someone investigating the sound of shooting? Or, and Joss's heart froze at the alternative, was it another of Lombard's hired murderers? Lombard's response gave him the answer.

'Fucking hell!' he cursed. 'Get in the bloody plane!' He started running towards the Navajo and Malcolm shoved Joss through the door. He jumped up behind him, followed promptly by Lombard.

'Get this fucking thing off the ground,' Lombard was saying, looking anxiously out the tiny window. 'Get a move on. Get up!' he roared. 'Do your map reading later.' Joss turned to encounter his enemy's eyes. 'I can have Malcolm off this aircraft,' Lombard reminded him. 'I can make a phone call right now,' he threatened. 'Those two women won't be hard to find.'

Joss started the two engines up, taxied out onto the rough runway, and then on full throttle rattled down the strip, past the body of Ignatius Ho sprawled beside two pools of blood, one bright, one dark, until the airspeed was sufficient to lift the Navajo's nose off the ground.

The coast was only a few miles north and then there was the long hop across the Celebes to the South China Sea. He thought of his father's WAC chart and wished he'd brought it on this flight.

On the first turn, which he made right at the edge of the aircraft's limit, Joss was pleased to hear Lombard groan with discomfort. The steep bank had put him almost on top of the road and two racing police cars.

'Nothing to do with us,' Malcolm said, watching. 'Territory cops.' Joss continued to climb, heading north. He hoped Dennis Johnson was every bit as smart as he remembered.

But for every hundred cops as clean and smart as Dennis, there was a Malcolm, thought Joss. And as long as there were men like Malcolm, criminals like Lombard could buy their way out of any problem, in any country. And even if Dennis Johnson was putting his what-ifs together and alerting his counterpart in Manila, contacting Interpol, Lombard would be contacting his equivalent of Malcolm in the Philippines police force, the friends in high places with the money and the power. The judges and the government officials who would smooth things over, lose files, remove records, organise passports and papers. And do all this simply for a sum of money. Men like Dennis have no show against men like Malcolm, Joss knew. And men like I was are worse than powerless against men like Lombard.

Five hours later, they were cruising north. The sun was low in the sky; it would set in an hour or so. There had been some turbulence at the start of the flight, but once the Navajo settled down above the misty cloud the two Lycoming engines sang. Underneath them lay an immense greyblueness. Occasional specks and blots of larger land masses dotted the wrinkled sea.

Joss exhaled and turned his neck one way then the other.

It was freer than he could ever remember. His mind felt clear and cool. Although he was frightened he was excited about this next step. He thought of the time Wal had switched the ignition of the Cherokee off and put the key in his pocket. 'Okay,' Wal said as the engine died, 'you've just lost all your power. What are you going to do? Where's your emergency landing field?' Wal had made him glide for a while, controlling the descending plane with rudder and flaps. Joss recalled searching desperately for a place to put down in that summer tableland with the winding river, the only sound the high wind outside and the creak of the Cherokee as it glided, cradled in air.

But this was a very different place and situation. If his calculations were off and he had to put it down on the water, he didn't think there would be much floating time; the two heavy engines would surely tip the aircraft forward. He knew there were sharks. And it would be hard later on, he knew, if the landing were successful.

He turned around briefly. Behind him, the two Japanese had fallen asleep and Malcolm had been silent for some time. Even Lombard appeared to be dozing on Joss's right. He glanced at the map, then peered down nine thousand feet. The island of Samsura should be only about seven nautical miles away, in the hazy sea. He glanced at the heavy man beside him. Joss could see the glimmer of eyes under stubby lashes, but Lombard's lower jaw had dropped. He looked at his calculations pencilled on the map. The time to act was now.

Cautiously, Joss put his hand out and felt under the control panel for the switch that isolated the radio from the battery. He pushed it across to 'off' and withdrew his hand. Now, no matter how much he worked the radio, he would find only silence. He glanced at Lombard. The slitted eyes did not move beneath the lashes and the big man's stomach was moving slowly up and down. A slight turn of his head allowed Joss to see that Malcolm was out of the line of vision, resting back in his seat. Slowly, Joss reached behind him with his right hand. He found the fuel shut-off valve and turned it silently, carefully. Lombard didn't move. No one stirred behind him. The Navajo flew untroubled through the rose-coloured sky.

It would all start to happen now. Perhaps he should make a formal declaration, he thought. With his ambush he recognised he was carrying out the first and only rule of war: hit the enemy when they least expect it, where they least expect it, and with everything you've got.

# 18

It seemed to take a long time in Joss's heightened state for the fuel pressure light to wink red. The dials dropped to zero. He felt a shiver of fear. This is it, he thought.

Within seconds the starboard engine was starved of fuel, failed to deliver its 310 horsepower, backfired once, then stopped. The propeller became visible, its three petals windmilling. The backfire woke Lombard, who sat up with a jerk.

'What's that?' he asked. 'What's happening?'

'We seem to have lost power in one engine,' said Joss, automatically altering the trim. 'I'll try and start it again. Maybe a little blockage in the fuel line.' The surprised pilot, doing what is necessary to cope with engine failure.

'I can see the bloody propeller!' cried Lombard, pointing at the windmilling tri-star.

'I'm trying to start it,' Joss answered, and the tension in his voice was no act. As he spoke, the port engine coughed and its propeller danced, sometimes blurring into action, other times clearly visible. The first engine started up again briefly, so that the stereo sound of the motors resumed, then cut to mono, then both cut out together as the second engine stopped delivering forward thrust and settled down to windmill like its twin on the starboard wing. The sudden silencing of the engines, the fifty-knot drop in airspeed, the change in altitude was shocking. Now there was only the sound of windrush at a hundred and thirty knots dragging on the propellers.

'Do something!' Lombard shouted, staring at the dawdling propeller on the starboard motor. Joss felt the cabin of the Navajo surge alive with tension as the five people on board leaned forward anxiously in their seats. He could feel their fear. It mixed with his own, and his excitement.

'What's that red light?' Lombard asked, pointing to the fuel pressure gauge.

'It means there's no fuel pressure – no fuel's getting to the engines,' explained Joss.

'Why?' demanded Lombard. 'Why is no fuel getting to the fucking engines?'

'I can't understand it,' said Joss. 'There's plenty of fuel in both tanks.'

Lombard was straining to make sense of the alien controls.

'The radio,' said Malcolm. 'Tell someone where we are.' He leaned across and Joss felt the pistol hard above his right ear. Malcolm grabbed the WAC chart. He jabbed at it. 'Tell someone where we are. *Do it.*'

Ignoring the bruising end of the pistol and keeping his head perfectly still, Joss reached his hand over to the radio and switched it on. Silence. He fiddled with the dial, moving up and down the frequencies.

'Turn the fucker up!' screamed Lombard. 'Where is everyone?'

Joss turned the volume control. There was nothing. No static, no strange noises, just the silence of a dead radio.

'Whatever's stopped the fuel pressure seems to have stopped the radio,' he said, fearful that part of his head might be shot off in Malcolm's rage. 'It's dead. I don't understand.'

'Give it to me,' hissed Malcolm, transferring the pistol into his left hand and pushing his way forward. He switched the radio on and off, moving the frequency dial. 'Shit!' he swore.

'Get this thing flying again!' The sharp edge of fear in Lombard's voice cut through the dead silence of the cabin. 'You're the pilot. *Do it!*'

Joss felt their panic. It cooled him. 'I'd be able to concentrate better without a gun in my ear.'

'Put the fucking thing down, Malcolm.' Lombard's command sprayed Joss with saliva. The cruel pressure on

Joss's skull was relieved; he could hear Malcolm's hard breathing. The Japanese made explosive sounds in the back.

Joss ran through a repetoire of plausible actions, switching the fuel booster pumps on and off, moving the mixture control to full-rich, moving the throttle. Nothing happened. The Navajo continued to glide forward, losing altitude as the heavy drag of the windmilling propellers resisted air.

*'What are you going to do?'* Lombard's voice was close to hysteria.

'I'm going to have to put it down somewhere,' said Joss, keeping his own voice steady and low. 'An emergency landing. And I don't need a panicking passenger. And I don't need a man with a gun pointed at me.' Now he was really in charge. Now *he* had *them*.

'Landing?' screamed Lombard. 'Where the fuck?' He was craning to look down at the wrinkled sea beneath them. It was much closer than it had been, the texture more richly detailed than only seconds before.

Joss moved the propeller pitch control to full feather so that the blades edged into the airflow, offering the least resistance. There was an immediate and noticeable easing of the steep glide and this brought with it some amelioration of the terror in the cabin.

The Japanese voices fell silent. 'Damn you, you stupid bastard!' screamed Lombard. 'Why can't we make radio contact? You fuck everything you touch. You're a fucking loser, Pascalll.'

Joss concentrated on trim. The Navajo was gliding fast, but the angle of descent was less sharp since he'd feathered the blades. He was thinking about losers and loss. I didn't lose my family, Joss thought. This thug beside me murdered them, him and his mercenaries. He was aware of the silent bulk of Malcolm sitting behind his boss and it somehow seemed fitting and right that the three of them should be on this final flight together.

The Navajo fell steadily through a few thin clouds and Joss blinked to clear his eyes. And then he could see it ahead, Samsura, a smudge in the misty water. He frowned, concentrating.

'You did this on purpose!' Malcolm's voice came from the seat behind his boss. 'Didn't you? You set this up.'

Joss turned. Malcolm, hard and controlled, stared from behind the narrow barrel of his .45.

'What are you going to do with that, Malcolm?' said Joss. 'Shoot the pilot? Have you ever done a deadstick landing in a Navajo on an island in the middle of the ocean?'

'You haven't either, you fuck!'

Joss turned back. Obscenity aside, Malcolm was dead right. He remembered Wal saying, 'It's always the same goal, whatever the conditions, put it down safe. Powered or unpowered, airstrip or no airstrip, fuel or no fuel. Put it down safe.' Their airspeed now was a hundred and twenty knots, altitude twenty-five hundred feet above the South China Sea. He peered at the landform ahead – very small, perhaps five kilometres long, two kilometres wide. He had never imagined it so small.

'Where?' screamed Lombard, looking at the vastness of the sunset sea. 'Where are you going to put it down? What fucking island?'

After his question came a silence so profound that Joss could almost see the thoughts in his passengers' heads crowding the air of the cabin. Outside, the roar of windrush and the whine of taut control lines made a dense backdrop of sound to the eerie silence. The Navajo rocked through turbulence on its inexorable descent. Beside him, Lombard, leaning forward in despair, had fastened his attention on the island he had finally caught sight of ahead, as if by sheer will he could force the land to receive the plane without incident. His expensive Italian suit coat shone in folds across his belly in the low sun.

Joss gathered himself up for the approach. This was like the moment of the cut. The surgical wound had to be exact, perfectly clean, the opposite of the messy wounds of injury. The Navajo sliced forward, Joss guiding it as he would a scalpel.

He was nine hundred feet above the sea. Samsura was rushing up to meet him, lying on a sea of liquid gold. Joss thought the misty isles of Avalon could not have been more beautiful than Samsura with the mauve sky floating behind it. Six hundred feet and he lowered the flaps, dragging the air, slowing the aircraft. He was aiming for a touchdown speed of about ninety-five knots, but he was still too high and too fast and there was no way he could go round again. The island opened out and flattened, rushing under him. This was it. Sand, trees, a beach, rocks, vegetation. This was the first and last approach. As he lowered the gear, someone cried out in terror at the clunk and thud, and the Navajo slowed a little more. Below, the tops of palm trees sped towards him, and beyond this racing mass of green he could see his father's airstrip, cutting through the vegetation. He knew that many of these island airstrips were still landable; he prayed that this was one of them.

'Get down,' he called out to the others. 'Put your heads between your knees. Arms over your heads. When we're on the ground, get away from the plane as fast as possible. There's the rear door that you came in, and this canopy above my head pushes out.' Somewhere, he recognised he had a duty of care for his prisoners of war. He concentrated like he'd never done in his life before. He felt benevolent, in this extreme moment. 'Good luck!' he yelled.

Beside him, Lombard was doubled over. There was a second when Joss thought of putting something between himself and the stick, but there was no time now and he was going to hit his father's strip at a hundred and five knots an hour. With luck, the trees flying forwards to meet him might shear off one or both wings and bring the Navajo to a slower stop, but he knew the aircraft might just as easily explode on impact, particularly if the gear collapsed and it screamed along the hard surface, spraying white-hot sparks through vaporising fuel.

Tree tips lashed the aircraft, whipping it, bouncing it. Suddenly Lombard was bolt upright again, trying to hold himself away from the expected impact.

'Get down!' Joss screamed. He had a sense of Malcolm bulked over in the seat behind his boss. Then all his attention was concentrated ahead again. He eased the stick, rounding out. The smashing treetops suddenly cleared and there was the airstrip rushing much too fast to meet him, palm trees far too close and racing towards him from the far end. He was already nearly halfway over the strip; he was overshooting hard. Trees loomed up, light and dark flashing together. The aircraft shuddered, the weird rush of unpowered metal through air at over a hundred knots an hour.

At the last moment he had to fight the desire to close his eyes, fearing the fireball of crash, burn and die. Thinking in a second we – should – hit – about – *still far too high and here's the metallic surface, right in front* – right under – should – hit – *NOW*.

Screaming. Swearing somewhere. The crushing grip of his hands on the stick. Let it go, let it go, he ordered himself, remembering the broken wrists of dead pilots. He stood on the brakes as the earth hit them with a tremendous crash. The impact of his body hitting harness at a hundred knots an hour, something sharp jabbing his side, the breath hurled from his body, the sound of a sharp explosion close by – he prayed it wasn't a tank. Lombard flying forward, crashing face first into the instrument panel. The screeching sound of metal tearing as the undercarriage leg collapsed under him. The whole world skewing to the left. Suddenly dark, the windscreen jammed with trees. A sickening jolt forwards and the airplane stopped. Joss was whipped back, winded, against the seat, then thrown forward to collide again with the harness.

He came to in the shock of stillness, the sound of fluid swilling in pipes and lines, the stench of avgas. The impact had winded him, smashed him. He choked and breathed, scrabbling to unbuckle his belt, every second waiting for the explosion that would cremate them all. He felt a burn where the harness had caught him. He struggled free of it somehow and went over his body in a quick check.

Nothing seemed broken. His wrists eventually responded to commands, though his fingers felt a little numb. There was a soft ache near his spleen. He turned to see behind him.

The rear door didn't exist any more, nor did much of the aircraft beyond it; there was nothing but buckled metal and seats and a profusion of trees. The birthmarked Japanese, still belted in his seat at an acute angle, sat staring stupidly. The seat where the second Japanese had sat was gone entirely, along with its occupant. Lombard was still slumped against the panel, the neck and upper back of his expensive suit blood-soaked. Joss reached out and felt for a pulse on the hand that hung limp near the tilted seat. Nothing. He checked briefly for other vital signs. Another entry for the little black book.

Behind the body of his boss, Malcolm was struggling with a suitcase that had become wedged across his lap between him and the seat ahead of him, partly blocking the aisle. There was the strong smell of blood.

'Out, quickly,' Joss commanded. He pushed at the overhead canopy but to no avail. The Navajo was wedged deep under trees. Next to the fire extinguisher was a small hatchet, but he was incapable of prising it out of its housing with his shaking hands. The birthmarked Japanese, now liberated from his angled seat, tore it out and started hacking at the densely packed leaves and timber that filled the rear section, cutting and bashing to create a way through the mashed undergrowth and foliage. Timber and leaves and splinters flew around the cabin. Finally he managed to hack out an aperture and he vanished through the crushed green mass of undergrowth.

Malcolm was swearing, still trying to extricate himself from the imprisoning suitcase. Joss took another look at Lombard and saw the small dark hole in the back of his head, near the occiput. It was a bullet entry, neat, close range. He looked at the seat Lombard had been sitting in and couldn't immediately find the corresponding hole. Then he saw it, almost at the bottom of the back of the seat.

It looked as if the bullet, on an upwards trajectory, had entered the base of the seat, travelled unhindered through its length in a diagonal, finally to penetrate Lombard's jerked-back head at the base of his skull. The gun must have discharged on crash-landing, possibly as it was hurled from Malcolm's fingers. Joss lifted the fallen face of his enemy but could find no exit wound. The bullet, slowed by its journey through the aircraft seat, must be lodged somewhere under the skull.

He looked around for the gun and found it on the floor, Malcolm's .45. He picked it up and checked it. He saw that two rounds were missing. One for Ignatius Ho, one for Lombard. Malcolm was deadly even when he didn't mean it. He wiped the gun down and shoved it in a pocket. He went to the control panel and flipped the isolating switch. He played with the radio. Nothing. The crash-landing had made an honest man of him.

He turned his attention to Malcolm in the seat behind, who had finally managed to shift the suitcase that trapped him. He gave it a huge shove and it fell sideways into the aisle. As it did so, two extraordinary things happened. A brilliant sheet of arterial blood appeared in the air over Malcolm's head, hit the roof and splashed down again, while from the bursting suitcase dozens of wrapped bundles of American dollars spilled out in a bloody avalanche to land at Joss's feet.

'Jesus!' Malcolm whispered, mesmerised by the pulsing crimson display above and around him. Joss grabbed for his neck, and Malcolm lurched away in automatic defence. But he stopped, the red geyser spurting up from his thigh commanding his attention. 'What are you doing?' he said as Joss pulled the tie from his neck.

'I'm tying off your femoral artery so you don't bleed to death,' said Joss, now wet with Malcolm's blood. He pulled the loop around the bloody thigh, noting the length and depth of the flesh wound, the glimpse of pearlescent, bloody bone sheath. Already, Malcolm was ashen. It was quite possible he was dying right now. The pressure of the wedged suitcase had contained the injury, but Malcolm had been losing blood since touchdown. Squatting beside him to pull the tie tight, Joss noticed the huge pool under him.

'Get me out of here,' Malcolm said. Joss looked up into his enemy's eyes. They flickered, dilated. Joss could see them wondering why he should help him.

'Tell me about Sybil,' he said. 'Tell me how you killed my wife.'

The stench of avgas had grown stronger than the powerful smell of blood. Malcolm's eyes were rolling; they flickered unfocussed, first at Joss and then down at the tourniquet. The bleeding was now just a slow ebb through the protruding lips of the wound and the matted fabric of Malcolm's trousers.

'I want to know about the death of my wife.'

'Lombard!' Malcolm tried to call out, but his voice had no power. He went to stand up, but fell back.

'Your boss is dead, Malcolm. Your gun went off while we were landing. You shot the boss.'

Malcolm tried to stand again. 'Don't leave me in here,' he said, falling and trying to stand again in a wavelike motion that he repeated several times. His teeth were chattering and he was looking disoriented. Comprehension flickered and died in his eyes. He slumped back, almost unconscious. He had lost a lot of blood.

Joss looked at the passage cut by the Japanese through the mangled growth jamming the aircraft amidships. It would not be space enough to drag Malcolm out. He retrieved the hatchet and set to work chopping away more bough and leafy mess. He was aware of the shaking of his body, but as the aircraft cooled the threat of fire became less pressing.

'I'm going to get the kamikaze brothers to shoot you,' said Malcolm, suddenly lucid and savage.

Joss continued working. Suddenly the aircraft lurched violently to one side, throwing him hard into a window. He picked himself up, dazed from the force with which his head had struck the pane. He had to stand quite still for a moment to let the pain recede. Something had given way underneath the plane, taking a mass of vegetation back outside again. There was sufficient room now, at least, for both of them to get through. Joss came back down the skewed aisle, tilted at a crazy angle, placing his feet carefully like a tightrope walker around the blood. He stood looking down at Malcolm.

'I don't think you fully appreciate your situation, Malcolm,' said Joss. 'Let me explain it to you. From the most cursory examination I can tell you this much: you have a severe laceration about ten inches long on your left thigh, which has cut through your femoral artery. The bone is exposed.' He saw Malcolm wince at that. 'It requires urgent surgery. Without surgery, you will either die within minutes of that tourniquet being loosened, or, if we keep the pressure up, the tissues below the area serviced by your femoral artery will start to die. Once gangrene sets in, you die by inches. I could try amputation, but under the circumstances it wouldn't be a good idea. Or you could die of an infection. And that's only three ways to die. There's still shock, blood loss, dehydration, heart failure, failure of any of your major systems. You are a critically injured man.'

Malcolm's eyes were black in his white face. He looked back down at the oozing gash in his trouser leg. 'I don't believe you,' he said, but he didn't sound convincing.

'Makes no difference to the facts,' said Joss, 'whether you believe me or not.' He paused. 'With surgery, your chances are a little better.'

Malcolm was looking at him, at the wound, and then out the window, as if he could find sense for all this somewhere in the dense mass of greenery pressed up against the pane.

'Now,' said Joss, 'I want to know everything. I want to know who killed Alan. And I want to know about Sybil's death. I've got enough drugs in my bag to make the operation on your leg almost comfortable. So, talk. If you don't tell me everything I want to know, I'll refuse to operate.'

'What about your oath?' said Malcolm.

'It is always tempered with discretion,' said Joss. 'I have other things to take into consideration. The lack of sterile conditions, the lack of any back-up help. The risk of emergency procedures at the best of times.' He looked at his enemy. 'Funny you talking about an oath. What about yours?'

Malcolm took no notice. 'What are my chances with surgery?'

Joss thought. 'Hard to say, really. About fifty-fifty.'

'And without?'

'Nil.'

Malcolm thought about that. He looked down at his thigh and winced again. He looked around the ruined interior of the Navajo. He looked up at the roof and the wide red patch where several thickening drops of blood that would never fall hung above his head. The seriousness of his situation was sinking in. He looked again at Joss, hating him for the power he held over him.

There was nothing he could do except start talking.

Later, Joss walked around the island a little, his thoughts with the dead. He had hauled Malcolm out of the Navajo – where flies were already swarming – as he began talking, and had propped him underneath a palm tree with Joss's medical bag for company. The Navajo had come to rest in a dense clump of palms, one wing almost torn through, the other pitched at an odd angle over its collapsed undercarriage. Across the trunk of the palm at the rear of the plane was half a trousered leg wearing a polished Italian shoe.

There was a warm, light tropical breeze, the humidity not unpleasant. A low rolling surf on the windward side and still water on the leeward enclosed the tiny island. Apart from three larvae-riddled pools, Joss saw no water. Malaria and other mosquito-borne diseases presented themselves as possibilities.

Malcolm had told him he'd been approached by someone

from Lombard's camp shortly after the bombing of the Mercedes. The amount offered him was more than he would have earnt in the rest of his career as a federal police officer. Sybil had died almost exactly as Joss had pictured. She had arrived on Malcolm's doorstep the night after the caravan park blind drunk and raving hysterically. She'd let slip Joss's whereabouts. Then she'd slumped into sleep on Malcolm's sofa, and when she was sober enough to comprehend he'd told her his own story. He didn't need her any more; she'd done what he'd always hoped and led him to Joss. Malcolm had forced her into meeting him one last time on that lonely beach, on the pretext that he could convince Lombard to let Polly live. She'd tried to get away from him but Malcolm had shot her in the back of the head. Twice. She'd been holding her medal of the Madonna in her hand, Malcolm said.

Joss felt the tears prick his eyes. He found now he could forgive her for everything except betraying the Sybil game. 'You have no sense of propriety, *Sivilla mou*,' he said out loud. He was relieved to hear about the medal. He remembered the Greek Testament beside her bed, opened at the psalms. Perhaps it meant she'd known what was going to happen, that she hadn't been hurled into the terror and confusion of her dying convulsions without some preparation.

Joss started walking back to the crash site. As he walked he was aware of the soft ache near his spleen. He felt around. There was swelling and a slight tenderness. Bruising? Or a slow and deadly bleed? Only time would tell. He came upon a small rocky outcrop – volcanic – some thin grasses near the rocks, and several brilliant flowers growing on vines. Across the other side of the airstrip was a low building that he wanted to investigate, but if he didn't fix Malcolm's leg now, the light would be gone.

Joss disturbed a black cloud of flies from around Malcolm as he came up to him. He could see, from the stiff way his enemy held himself, that he was in pain now, the first numbing shock having worn off. He had draped his coat over the tourniqueted wound to keep the flies away and it was already steeped in blood.

'Ready?' Joss asked his patient.

It was hard work getting Malcolm down to the sea. He was very weak by now and it took some time for the two of them, Malcolm leaning heavily on Joss and hopping on one leg, to make their way to the beach. Joss laid him on the coarse sand near the wave line, and undressed him from the waist down. His penis was pathetically shrivelled from having lain so still. Below the level of the tourniquet, his leg was corpse yellow. *Mavro*, the black one, Joss recalled.

When he had made his patient as comfortable as possible with local anaesthetic and Valium, Joss washed his hands in the sea. The surgeon was ready. Small waves rolled and unrolled against the rock outcrop further along the shore. *Ka-dosh, ka-dosh*, they whispered back at him.

Staring up at the milky sky Malcolm clamped his own artery as Joss directed, while the tourniquet came off. Then Joss allowed the waves to rinse over the bloody thigh and the wound was cleansed by the South China Sea. Its crusted edges softened as the water turned red from torn flesh and fat, drifting in the sea like bleached rags. Joss studied the leg. It appeared to be an impact wound, probably from a piece of metal that had then torn along the length of the thigh, slicing the great artery. He wouldn't be able to do anything fancy here, he knew. There was a lot of trauma to subcutaneous fat and muscle tissue; there was heavy swelling and bruising and inflammation in the areas where fabric from Malcolm's trousers was deeply embedded. Joss picked up his scalpel and started cleaning up, trimming away damaged tissue, removing tiny pieces of expensive wool. Seagulls wheeled and fished for scraps of Malcolm. Small fish darted at specks of him floating in the shallows. From time to time Joss looked up, relieved to see there were not triangular fins cruising. He knew sharks could charge into shallow water.

As he worked he found himself thinking of his oath, only

to do that which is helpful and never to harm. He remembered the sunlight slanting through the windows of the great hall, the mock-Gothic theatrical importance of it all. But it was important. It was the first of the only two oaths of his life. The subject of the second oath, his wife, had been killed by the man he was now repairing. He stitched the tear in the artery, kneeling sometimes in water, sometimes on wet sand. Malcolm had taken his hand away but Joss noticed how he still kept his fingers pressed together. Their tips were white and numb. *Ka-dosh, ka-dosh,* hushed the waves.

Once or twice he looked up from his work and thought of how he was actually here, really here, on Samsura. He thought of his father, long gone. He continued his suturing and thought of Sybil and her seals. But even she could never have imagined this scene, he thought. He saw that simply by being how he was, by doing what he did, he had ended up here. And so had the others. He had taken action to stop Lombard and Malcolm escaping, had brought an aircraft down on this beach, and that had wounded this man, possibly fatally. He, Joss, had indirectly brought death to others: Ignatius Ho, an unknown Japanese criminal, and Lombard. He had shot Eric Fuller without understanding, charged by an unknown energy somewhere from the past stored somewhere in mind. What an extraordinary mystery is the life of a person, he thought. He had made two children for this world with Sybil. Now Sybil and one of those children were already dead. And soon he would be dead, and later on so would Polly. Despite him, and without his comforting presence, his daughter would have to die too, eventually. This thought made him feel profoundly sad and real tears filled his eyes. I have done a lot of harm, he thought.

'But what else could I have done?' he asked Malcolm, as he snipped off a suture. 'How else could I have done it? I didn't know another way.' Malcolm stared at the sky, his fingertips pinched together.

'You didn't either, did you?' he asked of Malcolm. 'It's

not as if any of us get away with anything,' he said, thinking of what awaited him and everyone else at the end of their life sentence. 'There's only one way out of this world, and that's through the chimneys.'

Now Malcolm was staring at him. He looked as though he wanted to get away. He attempted to raise his head to see what Joss was doing, but, drained of energy, he sank back, ashen-faced.

'I didn't know another way,' Joss said as he joined the layers of flesh, dealing with torn muscle tissue as best he could, stitching the layers of fat. 'I just didn't know.'

Malcolm's ivory leg blushed rose, the colour spreading like a stain, and Joss couldn't help feeling pleased. Finally, he drew the edges together and started closing the wound. It wasn't a bad job, he thought, looking at it, considering he was working by twilight on a beach. Malcolm had turned his gaze back to the sky, flinching a bit from time to time, as Joss tugged, tying off and cutting. Faint stars appeared through the haze above.

The two men, stumbling and hopping, made their way up to the edge of the trees, away from the water's edge. Joss propped Malcolm back against the palm tree and powdered and bandaged the wound. He hoped the suture sites wouldn't tear. He gave his patient a shot of antibiotics and another intravenous Valium.

'You've got a nice pink leg again,' he said, like any friendly surgeon, while Malcolm struggled to sit up.

Joss washed his instruments in the South China Sea and left them to dry. He closed his bag and walked back to the crooked Navajo. He wondered if Polly had noticed the odd word her father said on the phone and repeated in the skirmish at Darwin. And had then told Dennis about it. He wondered if Dennis and Polly would work it out. Would they discuss it with Ashley? Or had it, like a nonsense syllable, made no lasting impression on his daughter, who, shocked by the murder of her ex-boyfriend on the tarmac and the whole sequence of violent events, would never think of it again? He wasn't even sure now if Polly knew about the magic island. Had he ever told her about his boyhood dream? He thought he remembered holding her up to the map to see her grandfather's airfields. He wasn't sure she knew about the faint purple pencil ring around Samsura. He was pleased that his daughter and Ashley were safe from Lombard, even if they could never be safe from their own life sentence and its aftermath.

He looked up and the sky was empty of everything except soft cloud. There was a chance he might be able to repair the radio from the manual. It was just possible that he and his companions would be found. He was climbing back into the Navajo with his bag, thinking to look for the manual, when he immediately noticed the silence, the absence of flies. At first he thought it was merely the time of the day when flies disappeared, but when he got inside the cabin and looked around he saw that the avalanche of bloody money was gone. The two other suitcases were gone.

And so was Lombard.


It was completely dark now. Joss's eyes were quite accustomed to the tropical night. Starlight and the soft luminescence on the water made things just visible. Malcolm was dozing under his palm tree, his leg packed up with part of an aircraft seat. Joss sat motionless, tucked out of sight against the rocky outcrop where it rose behind the shore, covered by vines. He was watching the low building on the other side of the airstrip. He had been studying it for a while and he thought it was some sort of bunker. The Japanese man was making a door for the building out of timber slashed with the hatchet from the Navajo. He worked skilfully, tying timber together with leaves and vines. It was almost in place now, and when he fitted it and closed it he would have a little fortress. And he probably had five million dollars in American currency in there, Joss thought. Maybe there were old provisions in that bunker. A radio that might still work if they connected it to the battery in the Navajo. Maps, charts, tins of food. Even water. He wondered about stores fifty years old. He thought of botulism. Maybe Lombard was already in there, waving his semi-automatic around, directing things, despite a bullet trapped at the front of his head. Joss knew that on occasions head injuries could be very eccentric, appalling injury causing little or no problems later. He knew of cases where people had lived for years with bullets in their heads. There had been no pulse when he'd checked him back there in the cabin, but Joss remembered how his fingers had been numb from the force of the impact. Or perhaps the violent jolting of the aircraft when the tree had snapped free had started that hard heart beating again. Lombard had the luck of the devil.

He dozed. When he woke, the moon had risen and the island was bright with black trunks and silver tips. The palms rustled in a night breeze. He was thirsty and hungry. Tomorrow he'd find a way to make a fire and boil some of the dirty water he'd seen in the rocky pools. He would set up something to catch rainwater. He would see what could be found in the way of food. Coconuts, palm hearts. Rock pools might yield molluscs of some sort. He would search for the manual and try fixing the radio. He thought about building his temple. The Japanese man might conceivably demonstrate to him how to make a simple structure. Or he might shoot him as he approached his fortress. Or Lombard might come from nowhere and kill him.

If he were able to begin work on the temple, Joss thought, he would do the heaviest work first, putting in the four supports while he still had some strength. It would be a tropical building – only a roof, really. A tropical temple of atonement, he thought. Because I have a lot to atone. In the temple, built near his father's airfield, he would have time to reflect on his life, on the way he had been, the way he had become. In the temple he would make offerings for all the dead, because he had been and would continue to be just another person doing things the only way he knew how. Just another lifer on a prison on an island. And perhaps in the temple he would find forgiveness. I only swore two oaths, he thought. And I've broken both of them.

He would have to care for Malcolm. There was quite a good chance now that he would live and that would bring new problems. Especially if he were able to fix the radio. And if Lombard lived on for a while.

He heard the sound of an aircraft, but it was a commercial airliner droning thirty thousand feet above. He slept again.

He woke yelling in shock at a sudden noise. It was light and he didn't know where he was. He jumped up and it took him a few seconds to realise what had happened. The Japanese was lying on the airstrip some twenty metres away, bleeding and heaving from a gunshot wound to the chest. Lombard was holding his semi-automatic pistol and staring down at him. Then he looked up and saw Joss, now completely exposed. At first, Joss thought that Lombard was somehow wearing one of Dennis's most hideous masks. His eyes were filled with blood and the entire area of his swollen face was bruised black. Joss wondered if he would have the chance to pull the .45 from his pocket and kill him.

Lombard came closer. Joss braced himself, his hand ready to grab the gun from his pocket, at the same time thinking that death by gunshot might well be the most merciful way out of here. Time off for good behaviour. His legs were trembling and he didn't think he could stay standing much longer. Then suddenly, and for no apparent reason, Lombard turned his back on him. Joss put his hand on the .45 and started to pull it out. Then he stopped. He knew beyond a shadow of a doubt that he had no heart to kill the disfigured creature. There was no point in any further harm to anyone. Lombard turned around once more and lifted his gun.

Joss wanted to pray but all that came into his mind was

the grace they used to say after meals at the Boys' Home. 'We give Thee thanks, O Almighty God, for all Thy benefits which we have received.' Then he remembered the negotiating skills that fear had driven from his mind. He was about to remind Lombard of his medical expertise when he realised that Lombard was speaking. His voice was slurred. The expression on his distorted black face was one of bewilderment; he looked like a badly beaten two-year-old.

'I was only playing,' he said. He lowered the gun and let it fall from his hand. 'Never point a gun,' he said. 'Even in jest.' Then he stumbled away, shaking that head. 'I was told,' he said, 'and now look what I've done. Dear oh dear.'

Joss saw something moving in the wound on the back of Lombard's head. Then Lombard turned round again and Joss noticed for the first time the huge bulge, just above the bruised frontal lobes. He realised that the bullet must be there, just above Lombard's nose, pushing out the forehead.

'I didn't know,' said Lombard. 'Dear oh dear. Will you tell on me?'

Joss carefully stepped down from his higher position to the level ground. Across the airfield, the Japanese man heaved one last time and died. 'No,' said Joss to Lombard. 'I won't tell.'

'Cross your heart and hope to die?'

'Cross my heart.'

Lombard seemed satisfied at that and turned away, continuing his walk. He started to hum a little song.

Joss wandered across the tough surface of the airstrip. I've lost too much of myself already, he thought. I don't want to lose any more. Every cell in his body felt that the force of life's events, and their consequences, was unavoidable, and that by resisting this long and this hard he had simply served to pull things down on himself. For the first time in his life he let things be as they were. He stopped fighting, and the power and enormity of life swept through him. His stranglehold was broken once and for all.

Although vegetation sprawled around the airfield and clumps of trees grew at either end, nothing had broached its metal mesh in fifty years. Joss looked up. It was a misty winter morning, hazy, steamy, a slight breeze in a dull white tropical sky. He looked at his watch. It said 6.40.

He went over to check the Japanese man. Unlike Lombard, he would not be be getting up. Joss took off his watch and hung it up on the new door to the old bunker. He would not be needing it again. He looked inside. It was quite empty but he couldn't help noticing that the window faced due west. He went back to the dead man, took him by the ankles and started dragging him towards the beach.

Malcolm watched from under his tree as Joss put the Japanese in the water. The body kept beaching in the low surf, staining the sand in bloody patches, until Joss took him out further, towing him along like a lifesaver, watching all the time for sharks.

'What happened?' Malcolm asked as he came back up the beach.

'Lombard shot him,' Joss said.

Malcolm's look told him that he clearly thought Joss had flown his coop.

'How's the leg?' asked Joss.

Malcolm shrugged, declining to answer.

'I'll have a look at it later,' said the surgeon.

Further down the beach Lombard had drawn a series of stick figures in the sand. He sat in the sea, facing the beach, his hideous face wrinkled with joy as he splashed water over his figures. He whooped as they dissolved back into smoothness. 'I'm hungry,' the brutish child called out. 'What's for eats?'

For a split then vanished second Joss was amazed to find the island beach and its inhabitants entirely lovable.

He went back to the edge of the airfield. He would have another look at the radio; he would try and pack that wound in the back of Lombard's head, try and clean up the fly strike.

What am I here for? he asked himself. He saw that four beautiful red flowers had bloomed on the vines that had hidden him during the night, and the intense red of the flowers, their radiant symmetry, made him smile. Perhaps the answer to his question would come.

On the ground beside the airstrip, walking back towards the crumpled Navajo, he started to pace out the measurements for his temple.